GOLLITOK

ANDREW NAJBERG

WICKED
HOUSE
PUBLISHING

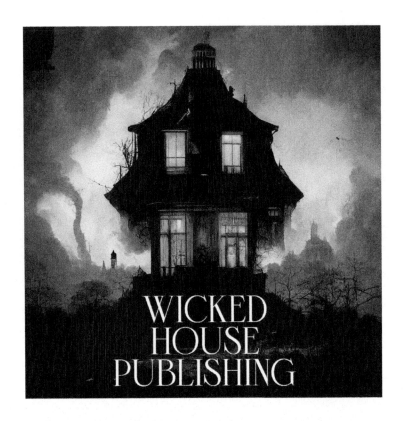

WICKED
HOUSE
PUBLISHING

Gollitok
By Andrew Najberg

Wicked House Publishing

Cover design by Christian Bentulan
Interior Formatting by Joshua Marsella

Contents

To Mom

DAY ONE

CHAPTER 1

THE CHANNEL, THE DOCK, OFFICES

The lantern at the prow lights our way across the channel. It is I, Hammel, my briefcase, and the ferryman. The ferryman chews an unlit pipe as he rows, and he wears a black fisherman's cap with a dead-man's hitch emblem on the temple. His face is brine-scoured with a scar from a badly closed surgery between lip and septum.

Fog surrounds us as it is not yet dawn. The stars look like meaningless specks of salt on a black tablecloth. I never learned my constellations, and my geography is juvenile at best. When I look back over my shoulder, I see the mainland lighthouse still, a distant dot of light on an otherwise black, craggy shore.

Ahead, the soft glow of the Midway dock. Beyond stands the watchtower, storehouse, the residence, and the official office, whereat I am to rendezvous with Brogden. Until then, the ferryman, who only grunted when I introduced myself, is my companion.

The pipe has slowly rotated under the grit of his teeth, the bowl now turned down. If it ever held anything, it doesn't now.

I lean against the stern and dangle my hand to the water. I barely feel the cold wet before the ferryman speaks.

"Wouldn't do that were I you," he says.

"Sharks?" I ask.

The ferryman spits.

"Jellyfish," he grunts. "Black 'uns. They wrap their tendrils 'round your fingers, and you'll be screaming until your next birthday."

The many papers the Bureau issued me upon departure include a small leaflet on local marine life. Perhaps I should peruse them. Until now, I've regarded them as a novelty.

"You been crossing these waters long?" I ask.

I can't tell if the ferryman shrugs or if it's just the roll of his shoulders as he rows.

"Ten years since I've had a working motor," he says.

"I'll put in a word for a replacement," I say.

This time it's clear that the ferryman shrugs.

"My successor will be grateful," he says. "I'll be dead before it arrives."

Then, he fixes his jaw and looks to the side.

As a cool wind sweeps and swirls the fog, the rhythmic dip of the oars and the lap of wavelets on the hull absorbs me until a man on the Midway dock, who I presume to be the customs inspector, hooks the mooring ring and ties us to a post. The ferryman doesn't respond when I thank him, but the inspector takes my hand and helps me and my briefcase out of the boat. On the horizon, first light breaks through clouds like a candle behind stretched silk.

* * *

"Welcome to Midway," the inspector says.

He used the motion of brushing himself off to call attention to a badge that identifies him as Customs Inspector, Third Class. His bearing paints him a proud man, all shoulders and hips, even though customs at a post where the only destination is an uninhabited island borders on Sisyphean futility. Nonetheless, I should treat him with politeness. Lower officials teeter on the brink of despair. Better, I suppose, than life in the work halls, but that's like saying that a chronic cough is better than the flu.

As the inspector leans his mooring rod against a bench and picks up a clipboard, I check the latches on my briefcase and make sure to scramble the lock. The inspector is tall and unshaven and smells like sour hibiscus, the scent of nearly all petty officials.

"Name?" he says, though he already has it at the top of his form.

"Hammel E. Varka," I say.

"Place of origin?"

"New Zagreb."

"Purpose of visit?"

"Inspection of government site in response to a report of disturbance," I say. These are all matters of his knowledge. He, after all, filed the disturbance report. His smug lips indicate he is pleased that the Bureau approved an investigation. He does not know that his report is most certainly a pretext, nothing more.

"Do you have anything to declare?" the inspector asks.

I shake my head. Onsite caches delivered in advance with the prep team will supply most everything I need. Brogden has the rest. Travelling with luggage through coastal checkpoints can be an outright nightmare, an invitation for bribe solicitation at best.

I pat the briefcase.

"Just official papers."

"May I see them?" the inspector asks.

"No."

A light leaves the man's eyes. I knew he'd ask, and he knew I'd say no. I am higher ranked, our ritual empty, performed so he can feel purposeful. My arrival, the arrival of our supplies, and the arrival of the rest of the survey team are likely the highlight of his decade.

He jots a few notes on his clipboard and then extends it to me. I sign his form without reading. Who knows when it will prove advantageous to prove that I was here? Who knows when it can be used against me? I hand the clipboard back.

Without further word, the inspector takes up the mooring rod, helps the ferryman shove off, and then trudges down the secondary pier, I assume to prep the boat my colleagues and I will take to the prison as soon as able.

* * *

As an island, Midway does not impress. The twin-pier dock ends at a short, paved road that splits into four stairs, one stair up each of the island's four low hills. Clockwise from the dock starting at my left, each hill holds a single structure: the watchtower, the government office, the storehouse, and the residence. Each building is stone around wooden frames and thick, thatchwork roofs. They are old as any structure in the nation. Impressive they've survived so long through winter storms. Their durability is a reminder that the harshest conditions cannot wear us down.

The wind blows fresh brine over the ocean, and a school of mullet splashes in the shoals. The tide will lower soon, and tidal pools will trap those mullets. There, gulls will devour them. I head up the stairs toward the offices, a squat building with a roof slanted against the direction that houses the prevailing wind. At the far end, the roof nearly reaches the ground. The path leads toward the high side and the propped-open entrance.

An electric bulb burns in a sconce beside the door, and in its light Second Liaison Brogden waits for me. I recognize him from his file photo. His skin is of that brown so deep it is almost blue, and his eyes are very white. His heavy, official peacoat looks black in the orange glow, but I know his, like my own, to be the same navy blue as in the national signet.

"Mr. Varka," he calls out. "It is true that you have arrived."

"It is," I say.

"Was the journey trying?" he asks.

"Not as bad as I'd feared," I say.

I reach him with my hand extended.

He holds his hands up, leaving mine empty.

"Did they not inform you of the protocols?" he asks.

I nod. In my fatigue from such an early journey, I'd forgotten.

"Minimal contact, yes," I say. "I'd been under the impression that we needn't follow that until we arrive on the island."

"You speak correctly," Brogden says. "But best start now, yes? Otherwise, we get there and find ourselves slipped."

"I'd heard you were a clever man," I say. A fetching, welcome scent wafts from the open door. Nose in the air, I ask, "Is that—"

"Yes, coffee," he says, motioning me inside. "A cup?"

"Maybe two," I say, and enter.

CHAPTER 2

CARD TABLE, WATCHTOWER, REPORTS

Brogden and I settle on either side of the card table in the back corner of the offices. The pre-war chair cushions upon which we sit are almost disintegrated. On the table are an ash tray, a small pyramid of government-label cigarette packs, a pile of matchbooks, and a deck of playing cards. The rest of the office is little more than two desks facing each other. On each desk there is an inbox and outbox, an old mechanical typewriter, a pencil cup, and a reading lamp. Both desks have blank nameplates.

We raise mugs that Brogden produced from one of the desk drawers. The coffee maker is an old-style iron pot on a hotplate. The drinks are not steaming. Perhaps the hotplate is failing.

"Where are the others?" I ask.

"Lieutenant Yost is in the residence," he says, sipping his coffee. "She will meet us at the boat. Mikael and Efta left with the forward team to set up camp."

"I've looked forward to speaking with Efta," I say.

"You've worked with her before," Brogden says.

"At the quarries, yes."

Brogden opens one of the packs of cigarettes and lights one. I am not partial to the habit myself. Funny that it had all but vanished before the war. Once the fallout cancers started, it didn't matter so much to most. As the saying goes, life's too short to let the world choose what shortens it.

"I have not, but she speaks Eastern Provincial," Brogden says. "Like conversing with a neighbor."

"I was born just outside New Zagreb, so nothing but Official sounds right to my ears."

After a long drag and exhale, he says, "A burden to speak Provincial. You always miss some nuance in Official, especially when standing before review panels. Did you know that by testing, I should have made First Liaison by now?"

"You were held back because you're from the Provinces?"

"Hell if I know," Brogden says with a wheezing laugh. "It's what I tell myself when my paycheck is gone and all I have to show for it are empty liquor bottles and dirty bedsheets."

I laugh, though he isn't exactly joking. The prejudices against the outer provinces are known. The barbarians are never where one lives.

"You know what they say," I add. "If they can't find a way to hate you, they'll hate you because they can't."

Brogden sighs, and it rattles. I expect him to cough. He draws on his smoke like it is medicine. His constitution concerns me. Something on his breath suggests he may have fortified himself with something stout. I avoid categorizing him as beyond his prime, because such a claim could be made about myself.

Then, Brogden stubs his cigarette.

"Let us get down to business," he says. "What do you know of our purpose?"

"A fortnight past, the customs inspector reported a flickering light in the ruins of Gollitok prison on Albertachen. Then, the island's radio beacon ceased broadcasting."

Brogden shifts in his seat; says, "That's the official report, yes, but you and I both know."

Of course I do.

"Tech?" I ask.

"Possible," Brogden says. "And classified records."

"So, search and retrieval," I say. "But records recovery doesn't need pretext, not from a place like Gollitok. You've heard as many stories as I, I'm sure."

"They don't want it on the official record," Brogden says. "Apparently, a naval drone detected movement among the buildings, and they are convinced there are other players on the board."

"That was not in my brief," I say.

Brogden reaches into his peacoat and extracts a large pistol with a caged muzzle. It's an outdated model, most likely passed within his family. On paper, all Bureau officials are expected to carry standard issue equipment, but general shortages created a long tradition of looking the other way. He places the gun on the table and asks, "Are you practiced with a firearm?"

I shake my head and say, "Not outside the training course."

"A shame," he says. He gestures to the pistol. "Keep this one. I have another."

I heft the gun. The weight is considerable. There is no safety mechanism, so I remove the clip and check the chamber. Then, I slip the weapon and its parts into my coat pocket.

"Are you prepared to use it?" Brogden asks.

"No," I say with a shake of my head. "But I'll sign the form that says yes."

"Spoken like a true patriot," Brogden says.

Then, Brogden nods, rises, and leaves. I sit a moment and gaze off into space. I drain my cup, though it has grown cool. The coffee is bad, but that is welcome. Even in the capital, good coffee only comes from the black market. A lot can be bought with black market coffee, certainly something so cheap as loyalty.

* * *

As I ascend the slope to the watchtower, I pause to look over my shoulder in the direction from which the ferryman brought me. My whole life, I've never seen a clear sky, but the particulate suspension in the coastal atmosphere is thinner than anywhere closer to the mainland blast sites. The colors of the sunrise are especially deep today, and I consider that if nothing else, the survey promises many such views.

The watchtower hill is the tallest of the four and the most weathered. My feet threaten to slip on the damp stair edges. Above, the tower, a wooden affair atop a square base of stacked stone. In a juncture of some of the largest joists, an enormous nest with bird feces streaking every surface beneath. In the structure, numerous replacements mark a visual record of decay and rot. The structure cannot possibly meet official code.

I approach the stone foundation as the path curves to the ladder that runs up to the observation platform. Steel plate reinforces the rungs, but the steel has rusted from constant salt exposure. I set my briefcase down. The wind is strong here, so I pull on a little woolen cap kept in one of my pockets. It is damp like everything else is damp.

I climb the ladder to the deck. I take a moment to thrust my hands into my armpits. I would hate to feel winter here. No doubt, the air is desolate. Unaided, I can't see Albertachen, but the scope aims in the correct direction. I lean to the eyepiece, ignoring the chill from the brush of metal housing against my cheek.

The island is nothing but a dim lump, a black rock on a blue sea. The island's highest point is closest to where I stand, obscuring its size, and the light is too poor for me to make out more than the dormant lighthouse's peak which, oddly, seems to barely rise above the main height of the plateau. I can't even see the docks or the labor yard where Mikael established our camp.

I slump back from the scope and turn to the ladder. I startle to find the inspector at the base. He is examining the locks on my briefcase. I climb down, my boots clanging on the rungs. He clears his throat, straightens his collar and cuffs.

I descend to meet him and ask, "May I be of service?"

"I did not want to speak in front of the ferryman. He is a terrible gossip and hopes to put himself enough in someone's pocket they post him to a busier channel," the inspector says. He checks once over each shoulder as if the ferryman hadn't already departed to the mainland. "I want to give you warning. The report that summoned you is not my first report."

"This is the first I've heard of this," I say.

The man leans forward. Spits. Again, I smell sour hibiscus, and this time, something underneath it, a faint fishy odor.

"I'm not surprised. I can't say they've been well received," the inspector says. He kneels and plucks some sort of purplish moss. A bitter scent disperses, and I sour my nose. The inspector chuckles. He holds up a pinch of the moss and shoves it between his cheek and gums like chewing tobacco. He sucks hard through his teeth and says, "Orlot. Pungent when picked, yes, but it has a relaxing effect."

"So, Mr. Third Inspector," I say, trying to conceal that the odor of the herb is turning my stomach. "Were I to have been privy to your prior reports, what from them would I have gathered? What is happening on Albertachen?"

"You won't like what you find there," the inspector says.

"And what might that be?" I ask.

Again, he leans closer, his mouth hardly a foot from my ear, his hot breath ghastly from the bitter herb. I half expect him to say 'ghosts.'

"Insurrectionists," he whispers.

I press my lips together. Had he half a bit of sense he would have at least toned it down to a smuggling operation. It's expected from such a remote post, but this inspector is like every other low official distributed to posts such as these – placed there precisely because they saw insurrectionists around the corners and heard guerilla code in the static. Of course, a post like this could make anyone desperate to feel valued.

The inspector sucks through his teeth again, and he spits out a stringy wad of purple phlegm that quivers on the stone. He says, "You don't believe me, I can tell."

I open my mouth to object, but he holds up his hand.

"It is okay," he says. "I expect no less. You've lived in the heart of stability. I imagine it's been some time since last you've been to the fringe."

I clap a freezing hand on his shoulder.

"Too true," I say. "And the warning I appreciate. You know I must depart straightaway because that is what I have been assigned to do, but forewarned is forearmed. I will be doubly vigilant when I arrive there."

The Inspector seems pleased, and then he absorbs himself in the task of gathering more Orlot and placing it in his leather pouch. I collect my briefcase. It is time to head to the dock and make the crossing.

CHAPTER 3

GHOST STORIES, LEDGERS, PREDECESSORS

T he dock has become busier since my arrival. The pier where the ferryman delivered me is empty, but Brogden and a lean woman with a shaved head and black wire-framed glasses busily secure duffels and boxes. I cannot make the woman's features out clearly, but I assume from her military overalls and standard issue black shirt that she is Lieutenant Yost.

I descend the stairs from the tower hill. My boots clomp on the wooden planks of the landing. Ahead, the boat resembles a craft one would find in a book about Vikings. It has a long, upturned prow, and the oar locks are dull and rusted. At the back, a single, outboard motor with a rust-mottled housing dangles seaweed to the ocean's surface. Brogden rises as I approach. Yost hunches over one of the packs. A Kalashnikov rifle is attached by a loose sling to one side and a pair of black-bladed machetes are sheathed on the other.

The deck wobbles as I step onto it.

"Yost," I say. "I am pleased to meet you. I am—"

Yost snorts.

"My commander said you're more useful than I think," she says. "But I doubt it."

In one quick motion, she wraps the belt that straps her pack to the deck around her palm and jerks her shoulder back. Something oily churns in my gut. Already, I fear her management will be difficult. Best to clip the weed before the root gets deep.

"My regrets, Lieutenant," I say, "but have I given you offence?"

"Offence? About what should I be offended? That I'm placed under the charge of some third-rate bureaucrat and his handler?" Yost says. Brogden's jaw stiffens, but he looks to me as he settles onto the prow bench.

"I assume they placed you on my team because you are good at what you do," I say. "I will insist that you extend me the same courtesy."

Yost gives her pack strap a second jerk and rises. Each of her muscles is strong, even those in her face, and I can feel aggression emanating off her in waves as she takes a step toward me. "Let me run the survey. Then I can trust your judgment."

I have no doubt she can rip my arms right out of their sockets, or at least snap my neck in a heartbeat. I can tell that something burning drives her, but clearly, I will achieve little in this conversation and must focus only on diffusing it.

"Don't be foolish," I say. "You know the penalties we would both face. I'll be transmitting regular reports."

For a split second, I believe the lieutenant is about to strike me. Then, her cheeks puff out. The urgency leaves her eyes. Abruptly, she steps past me and onto the pier, disappearing up the steps toward the island's storage facility. I shake my head and sit on the middle bench.

Brogden chuckles and says, "You need reach an accord with her, or else you might wish to get more proficient with your firearm."

"The lieutenant will not risk a mark on her record."

Brogden sighs. "Don't think like you're in the central territory."

"The Central Bureau doesn't care about our distance from the capitol," I say.

"And how long you think, even if deemed important enough to dispatch them, it would take for police to reach Albertachen if Yost decided to silence you? The military thinks differently than Bureau, and things work different on fringes," Brogden says. Then, he heaves out a great sigh and pinches the bridge of his nose.

"Let me tell you little story. When I was still third liaison. My partner Leotov and I conducted audit of deforesting crews. Our second year working together. Always we'd been at odds. Then, we came across a collective whose export ledgers did not match corresponding import ledgers we'd brought. Apparently, Supervisor Welma's books differed from those of Supervisor Obal." Brogden rolled his shoulders and cracked his neck. "Simple enough issue, we assume one is taking, one not. So, Leotov says 'Brogden, you depose Welma, I depose Obal, and we figure out whose pockets are fuller than ought.'

"I visit Welma at her office," he continues. "She is upset. 'Dishonored,' she says. But I tell her it is procedure. Protocol. She swears up and down her account honest. Calls in her people, they show me their numbers. All details add up, so I return to Leotov. He is in office of Supervisor Obal. Disarray everywhere. Chairs knocked over. Leotov himself kneeling on Obal's chest. He had with his belt knife cut open Obal's testicles. Obal's face had been battered almost unrecognizable with drawer of file cabinet."

"God in Heaven," I say.

"Turns out Obal kept secret records, and refused to turn them over," Brogden says.

I sigh. So many problems could be solved if people just cooperated. I am about to say as much, but Brogden continues again, "The records made quite clear: Welma and her people were all in it together. Obal had hoped to bring his evidence before tribunal, but he'd feared that Leotov could not be trusted."

"That's a true shame," I say.

"Indeed, especially since Leotov then tried to kill me as we went to leave Obal's office. Turns out his name was in the ledgers," Brogden says. "But I was much fitter then. I cut his carotid artery with his own knife. That's also how I became Second Liaison."

"Are you saying that Yost is in league with...?"

"I'm saying that you don't know who is in league with those whose interests do not align with your own," Brogden said. "And that Yost intends to act in her own interests. Efta and Mikael too. Even myself for that matter."

I hesitate. Scratch the back of my head. I have a flash to a time when I was a child, maybe twelve. My father had been made Chief Clerk in the Central Appropriations Office. We expected a new housing assignment but still lived in one of those giant apartment complexes most people call 'hives'. We lived high enough that we weren't too vulnerable behind locked doors, but one time we were coming in from market when a gang of local thugs arrived to shake down the lower floors.

We'd fled to the basement and hid in the building ossuary. The bones crunched and shifted under me as we knelt in the dark and listened to shouts, thuds, and the occasional gunshot. When one of the gang members found us, my father stabbed him in the lung with a splintered femur without hesitation. The look on my father's face as he twisted and jerked the bone hadn't been human, and I learned that day that inside, everyone wears another face they never want to show the world.

"I think we all can do our worst when it is what we must," I say. "And that we must try to do everything better before it comes to that."

Brogden is about to light a cigarette when his attention shifts to the hill. Yost is returning, carrying a bulging rucksack. As she proceeds, the inspector trots behind her. For lack of a better word, there's simply something smarmy about his demeanor as he talks at the back of her head while they walk. Yost doesn't look at him, though the annoyance on her face is unmistakable. When she gets to the boat and her eyes fall on me, the annoyance grows. Immediately, she secures the rucksack behind my seat, her mouth a tight line.

The inspector stops short of boarding the boat at the dock's edge. He extracts a small parcel from his pocket which he extends toward me. It is barely larger than his palm, wrapped in paper, and bound together with twine.

When I don't immediately reach up to take it, the inspector frowns.

"For your journey," he says.

I still do not respond. I do not trust the inspector, and the conversation with Brogden has made me further apprehensive.

"It is Orlot," the inspector says. "To bolster your immune system against contaminants."

My stomach twists as I remember the herb's foul smell. I do not want it, but I reach out and take it anyway.

As I stash the little package in the gear under my seat, I nod a thanks to the inspector and bid him goodbye, but he lingers.

"Is there something else?" I ask.

The inspector draws a slow breath and says, "Just that I wish you better luck than your predecessors." At the end of the word 'predecessors' he clamps his mouth shut and takes a jittering step sideways.

"Predecessors?" I ask.

"Y-yes." He hesitates as if I have caught him in a slip, though it is quite clear the 'slip' was intended. "The supply ship—"

"Mr. Inspector," I say with a sigh, "if you wish me to take you seriously, then I would ask you to at least maintain a consistent story."

The inspector puffs his chest out and raises his chin.

"If you don't appreciate—"

"I don't appreciate," I say, "the way you dole out information one morsel at a time. I fear you hope to bait me – badly I might add – and that even if you are in earnest there is no longer any way I can believe you."

"There was," he insists, "an expedition just like yours—"

"Unless you can tell me something clear and concrete about what is happening on that island," I begin, but I never get to finish the sentence. In an instant, the boat jerks wildly, and Yost is on the dock's edge. Her fists twist the fabric of the inspector's shirt, and she drives him backward with powerful lurches of her legs.

I hear her whisper something violently at him to which he babbles a frantic response, but her boots slamming the slats interferes too much for me to make any of it out. Then, the inspector trips where the wood gives way to the island rock, and he falls onto his ass. He continues to push himself backward, driving himself across the stone with his heels, but the energy ebbs from Yost's charge.

Then she pivots, and before I know it has resumed her seat at the boat's stern. I am aghast at the abrupt violence, and it takes me a moment to formulate a thought.

"Was that necessary?"

Yost looks at me with hard eyes.

"Yes," she says. Then, her gaze shifts ahead of the boat, her jaw rigid as if it were sculpted. I will get nothing from her.

CHAPTER 4

TRANSIT. TRANSIT. TRANSIT

The water rustles around us, and the shore wavelets slosh against the hull as Brogden rises and uses one of his oars to push us away from the dock. He removes his peacoat and slides the oar back through its lock in the raised position. Age has grown his belly, but the build of his shoulders is formidable. He appears eager. I look back at the motor. I cannot say that I have faith in its condition, either. I'm no stranger to exertion, but I hope we don't have to do much rowing. Just another concern to sit on the uncertainty of this survey's start.

Behind us, Yost sits at the rudder. She makes no unnecessary motion, and her body seems unnaturally rigid. Her gaze remains fixed on our destination. Albertachen is a barely visible dot on the horizon, but she has it deadlocked.

"If the sea gets rough," she says, "follow every instruction when I give it."

I don't dream of contesting that.

With a sharp twist of her hip and a pull of her shoulder, the motor roars to life and the boat shifts into motion.

Meanwhile, I reach under my bench and pull out a rectangular, waterproof box. Inside, a radio transmitter. I adjust the frequency to Mikael's channel. Static crackles. He does not respond to my hail on any frequency.

Then, there's a sharp hiss.

"...camp...complete..." a voice bursts between squelches. Though I can only understand every third or fourth word, the tone is calm. "Approach...South South...the lighthouse, repeat..."

I try to fine-tune the frequency, but it doesn't help. The signal drops below the threshold and only static remains. I cycle through the channels again, hoping Mikael will find a more stable connection.

Suddenly, a robotic voice breaks though, speaking syllables with identical pace and rhythm: "Albertachen. Clover. Seashell. Wormwood. Caldera. Coral. Albertachen. Transit. Hedge clipper. Tally. Quill. Grave. Albertachen. Clover. Seashell..."

When the message falls into repetition, I lower the volume and check the frequency. I look to my companions.

"That's the Albertachen beacon," I say. "Were any of you aware it was operational?"

"Perhaps they repaired it as a task of opportunity," Brogden says.

I nod. Certainly possible.

"But what gibberish is this?" I ask. "Where is the security status? Approach coordinates?"

Brogden does not reply. Yost lifts her head and eyes something in the water. A rock maybe? Sandbar? Then, she adjusts the rudder a couple of degrees. If she knows anything, she doesn't say. No surprise there.

I turn off the radio. No good to guess at riddles with missing clues. Best now to make all speed ahead and find with our own eyes whether more information will make itself apparent. Over the water, a cloud cover in the distance. A mist rolls over, the sea beneath. If we don't make good time, this boat journey might get a whole lot more interesting.

Our path meanders among dead reefs and submerged rocks,

but the water is clear with a crystal-blue tint, and the hazards are easy to see. Yost navigates the rudder with deft skill. Occasionally, clouds of white silt kick up from underneath us as the force of our prow alarms bottom feeders.

Then, our course evens out. I try to let my mind disassociate. The motor has a cough in it that makes clear we shouldn't push it too hard, so the trip will take some time. I remember the train I rode from the Capital to the outskirts where my mother had purchased land with my father's death bond. We rode one car off from the livestock car, the cheapest spots that ran the length of the line. We couldn't smell it in motion but at every station, the chicken, goat, and donkey feces billowed into the cabin like a dust cloud barreling down an erupting volcano. I'm sure we inhaled every manner of parasite.

The track we took travelled through the mountains. I'd once thought the Capital the most majestic place one could imagine. Yet, entering the mountains, I'd felt so dwarfed that I cried.

We passed into the first tunnel. I'd been in total darkness before of course, in basements, under the streets working for extra rations, but entering the tunnel felt like I was descending into the heart of the earth. Despite the darkness, I'd found myself drawn to the windows. I'd pressed my palms to the glass and tried to cup fingers around my eyes to keep the light inside the car from tainting the view beyond. When looking at the dark of the world, it is always veiled by the light inside of us.

I don't know what I saw out there beyond the window, whether it was earth or nothingness. I don't remember anything beyond the cold, hard barrier my breath clouded. Even then, with my whole life ahead of me, it was easy to believe that barrier was all that was real to begin with.

* * *

The motor dies a mile out. It does so with little aplomb: a simple, single sputter is followed by a gasp. Then, silence. A couple wisps of black smoke waft up and are immediately stolen away by the wind.

Yost's face remains impassive as she inspects the motor. She gives a tentative tug to the pull cord, but I assume the mechanism is locked up because she lets go of it with a swear almost immediately.

"Maybe we fix once we arrive at Albertachen," Brogden says.

He lowers his oars into the water and gestures at my set. I lower mine as well and take a couple deep breaths. The going is slow from the start, but it is unquestionably better than being adrift with a storm coming.

The shelf gradually drops into the lips of the channel, and the water around us darkens. The wind chills and the cloud cover spreads across the sky like we are in a closing drawer. The chafing has begun to damage my palms. I have too long manned desks and sat in offices. I will blister soon.

Then, something wet slaps the deck beside my boot. Something that splattered from the object glistens on the leather and on the wood beside. On first impression, the object is a kelp knot the size of a fist.

No, it is a jellyfish. Black, pulsating, helpless. No doubt one of the same jellyfish of which the ferryman spoke.

Yost's eyes widen slightly, and in an instant my gut knows the ferryman did not exaggerate.

"Brogden," she calls. "Don't jerk your oars so high."

Brogden's oar had flung the jellyfish into the boat. I am grateful that it struck no one. Yost unsheathes one of her machetes, reaches with the blade like a shovel, and scoops the creature over the side.

The second time, it is I who throws a jelly. It splashes into the water just by the port hull with a dull slap.

"Slow," Yost hollers. "We're entering a bloom."

Our rhythm subdues. Dark shapes hover below the water's surface. Fat at the top, they taper and fade. At first, they are scattered meters apart, but the distance between them halves and halves. Clusters form and then a blanket under the gentle chop blown by a rising wind. The bloom is like ink poured into water.

If one of them is as bad as the ferryman said, I wonder what of falling into a dozen? Sweat runs down my back and down my ribs. I'm no stranger to pain. I've been stung or bitten by pretty much every insect that flies or crawls and stings or bites. I've broken my forearm twice; my eyes drop to the pale scar where my radius broke the skin. However, I've heard that poisons that come from the sea bring pain like no other.

A tremendous splash behind us startles us all. In my own shock, I find myself half standing before I even realize what I'm doing. The shape rising from the water looks totally alien, a whitish-gray thing the size of my torso. Enormous shoulders bulge, and wings that must be a meter long unfurl to beat the air with strokes powerful enough to crack a skull. From gnarled claws dangle a knot of jellyfish.

My eyes follow the creature up until it is a silhouette against the impending overcast, and it joins a dozen circling birds high up enough that they don't cast a shadow. Most are the same size as the one that snatched the jellies, but some are larger. They must have emerged from the cloud bank.

One of the larger birds dives next, this one with a piercing shriek that cuts straight into my soul like a razor into boiled fish. White, frothy spray erupts where talons strike the surface.

Then, another shriek, another splash, this one just beside the hull. The saltwater sloshes onto my legs and the deck. My legs twitch, and my flesh pimples everywhere. A deep enough chill rests in the water to kill us should we sink and be forced to tread within it.

The two birds lift off, and then the sky comes down.

In twos and threes they crash. The noise buffets my ears and frays my nerves, because I never know quite which direction the next set will erupt from. I try to follow them in their climb toward their clouds, watch as their beaks stab straight through jellyfish hoods and rip out their innards before they release whole fistfuls from their clutch. The dead jellies rain down on the ocean like hail.

Rain down on the ocean and on us.

The first splatters that hit us smack harmlessly against the horsehead prow.

The second scores a direct hit onto Brogden's exposed forearm.

His hand claps onto it and flings it away.

Already, the skin beneath it streaks fiery red. A clear liquid oozes from a welt. Brogden roars, his baritone hard and raspy and wild like a deranged grizzly. His hand slaps back to the wound site and squeezes so hard his knuckles whiten and the tendons raise like tent wire. He draws a deep breath that spreads his shoulders, and he shrieks, this time high and shrill.

Already Yost is in motion, her arms flying up as she rises, a black length of cloth held in her hands.

"Your coats!" she shouts. "Over your heads!"

She falls on her knees beside Brogden, who has tumbled onto his side and is thrashing his arms and arching his back. His coat is crumpled on the deck beside him. Immediately, she is upon him, pressed against his back, her arms winding around him, her legs hooking against his. Her attack reminds me of a spider coming down on its prey in a web. Though he clearly strains against her, all Brogden's large motions cease. I'm sure it must be part adrenaline, but her strength is astonishing.

"Don't just sit there, you dolt," she bellows. "Cover us!"

I stumble forward, grabbing for Brogden's coat even as another cluster of jellyfish splatters across the boat, streaking the seat Yost had just left. As I crouch down, my hip jostles the radio and something on its face clicks. Static squelches. A high-pitched whine follows that makes my teeth hurt. The mechanical voice begins, "Albertachen. Clover. Seashell. Wormwood. Caldera. Coral. Albertachen. Transit." In the background, garbled, the same message again, offset by a couple seconds.

More jellies strike the water as the birds keep shrieking their feeding frenzy. Water sloshes onto the boat, and a plunging body strikes the side of the hull with a reverberating thud that shudders the whole frame. I am shouting. Maybe there are words in my voice, maybe not.

CHAPTER 5

NEUROTOXIN, CHANNEL, STORM

The attack might only last for a few minutes. Probably, it only lasts for a few minutes. It is hours on our hearts. When Brogden ceases his fight against Yost, I assume he must be dead, his heart stopped, his tongue bitten in half. We will bury him on the shore of Albertachen, I suppose, unless we receive other instructions. The Bureau frets little about the internment of those who die in the field.

When it has been several moments since the last strike, I am trembling. My teeth grind. My temples twitch as if jellies still thud about us. All my limbs are fatigued, although I've done nothing but quiver. The musty, sour smell of fear emanates off my companions. No doubt I am myself rife with it.

I count twenty breaths, each a fraction longer than the last. The stillness unravels knots in me. I wince at nothing but expectation of that nothing shattering.

Then, I lift the edge of my peacoat. As the fabric rises, a couple of jellies roll down it, tumble to the deck behind me with graceless splats. Their barbs can still sting, because they are designed to inflict damage no matter what. We will need to remove them with caution. People fight to the death, but these creatures fight beyond. I let the coat settle on my shoulders and hold it closed at the neck as I rise to a crouch. The hull is littered with jellies, white feathers with grey tips, and spatters of guano.

Above, no sign of birds. They have vanished into the clouds. What kind of bird were they? Some sort of heron? The clouds have thickened, and their crawl across the sky has grown more pronounced because the wind has strengthened. The surface of the water laps and curls almost as if birds still strike it. Gutted jelly hoods and tentacle clumps bob and roll on the turbulence. The school is still there, though descended a couple meters, its density undented.

I help uncover Yost first and then Brogden. Yost sits up, checks the hull behind her for jellies and then leans back. She snorts up a drop of blood that had bubbled from one of her nostrils and wipes her upper lip with the back of her palm. She proceeds to massage her left shoulder with her right hand and her right quadricep with her left hand.

"Are you okay?" I ask.

Yost tilts her head back against the hull and closes her eyes. She licks her lips and flexes her jaw. Blood smears her front teeth. "He is a strong ox. I'll be fine."

I examine Brogden's arm and check his pulse. His heart is racing. His entire upper arm is massively swollen. Purple stripes raise even higher where the tentacles touched his flesh. The welt where the barb pierced is puffed the size of a strawberry and oozes a red pus that stinks like fish oil. Even in his unconsciousness, his face is screwed up in suffering. His eyes flit under the lids, and his lips twitch back from his teeth.

I turn to the nearest rucksack. It is covered with jellies. I borrow Yost's machete and scoop the carcasses back into the sea. I dig through the bag until I find a medical kit and remove an ampoule of morphine.

Yost says, "Don't bother."

I look at her blankly.

"Won't work," she says. "The toxin attacks the pain center of the brain. You need to neutralize the poison."

I want to curse, but there is no point. The only option is to adapt. I repack the medical kit, take up the machete, and continue to fling dead jellies into the water.

* * *

By the time I clear the boat of jellies, Yost appears less jarred. Brogden hardly moves except for small spasms. Meanwhile, the storm surges toward us. The clouds cover nearly the whole sky, and the wind buffets my ears. As I sit to row, I am forced by the growing chill to pull on my peacoat even if it will inhibit my motion.

Our progress is slow at first. Without Brogden's massive shoulders, our strokes feel ineffectual, and Yost and I struggle to synchronize. My hands grow numb in their grips. Fortunately, we're on a straight course for the deep channel, so Yost's hands are free from the rudder to row. Even then, her pace falters often.

Meanwhile, the first peal of thunder arrives as the gods of storm and winter clear their throats. Flashes flare within the nimbus hearts. Soon, ocean swells will rise. If we haven't arrived on the island before the storm reaches us, it will be a miracle not to be swept off course.

Yost, however, stops rowing. For a moment, I think she needs rest, but we still move quite fast, faster than when Brogden had been rowing too. The water has grown dark around us. We have entered the channel current, and it pulls us like a great river. I release the oars, all my muscles trembling, and I cup my hands at my mouth, and blow hotly across my tender blisters.

"I hope Mikael has a pair of replacement arms for me at camp. Maybe a new lower back," I say.

"The storm could still overtake us," Yost says. "The wind is strong."

I nod.

"We'll rest as long as we can," I say. Yost massages her shoulder and leg again. It could not have been easy to restrain Brogden. She is strong, but so is he. No doubt there is damage to muscle or tendon or both. I retrieve the med kit and for the second time remove the ampule of morphine. This time, I ignore Yost's protests as I draw a low dose and say, "The rest will make you stiffen. The pains will grow. You know this."

Yost sighs and extends her hand. I pass her the painkiller and then sit back. For a moment, I don't really think about anything, just let my gaze blur in and out of focus on some arbitrary point in the woodgrain of the hull. The water underneath, with its steady pull. The lapping wavelets, our prow severing them.

Then, I lift my gaze to Albertachen. It is still distant. I can't see it grow, but I know that it is growing. If I squint, I can discern a couple of roofs, including the peak of the lighthouse. Some sort of house stands on the bluff closest to us, half concealed by a rocky crag.

The distance amplifies the haze caused by the particulates suspended in the air and makes my eyes ache in their sockets. I shift my focus into the water. The jellies are gone, vanishing into the increasing current. I imagine sticking my hand through the water's surface, the cold embrace of the water, the tug of the current on my fingers. Like sticking one's hand out a train window into the wind. The simple pleasures, they say.

The water itself is a rich blue-green, and the longer I peer into it, the more it strikes me just how deep I can see. It's difficult to gauge the depth, because so little provides frame of reference. The rocky crags that rise from the sea floor could be two meters high or they could be twenty. Maybe they're two hundred.

Among them slide long, dark shapes. Are they two meters

long? Twenty? Are they tuna or sharks? Dolphins or whales? How many are there? I try to count them, but the number slips through my fingers as I second-guess whether I'm seeing different ones or the same. The way they weave among the rocky outcroppings is difficult to track, like some living shell game.

One of them darts at something I can't see and thrashes. The motion reminds me that fish aren't composed of parts in quite the way humans are composed of parts. Their whole body is one unified thing, a single arc of graceful, dire force. They don't tear a quadricep like Yost. They'd tear their whole being or not at all. What would it be like to watch them on their level, perhaps hiding in some crevasse like a camouflaged octopus or a moray eel waiting to grab the weakest hunter? Sharks can smell blood from distances hard to fathom smelling anything from, but what, under water, do the sharks smell like? I envy their single-minded hunts, the singularity of their form.

I lean toward the water. At the bottom, rocky heaps on the channel floor seem to move. It must be a trick of the water, of the motion of the water, of the turbidity caused by the motion of the hunters, but they tilt and sway. What must be tons of basalt rocks wafting like leaves.

It's not just the basalt pillars, either. The whole sea floor seems to rise and fall, slowly, and I'm reminded of the way blankets rise and fall. It strikes me, impossible as it is, with a certainty that the sea floor I see is not the sea floor, but the back of some gargantuan beast made of the earth itself. I imagine it crouched; its enormous limbs folded underneath itself like collapsed mountains. What if it were to awaken and rise up beneath us? Our boat would pour off its shoulders as if it was just more water.

A large cluster of rocks seem to twist in a way that feels like something in reality is breaking, and as hands on my back pull me away, I realize that I'd just seen two enormous, pale-green eyes open.

* * *

Yost slaps my face. My cheek is numbed by cold. The meat feels rubbery as a fat lip, but the slap is hard. My vision flashes white. Yost looks cross, even for her.

"What the—" I start, but Yost's steely eyes shut my mouth.

"You nearly went over the side," she says. "Are you mad?"

I rub my jaw and flex the joint. Something stiff hurts when I do.

"No, I..." I begin, but I trail off, looking slowly around the boat, and the choppy water surrounding us. It's gotten a good bit darker. What just happened? I'm not at all certain how long I'd been so engaged. "I'm sorry," I say. "I think I may have fallen asleep."

"Osh!" Yost exclaims. "Asleep, my ass. You were staring into the water. You started muttering to yourself, and then you leaned toward—"

"Muttering?" I ask. "What was I saying?"

"Same bullshit that came over the radio," Yost says, folding her arms across her chest. "Albertachen. Transit. Caldera. Whatever."

Frowning deeply, I glance over the side. The eyes are not there, and the seabed looks dead and abandoned, not just lifeless but as if life has forgotten about it.

"Apologies," I say. "I do not know what to say. I must have found the seabird attack more straining than I'd supposed."

Yost narrows her eyes at me, but then she points over the port prow.

Albertachen has grown enormously. We have crossed perpendicular to its narrow peak, and I'm peering down its length. Whereas before I could only see the lighthouse and a couple scattered roofs, the whole tableau of the island now spreads before me.

From above, it would likely resemble something akin to a croissant with the bulk being the rising bulge of the island's dominant hill. The Midway viewing side is predominantly a sheer cliff, but from this side, the whole island is a mesa with a gradual slope down toward the far end. To port now spans a cove nearly the whole length of the island, the croissant's belly of exposed beach. I see the docks, a covered design for sheltered unloading, the moored supply boat that brought the rest of the team, and the base camp that is little more than a cluster of tents surrounded by a razor-wire fence.

Beyond the camp, a long building with a half-circle steel frame reminds me of the greenhouses of central farms. A few sheets of rotting canvas still dangle from the frame, and along with the double door at one end, form the only solid wall that remains. I know it to have once been a barracks. The newest structure on the island, it was constructed shortly before the prison was decommissioned. It seems a bit odd to have built quarters large enough to house so many in a place on the verge of abandonment, but I won't say that the Central Bureau is always tremendously judicious in its expenditures.

A broken fortification and a collapsed tower stand across from the barracks entrance and past them both stands a stone structure with a timber roof. Beyond, a sixty-meter cliff with broad stairs carved into it. The stairs lead to the plateau, all the buildings on which stand in varied states of decay. The plateau is the destination for our survey.

"An ugly place," I offer.

"I don't think they intended it to look otherwise," Yost says.

I can't make out her expression. It's not that her face is blank, but rather something complex is happening beneath the surface and she is saying none of it. Then, her attention fixes on the dock. She calls out to row, and we set our hands on the oars.

I am focused on the chop. Yost steers us out of the strongest part of the channel current, but the sea has begun to swell underneath us. Each rise and fall threatens to carry us a little further out, and we row against our own motion. It is good, then, that we found some chance to rest. Had we fought this right after the jelly frenzy, I doubt we'd have overcome.

The wind howls over the island's shoulders with a sound like a flag flapping in a gale. It sends a cold straight into my ears that makes my eardrums ring. My hands shake on the oars. I fight the urge to keep checking over my shoulder because it breaks my rhythm to do so. The waves cap white.

The boat lurches to the side with a shuddering thud. The oars swing wild, and mine strikes with a glance off my forehead. I recover, no more than a bit dazed, but aware a firmer blow could have cracked my skull.

Then, my eyes widen at the black silhouettes of sharks. Two of them the length of our boat outstrip our pace. A third emerges from underneath us, swimming perpendicular to our course. Any one of them could swamp us. My bowels quiver like they're going through a laundry ringer. Yost's fingers twist on the oars. She opens her mouth to say something but does not.

Are they going to ram us? Dive and surge up from beneath, fracturing the hull? Or maybe launch up from the surface to crush us beneath their teeth and weight?

I check if the first three circled back toward us and realize I see more than sharks. Too many fish to count all swim along the current as if in migration. They range in size from sardines to large sleek shadows one might mount on the wall.

"Maybe they're escaping the storm," I say.

"Maybe they know something we don't," Yost says. "Animals are usually smarter than people when it comes to danger."

I am reminded of what I thought I'd seen on the sea bottom.

Moments later, the sea breaks its hold on us with a palpable surge as we cross into the space a sand bar shields from the surrounding flows. We ride the shoreward swells toward the docks. The first drops of rain plunk concentric rings all across the water. Something stings my cheek, and I look to my feet where something knocks to a stop. A stone of hail the size of my fingertip to the last knuckle. They rattle in the boat like tossed dice.

On shore, a man I recognize from file photos to be Mikael rushes down the dock with a mooring hook.

I cannot possibly contain more relief when our prow thunks against the dock.

Chapter 6

Mikael, Irregularities, Inverterbrates

We waste no time unlashing our packs and thrusting them under the dock's roof. Every hail stone that strikes Brogden makes me wince, even if he is unconscious. We must get him to shelter as he is unable to shelter himself. I am hesitant to ask Mikael to help, but he's been on the island longer. Records indicate several strains of the virus can survive inside their protein capsids for decades in favorable conditions, and the high levels of exchangeable aluminum in Albertachen's soil is quite favorable. The official reports grow fuzzy accounting for all Gollitok's deaths, but they're generally attributed to rampant infection.

Without a word, Yost climbs onto the dock, crouches, and reaches down. Careful not to rock the boat too severely, I crouch and shove my hands into Brogden's armpits. He's as dead weight as a burlap sack of potatoes, but in a moment, I'm on shaking knees and Yost is grappling under his shoulders too. Tired and sore as we are, large as Brogden is, we manage to heave him up onto the dock, muttering swears all the while. Hail bounces off the boat's surfaces at all angles, strikes my cheek, my neck, any other exposed spot as I drag myself from the boat. The dock creaks under our weight, but a few planks of fresh lumber shore up rotted sections.

Mikael and Yost walk to the end of the dock and exchange hushed words. Mikael is unshaven with olive skin and nearly black, wiry hair. He is thinner and shorter than Yost, but he wears the same camouflaged overalls as her and a white turtleneck with a silver wrench embroidered into the neck that signifies that he is a military engineer.

Yost cracks her shoulders and neck, and she flexes her knees while they converse. They stand in close proximity with the posture of old friends. Their body language is so familiar, I half expect them to embrace. Of course, they make no contact. Fortunately, the risk is minimal until we are exposed to the soil and dust of the plateau.

When Yost and Mikael return from their conversation, I say, "We need to move Brogden to his tent."

"Indeed," Mikael says. "I will see to your gear. You go straight to the camp."

"Has something happened?" I ask. "What have you found?"

"Much," Mikael says. Then, he gestures to Brogden. "See to your companion. When the hail abates, I will apprise you of the state of things."

"Very well," I say. "Are we under threat?"

"Always, and don't forget it," he says. "But our camp is the safest place you can be for the moment. Do not attempt to go beyond the camp until I can debrief."

"Understood," I say. I squint into the rain. Electric lights glow in the camp, but no one is moving about. The rest is gray, hard, and still. "I appreciate your directness."

"Lieutenant Yost informs me that your man was stung by black jellies?"

"Yes," I say. "One landed on his arm."

Mikael nods, but his attention roves around the tents and rocks onshore with the clear look of a man who has other things to think about. It is no surprise when he excuses himself.

* * *

The path from the docks was once paved, but every other stone is broken. A banister once ran its length past our destination, past the old watchtower and admitting building, to the stone stair up the cliff face to the Gollitok, but all that is left are broken posts and tumbled rails. The ground of Albertachen is an almost uniform gray, littered with broken stones, chunks of driftwood, clumps of desiccated seaweed. A few rocky outcroppings shelter what appear to be some sort of abandoned avian or reptilian nests.

Most distinct of all, there is no vegetation. No grass. No shrubs, not even the scrubby succulents that grow all over the shoreward islands. The name "Gollitok" was created by linguistic drift from the island's original name, Goli Otok, but the prison long held the nickname "the Naked Island" because it was, in essence, a naked rock on the sea. No shade. No natural sustenance. No beauty. The soil was not arable, leaving those interned here utterly dependent on their custodians. Looking at it now, its bleakness is beyond doubt. What better place to deposit your enemies?

Without a word, Yost and I heft Brogden between us and haul him into the stinging hail. The stretch we carry our companion through was once a labor yard where the prisoners would engage in useless toil, forced to dig holes to the waterline and then refill them, forced to move a massive pile of stone twenty meters to one side only to reconstruct it in its original place the next day. Sometimes, as a warning to the others for how disposable they all were, the guards would demand a prisoner dig down six feet and then bury him or herself alive. How it must have felt to sit at the bottom of a pit you dug and begin pulling dirt over yourself. It's always been said about Albertachen that the reason nothing grows is that the dead drag everything down by the roots.

As the degradation of the path forces us to carry Brogden beside it, I wonder how many people's bones we step over. From the docks to the camp, it's only about a hundred meters, but the burden of an unconscious man and our packs make it feel like a kilometer. Finally, the path forks, and we branch through a break in the razor wire fence. The wire is a nasty, coiling affair meant to strangle and slice anything fool enough to attempt crossing through it, and it stands over six feet high, coil over coil.

Inside the camp, five tents and a latrine shack surround a firepit. Several crates are stacked in between the tents, a couple open to reveal straw-packed bottles, canned goods, and pickling jars. The tents are top quality military issue, the kind they reserve for troops in combat zones. At first glance, they look like standard Mylar, but they're a pre-war reinforced weave. We were issued similar in the quarries to protect against falling rocks.

The tents to either side of the camp entrance are occupied, and one has been set up as the camp headquarters. The flap is closed, but the portable radio antennae array standing beside it tells me that inside, I'll find our comms equipment. The other two tents are empty. I nod to the left tent, and we hustle Brogden inside.

The tent inside is tall enough to stand in. Just barely, but enough. Two cots with a bedroll and blankets stand, one on each side. The hail clatters as we lay Brogden on the right and cover him with the blanket. His body tenses, shakes, then goes limp again. While I remember the ferryman's words, I hope he was exaggerating about the duration of the poison. With any luck, Brogden will remain asleep through the worst of its effects.

I slough off my pack and sit on the edge of what is going to be my cot. The relief is glorious.

"Yost," I say with an exhausted smile, "I will not say anything remotely pleasant about our journey together. I do not know what tonight or tomorrow will bring us, but right now we are concluding a segment of terrific ordeal. I am glad of it. And I am glad for your company."

Yost nods. It is neither friendly nor hostile. The best I could hope for, I suppose. Then she turns and leaves the tent. I don't fault her. Even if I wanted to, I don't have the energy. All I really feel is an unsettled nausea.

I sigh and rub the sides of my nose with my index fingers. The stress of the day has left me with a mild headache, and the day isn't even over. Who knows what Mikael is going to heap on. What if the strain here was the hemorrhagic strain? Who knows if there are smugglers somewhere on the shore or perhaps waiting behind some ocean rock a few kilometers out to ambush us? What if I wake to bullets striking my tent? The memory of those enormous green eyes under the water resurfaces, and I shudder.

"Maybe you're lucky," I say at Brogden. "Maybe you'll sleep through our deaths and wake up to a rescue team and a survivor's medal."

Tired as I am, I take a moment to sift through my pack. Aside from the standard issue of thermal underclothes and beige Bureau top clothes, I find my official survey ledger, a reflective, insulated blanket, matches, lighter, flashlights, emergency tinder and kindling, three packs of government cigarettes, two types of iodine tablets, toilet paper, a canteen, and the med kit I'd already opened. There is also a variety of disinfectants and a multitool intended to be a shovel, pick, prybar, and hatchet all in one. Finally, I extract a calf-holstered 9mm HS 2000 pistol and two sixteen-round magazines that I strap underneath my slacks, an Orion flare gun with four flares that I stash in the pocket opposite the pistol Brogden gave me, and a thumb-sized New-Tech radio transmitter and earpiece.

Reaching into the very bottom of the bag, my fingers scrape against a plastic back, and I pull out a piece of old tech that I don't recognize: a rectangular panel with a blank, powered down screen and several buttons on the front. I thumb on the power button, and the screen lights. Several numbers indicate some sort of rate per hour, though I don't recognize the unit, and the device emits a steady clicking sound. At the top left corner blinks a circle with three triangles fanning out from a central point. I am not familiar with the symbol. The device itself feels vaguely military, so I figure I can ask Yost about it, though I do not know if she will be forthcoming. A rigid clip is attached to its back, so I hook the clip to my belt where it vanishes under my coat.

Then, though I know I should make my notes about the crossing in the survey ledger, I lean back on the cot. I only intend to do so for a few moments, but the moment I'm flat on my back it strikes me as simply too difficult to get back up for it to be worth the trouble. Seconds later, I am asleep in fitful and irrational dreams.

* * *

I wake to someone poking me in the chest with a stick. I open my eyes to a brick house of a woman in construction overalls and a thick, button-up shirt. Even from here, I can smell alcohol on her breath. I can see beyond her through the open tent flap that it is now evening, but the tent is lit by strip lighting embedded in the seams.

"Time to wake, they're by the fire," she says in a gruff voice laden with disinterest. She gestures at Brogden. "Mikael is preparing an antivenom."

Then she is gone.

I sit up straight through a cloud of my own breath. The temperature has dropped at least fifteen degrees. How long have I been asleep? Brogden does not seem to have moved, though someone apparently entered while I slept and spread an additional blanket over him.

I breathe into my hands. Despite having slept fully clothed and in my peacoat, the air bites my cheeks and fingers. My cap has fallen off, so I pull it down as far over my ears as I can and retrieve a pair of work gloves from my pack. Then, I grab my ledger and a sanitizer bottle and step to the tent flap.

Outside, the wind shrieks over the barren landscape, but the rain and hail has ceased. A large fire has been built in the pit at the camp's center. A camping grill sizzles with food and a large soup kettle hangs over the flames. Already, Yost, Mikael, and the forward team have occupied folding chairs around it.

I amble to the latrine and relieve myself, but when I emerge, I find myself facing a woman in standard issue brown khakis and a navy t-shirt. Her broad face has aged considerably since I last saw her, but I'd worked across from Efta in the quarry offices a long time. Burn scars trail down her left arm and up from her collar to her chin on the right side of her neck. Even if I could have forgotten her face, I'd never forget those scars.

I smile immediately and clap her lightly on the shoulder.

"Efta, it is fantastic to see you."

Indeed it is. The Bureau typically eschews assigning the same officials to multiple tasks. As the saying goes, fraternization is the root of corruption.

Efta does not smile in return. Instead, she raises a bundle of papers she clenches in a single fist so that it has crumpled up.

"What nonsense is this?" she says, her voice low.

I take a step back and politely pluck the papers from her hands. I carefully smooth them flat against my thigh before I regard them. I immediately recognize the Bureau seal and watermarks. These are official orders.

"My apologies," I say, "but I do not know of what you speak."

"My assignment," she says. "Nonsense. Bullshit. There is real work to be done at Albertachen."

I glance toward the fire. We are close enough to hear that people are speaking, but far enough their words are lost. Though it is unlikely they can hear our exchange, I must comport myself diplomatically as my post demands. Who knows who will write what in which report or whose unintended eyes will intercept.

"Forgive me," I say, "but I will remind you that all Bureau work is real work."

Efta snatches the orders back from me and points to a paragraph. It might be what she wants me to read, or it might just be a random spot, but she speaks as if quoting when she says, "Determine if the lights characterized in the incident report are of natural origin. Write up a geological report that would justify the phenomenon should they prove insubstantial."

I cross my arms. I do not wish to sour my working relationship with Efta, but her response will not do, especially at such an early juncture. I have misgivings too with Yost's hostility, Brogden's injury, and now this, but my job as survey lead is to maintain team discipline and ensure everyone applies themselves to their assignments, whatever those assignments might be.

"If the Bureau saw fit—" I begin.

"I don't give a damn what the Bureau sees fit," Efta interrupts, but I speak over, as urgently as I can while keeping my voice down.

"You know full well from what happened at the quarries you should," I say.

Her jaw clamps shut. Her eyes harden.

"You weren't there," she says.

"I'm glad of it," I say.

There is a glacier between us.

"Shit," Efta says finally, with a shake of her head. "I shouldn't be surprised you're as orthodox as ever. They wouldn't have made you lead otherwise."

Then, she turns heel and heads to the fire. I follow and join everyone in warmth and light.

When I sit down between Yost and Efta, Mikael passes me a mug of coffee and introduces the rest of the forward crew, who all sit on the far side of the fire. The woman who woke me is Tompka, the engineer. The dock repairs and the fence both were her handiwork. She is also, apparently, our team virologist. The combination of specialties is odd, but often training is based in pragmatism. Yammut, the first technician, shivers underneath jeans and a heavy woolen sweater, chewing thoughtfully on an old pencil she pauses to scratch her scalp with. The second technician, Jones, is a hulk of a man with pale skin and enormous hands that look like they could crush a grizzly skull.

Mikael stirs the kettle over the fire. It contains a simple vegetable stew that smells of garlic and turmeric. He then turns to the grill and tends sausages and onion halves cooking there. I notice that the bundle the inspector gave me is on a cooler next to the grill. Did he actually add the foul-smelling herb to our food?

As we eat, I try to detect traces of what I would imagine Orlot tastes like in the food but fail, and before long, the welcome warmth of the meal makes me forget the effort. As the wind continues to gust around us, I wonder what the island must have been like for the prisoners in winter as they toiled on the shore to dig their holes and pile their rocks. How many lost fingers, toes, or noses to frostbite? How badly did their skin crack and peel? How many wandered off in the late stages of hypothermia to cram themselves into an unseen cranny to die? Would the guards have stopped them? I am glad I do not believe in ghosts.

For some time, we eat quietly. Only the technicians converse amongst themselves. Apparently, they both enjoy pre-war art, especially a style called impressionism. The first technician has been sketching features of Albertachen in a pad. The second technician nods appreciatively. More than once, Tompka takes strong pulls from a flask she produces from her coat. Though there is no regulation against drinking off-duty, what is off-duty in an assignment such as this is subject to debate.

I drain the last of the broth from my soup and say to Mikael, "A fine meal. Thank you."

A murmured agreement passes around the fire.

I lean back, pat my belly, and say, "I remember a survey I was assigned to in the inland swamps. One of my first assignments. No one told us the locals wouldn't allow outside consumables into the region. Believed that strains of contagion would survive processing."

"Ah, yes," Efta says. "Those are the folk who eat EVERY part of the animal and call anything questionable—"

"—A delicacy," Mikael finishes with a chuckle.

"Ah, but these folks," I say, "they didn't eat animals – leastwise, they didn't eat vertebrates."

"Oh, Lord," Efta laughs. "Crème de caterpillar was it then? Sauté of snail?"

"Close," I say. "Their principal proteins were spiders and scorpions. Holy shit, you wouldn't believe what their plates looked like all served up."

Yost shakes her head and says, "I'll cannibalize myself before I eat anything with more than four legs."

The laughter lasts several seconds then subsides. I look across their faces. Yost and Efta appear more relaxed. Funny how food and conversation can turn your view of the world.

Everyone finishes their meals, and we set aside our plates. Mikael clears his throat. He leans forward and props his elbows on his knees, extending his palms toward the fire.

"We must turn our attention to more serious matters," he says.

A general stillness falls on us all.

Mikael checks a pot on a kerosene burner by his foot. He removes a digital thermometer from his pocket and sticks it into whatever is heating there. After checking the temperature, he nods. Then, all emotion leaves his face.

CHAPTER 7

NEW PROTOCOL, SMELLING SALTS, THE REMAINING SKY

Mikael begins.

"We arrived at ten-hundred hours. Dock was unstable, so dropped anchor and disembarked in the shallows. Everything appeared deserted, though we discovered the buried remains of multiple fires a little closer to the stairs to the plateau. A number of footprints as well, but none were fresh. Most clustered near the fire sites, but we traced some of the older ones as far as the admitting building. No trace of anyone heading up to the Gollitok. The evidence is consistent with smugglers using the cove and beach as a campsite."

"What about other landing sites?" I ask. "Other stairs up the plateau?"

Mikael shakes his head.

"We took the cruiser around the whole island. The cliffs sheer to the water most of the shore, except this peninsula and a small stretch across the far peninsula that appears to be used as a gravesite," Mikael says. Across the cove, the other peninsula rises high above the water, but even in the dark, an old mechanism is visible. "A cargo elevator on the far side once brought up heavy loads, but it's non-functional. It's not impossible they've come to shore at the graveyard, but access to the plateau from there is extremely difficult."

"What about the lighthouse?" Yost asks. "Its foundation is only slightly above sea-level."

Mikael shakes his head. "Unapproachable. The rocks off that spur would be impossible to navigate with any craft bigger than a raft or dingy."

"Why build it there?" I ask. "Why not on the bluff? It's barely taller than the cliffs."

Mikael shrugs.

"Beats me. The lighthouse does not seem to serve a functional purpose."

I nod. I make a note in my ledger that the lighthouse might be worth prioritizing. A lighthouse that doesn't function as a lighthouse is just a building that looks like a lighthouse.

"The most important finding of our preliminary investigation is that while there is clear evidence of activity," Mikael says, "there is no evidence of activity in a time frame that lines up with the inspector's report."

"So, the inspector was lying," I say.

"If you mean about observing figures on this shore two weeks past, then yes, the evidence indicates he has fabricated his statement," Mikael says.

"But he's telling the truth about what?" I ask.

Mikael chuckles, but then his expression deadens.

"That a prior expedition was dispatched," he says.

Yost straightens. What did the inspector tell her when she had him by the shirt?

"So he told you that as well," I say. "What evidence have you found?"

"Their boat," Mikael says.

"Where?"

Mikael points to a long, low building at the top of the plateau stairs. It is made of stone, but chunks of its walls have crumbled. The roof is half collapsed, but it looks sturdy at one end.

"Inside what records indicate was once the mess hall," Mikael says.

"How'd they get it up there?" I ask. "What did you find?"

"I've not been up there. Jones spotted it on the way to the radio array," Mikael says. He removes a Polaroid from his cargo pocket and passes the photo to me. The photo was taken through the collapsed wall of the mess. The name of the boat is familiar in the hybrid of Cyrillic and Kanji used by regional government in the period following the war until Official was codified. The *Sarru*.

"The Maritime Activities Bureau indicated that the *Sarru* is a government-registered ship reported lost off the western coast of Africa last year. Its service history indicates it was a medical research transport."

"And that brings it here how?" I ask, though I already know the answer.

"Likely its presence here is unofficial."

I pass the photo back to Mikael. His explanation makes sense. Given the failure of contact from an unofficial investigation, there would then be no choice but to open an official log. It also explained why they would take a high caliber field agent like Efta and assign her to write what are, on the books, bullshit cover stories for a tenuous incident report. Having her here to create credible cover for the loss of an illegal expedition, on the other hand, sounds in line with the Central Bureau's modus operandi.

"Any sign of the expedition members?" I ask.

Mikael shakes his head.

"Haven't searched. Jones only went to the plateau for the beacon. It was an unacceptable risk to further explore the Gollitok until basecamp was fully established and you had arrived."

Mikael gives a slight smile. I hadn't realized he'd been perspiring, but now I see it in the light of the flames. As the leader of the forward crew, the part of his job upon which his merits would be most significantly judged is now complete.

I ask, "Do you know why we struggled to maintain radio contact during our transit? Or the meaning of the message broadcast by the radio beacon?"

Mikael shifts his attention to Jones. The technician coughs slightly and runs his fingers through his hair.

"Um, yes," he says softly. "The island itself seems to have a strong electromagnetic property that disrupts incoming and outbound signals in an oscillating pattern. I believe it may have been one of the original selection criteria pre-war for designating this site a prison. Whether that effect is the result of some unstable geological properties or something man-made, is unknown."

"I see," I say.

"However," he continues, "though there is no recent evidence of any activity in the Gollitok, the radio equipment may have been tampered with, maybe even decades ago, to give outside parties access to the broadcasting capabilities. When I restored power to the transmitter, the iterating message began to broadcast immediately. If I had to guess, the message may well be an old smuggler's code. How to interpret it..."

He trails off with a shrug.

"I will need you to return with us in the morning to the plateau and see if you can resolve the tampering," I say. The technician's expression seems nonplussed, but he does not dispute.

I continue, "Mikael, after we establish the general security of the Gollitok, help sweep for signs of the prior expedition. We need to secure their team leader's records and any observations they may have recorded."

"That presumes," Yost interjects, sitting forward, "that something has befallen them."

"We must operate under that assumption," I say. "Given that they've not made themselves known since our arrival."

"No one has come or gone from the mess hall for some time,"

Jones says. "I saw no indication that anyone has been active on the plateau."

"I see," Yost says. "And you are a professional tracker?"

The technician cocks his head, his brow furrowed.

"That's what I thought," Yost says.

I lean back and bring my hand to my chin. I watch Yost a long moment. Her jaw quivers, and her molars grind. Her tendons are tense in her neck and the backs of her hands as well. She has some investment in the prior expedition. A supposition, of course, but certain enough that I may enter it into the expedition log before I sleep.

A buzz from Mikael's watch interrupts. He silences the alarm, checks the temperature of the liquid on the stove by his feet, removes the pot, and dowses the kerosene flame.

"The compound needs to cool," he says. "Then we will be able to assist Brogden. Until then, there is another matter we must discuss."

He gestures to Tompka who slides a canvas satchel from underneath her seat. The bag unzips with a whine, revealing bulky, black contraptions. She pulls one out and holds it up.

Respirators. Most likely standard high-filtration units issued for government activities in contaminated zones. .3 micron, maybe finer given the known high aluminum content of the soil. They cover the full face and strap tight around the back of the head; feels like wearing an upset octopus. I've only worn them in training scenarios.

"Under no circumstances will anyone ascend the cliffs without a respirator," the engineer says. "Check the seal on your respirators before descending. If your respirator has become compromised, you will not return to camp. We will disinfect all possessions you bring to the plateau after each trip."

The masks indicate high risk of exposure. Perhaps the prior team was infected, and the Central Bureau knows it.

"What do you know about the strain here?" I ask.

"Next to nothing," Tompka says. "Other than that the Gollitok was subject to the Starvation Quarantine and that I detected intact protein capsids in soil tests."

"Fucking disease," Efta mutters. "Dormant for decades, waiting for someone to poke it."

"I was briefed to expect a resilient strain," the engineer says with a dour nod.

"What are the projected odds of infection occurring within survey members despite protocols?" I ask.

"Eighteen percent. If infection reaches camp, odds of infection of the entire team are projected at ninety-six percent, regardless of interventions."

"So then, contact protocols within the camp are irrelevant?"

"Irrelevant? No. Restraint is prudent, but necessary contact is acceptable."

A curious smile passes between Efta and Tompka. There is some private joke.

"We have also set up decontamination protocols in the Admitting Building," the engineer says. "We will each be subject to a chemical shower and a UV bath. I hope you like chemical burns and aren't prone to skin cancer."

My heart drops. The protocols are not unexpected, but they will add a painful tedium to the expedition. Lord help us if the survey drags on too long.

The gathering devolves into contemplative silence interspersed with light conversation. The team members eat and drink and talk about prior assignments. Efta and the engineer fall into an involved conversation that displays an easy chemistry together, and the technicians argue softly about electromagnetic frequencies. I listen with half an ear and let my mind wander to evenings in the family orchard.

It was mostly just my mom and I, occasionally members of our distant family. When they visited, we'd build fires in the yard and spend evenings much like this. Of course, the difficulties of arranging travel permits meant no one came on the regular, so they felt more like guests than family. In many ways, folk I work surveys with feel more like family.

Suddenly, I realize that Yammut, the first technician, has crouched beside me. He's a slight man with lank black hair. A string of beads is wound around his hand. He asks if I have a moment.

"My briefing documents contained a very old geological survey of the island," he says. "The island rests atop some pretty extensive mineral deposits, and the prison was initially built to provide forced labor to extract those minerals. Once we restore radio functionality, I'd like your authorization to explore those mines."

"To what end?"

"I found a comm line that appears to run into the mine," he says. "I wonder if I might find a cache of old tech down there. Would look good on a report, eh?"

I shrug.

"I don't see why not," I say. "But watch the mine for signs of structural instability."

The technician gives me a thumbs-up and the beads dangling from his palm rattle softly.

Then, Mikael rises and lifts the cooling pot. He removes a small funnel and a narrow-neck flask from his coat pocket and fills the flask. The liquid inside is nearly transparent with a slight amber tint. He holds it up the firelight and swirls it around.

Satisfied, he brings it to me.

"Your man will need to drink as much of this as you can force him to," he says.

I reach up and take the flask. It is warm from the residual heat of the liquid. The liquid itself is more viscous than it had initially appeared, closer to a maple syrup in consistency.

"You will need assistance restraining him to ensure he takes enough for it to matter," Mikael says.

I rise, as does the second technician, Efta, and Yost.

"All four of you?" I ask.

Mikael gives a sober nod.

"The pain intensifies as the venom takes hold," Mikael says. "Adrenaline will flow through him unchecked in response. He will be irrational."

A cold iron rolls in my belly, and the wind re-embraces me as we step away from the fire. It is only a few meters to the tent, but the temperature drops with each step. As we walk, I remember the size of Brogden's shoulders, how Yost strained to hold him down. It is true that she did so by herself, but those circumstances were extraordinary. She too had been charged with adrenaline. Now might not be the same. I've seen the drug-addled and the deranged wrestle off entire clusters of peace officers. I've seen them snap people's bones.

Inside the tent, we drag Brogden's cot toward the center of the space so we can position ourselves around him. Thankfully, contact protocols can be relaxed. Yost and Jones brace themselves against Brogden's shoulders while Efta and Mikael wrap their arms around his thighs. Everyone's face is grim.

I remove my medical kit from my pack and pull out a capsule of smelling salts. Everyone takes a deep breath and holds it as I break open the capsule under Brogden's nose.

His chest rises. Rises more. His eyelids flutter.

And then his back arcs like he's being electrocuted, thrusting his abdomen up with such force that Efta and the technician stagger back against the walls of the tent. The reinforced fabric keeps the tent from ripping.

Brogden sputters and thrashes his shoulders side to side. He sucks in an enormous breath and lets out a wail that reminds me of the howling winds before a tornado. The kind of wind we heard in the quarry through the crevasses every time a storm rolled through.

Then, the tech and Efta are back on their feet. The tech swings himself over Brogden's legs so that he is straddling them, and he wraps his arms around Brogden's thighs. The liaison's back still remains arched despite the added weight, so Efta climbs across his abdomen. For a moment, Brogden manages to support both their weight, but then his back collapses and his frame drops to the cot like a balloon deflating. His wailing does not cease, and my ears ring even as he swings his head about. I must be careful as I raise the flask that he neither strikes it nor bashes me in the face.

I pour a bit into his mouth, but he immediately sputters it out. I wish we could simply tranquilize him, but then we would risk aspirating him. We might aspirate him anyway.

The second time I pour into his mouth, I clamp my palm over his face. A bubble of it wells from his nostril, but finally, his throat works and drags it down to his belly.

"If you could kindly hurry this the fuck up," Yost says through gritted teeth.

I spare only the slightest glance, but it is immediately apparent how badly they are all straining to keep Brogden's body pinned. It wouldn't surprise me if I heard a tremendous crunch and Brogden's bones simply collapsed into dust. A miracle the cot has not collapsed.

I give Brogden the second dose. It is no easier, but it seems easier because I've already done it once. I let him take a breath and shriek a couple seconds before I pour in the third dose.

Then, a tremendous shudder runs through Brogden, and he begins to convulse.

"Don't stop," Mikael says. "He's having a stress-induced seizure. He must receive enough antivenom."

The smell of urine blossoms in the tent as Brogden loses control of his bladder.

A beat later control of his bowels goes.

"Next asshole who gets stung by a jellyfish is getting left in the ocean," Yost growls.

And then, it is done. The last two pours are out of the flask. I just pray that Brogden has ingested enough and that the damage his body has sustained is minimal. The pain wrought on Brogden's face is hard to imagine, but the physical throes subside as the seizure ends. Mikael slides off our patient's legs. Brogden's eyelids flutter and droop shut.

"Let's hope he stays out until the antivenom takes effect," Mikael says. "We will know better in morning if there will be permanent repercussions from this incident."

We all heave a collective sigh, and the hands and weight withdraw from the big man between us. Brogden's dark skin and now pale lips look strangely artificial.

Then, we set about the unpleasant task of cleaning the big man up. We open the flaps to vent the stench. I suppose it's a little better than dealing with someone suffering a severe contagion, but the survey is still young and there's plenty of room for that after we really get into our forays on the plateau.

When we are done, I thank everyone.

"The first day of our survey has been awfully fraught," I say. "With any luck, dawn will bring better luck."

As everyone files out, my hands and knees shake. I sit on the floor of the tent and remove the survey ledger. It takes all of my focus to steady myself enough to write legibly the events of the day, though I keep them sparse and decide to reserve most of my judgments until they are further substantiated. I speak positively of everyone's contributions, sign the day, and close the book.

Brogden's chest rises and falls steadily. His lips work as if he's muttering about something. The smell is still overbearing, so I step outside.

* * *

The camp's activity is low. Only Mikael has returned to the fire and sits watching a metal coffee pot. The technicians are nowhere to be seen. Yost stands at the camp fence gazing out toward the plateau. A couple voices come from one of the tents, Efta and the engineer, I believe.

I approach the fire. Mikael offers me a cup of coffee, which I accept, and gestures for me to take a seat, which I decline.

"You got anything you care to share about our central objective?" Mikael asks. He stirs his own cup of coffee absently. "I don't relish spending a minute longer on that plateau than necessary."

"Any specific reason?"

Mikael sips his drink and leans forward.

"You won't find many folk comfortable tramping around an old plague ground," he says. "Tompka seems like she knows her stuff, but they didn't even send with us a full specialist, and she's half-drunk to boot."

"Maybe Central deemed the threat lower than we expect?"

"Or maybe they don't want us looking too close at what's in the soil here," Mikael says.

I sigh. I try to sip my coffee, but it is still too hot to drink so I set it on one of the empty chairs.

"What if this, maybe that," I say. "I am thinking that we have apprehensions, but very little to rest them on outside forty-year old stories of this place and frustration with the ins and outs of the Bureau."

"True," Mikael said. "But this is remote territory. Even if a rescue team stands ready as we speak, we cannot expect swift rescue and so far, everything I've seen has framed this dispatch as exceptionally routine."

I can't argue. They sent me with the thinnest of briefing files and a couple leaflets on animal life. Of course, we had the incident report, but that hardly seemed reliable, and the evidence that smugglers had been about is hardly enough to raise flags. However, the presence of the *Sarru* changes things. Something has been downplayed.

"The thing about a map," I say after a moment's pause, "is that you do not know where the road goes until the pages are unfolded. I appreciate your candor about your reservations, however. I want you to feel you can always speak openly about our purpose."

I pick up my coffee. It has cooled enough for me to take a generous swallow. Then, I set the cup down and walk from the fire. I consider heading toward Yost, but instead I let my feet carry me outside the camp entrance.

I do not wander far, contenting myself to stop with my arms crossed about twenty meters up the path toward the plateau. The ground beneath my feet is soggy and wet, and moisture hangs in the air from the abated storm.

Ahead, along the cliff's edge, nothing moves. The breeze rakes ripples on the water and blows laterally across the cove. If it blew down to us from the plateau, in all likelihood we'd need to wear protective gear everywhere but inside our tents.

The half-orb of the moon is visible in the sky along with a handful of the brightest stars. The rest are shrouded by lingering clouds. I'd hoped for clear weather on our arrival, because I'd been told that during good weather, I'd see more stars here than I've ever seen at once. Before the detonations, of course, the books say the sky had been swarmed with them. I once saw a photograph of what they called the Milky Way. It's hard to believe it to have existed. Of course, the mandate of our Bureau is to maintain the hope that the world may one day be restored to what it once was. However, even with forty years to clear, and despite every possible resource being thrown into it, the haze has never left the atmosphere, and its shadow never quite lets us feel the full warmth of day.

I wander to the shore rocks. A handful of crabs scuttle in and out of the water. They know little of the worry of living in the ruins of our ancestors, and for that I envy them. I scoop up a bit of dirt and gravel and toss it carefully among them. They scatter with little plops off the rocks, disappearing beneath the surface. I smile.

The smile fades as vibration thrums under my feet. A minor tremor perhaps. We used to get quakes in the Capital every few years; nothing powerful, just enough to feel in our bones. Only once, when I was not even a teenager, I remember people talking about a shake strong enough to bring down the bell tower of the derelict cathedral across the city square from the central government office.

A new distant churning sound, this something more like a wide bore drill perhaps, draws my attention back to the plateau. The mess hall at the plateau's edge is dark and still. The wind still blows, and the water still murmurs. My ears try to fill in sounds that aren't there too, sounds from the orchard – the flutter of leaves, the creak of tree trunks, the call of night birds. They try to fill in the sounds of the Capital – the buzz of power lines, the pneumatic whine of the bus breaks, the arguing of couples through apartment walls, the surge of sewage and bath water through pipes. Despite the chaos of the day, this stillness brings a restlessness into my heart but also tears to my eyes.

Then, a bubble of glow takes hold of a small segment of the atmosphere above the plateau. It is so diffused that I'm scarcely sure I see it, and it might just be a trick of my perception, might just be an effect cause by shifts in the air currents of the upper atmosphere or on the plateau. For a few moments, I simply stand and breath the night air, and then the glow is gone.

Because it would be senseless and dangerous to head anywhere else, I return to camp. Mikael walks the fence on watch. Though it appears like no one else is out, I run into Tompka as she exits the latrine. She looks a little disheveled, and her path weaves a bit. One hand holds her open flask. When she sees me, she takes a swig. The alcohol is pungent.

"Tompka," I say, "I appreciate the volume of work that you have done, but I am concerned. You may want to minimize your drinking."

"It's no concern of yours what I do off duty," Tompka says.

"I do understand," I say. "But we have sensitive work and rigorous protocols—"

Tompka lets out a single, harsh laugh.

"Last time I was assigned to an off-coast survey, I received word my wife's cancer had advanced aggressively," she says. "I tried to get assigned leave and transport to see her, but she died before I got there."

"I'm sorry," I say, looking at my feet.

"You ever come home to your spouse four days dead?"

"No," I say, my face flushing a fierce red.

"How about to children alone in a house with a corpse?" she asks. Then, she takes a long, hard pull off the flask and shoves past me. As she approaches her tent, the flap unzips, and Efta ushers her inside with a smile.

Inside my own tent, the air still smells foul, but it is passably tolerable. The outside air is far too cold for me to keep things open, so I zip up the tent. After tossing an extra thermal blanket over my infirmed tentmate, I dump myself onto the cot, drag a heap of blankets over myself, and fall asleep immediately, again fully dressed.

DAY TWO

CHAPTER 8

SIGHTLESS, RATIONS, RADIO-TEST

I dream of the war, but instead of my usual dream of being a child carried into a below-ground shelter, I am an adult, maybe my father, and I tread water in the open ocean. I am wearing an official uniform whose wet weight works to drag me under. I'm trying to pull it off, but the buttons are somehow caught. Below my feet, a reef upon the rocks just out of reach. Hardly a meter too deep, but it may as well be a mile.

In the sky above, white flashes consume the world. Dazed birds fall from the sky in their wake. Then, explosions like miniature suns. They're hundreds of meters above the ocean so that their fire bellows down savagely. Billowing pillars of steam launch upward in retaliation. The heat scalds my skin and drives me under the surface with nothing but a lungful of superheated air to hold onto. I am burning from the inside.

When my head dips below the surface, I see a sea teeming with clouds of jellies, pulsing pink as if the water is blushing. Fish dangle, wrapped in their drifting tentacles. In their shadow, eyes the size of dinner plates open and close among the coral and anemones. Sharp coral edges glisten like teeth. They spread wide, revealing a gullet into the earth, and reach for me.

I roll out of bed with my head in a daze. The tent is dark though Brogden snores loudly. I sit up with cold sweat on my brow. I should be able to see the glow of the fire and the other camp lights through the fabric, but nothing. Did Mikael fall asleep and let the fire extinguish? I pinch the bridge of my nose, pull my blanket over my shoulder, and reach for the tent zipper.

A whirring sound outside makes me freeze. It reminds me of a cord being quickly pulled from a spool. It is similar in character to the distant churn I'd heard from the plateau while I stood by the shore. I can't tell if it is quiet or far away, so I slowly unzip the tent. Not a single glowing coal remains in the campfire.

The camp is dead still. The moon is out behind the haze. The thin light provided makes the shadows darker by illuminating edges. An electricity in the air makes me want to pop my ears. Across the dead landscape, nothing moves. I shiver and pull my blanket tighter as my breath clouds in front of me.

"Mikael?" I whisper. "Yost?"

Somewhere outside the fence, gravel scatters. I instinctively duck and try to peek above the tent. Unless the ground has pits and contours of which I am unaware, nothing could move openly across it even in this dim light without making itself visible. Still, I hold my breath.

The whispers come from behind me, and I whirl. I can't see the source of the sound, but I realize that it's coming from the direction of the technicians' tent. I creep across the camp, stepping around the firepit. Another scatter of gravel outside the fence startles me, but the whispers sound louder, more urgent. I squint and bob my head like a bird, hoping the changing angles will help me see the source of the disturbance. In my peripheral vision, flits of motion draw my gaze to depressions, stones, shadows, but never to anything solid.

Twice, I nearly convince myself that I can see full silhouettes in motion before they seem to dissolve into nothing, and I must reassure myself that it's more likely my mind is attempting to assert form on formlessness, the familiar into the empty. Nonetheless, apprehension grows, and a tingling sensation creeps around my shoulders. I step as gently as I can on the rain-soft ground, wincing each time the earth squishes wetly around my soles.

Finally, I'm at the techs' tent. The whispers sound just as distant as they had when I first heard them. Either they get quieter as I approach, or they get further away. I'm no longer certain that they're coming from the tent. Still, I take hold of the zipper tab, inhale deeply.

A hand on my shoulder.

Another on my mouth even as I yelp.

"Shhhh," Yost whispers.

With pressure on my back at the base of my neck, she indicates I should follow her low. We creep toward the comms tent. Inside, Mikael crouches, cleaning a shotgun.

"I was starting to think I was dreaming," I whisper.

Yost shakes her head.

"Movement on the plateau. At least two to three."

"Reconnaissance, no doubt," Mikael says.

"Smugglers?" I ask.

"Doubt they're locals," Yost says.

"Where'd they make landfall?" I ask.

"Would have to be the graveyard," Mikael says. "Don't know how they could have made it up the plateau though."

"Threat?" I ask.

"Doubtful tonight," Mikael says. "No doubt they'd want intelligence before they try anything – *if* they try anything. They can count our tents, but they don't know our composition."

"With any luck, they know we're on guard," Yost says. "They'll also know if something happens to us, more will come."

"What about on the plateau?" I ask. "Did you all feel the tremors?"

Mikael shakes his head.

"You need to get some rest," Yost says. "They gave away their presence, and they know it. They'll think twice before their next move."

I nod. I don't know that I'll be able to sleep again, but by the time I am halfway to the tent, a deep fatigue sets into my being. I feel mildly vindicated, too, that I hadn't just spooked myself. Behind me, Yost and Mikael glide out of comms and fan out to opposite ends of the camp. I can't really say how grave a threat the smugglers pose, but I doubt they will succeed in an ambush right now.

Back in the tent, I settle down on my cot and realize I've been wearing my blanket the whole time. A strange embarrassment strikes me, and I fall asleep wondering what kind of impression that left upon them.

* * *

Cold sweat on my brow causes me to shiver. My whole body aches as I roll over. My eyes pop open like old window shades from another dream about the war. My earliest memory was witnessing one of the great explosions in the sky. I was two at the time. I don't have another memory until I was eight. My vision didn't recover until I was five, and not without the help of government surgeons that I would later learn were what could be considered an advanced payment on my father accepting a role within the Central Bureau.

Mother never talked about what he did in that role, but nevertheless, I grew up proud of him, especially as I watched so many starve in the streets, their bodies dumped into the enormous mouths of the city graves. At least being a bureaucrat bestowed on my father the dignity of being interred underneath his own home. How could I not take pride in someone so willing to sacrifice for his family?

I toss my blankets aside and sit up. My knees pop, and I stretch my arms behind my neck one at a time and crack my shoulders. The chill in the air is deep. I will need to pull on a light jacket under my peacoat. It's hard to believe it's only been a little over twenty-four hours since I first set foot on the ferryman's craft. I feel like it has been a lifetime.

On the cot, angled into the middle of the tent, Brogden sleeps still. I hadn't realized that we didn't move his bed back into its original place after we cleaned him up. His face is much calmer now. Something seems to have returned to his complexion, and he no longer looks so unreal. I wonder how long he will remain asleep. Ostensibly, his role as second liaison to the oversight committee means that his duties are essentially a reinforcement of mine – but right now, I feel I could use all the hands I can get.

I rise and exit the tent. The morning light makes me squint. The storm's dissipation left hardly a cloud, and I'm unaccustomed to sun filtered through such a thin particulate haze. I should have realized that more stars at night meant watery eyes in the day.

I sniff the air. Coffee. Something cooking. Sausage, I'd say, though it could be any greasy meat.

The fire has been rekindled. Mikael, Tompka, and Yammut sit beside it and regard me as I approach. Mikael and the tech hold tin mugs and prod the sizzling sausages on a grill, standing over the fire with long, pronged skewers. A broad steel pan sizzles shredded potatoes glistening with oil and speckled with black pepper. Clearly enough breakfast for the whole camp is preparing.

Mikael offers me a cup of coffee and a plate and informs me that Jones took the final watch rotation and is still asleep and that Yost is attempting to establish radio contact with her superiors to deliver a sit-rep.

I take a cup of coffee and tell them I will return. They resume whatever conversation they'd been having when I approached, and I follow the path down to the docks. I am uncertain of the time, but I know that given the strain of our first day, prudence lays in taking a slow start. Stress numbs judgment, leaves it buzzing dull like a swollen lip.

I find Efta sitting cross-legged on the dock's edge. She wears her jacket over her shoulders. Beside her, her cup of coffee is empty, but she has a thermos. She is looking out over the water. The sun has sloughed off its morning robe of colors, but it streaks shine on the wavelets in the cove.

"Beautiful morning," I say.

"The light reminds me of the reflection on the quarry pools," Efta says.

"I can't say I saw that too often," I say. "I was mostly assigned evening duty."

"A shame," Efta says. "It's a waste not to see the beauty of the places they send us to."

"I didn't find the quarries beautiful," I say. "It was like a gash in the earth."

Efta looks up at me and refills her coffee. I take a drink of mine.

"There is beauty in the wounded," Efta says. "Perhaps more than in most things. The only control I now have over what happened at the quarries is in what I focus on in my memories."

There are a lot of ways I feel like I could respond to that; that I can see that beauty, some different form of beauty that I see – but I don't feel like any of the responses that come to me seem exactly true. I want to instead insist that the scar of the brutal violence that happened there after I left is the only thing that will ever remain. The truth is that since that day in the tunnel on the train where I peered out into the darkness, I'm not sure I've seen anything as beautiful. It occurs to me for the first time that I might have found something in common between that darkness in the tunnel and my lack of vision following the explosion as a child. Perhaps I feel most comfortable when I can see nothing at all.

I crouch, take another sip of my coffee. I focus on the water, the light dancing across it. I am both considering what Efta has said and wanting Efta to see that I am considering what she has said. I can ask her something personal. When we worked on the quarry reports, I learned that she has two brothers. I can ask about them. But I don't. Maybe I'm about to, but she takes a drink and then asks, "Do you ever wonder what the world would be like now if the War had never happened?"

"Not really," I say with a shrug.

Efta's eyebrows raise. She turns to me, and leans away, propping herself with one hand.

"You're kidding, right?" she asks. "You can hold something like a photograph in your hands and not wonder what it would be like if everyone still had all the old tech? You can bite an apple and not wish the stores always had mountains of them?"

I shake my head. The truth is, of course I'd wondered if before, but it feels little different than wondering what it would be like if my father wasn't dead. What use in making myself want something I can never have? It stings a little that she chose to mention apples. I'd told her how much I loved the orchard at the quarry, what it represents to me.

Efta continues. "People could access any information they wanted whenever they wanted. They didn't need to sort the facts out of the propaganda. They didn't have to read books sanctioned by the Mass Diversion Bureau."

The line of thought further upsets me. To concede the point would be to acknowledge the reality in which I lived was insufficient.

"If you had that," I say, "would you be sitting here and watching the light on the water? Would you have spent the evening with the engineer last night?"

"You noticed?" she says.

"Don't worry, I won't put it in the reports," I say.

"Anyway, who's to say where we'd be now?" Efta shrugs with a sly smile. "But I've read that everyone had cars, computers. You didn't need to work for one of the bureaus to get real medicine. You could buy whatever food you wanted, instead of collecting the food allocated by rank and status."

Heat blooms in my chest. My face reddens.

"Did those medicines save them when the epidemics started? When the smell of the dead in their neighbors' houses seeped through walls and vents? Did the choice of food keep them from starving when the dust plumes from the bombs darkened the sky?" I ask. Then I point to the plateau. "Did the computers and cars prevent places like the Gollitok?"

Efta sighs and sloshes what is left of her coffee out over the water.

"Something I remember about you from our survey in the Quarries," she says. "You were always so serious. Not one for pipe dreams."

"I don't smoke," I say.

Efta shakes her head, laughs, rises.

"Lord, there's no helping you," she says and then points to the thermos. "Help yourself to what's left of my coffee."

Then, she clenches her jacket shut over her shoulders and marches back toward camp. I watch her dwindle, and then look out at the water. I want to appreciate the view. Objectively, it is quite lovely, soothing. Somehow, when I look at it though, I feel like I'm looking at the water in a bay berthing a cargo ship with a leaking engine. A corruption underneath the shimmering rainbow. A slick that drowns whatever life blunders into it.

Back at the fire, Mikael and Yammut are checking gear and discussing tabulations about something or other that I assume concerns our communication hardware. Jones has awakened and is simultaneously checking his field kits with one hand while biting a pair of sausages he holds in his other.

Tompka has retired to her tent. She will likely sleep the better part of the morning before she tackles the camp's defenses. I'm not especially worried. Smugglers typically travel on single ships with crews of between five and nine. They'll wish to avoid open engagement with us, especially by daylight – and they'll be actively seeking to conceal their base of operations. It wouldn't surprise me if they simply pull anchor and move on until they're certain we're gone. After all, even if they win and drive us off, how much damage can they do to us before the Bureau decides to move against them in force?

I grab a few bites of breakfast and return to the tent to prepare. Inside, Brogden is still asleep, and he doesn't stir as I change clothes and shift gear from my pack into my footlocker. I check my firearms, attach a knife to my boot, and re-examine the piece of old tech the outfitter provided to me. When I click it on, the numbers run up a bit and the ticking stutters, but I don't know what to make of it. Again, I remind myself to ask Yost or Mikael about it. With all the stress of the prior day, I'd outright forgotten.

Secure that I have everything I need either attached to my body or tucked into my various pockets, I emerge from the tent and head through the camp entrance. I double check that I've brought my disinfectants. The disinfectants include chemical abrasives and milder, regular-use sanitizers, but both will be of an efficacy higher than available to even influential citizenry. Of course, we are going into a place that speculation believes may be a hotbed of high levels of some more virulent strains. I was briefed on the full list of likely contagions, but they were too numerous to remember, and, if one did kill me, it wouldn't matter much which one.

I do not see Yost, so I cross camp to the comms tent. The whole team is nearly prepped, so I do not want delay to dampen morale. When one is venturing into a site as hazardous as we've been prepped to believe the Gollitok will be, morale is crucial.

Inside comms, Yost sits at the radio table with the receiver in her lap and a photograph in her hand. Immediately, she straightens and sets the photograph face down on the table.

"Have you raised the mainland?" I ask.

"No," she says, her brow furrowed. "Yesterday's interference has not resolved."

"I'd hoped it was the storm," I say.

"I had too, until last night's activity," she says.

"Do we have reason to believe that we will face conflict?" I ask.

Yost hesitates.

"That depends," she says.

I wait a moment for her to continue, but when she doesn't, I say, "You can only shut me out of your mission so long before it puts us in danger."

"Depends on whether or not they're simply using this place as a waystation or if they're here looking for tech," she says. Something clipped in her delivery tells me it goes further than that, but I don't press it.

I nod. Then, I point to the photograph.

"I don't assume you'd be interested in telling me about the photograph?"

She looks up at me and passes me the photo after a long exhale. The likeness is of a young man, likely between twenty and twenty-five years old. His nose appears crooked from a poorly set break, but the rest of his features have a boyish beauty to them and a clear structural similarity to that of Yost, especially around the eyes and the jaw line.

"My younger brother," Yost says. "Kirsch."

She watches the photo in my fingers like she is made of glass. I pass it back, and she folds the photo in half and tucks it into her breast pocket.

"He is my only family," Yost says. "My parents succumbed to cancer two years ago. A couple months apart. They'd taken a settler's purchase in the Southern Delta."

"Southern Delta?" I ask. "That's a restricted zone. The fallout was awful there."

Yost nods.

"They decided they'd rather die comfortably than live starving in one of the certified districts," she says. "You're from the Capital. You know what the cities are like. Urban Resettlement licenses offer double rations to anyone willing to help clean-up efforts."

I'd heard of the program of course. They also offered a similar deal to convicts, though it wasn't double rations, it was halved sentences.

"So, what about Kirsch?" I ask. "Where does he live?"

Yost looks down at the radio, clips the receiver to her belt.

"He is military ops. His location cannot be verified, but..."

She trails off, but I can follow her line of thought without her saying more.

"You believe him to be a member of the unofficial survey," I say.

Yost nods without raising her head.

"I have reason to believe so."

"If there is evidence," I say, "we will find it on our sweep."

Yost rises and picks up her Kalashnikov, which she'd left propped against the tent wall. She removes an extended magazine from her loadout and inserts it into the rifle, which she then slings over her shoulder. Then, she straightens her cuffs and the straps of her overalls. She makes eye contact with me for a moment and then leaves the tent. There is a twist in my gut. I cannot let empathy effect my judgment for her, but she is younger than I. She is still learning not to trust in the permanence of family.

I follow her out and survey the waiting faces. Yost stops at the head of the group to wait for me to lead us out. Then it is Mikael, Efta, and the techs. They each hold a respirator. Mikael wears a long-barreled shotgun with a drum magazine slung over his shoulder, the same one he'd been cleaning in the middle of the night. If anyone else is armed, they have not made it visible.

I take a respirator of my own and hold it up high.

"Remember that this thing of rubber and plastic stands between you and whichever strains of the dozens possible brought this place down," I say. "Adhere to the protocols. We will have enough variables that we must control what we can."

They murmur assent. I knew they would. It's the first day. A week from now, I'll see a different mood. The longer you work to keep yourself safe, the less you feel you needed to work to keep yourself safe.

I set an even pace toward the gap in the razor wire and onto the trail to the plateau stair, and the only thing I say, just before I insert my earpiece and pull on my mask, is, "Let's move."

The respirator amplifies the volume of my breaths, and my exhalations splash off the mask, suffusing my face with a stuffy warmth. The pale blue lenses tint the ovals of vision amid the field of black polymer. The mask's strap is constricting, and its edges dig into my skin and scalp. In a few hours, I will be eager to tear it off. The impulse to pull it away for even a split second will be difficult to fight. It is considerations such as these that make discipline and compliance such a valuable trait to field workers. If Yost were not military and Efta so experienced, I would harbor serious concerns that they might risk self-exposure.

Yammut performs radio equipment checks while we approach the stairs. Twice, my frequency bursts with his voice saying, "Check, reply," and I offer an affirmative. Twice also, he activates our global frequency and links it to the island's beacon and its drone of, "Albertachen. Clover. Seashell. Wormwood."

After the second cycle, the tech's voice enters global. "Equipment functioning on our end."

The path swings us by the admitting building, but we ignore the branch that curves to the side entrance. The admitting building itself is a squat, gray and brown brick building with an old-world red-clay tile roof. Quite a few tiles have fallen loose.

I hold up a closed fist as we reach the base of the plateau. The steps up, approximately four hundred of them, contour the curves of the slope. Ahead, to our right, stands the shell of the barracks. It will need inspection too, but its close location and lower contamination risk make it ideal for target of opportunity windows between the more involved work on the plateau.

"Okay everyone, once on the steps, we begin no return protocol," I say. I point to the building that was once the admitting building. "Nothing we bring to the plateau comes to camp without full decontamination. Especially us."

A series of affirmatives comes back through my earpiece.

"Our first priority is to determine what we can about the *Sarru*, restore comms with the mainland, and begin a sweep looking for evidence of unauthorized activity. You all know your business, but letting your guard down lets the team down."

A second round of affirmatives.

"We return for lunch in four hours. Remember to keep your feet low to the ground but don't drag them. Do not run unless running is a matter of life or death. The less we kick up the dirt, the less we kick up what lives in the dirt," I say. I could list other protocols, but I know I'm delaying.

I run them down on the prior night's activity and ask, "Does anyone have any questions before we proceed?"

"What procedure if we encounter hostiles?" Mikael asks.

"Do not engage unless engaged," I say. "If your position is compromised, fall back, and launch a flare. If you hear engagement, fall back to defensive positions, and make your way under as much cover as possible to the mess, where you hold ground until all are present."

I pause. In one step, I begin my investigation of the Gollitok proper. Already, we have found our intelligence change repeatedly. One of our members has suffered serious injury. I've faced dissent from within the team, had verified that hostiles are active in the area, and all of us have undergone a period of stress in excess of what one would expect in most short-term survey expeditions. I feel I've been dropped holding a hornet nest down a well.

I begin up the steps. A metal railing runs up the stone climb, but it is metal, and the salt air has badly corroded it. Its surface is rutted, pitted, and brittle. Entire segments have simply crumbled away. The wind picks up with cold teeth as I ascend, ruffling through my hair that sticks out of my respirator. How easy would it be to land a foot on a stair's edge, twist an ankle, and tumble over the side? What if the smugglers attack from over the cliff's edge? They wouldn't even need to open fire. They could simply dump rocks onto us.

As if the island itself could read my mind, a mild tremor like I'd felt last night, vibrates the cliff face. Though a slight dampness clings to much of the stone, pebbles sift from cracks and dust rises from dry places. I pause a moment and place a palm to the cliff face to steady myself.

"Is something the matter?" comes Efta's voice through the comm.

I examine the stone. Could the tremors create a serious landslide? Could an earthquake collapse the stairs? Set the whole plateau sliding into the ocean?

"Minor tremor," I say. "Concerned for the plateau's seismic stability."

Mikael's voice responds.

"The seismic history of the islands indicates nothing higher than a five on the macro seismic scale for at least two centuries."

"Understood," I say.

I take a deep breath. My nerves are on edge. I remind myself that my apprehensions are the result of internalized anxieties – analytics of events. The survey is just beginning, and I'm attempting to feel out its tone. Things will get better, normalize. The smugglers will depart. We will settle into a routine search and catalog. We will turn every stone on the island over and find nothing further to indicate that Yost's brother Kirsch has ever been here. I hope Mikael conducts the dullest grid search possible, that the techs find a burnt capacitor, purge the system, and restore the beacon.

The top of the stairs comes as my thighs and calves burn with the exertion, and my eyes rise clear of the cliff face, giving me my first view of the Gollitok.

CHAPTER 9

FIRST SIGHT, MEALTIME, TROUBLING SWEET POTATOES

E ven when I was young, I'd heard of the Gollitok, the Naked Island, the place where they sent the undesirables. Its history spanned back to an earlier era, back to the hot and cold wars between Capitalism and Communism, back before the world was brought to its knees by plagues; before we shattered what remained in the great nuclear exchange. Through nearly all of this, the prison persisted, perhaps a testament to the fact that some dark parts of human nature never change. I'd learned it to be a political labor prison for the most dangerous enemies of the state, characterized by its total lack of vegetation. It caused public outcry and protests. People demanded it be shut down, that those in charge be held accountable.

Then, a particularly virulent epidemic burned through the prisoners with a near perfect mortality rate. The few who recovered continued to shed the virus, so it became necessary to write off the whole population. After that, no one talked about it anymore except to tell mythlike stories full of tortures only limited by the imaginations of the teller. The reasons for internment were guided by the conspiracies either most popular or longest standing. People told of escape attempts and rebellions. Some said the prisoners ate the guards and others that the guards ate the prisoners. Parents would say, "When I was your age, they'd have shipped me off to the Naked Isle for saying something like that."

At the top of the stairs, the wind buffets me, sweeping nearly unobstructed over the plateau. The elevation isn't especially high, but out here, the wind holds the urgency of ocean currents. The salt will crust on my skin even if the mask prevents me from smelling the brine. The sun itself, visible again in its climb, is a hazy disc through the particulate sky. I've before read that it was once pure blue on a clear day, that it looked weightless instead of like stretched gauze that wrapped a wounded planet. The older generation regards the atmosphere with a particular pain that is lost to me.

The plateau itself is barren rock, gravel, and a steely dirt within which deadly infection might wait. The slope inclines gradually from east to west, rising to a craggy peak upon which a cluster of three buildings stands behind a decayed fence. Beyond them, I can barely make out the peak of the lighthouse roof. To the left of the stairs stands a squat stone building with an open arch entry facing me, and inside I see a broken well mouth. A couple more buildings stand on the northern edge of the plateau, built close enough to the cliff's edge that one of them appears to have collapsed partially over the side from erosion or perhaps a rockslide.

To my right stands the mess hall. It's a long, T-shaped building with a stone foundation, with the base of the 'T' nearest us. The remainder of the walls is rotted wood, six-inch thick posts with a triple layer of paneling that had long engaged in a dance with disintegration. Its roof collapsed in several places, its windows tumbled from their frames and shattered, and its doors have fallen off their hinges. Even from here, I can glimpse the boat's hull through the breaks in the cove-ward façade.

More buildings stand on the far side of the mess including the warehouse, the entrance to the old mine, and the giant stone eye of the cistern collector, but I cannot see them. However, if I follow the edge of the cliff, I can see better the pulley platform above the cargo dock, a small receiving building with what is likely a short-term storage shed attached.

In between, all is gray dirt and pebbles that could just as easily be the surface of the moon. Piles of stones the size of basketballs. Half built, low stone walls about waist high that define nothing and go nowhere. Every bit of it simply more remnants of the useless labor performed by the prisoners here, year after year spent hauling heavy rocks, learning just how little the sun cared about what happened below it. It's almost comical now that the sun never shines strong enough to burn a naked toddler.

They say it will take perhaps another twenty to thirty years for the airborne particulates to sweep away, but I don't think they really know. Either way, will that be long enough for the memory of the Gollitok to vanish? What would my mother have thought of my standing here? My old teachers? The people I see in the halls around my office at the Bureau? Am I exploring the ghosts of the past, or am I the ghost in the bones of this place?

Maybe our survey will be the one that closes the books on it for the last time.

Yost clears her throat behind me. She has unslung her rifle and holds the weapon loosely with the barrel aimed to the ground. Mikael stands beside her and holds up a pair of ancient binoculars. The techs examine a document and discuss the beacon array. Strange that the beacon had continued transmitting so long after the decommission. Who maintained it? From where is it powered?

I approach the techs and ask, "According to the initial report, we are here to investigate movement on the plateau, unexplained lights, and loss of contact with the Albertachen beacon. Last night, you told me that you restored power. Had it been broadcasting for forty years before it stopped? Why were they even monitoring its broadcast?"

I cannot determine their precise reactions behind their respirators.

"Unknown," Jones responds. "My briefing merely indicated that contact had been lost, that I was to restore contact, and, if possible, determine cause."

I nod. Typical that they'd be provided the bare bones alone.

"Was it difficult to power up?" I ask.

"No," the tech says. "Just hooked it to a battery and turned it on."

"A battery? From where did it come?"

"We brought it, of course," the tech says.

"Then what was powering it before?"

The tech shrugs.

"We couldn't trace the primary power conduit," he says. "Perhaps we will learn more as the survey progresses."

"Indeed," I say. Then, I send the technicians toward the beacon. I find it troubling that there might be still active power sources on the island. However, the priority is to re-establish the mainland comm connection. The sooner that occurs, the more secure I'll feel.

As the technicians disappear around the mess hall, I realize Efta has yet to step off the stairs. Her hands are clasped at her waist. Her shoulders have shrunken in, and they shake.

I drop back to the stairs. Efta startles. Her hands unclasp.

I keep my voice as low as my mask will allow while remaining audible, leaving the comm channel off to maintain our privacy.

"Is everything okay?" I ask.

"My grandparents died here," Efta says. She seems to be gazing at some indeterminant point past the plateau.

"I had no idea," I say.

"It was a long time ago. I barely knew them."

Even through the muffling respirator, a catch and tremor in her voice betrays deeper feelings than that, but this is not the time to expose it. However, I find it nagging that she too has a connection to Albertachen. Her interest must certainly be known to the Bureau, even with so many records having been lost.

Maybe I should not accept her on face level, even if I feel I knew her well before. Maybe it is dangerous that I feel I knew her well before. Brogden's story about Liaison Leotov comes to mind.

I say, "Do you need some time? Head back down to camp while we begin our sweep?"

"Absolutely, not," she says, walking by me. "We all have jobs to do."

So, we approach Yost and Mikael.

"It is time to get started," I say. I point to the wellhouse. The threat of smugglers necessitates that no one travel without armed and trained company, so I say, "Mikael and Efta, you both assess the wellhouse. Yost and I will examine the mess and the boat. Rendezvous here in fifteen."

* * *

Yost and I approach the mess. Yost takes point in the approach to the doors, her rifle raised. I don't draw my pistol. Yost is vastly better equipped to mitigate danger. I'm more likely to shoot her accidentally.

Once Yost positions herself by the door, she steps in, sweeping her weapon from one side of the hall to the other. Keeping my knees bent, ready to react, I follow her inside.

The building is one long hall up to a heavy steel door in a metal frame at the far end, which separates the kitchen. A large square opening in the wall with a serving counter still remains. In the main space, dozens of plastic tables with rusted metal legs and long benches fill the space. Many have collapsed.

Of course, the feature that no one could ignore is the large boat that dominates the right side of the cafeteria. I've only seen a small handful of boats out of the water, and I've always been struck by how much larger they are when you see them in their entirety, than when they're bobbing on the surface. This boat is no exception. It leans at a forty-five degree angle against the remaining wall on the cove side of the mess. The hull is dark gray with a white band just below the deck level. The word "Sarru" is written in that band, in the blue of the signet sky.

The wind howls through the hall from one end to the other. Its current swirls into some sort of eddy as it scrapes the walls.

Yost shuffles forward between the tables, stepping over cups and plates half buried in blown dirt. The whole floor is slathered in a muck of sediment and rain, with several broad puddles spanning swaths of the ground. The floor might have been at one time some form of tile or laminate, but it's so decayed it might as well be carpet with its softness under my feet.

I follow about five meters behind Yost as she shifts into an arc alongside the hull.

"Varka," Yost whispers. She points to the floor by one of the collapsed tables at a pile of broken plates. "Why are there so many plates?"

I look around. It's hard to say how many there are, but there are clearly dozens, broken shards all over the floor. For a moment, I'm surprised that they would have used any ceramic given how easily an inmate could use broken shards as a weapon or to kill themselves, but I suspect that the wardens didn't particularly care if the prisoners killed themselves or each other. After all, even if they killed all the guards, the mainland need only stop sending boats and let the population starve to death. In the end, that was how they'd responded to the outbreak.

I also note that on the tables that still remain standing, some plates still sit. It enters my mind's eye that many of the plates on the floor may have once been on the tables as well, knocked off and broken by hailstorms and high winds.

"Because the tables were set," I murmur, trailing off.

There are also small bones everywhere. Most are a couple knuckles in length. A couple the length of a whole finger. If I had to guess, chicken bones.

"They were eating," Yost says. "They didn't clear the table."

"If they abandoned this place," I say, "they did it during mealtime."

"Doesn't make much sense for a place under starvation quarantine," Yost says.

I frown at a pair of plastic lanyards half-buried in the debris. Surely, those would not have been given to prisoners, though whatever they contained had decayed beyond recognition.

Yost reaches the far side of the room and inspects the serving portal with caution and checks the kitchen door. The hinges screech sharply for a moment at her pull but then cease, having hardly budged a couple of centimeters.

"Clear," she calls out.

I step carefully over plates and bones. The remains seem simultaneously sacred and profane. Defiling their evidence might anger gods and devils alike. Though the organic matter has long decayed entirely away, I am glad to only smell the oily vanilla of the respirator's interior lining.

I approach the boat's stern. The vessel is approximately ten meters long. A depressed seating and storage area aft houses two storage benches. To the bow stand a raised cockpit with three seats, pilot and copilot in the front, side-facing navigator behind with a detachable sonar and weather tracking console. Removed, it would fold up into a design much like a briefcase. Sophisticated equipment. Rare. Highly disconcerting that whoever managed to get this boat up onto the plateau elected to leave something that precious behind. On the open market, that console is worth the price of the rest of the boat and then some.

I take hold of the deck rail and push up hard. The boat does not budge. Satisfied with its stability, I grip the rail and pull myself up so that I can swing my leg aboard. When I rise up and find my balance, I'm standing at a forty-five degree angle, one foot on the deck, one foot on the bulkhead. I reach into my pocket and remove a headlamp. It is difficult to aim it effectively over the mask, but with a bit of fiddling I get it. It won't be as effective at lighting an open space as a lantern would, but it will do.

A hatch in the middle of the cockpit floor descends to a small cabin. The cabin is dark. The beam dimly illuminates the far edge of the deck below. If there is someone hiding here, surely they would have made themselves known already.

I turn my attention to the storage benches. They are closed by a simple bolt latch that I draw back. I note that, although the boat is clearly dirty from use, it doesn't share the same sedimentation as the mess hall around us. There is no question that this boat has not been here long.

My eyes widen when I open the first storage bench. Every cubic inch is filled with canned food. I lift up a can as Yost comes around to the corner of the boat where I climbed aboard.

"What is it?" she asks.

I hold the can out to her.

"Tomatoes," I say. I point into the bench. "Roast beef. Carrots. Sardines."

Yost rises up, probably on her tiptoes. I'm glad she doesn't try to climb aboard, though. The boat has been stable for me, but it is a bad risk for us both to be mucking about.

I open the next compartment. More cans, some vacuum-sealed packages.

"Enough food to feed a crew for a month," Yost says.

"And they left it behind," I say.

I open three out of four of the remaining compartments. More of the same.

The final compartment is full of ammunition. Boxes of shotgun shells, .308, and 9mm rounds. A wooden box divided into sub-compartments that holds eight hand grenades.

"Ammo cache and explosive ordinance," I say. "You'll want to secure this."

Yost rounds the base of the boat into view. She's lowered her barrel, but the stock of her assault rifle is still pressed to her shoulder. I don't need her to have her mask off to guess she is surprised. Equipment, ammo, and food. If I find potable water, the boat will be loaded with the four most valuable things in the world if you're outside a city.

"I'm going to check below decks," I say.

I approach the hatch. The ladder is only two steps, the hatch only a meter high. I squeeze myself into a claustrophobic living space. I am immediately hit by stale, rancid fish stench. Somewhere in the cabin, something has rotted.

Ahead, there is a seating area with a right-angle cushion and then a small desk completing a horseshoe arrangement. Small overhead compartments line the top of the bulkhead, and one of them has broken open, spilling out plastic water bottles. A small oven crowds me on the left, and a tiny water closet to my right. Under the ladder, a single bunk wide enough to maybe sleep two people.

On the desk, there is a book. It is cheaper quality than my official log but the same design. The cover reads,

Pruitt, D.V., K. Kapetan
Survey #0x29A
Operations Log

I carefully open the cover. It is damp, but it's been sufficiently sheltered to keep the storms from waterlogging the pages. The ink is blurred, leaving only small, legible portions. The book smells like rat skin.

Kapetan Pruitt writes in a crowded, uneven hand, and aside from the weather damage, the page also bears numerous palm prints in ink where the man pressed his hand against his own fresh writing. From the segments I can decipher, the first pages read like any other survey log dating back to about two months prior to my arrival on Midway. He charts their arrival, detailing his first meeting with his second in command, Nadnaredik Jemen, and he complains as I did about the inspector's dubious voracity. There is even a mention of Orlot, though Kapetan Pruitt himself refused to partake. I can't help but chuckle.

Then, I stop. The next entry, more legible than anything else thus far, chills my blood.

It opens with, *Kirsch and Omar drew me aside moments ago to inform me that the inspector intimated to them that a prior expedition to the Gollitok had passed through two months ago. It would seem that the inspector would have us believe that the old prison is home to insurrectionists. He might even believe he's telling the truth. Lord knows what he's cooked up in that isolation-addled head of his. Still, he does have my sympathy. I've known my share of isolation, and I can't imagine the ferryman provides good company. He seemed he'd just as soon kill the inspector as to look at him.*

I look away, back to the ladder. I cannot hear Yost, but no doubt she grows restless. Returning to her makes my stomach churn. While I have not discovered definitive proof that Yost's brother is dead, the log makes it feel a foregone conclusion.

Returning to the book, a substantial portion of the following pages is illegible. I can make out occasional words like 'canteens,' 'excursion,' and, curiously, 'blast door.' I also spot the name Kirsch twice more. Then, the next entry is entirely obscured by reddish brown smears. Blood on the captain's hand, no doubt. Perhaps he was wounded and not in his right mind. I look around the stove, the seating area, the bed. No blood that I can see. Either that entry was written elsewhere, or someone cleaned up. Either way, if the captain died, someone remained alive after.

Three blank pages follow, each one increasingly less stained by the blood of the captain's final entry. Then, on the fourth page, a new hand takes over, this one larger and more rounded. Even where it smeared, it is easier to read than almost everything the captain wrote.

The first and only entry in the new hand reads, *Nadnaredik Jemen recording as acting team lead. Kapetan Pruitt is dead. So are*

Omar and Leads. K believes the objective to be in either the warehouse or the lighthouse. L was barricaded in the kitchen, but I couldn't tell against what through his babbling. I have no idea how the ship got onto the plateau and my nerves can't handle considering the implications. What I do know is that here, I have food and an entrance smaller than a square meter. If I can stay awake long enough, I can survive until dawn and try to repair the beacon array when I have the light. If only K had run here instead of toward Sanchez, we'd be able to take shifts.

Nothing more is written in the book. I close it gingerly and remove a plastic bag from one of my coat pockets. It's possible the book might crumble. Normally, it would have been best to leave it in place until I could mention better preservation materials, but given the contents of the journal, I fear that careful preservation might become the least of our concerns.

When I emerge from the boat's cabin, Yost appears to be walking a circuit of points of exposure, approaching any place where the outside is visible through the broken walls. Her footsteps are silent and her motion fluid. My movements are loud in the stillness as I climb over the railing and let myself down as gently as possible.

"Find anything?" Yost asks, starting toward me in that same graceful gait. Were she to continue her approach and drive a knife into my throat, it would seem perfectly natural for the posture.

Instead, she stops a few feet away. I can't really see her eyes through the tinted portals of her mask, but I suspect they're eager. They won't be in a moment.

"Captain's log," I say.

A faint rattling sound causes me to glance down. Yost's hands are shaking around her assault rifle, causing the little hook of the strap to scrape slightly against its anchor.

"The log is nearly illegible," I say. "But I can clearly read the name 'Kirsch'."

Yost swallows, turns her head away, then turns it right back.

"Dead?" she asks.

"It does not say, or, if it does, I cannot read it," I say. "But it does clearly indicate that several of the team members were killed. It does not say how."

Yost nods.

"They were looking for something," I say. "Believed their objective was either in the warehouse or the lighthouse."

Yost nods again.

"Why did they assign you to me?" I ask, feeling a powerful deja vu from my conversation with Efta. "Are you emotionally compromised for this duty? Do you know if any other team members have complications?"

Yost does not answer. I want to tell her about Efta, but I do not feel it is prudent to do so until I know more. If I wasn't before, I am certain now that it can't be coincidence that two of my team members have compelling personal motives. If it is, the level of oversight failure is stunning. Could the Bureau be faltering so badly?

"There is something else," I say. "According to the kapetan, the customs inspector indicated that the *Sarru* was not the first survey to embark toward Albertachen."

"Pezzo di merda," Yost mutters, barely audible through her mask. She straightens her back and rolls her shoulders. Whatever impact my news had on her seems to slough on the motion, and her composure restores. "How many people have they sent here?"

"I don't know," I say.

"I suppose it doesn't matter how many they've sent. Dead teams don't pose a threat. Our concerns haven't changed."

"No, they haven't," I say. "Though we must assume that whatever killed the crew of the *Sarru* may be a threat independent of the smugglers."

We climb through the serving window into the kitchen and find little more than rusted crockery, empty cans, and empty plastic containers that looked to have been chewed by rats or some other vermin. The drawers are full of metal, plastic, and wooden utensils. An enormous block of carving knives stands on one of the counters, the handles so rusted I doubt the blades could even be removed. The counters themselves, made of some sort of once-sealed butcher's block, have taken on a foamy-looking texture from decades of decay.

I pause and activate my radio mic.

"Radio Team, check in."

There is static a moment, then Yammut's voice crackles in.

"We're at the beacon," he says. "I'm about to purge the cache and reset the hardware."

"Check," I say. "Anything we should be concerned about?"

"Going swimmingly," the tech says. "I'll check back in when the repair is complete."

Yost approaches a tall, black pantry cabinet that dominates the entire northern wall and slings her rifle over her shoulder.

"Mikael and Efta?" I ask through the radio.

"All clear," Mikael's voice returns. "We're waiting outside the wellhouse."

"Outstanding," I say. "Anything of note?"

Mikael's voice responds, but indistinct and barely audible. I realize that I'm hearing him through Efta's microphone as she chimes in and says, "Someone poured cement into the well."

I frown.

"That's odd," I say. Even though the evidence that the mess was disrupted during mealtime suggests otherwise, I add, "From the starvation quarantine, I suppose."

Yost laughs. She has opened the black pantry. Though she is standing in front of it, blocking much of my view of its contents, it is clearly stacked to the ceiling with unopened canned goods.

"They're not very good at starvation protocol," Yost says.

I thumb off my mic and step up beside Yost. She reaches inside and pulls out one of the cans. The can is large enough that she must hold it with both hands. It could serve fifty people. The label has disintegrated, but I see in the light streaming in from the back door that there is a raised type on the can. Yost runs her thumb over it.

"Green beans," she says.

I reach into the pantry and take out another can. I never would have thought I would find sweet potatoes so troubling. No doubt, if I continued to inspect the cans, I'd find the full range of institutional staples. Carrots. Mushrooms. Beets.

Yost sets one of the cans on the ground, unslings her rifle, and bashes the lid with the stock. The can's seal ruptures as its sides buckle and fistfuls of smashed peas tumble out amid a spray of briny water.

"Perhaps the smugglers?" Yost asks.

I shake my head.

"No reason they'd stock the pantry. The mess and kitchen are filthy and unusable," I say. I reach to one of the stacks of cans. Despite being behind closed doors, a thick layer of dust sits on top. "And no one has disturbed these for some time."

I want to scratch my chin, but I resist the urge to bring my hands to the respirator lest I disturb the seal. If the starvation protocol was a lie, then what really happened here? What are we really looking for?

I regard Yost carefully. She seems as bewildered as I, but is it just an act? What is her mission here? I find myself itching to return to camp so that I can take another look in Kapetan Pruitt's logbook. Perhaps in better light I will be able to read more of his scribblings.

CHAPTER 10

WHEELBARROWS, OFFICES, WIRE LOOP

We rejoin Mikael and Efta between the mess and the wellhouse. I find their report troubling because it contradicts what we found in the pantry. Capping the well with concrete would seem to confirm starvation protocols – so why stop there? Why leave enough food to feed the population for weeks if you cut off their water supply?

I feel glad to be out of the kitchen and standing in the sun, no matter how feeble its warmth. Being in that boat felt kind of like being in a coffin. I try to take a long deep breath, but the respirator annihilates any freshness it might bring. Maybe I will have some sort of epiphany when I fill out the morning's log. Perhaps Brogden will see something I do not when he has recovered enough to debrief. After all, protocols and procedures are his principal purview.

When we rendezvous with Efta and Mikael, Yost and I fill them in on our findings.

"Keep a careful eye out for bones," Efta says.

"What do you mean?" I ask.

"If they really did starve," Efta says, "they had to starve somewhere."

"She's right," Mikael says. "When I first enlisted, I was assigned clean-up duty at a tungsten mining op that underwent starvation quarantine. They'd designated one of the barracks to send the weak to die and a storage shed as depository for the dead. Eventually, no one cared to steer them to their death, and they dropped where they stood."

"What did you do with the remains?" I ask.

"Loaded them onto wheelbarrows," Mikael says. "I presume they were cremated. They could have been buried. Why?"

"We have reports of two teams dispatched here before us," I say. "One confirmed. Who's to say if one of them was sent to clean up the bodies?"

"And perhaps one of these teams might have cemented the well," Efta offers.

"But left the food?" I ask. "And why would any of this be kept off the official record?"

"They may not have found the food," she says with a shrug. "Those sent to haul bodies might not check the pantry."

It was a fair point. There would need to be a reason to seal the well, but at least the well supported the official record of starvation protocol. A headache forms at the back of my eyes. For all I know at this point, Efta could be trying to confuse me. Or Yost. Or Mikael.

A groan from Yost refocuses me.

"I realize circumstances might be deemed mysterious here," Yost says. "But we're structured to sweep and document. Perhaps we can discuss nuances later?"

I check my watch. She is right. We will need to descend the plateau for lunch, and decontamination will take time. All told, we will spend no more than six hours on our investigation today, even with the apparent urgency. Best we contemplate findings in camp. Otherwise, we speculate on legs when the body has not yet been seen.

I glance to a long building on the eastern edge of the bluff. The warehouse, as I understand it. On the far side, the transmitter array. The tip of the antennae juts over the warehouse roof, but I'm not able to see the technicians.

"We move on then," I say. I point up the path that runs up the bluff toward the cluster of buildings behind the fence. If memory serves, they are the official offices, the warden's residence, and the armory. The heart of the facility. I don't recall the last warden's name from my briefing file, but the prison had a live-in staff of twenty: the warden and the assistant warden, two secretaries, a cook, five maintenance staff, and ten guards.

Up the hill, the decrepit buildings seem ominous. The offices are a two-story rectangle with diagonal cracks all across the façade. Holes gape where the mortar caved and the stones simply fell out like rotting teeth. Its roof is made of heavy lumber that seems to have withstood the elements better than most, but a couple gaps allow in the elements. The windows have not fared well, nor have the bars that once covered them. Most have fallen from their casements.

Next to the offices is the armory, a low cement slab of a building. Its frontal double doors have fallen outward, the entryway badly fire damaged. Though it's only a guess, I suspect the prison staff scuttled the cache to prevent a riot when –if— the starvation protocol was ordered. Those sentenced to death by wasting, maybe cannibalism, would have little to lose. The burned-out bunker summed up my impression of this place – if every building looked just like it, I wouldn't bat an eye.

In contrast, the warden's residence feels out of place. Everything else was stone and wood in Spartan designs. The Gollitok might have been old, but the warden's house felt more antiquated, like a cottage from an old fisherman's story. According to record, it was the only building on the island before the prison was established. It too is made of stone and wood, but its entire façade is more refined. Its stonework is skilled and precise, even though it has worn. Its triangular awnings still have all their shingles. The glass is intact. All told, it looks brought forward in time from three hundred years past. If someone steps out the front door wearing a sun hat and holding a watering can, it will strike me as the most natural thing in the world.

Approaching the fence, the stretch of open ground contains numerous sharp spikes and posts at various angles. Eyelets dangle off nearly all of them, and I suspect that affixed to the eyelets once ran razor wire. Some lengths still dangle impotently, though most disintegrated with time. The fence has mostly collapsed and is a combination of barbed wire, gates, and segments of thick lumber palisade. With guards behind it and in full repair, no doubt it looked formidable.

The gate has, of course, fallen off its posts. I face my companions.

"Search in the same pairs," I say. "Mikael and Efta in the armory, and Yost and I—"

"I will take the warden's residence," Yost says. She angles to face me full-on and squares her shoulders. "Alone. Mikael will search the armory."

"That's—" I start, but Yost cuts me off.

"I have my orders," she says.

"And you don't give me mine," I say.

Her fist, fast as a viper strike, connects with my temple with a dull thud. White light blots my vision. My feet stagger and my arms pinwheel as my center of gravity veers. I thrust my arms down to break my fall. Pain rockets from my right forearm, and my body carries forward. Another sharp pain lurches from my shoulder blade as I strain my neck to keep my head from striking the ground.

I come to a stop on my side and roll onto my back. My forehead throbs. My forearm aches, as does my shoulder. Instinctively, I cradle my right arm to my torso with my left and prod my way down its length. I do not think I broke anything.

"I've got you," Efta says, her face beside my ear.

As she helps me to my feet, Yost continues up the path toward the warden's residence. Despite the pain and a general wobbliness in my head, I step forward to pursue, but Mikael inserts himself in my path with a smooth motion. He places one palm onto my chest.

"I cannot allow this to stand," I tell him.

"And I cannot allow you to pass," Mikael says.

Even though either Mikael or Yost could grind me into dust, my impulse is to draw my pistol. Unfortunately, that fall banged me up pretty good, and I'm addled enough that even if I managed to unholster my weapon fast enough, I would not be able to hit the island itself. Damn military. If it is a Bureau imperative that Yost proceed to the warden's residence alone, they could have apprised me of the matter and prevented the entire altercation. It's almost as if they deliberately manufactured the discord.

Efta tugs me gently backward by the sleeve. She says, "I do not think this ends well if you proceed."

Then, she turns me, pulls on a latex glove, and begins a point by point inspection of my respirator. My heart feels like it ceases as she does so, certain that she must have spotted some visible defect in the seal. Finally, her hands fall away, and she drops the glove to the ground.

"Guess you return to camp after all," she says.

I picture sitting at the campfire tonight with Yost.

"Well, that's disappointing," I say.

Mikael lingers. I try to get a sense of his facial expression, but it's simply impossible through the mask. I half wish mine had broken so I could rip it off and let them see just how angry I am. My hands both shake, and it causes sharp pains in the injured wrist. I suspect I may have a mild sprain. I will know soon if I see swelling.

Mikael gloves his hands, opens a small case attached to his belt, and pulls out a roll of heavy-duty bandage. He wraps my hand and forearm with the bandage after discarding the plastic wrapping. I grit my teeth against the pain as he does so, but his hands are surprisingly deft, keeping the discomfort lower than I would have expected.

"You should head back to camp. The engineer can give you a proper brace," Mikael says, stripping his gloves and tossing them to the dirt. His voice sounds heavy and regretful. "If you wish to manufacture an explanation for the logs, please inform me and I will support your narrative."

I am relieved at being offered an excuse, but the temptation lasts only an instant. My role as survey lead is to know when it is appropriate to relinquish control and when to keep it. Now, I must keep it. Fear of my team member is not a reason otherwise, and clearly Mikael will only help me if helping me does not contradict Yost.

"Thank you, but I will keep an accurate log," I say. "The Bureau will want to know why I was forced to bring Yost to task."

"Suit yourself," Mikael says. "I am going to carry out Yost's instruction. I will bring Efta if you still wish."

"While I appreciate being given permission to give instructions to my team," I say sharply, "I believe I will now have Efta assist me in the offices."

"Again," Mikael says with a shrug, "suit yourself."

He veers toward the burned-out armory. As he approaches its entry, he unslings his shotgun and affixes a flashlight to its barrel. Then, he disappears from sight. Likewise, Yost has disappeared into the warden's residence to pursue whatever aim she deemed important enough to fracture the survey team.

A cold surge of anxiety washes over me now with them out of sight.

Efta looks at me.

"You might need to kill them," she says.

I am surprised at how casual she is in her comment.

"As far as I can tell," I say, brushing myself off as best I can, "at least two teams have arrived on Albertachen and never left. We will not add to the bones."

For a moment, I furrow my brow at the three gloves and the plastic wrap from the bandage lying in the dirt. Our footprints surround them, run underneath them. How quickly traces of ourselves accumulate. Why has so little from those here before remained?

"We should get back to camp," Efta says.

"Nonsense," I say. As distressed as something inside me wants to be, I need distance from the events that have just transpired. As I have much of my life, I seek refuge within a shell of professionalism. I point to the office and say, "We have work to do."

* * *

Backless wooden benches once stood on either side of the office vestibule, but at least two legs have collapsed on one and the other is simply tilted on a pile of rubble. The entry opens immediately to a single, large room that occupies nearly the entire first floor. On the far right, a doorway leads to a staircase, and a doorframe from which the door has fallen, is marked as a bathroom. On the far left, a partition blocks off a single, large desk and a horseshoe of file cabinets. Shards of glass still stand and dangle in the open spaces of the partition.

In front of us, a long counter interposes between ourselves and a row of desk stations. A transparent plastic barrier spans from the counter to the ceiling with three tarnished speaker grates mounted in it. A broken, wooden door at the end allows entry into the main space. I trace my finger along the edge of the counter as I walk its length. Once heavily varnished, the grain has grown coarse.

I pass through the doorway into the office area with Efta moving slowly behind me. She produces a Polaroid camera from inside her jacket that apparently has been hanging against her hip from her neck by a thin, leather strap. The flash bursts as she takes a photograph of the open area.

Three desks face the far wall, and in between each, a desk stands at a right angle, perpendicular to the width of the room. Each desk holds a typewriter and various knick-knacks and sundries. The chairs are all shoved in a corner and covered in dust and cobwebs. The main space of the floor is occupied by a pair of encampments – disintegrating mattresses and bedding around two half-assed firepits made of heavy stones. A heap of rusted and pitted iron cookware stands surrounded by dozens of opened cans.

On several of the bedrolls lie massively rusted firearms – rifles and shotguns, pistols, all clearly decayed beyond repair. A couple of fire axes with red metal heads and black wooden handles are tilted against one of the desks, and another desk is littered with all sorts of oxidized blades.

"I can only assume the staff attempted to fortify this space once the starvation protocol was imposed," she says.

"A reasonable assertion," I say. "Supports the official record."

Efta lets the camera dangle against her stomach. She sighs and looks at me.

"Do you really believe there is truth to the official record?"

"I do," I say with a nod. "I believe that every word of it is in its own way true, but that there is an important difference between the truth and the whole truth."

"Then why give it any credence?"

I kneel by one of the desks and open the drawers. The bottom drawer is full of nearly disintegrated clothes. The top contains crayon drawings on a heavy bond of paper that has long yellowed. A cat. A tree beside a house. A dragon. Clearly drawn by a child. I imagine that somewhere on the mainland, a little boy or girl waited for a parent who never returned home. Would they have learned of the quarantine order?

Efta still looks at me, waiting for a response. I hold one of the drawings up to the light to better see it. Unquestionably, it is of a father, a mother, and a child. The mother wears a green, triangular hat, the father a red tie. The child holds a teddy bear.

"Because when you read words on a page, the meaning is shaped every bit as much by the empty space on the page as the words themselves," I say.

"If you shit in a box, you don't have a box anymore," Efta says. She takes a photo of the space from another angle, then she looks at me again. "You have a boxed piece of shit."

I move on to the next desk. There is a large, leather-bound book on it. The cover reads, "Station Log." However, when I attempt to open it, the pages disintegrate. At some point, water soaked it badly. Next to the log, there is a framed photograph, but the photo is not a personal photo. My initial impression is that it came with the frame, but there is a brand logo on the photo that differs from the brand logo on the frame. Apparently, whoever enjoyed this sample photo removed it from the initial frame and placed it into this frame.

I open the wide, skinny drawer over the leg hole. Staples. Paperclips. Tweezers. All rusted.

In the next desk, more clothes in both drawers. A carton of cigarettes that is mush to the touch. A glue stick. An old government ID badge. The photo has been rendered uninterpretable by moisture. The name is Heldicka Ordwick. Order officer, 2nd class. P, F, and D permissions, L and T restrictions. Employee ID number 465F3AB. I wonder what Heldicka thought of the one who kept their child's drawings. What did she think of the one who liked a stock photo so much they bought a new frame for it? A twinge of sadness strikes me.

I feel like I'm walking on graves, or at least a place where someone died. A mass grave really. I know that before the pandemics and the war, people often believed that tragic deaths left a mark on places, but that was before tragic deaths occurred in almost every conceivable location. Now it only makes sense to cultivate ghosts in our hearts.

Efta gingerly twists the knob to the file room. The hinges groan, and she pushes hard enough to shake the frame. A large triangle of glass falls and shatters on the tile floor. I look at the small external windows over the desks. They are double-paned, insulating plastic. It goes without saying they are pre-war. Those types of things haven't been re-attained yet.

The file room does not have exterior windows, leaving it dark enough that Efta clicks on a penlight she'd been carrying in her pocket. I have one as well, but I don't have any need to deplete its batteries yet, and I won't rule out the possibility that we will need to conduct some night work.

Efta tentatively opens a few cabinets and shines her light inside. She removes a couple of folders, rifles through them even as the contents crumble and fall to the ground. The files, themselves disintegrating, end up in a lumpy stack on the corner of the desk.

I reach for one of the fire axes and use its head to lift one of the mattresses.

"Varka," Efta says sharply.

I cross quickly through the door into the file room. She is shining her light into the hollow under the desk. I step around.

A heap of clothes, crumpled, tossed on top of each other.

I assume Efta is going to explain so I say nothing. She points to a green shirt at the top of the pile. It is torn, badly, with a brown stain all around the tear. Blood?

Efta slides a telescopic baton from her belt, snaps it to full length, and probes the pile. The clothes in the desk drawers had all been neatly folded, but these all seem to be torn. A couple more appear similarly stained.

"If that's blood, that's the closest we've come to bodies," Efta says. "If that's blood."

"But why hide them under the desk?" I ask. "Why keep them at all?"

"Perhaps they could not leave to—" Efta breaks off. "But no, they could just have burned them."

A glint of gold at the edge of the bottom of the pile. I reach down and pick up a simple, golden band – an old-style wedding ring. The beam of Efta's light illuminates a date nearly a hundred years past inscribed on the inside. A family heirloom? I pinch it between thumb and forefinger and hold it up between me and Efta.

"What if they went crazy?" I ask.

"En masse?" Efta asks. "We'd need a cause."

"Of course," I say. I realize that Efta is focused on the ring and that perhaps she believes I am about to explain how the ring indicates a possible cause. As crazy as marriages can drive people, unfortunately, I had no such thing in mind.

Instead, I set the ring on the desk and step up to the broken window. From this angle, the encampment looks slightly more orderly, and I realize that everything down to the mattresses, the empty cans, the blankets, and the weapons all seems to be organized in something resembling a pattern of diagonals.

"Do you believe that any of the files will be readable?" I ask.

Efta shrugs.

"Don't know," she says. "But they're prisoner files. Doubtful they hold direct answers."

"What about personnel files?" I ask. "Duty logs? Incident reports?"

"Not sure," Efta says. "Might be here, might be in a separate file storage."

There is obviously far too much information here for us to sort through in a single morning. This was anticipated, of course. Records examinations are the most labor-intensive part of any survey, even if the records are in pristine condition. This room alone might provoke a month's investment.

So, we decide to move on, crossing the interior encampment again.

The stairs to the second floor are creaky, and two or three feel as if they might collapse. The upstairs opens into a single hall lined with doors. A uniform storage room. A workshop with bins of tools like socket wrenches, hammers, and saws in boxes. A whole mess of fishing tackle. An interrogation/observation room combo separated by a half-wall that clearly once held a two-way mirror, shards of which cover the floor.

Efta and I open the door to a private office. It is quite small, containing only a desk, a broken lamp, a wheeled chair, a small chalkboard, and a single, empty shelf. If the office's owner ever showed their personality in the office, they took it with them whenever they left.

The across door opens to a storage room filled floor to ceiling with food: five-kilogram cans, crates of freeze-dried meals, woven bags of rice and beans, cardboard pasta boxes, all untouched. Efta picks up a box of instant mashed potatoes and inspects the corners and edges.

"You'd think vermin would have been at this," she says.

"I'm not sure vermin can survive here," I say, "but it's like the pantry in the mess hall."

"What if something happened here after they imposed the quarantine but before they actually starved?" Efta asked.

"I suppose they likely kept a sizeable stockpile on hand given the remoteness of the location," I say.

"I'm sure they get cut off by storms with some regularity," Efta said. "If they rationed carefully..."

It bothers me that both the pantry and this storeroom don't just have food remaining. They're fully stocked.

"What if they ordered quarantine," I say, "and then executed the entire population?"

Efta grunts and closes the door. We turn to the final door at the end of the hall. The door itself hardly moves when we turn the knob and push. It appears blocked by debris, but after alternating steady pressure with more forceful pushes, we shove back the obstacle. At one point, we freeze as a terrific clatter erupts from the other side, but we can only assume that something has simply fallen from whatever obstructs us. Eventually, the opening widens enough for us to slip through, so we do.

We enter what I assume to be the warden's office. A bureau has been pushed to barricade the door, and we've managed to back it up through the dust. Beside it lies a broken wooden chair, likely the source of the clamor.

The room runs the full depth of the building and is lined with bookshelves. A massive desk dominates the far end. The ceiling is peeled with exposed, heavy cross beams.

A wire noose hangs from one of the cross beams.

On the floor beneath the cross beams, there lies a heap of bones.

*　*　*

The door closes on its own behind us. The room is dim, lit by a single, cracked window on the far side of the desk. The desk is clear except for the nameplate attached to the front:

Dr. Zjenicka Redgeleyisch
Warden

A green blotter with leather trim and corner pads lies bent and half-crushed on the floor beside the desk. An old-fashioned ink well and a fistful of fountain pens lie beside a black puddle. Several yellow pencils have rolled to a stop against various bits of unidentifiable debris.

My attention snaps back to the noose, the bones. A few strings of dried-out tendon and sinew still hold together a couple of the joints, but otherwise, they're bare and brittle-looking. Picking up one of the fallen pencils along the way, I step toward the bones and crouch, poke at what I'm pretty sure is the femur. Flakes of bone scrape away at a sweeping pressure.

Meanwhile, Efta's boots clop on the wooden floor as she steps toward the bookshelves that line the left wall. The right wall is bare except for a small bank of two-drawer file cabinets with several dust-burdened sculptures standing atop them. A bust of a woman with a cleft lip. A pair of baroque-dressed ocelots dancing bipedally. Some sort of fertility goddess in a crude style. Over them, an oil painting depicting the suicide of a soldier wearing a military uniform I do not recognize.

I use the eraser of the pencil to push a couple of the bones off the highest part of the pile. The head has broken off from the spine and rolled a few feet to my right.

Efta clears her throat and runs her fingers along the base of the bindings on one of the shelves. Her voice is sharp in the stillness.

"Legal codes," Efta says. "Procedural guides. History books. Anatomy guides. The warden, she must have loved a bit of light reading."

One of the books is open on the floor. I scoot over to it in a semi-crab walk. It appears to be some sort of massive technical manual full of circuit diagrams.

"Why hang herself?" I ask. "She had so much entertainment to keep occupied."

Efta freezes and looks at me. I smile broadly, but she stares until I realize that she can't see my smile through the respirator. I force a laugh. Efta remains still another moment, and then she chuckles and shakes her head. She pulls a book off the end of the shelf and says, "*Nerve Cluster and Pressure Points Subdual Techniques: A Treatise on Crippling Your Opponent with Minimal Physical Exertion.* Right next to Sun Tzu."

"Bet you she was a dash to have coffee with," I say.

"Perhaps her and Yost would have gotten on well," Efta says.

I edge around the desk, my feet leaving scraping tracks in the thick dust. An old rotary phone receiver lays at the end of its kinked spiral cord on the slats. A stack of stained file folders lies in the dust next to it. I brush the dust away from the label of the top one with my thumb. The pen is fuzzy from exposure to moisture in the air, but the label is legible enough for me to read "Shaft T-81m A-F."

I gingerly open the folder. A typed document in full, pre-war Cyrillic sits underneath a series of printed photographs. The photos depict two skeletons lying against a wall in a mineshaft from multiple angles. The composition is very grainy, the lighting poor, the camera insufficient, but something seems wrong with the skeletons. The structure looks all wrong, but it's hard to tell what is shape and what is shadow.

I set the photos on the desk and turn my attention to the documents. Initially, they seem to be gibberish, but likely they are written in some sort of cypher. I close the file. The key might be somewhere in the office, but that is not something to consider right now. It is similar to how neither Efta nor I feel the need to discuss the apparent suicide of the warden. Unless we find a suicide note or some corroborating piece of evidence that justifies the tableau, it is not a detail wise to speculate upon.

Efta reaches the final bookshelf and examines a couple of objects there while I approach the file bank. The first cabinet's drawers are labeled from top to bottom, "Personnel" and "Facilities." The next cabinet's drawers are named with paired strings of six-digit numbers separated by a dash. The last cabinet is much heavier-duty than the others. The label of both drawers reads "Classified." The edges of both drawers are blackened by fire damage; the interior of the drawers is incinerated.

I tug one of the numbered drawers, but the cabinet is locked. I doubt the mechanism still functions after all this time, but the keyhole is so brittle that it will be easy to drill out later.

Scraping metal snaps my attention to the desk. Efta is dragging one of the drawers open. She pulls out an unlabeled bottle of what I presume to be liquor, a fat portfolio binder, an ancient flintlock pistol with a plugged barrel, a handheld transistor radio, and an old black Bible with a gold cross on the cover. Efta fiddles with the drawer until something clicks. She pulls out a panel from the drawer and removes a ring containing three tarnished keys. I can tell immediately they're not file cabinet keys; they're far too large to fit the tiny locks I was just looking at. She deposits them into a plastic bag which she drops into her coat pocket, and then she examines the portfolio gingerly.

I cross over to the desk and review the objects lying there. I pick up the photographs. They are printed on thin, floppy, matte paper. Several of them appear to be personnel photos – some sort of event in the open office downstairs, mostly people in blue uniform shirts holding paper cups and standing in clusters. One shot features a sullen-looking man in a lab coat. He looks down and to the left, and the way he absently holds his cup suggests he's about to let it spill. The facility physician perhaps?

The last two photos differ from the rest. There is another photo of an underground shaft, this one black and white. Alternating steel and wood beams support the tunnel. The focal wall of the photo appears veined with some sort of rich mineral deposit. Though it is apparent enough in the photo, someone has circled the deposit in marker and written NME 34.20A-F.

The last photo was taken in some sort of clinical environment. It is taken from behind as a woman in a suit peers into the lens of a microscope. Her hair is gathered in a neat bun, exposing a ring of purple bruising around her neck. My eyes immediately flick to the noose in the room and the bones below. Was the woman with the hair bun the warden? Had she tried to hang herself once and then finished it here?

I slide the photos into my pocket and look around. Efta has opened the portfolio and is examining the top document.

"You know one thing I can't help noticing?" I ask Efta. Her attention doesn't shift from the materials in her hands, and I cannot read if she reacts through her mask, so I continue, "No old tech. This place is pre-war, quarantine, but there are no computers, no tablets, no camera networks."

Efta closes the portfolio cover and turns to me.

"Prior teams?" Efta says. "If we concede that there have been more than one before us, who's to say—"

"It's not just no computers or cameras." I point to each corner of the room in one rotating motion. "No camera mounts." I point to the wall under the window. "None of the old-tech wire ports. The power outlets are the only sign they used electricity outside ceiling lights. Have you noticed that there aren't even any exterior yard lights? You'd think they'd want to be able see the approaches in the dark."

Efta picks up the radio. Its antenna flops loosely on its little hinge.

"There's this," she says.

"Yeah," I say. "So, of all the 'wonders' of the pre-war era, the only thing they've got is a radio? One dingy by even our standards?"

Efta regards the radio and then sets it back down a bit roughly, visibly startling herself.

"It's like everything else here," Efta says. "Doesn't add up."

I step behind the desk and peer through the window. The window looks out across the channel. In the distance, a heavy cloud bank has begun to loom across the horizon. We will likely face an afternoon storm like the prior day. Are they a regular enough occurrence that we may need to adjust our schedule around them?

The channel itself is calm, the sun risen high above, reflecting off the ripples. The bluff is too steep for me to see the shoals, but if I squint, I can see Midway. I wonder what the inspector is up to. Sitting around a fire sucking on Orlot? Really, how does he pass his time? There are always logs and reports to fill out, I suppose, even in a place so remote. Someone who fully embraces the workings of bureaucracy can fill out incident reports over paper cuts and log the individual cans they open at a meal.

My earpiece squelches, startling me. We'd used it so little, I'd practically forgotten it was there.

Tompka's voice enters the transmission. "Varka, this is camp, do you read?"

"Affirmative," I say. "What do you need?"

"There is news," she says. "Brogden has awakened."

"What is his state?" I ask.

"In pain, but rational."

"Excellent," I say.

"There's something else," the engineer says. There is a hitch in her voice. She is hesitant to voice what she is going to say next.

"What is it?" I ask.

"The patrol boat. Someone has sabotaged it."

My stomach drops, and my blood chills. I ask her to repeat.

"Sabotage. The motor was flooded with corrosive chemicals. Whole thing is slagged."

"Understood," I say. "We will be back first opportunity."

The connection drops. Efta slides the portfolio into an envelope of thin plastic and holds it carefully in her arms. She looks at me and says, "We'll swim our way home, no doubt."

CHAPTER 11

DECONTAMINATION, POOR VINTAGE, DEFORMATION

Efta and I exit the offices. It is disappointing to cease the search of the Warden's office. Her records are more likely to yield useful information than anything we've found, though the downstairs record bank will also bear some examination. However, the majority of the stored files are likely to be fragile and will require delicate and patient treatment. I'm tempted to suggest she leave the portfolio behind until we are better geared to transport it, but after the altercations with Yost and Mikael, I do not find that to be a hill I should die on. I don't have time to fight her anyway. Sabotage of the boat is a threat on the camp. The logical conclusion is that smugglers are responsible and that an attack may be imminent.

I send an open broadcast to the team requesting we rendezvous at the stairs ahead of schedule. The reluctance and frustration in Yost's voice are palpable when she agrees, and I wonder from what she does not want to be drawn. Mikael's tone indicates he clearly understands the urgency. The technicians outright refuse.

"We cannot leave until the system is restored," Yammut says.

Because restoring comms with the mainland provides potential alternative solutions to our newfound transportation problem and offers the promise of reinforcements should we come under attack, I agree. I request they maintain a watch and that both immediately return if they make visual contact with any possible threat.

"Don't take any unnecessary risks," I say and switch off.

I follow the path through the fence in long strides even as I look to my right and see Yost exiting the warden's residence. She carries a bundle of papers in a brown leather folder along with a couple of plastic document tubes. Mikael emerges from the burnt armory with a black duffel bag over his shoulder. Everyone has brought something home but me.

I arrive at the stairs first. I look back to make sure that everyone is still accounted for, and then I start down. Efta is behind me, then Yost, then Mikael. I am glad that it is Efta behind me. Were it Yost, I would worry I might be thrown off the steps. Part of me wishes that I could reverse time to our first meeting and somehow break the ice more effectively.

When we arrive at the bottom, we continue to the old admitting building. When the prison was fully operational, the admitting building processed incoming inmates and employees. Tompka has converted it into a decontamination building.

Just as we arrive at a door that Tompka has marked as the entrance, I hail her on the comm. Her voice enters my earpiece.

"Do not remove any of your gear for first stage decontamination," she says. "Enter one at a time."

I enter the building. The first chamber was once used for prisoners and employees to dress before they ascended to the plateau. For us, it has been set up as a UV bath. There are mounts on the floor that once held the posts of dressing benches, but they are gone. Instead, along the baseboards and along the joint of wall and ceiling, the room is fully lined with banks of UV tubes.

"Please close your eyes and stand still with your feet at least shoulder length apart and your arms out," the engineer says. It is somewhat strange to hear her voice commanding me in a windowless room. Something about it makes me think of the voice of God. As if it were the voice of God, I comply.

The lights pop on with an audible click followed by an intense buzz that tickles the hairs inside my ears.

"You must remain still for five minutes."

I wiggle my fingers. I am glad of the mask because it protects my face from the light, but I can feel mild discomfort in my fingers. My arms start to get tired as I wait. It is easy to take for granted the weight of the sleeves of a coat until you must hold them up. My shoulders and triceps throb intensely by the time the engineer's voice finally returns.

"You may move on to the next room, and another may enter," she says.

Tompka instructs Efta while I open the door and let myself deeper into the building. It is unclear what function the next space initially served, but now it is simply an undressing room. One wall has a large bin operated by a foot petal with a rubber seal around its lid. There is also a container of large zipper-seal plastic bags that we are to use for personal possessions.

I empty everything I am carrying into two plastic bags and then dump all of my clothes into the bin. I discard my peacoat. I've worn this particular coat some time now, but I know that another awaits on the procedure's far end. The original will be disinfected and returned.

When fully nude and shivering in the cold air, I indicate on the comm that I have disrobed. The earpiece transmitter is impervious to fluids, so it and the plastic bags are the only things that remains on my body. I proceed to the next room. It is tiled, floor to ceiling. A huge shower spigot is in the ceiling and both walls. The floor has a gentle gradient from the center to the sides into slot drains. The showerheads normally feed from the island water system, but I know that the engineer will have re-routed it to a chemical drum and pump system.

On the wall by the exit, a row of goggles dangles from a row of hooks. I set down the plastic bags and take a pair of goggles. I put them on just seconds before I'm instructed to do so. Goosebumps cover my skin. It is uncomfortably cold. I wish we could have outfitted the building with a heating system.

"Hold your breath when I give the signal. The chemical spray will last fifteen continuous seconds. Remain with it on your skin for thirty seconds and it will evaporate."

"Are the fumes damaging?" I ask.

"Yes," the engineer says. "But the risk is minimal as long as you do not breath in while the spray is actively filling the air with mist."

I sigh. No point in arguing. The nature of the world, the nature of service: most of what we do shortens the span of our life. I've read that once people lived to eighty or a hundred years. I can only imagine their health was better back then, but the only octogenarians I've met make me hope I don't last that long.

Tompka signals and I take a deep breath.

A hiss escapes the plumbing as the pressure surges, and then a wetness on my body immediately follows. It feels thicker, more viscous than water, and this creates a dissonance between how fast my nerves think it should flow down my skin and how fast it does. It contains a deeper chill than the air, and I shiver, fighting the urge to cling my arms to my body. Beneath the cold, my skin tingles as the chemicals interact with the salts and minerals. My testicles feel like they're going to fully retract into my body. I press my lips together even as my teeth chatter behind them. The last thing I want is this goop in my mouth.

And then it is done, and I stand there shivering violently. My muscles spasm hard enough that I feel like they're knocking my heart about in my chest. Or maybe my heart is knocking about in my chest so hard it makes my muscles spasm. I really can't tell. My nervous system is haywire. Hearing the engineer instruct Efta in the undressing room and Yost in the UV chamber helps keep me grounded.

Then, the chemical wash leaves my skin. Its wake is tingling frostbite. My knuckles and elbows are stiff. There is a deep ache between my legs and in the seat of my belly like I'd been kicked there hard.

"It is okay to breathe," the engineer says.

I try to keep holding my breath until I can make it into the next room, but in a second I breathe in sharply, exhale short, almost a hyperventilation as I shiver. Though the goggle lenses stain my vision, my body is a bright pink head to toe with every hair standing on end. My toes and fingers curl on themselves like they're arthritic.

My weight hits the door even as I turn the knob. I feel like my feet are going to freeze to the tile. I pull my goggles off and drop them, grab my bags and then stagger out of the shower.

My feet hit wood, and I'm in a long, dim room. It had once been several rooms before the walls either decayed or were knocked over. To my right, the row of lockers that remain was once part of the personnel changing room. One of the lockers even has an old padlock hanging from its latch. To my left, a janitorial closet. There is still an old-fashioned yellow mop bucket. Ahead, the main space was once a reception and processing area with a long receiving counter and several substations set up for individual interviews.

Next to me stands a long, low bench with six bundles of clothing on it. They're all identical in design, but each bundle has a name on it because of our different sizes, so I grab the one that has mine. I pull on the charcoal gray pants and light gray, long-sleeve shirt. A second bench contains belts, socks, and boots, so I don them too. At the end, a pair of coatracks holds our peacoats, one of which I am eager to slip into. It will take several moments for the new clothing to warm from my body's heat, and the cold is causing my chest to feel constricted and my breath to catch.

Once fully dressed, I take my plastic bag to a small pile of rags and a row of bottles of disinfectant. I set about disinfecting my possessions one by one, and I am nearly done when Efta emerges from the shower room.

I do not mean to look at her, but it is the effect of the sound of the door opening. She does so as violently as I did, and I am startled.

She is, of course, naked, her skin pink and shiny like mine. However, now I see that the burns on her neck run down the right side of her chest and across half her rib cage, curving under her right arm. Her right breast does not have typical definition, the nipple being entirely gone, the overall shape heavy with scar tissue. Her left leg is also heavily burned from the knees to her pelvis with a swath running up to her navel.

She walks over to the clothes and selects her set, and then she methodically gets dressed. Once she has pulled on her coat, she approaches me, takes a rag and begins to disinfect her own materials.

She pauses, however, when she sees what I am holding. I had picked it up as I moved through my items methodically and hadn't been entirely aware of exactly what I held. It is the piece of old tech, the one with the numbers that rose and with the three black triangles on a yellow, circular field.

"That device," she says. "What is it?"

I hold it up so that it is clearly visible to both of us. I shake my head.

"You tell me," I say. "It wasn't in my briefing."

"I have seen one of those before," she says. "On an expedition into one of the abandoned cities. Our physicist carried one to measure contamination levels."

"What sort of contamination?" I ask.

Efta holds her hands out, palms up.

"They hadn't been told either," she says. "But they didn't want to see a number over one hundred fifty."

I finish wiping the device down and turn it on. It immediately makes a steady clicking sound. The digital gauge climbs to seventy-two or seventy-three. I rotate slowly. The number fluctuates up and down a bit, but it climbs to eighty when I face the plateau.

"Would be nice if it came with some instructions," I say.

* * *

I exit the admitting building as Tompka instructs Yost out of the chemical bath. I know that I will have to deal with her, but I wish to take a few breaths of fresh air before I do. I had not fully been aware how stifling the respirator had become. My whole world had felt compressed to a little bubble. Even as the coolness of the approaching noon strikes my skin, I am immediately overcome by the urge to scratch a dozen tiny spots on my face, and I already dread that our afternoon excursion will demand I wear another respirator all over again.

For the indefinite future, my days will be spent largely in that bubble.

The cool, damp air also soothes my skin, which the decontamination protocol left quite tender. On the horizon, the thunderhead continues to gather. There will be a storm of significance from those clouds.

I attempt to raise the technicians but experience no success. I check the beacon broadcast, but it still broadcasts the gibberish. In most surveys, there is something of a relief to periods spent out of contact with the Bureau, but this time, it makes me uncomfortable. Nothing yet has gone wrong that cannot be remedied, but that can change quickly with so many uncertainties. When Efta and I worked the quarries, the project had been difficult but straightforward, at least in regard to the work I was there to do. I'd never doubted the fundamental premise upon which I'd been dispatched.

The radio squelches, but nothing intelligible comes through. For a moment, I think I hear Jones, then nothing but static. I doubt that signals will travel any better as the storm approaches, but I'd like them down from the plateau before it hits. If I haven't re-established contact with them by the time I can eat, examine the damage to the boat, and assess Brogden's condition, perhaps Mikael could retrieve them.

As I enter the camp, a powerful flood light illuminates, I assume triggered by a motion detector. Looking around, each razor wire post has a bulb attached to it.

On the far side of the campfire, Tompka is securing a wind-shield over my tent. She has already done the others, except for the one she shares with Efta.

She looks up to me and adjusts her cap as I approach.

"I need to finish this," she says.

I nod.

"Is he in the tent?" I ask.

She tightens the tent wire on the stake. I unzip the tent and step inside.

Brogden is sitting on the edge of his cot. He is fully dressed, but his clothes look huge and rumpled on his frame. He couldn't possibly have lost much weight, but the hollows of his cheeks seem magnified, and his complexion is blotchy and ashen. A mug of something steaming is cupped between both his hands, but his arms shiver heavily.

He acknowledges my entrance with a partial turn of his head.

"Have things gone to shit yet?" he asks.

"Gone?" I say, chuckling. "We sailed straight into shit when we left the mainland."

He takes a sip from his mug and grimaces.

"Imagine that I am laughing," he says. He coughs, clears his throat with another wince.

"I take it you are still in pain?"

Brogden nods.

"Tompka says morphine won't block pain. I said, fuck you, I take morphine anyway," he says. He wags his finger at me, but that too seems to cause him pain. "She was right. Hurts like son of a bitch, but I care less that it does now."

My cot creaks as I settle down onto it. I lay on my back and lay my arm over my eyes. I decide there's not much to 'assess' about Brogden. He's not dead, and he's clearly still too weak to participate for duties. Unlikely that he would make it out of camp if he tried.

"So, who turned on you first?" Brogden asks. "It was Yost, wasn't it? Thought she'd turn out just a blowhard. My money was on Efta."

With a sigh, I explain the altercation about the warden's residence.

"You're going to need to rein her in," Brogden says.

"If you have a set of reins to yoke a military woman like her, you've been holding out." I reach into the ration box under my cot and pull out a pint of water and a compact protein bar. I drain the water in one long chug and then ask, "What can you tell me about her?"

Brogden shakes his head.

"Not much," he says. "I don't deal much with military circles. As they say, guns stick to guns, pens to pens."

"There has to be something," I say.

"There is something in that there is nothing," Brogden says. "Yost's records read like they've been cleaned. Of course, my access is limited—"

"Better than most," I say.

"Better than most," Brogden says. "Still, the Bureau likes to put doors rather than windows on its secrets—"

"Lest we fool ourselves thinking the sun is a light bulb," I finish. "Listen to us, like two old school Toms who find platitudes wisdom."

Brogden coughs lightly; then, after sipping his beverage, he leans over with a grunt, picks up a plastic cup by his foot and spits into it. Either there is blood in his spit or whatever he is drinking stained it.

"You're spitting up blood," I say.

"Tasting first. Poor vintage."

I scratch the back of my head. It sounds like our tent is done. The camp is almost secure, and it will be time to see the boat. Although I want to respect how weak Brogden appears to be, I can't beat around the bush too much.

"How much do you know about this situation?" I ask as Brogden raises his cup back to his lips. He freezes without yet having drunk.

"What have you learned?"

I tell him about the *Sarru*, what I learned from the captain's log. He hardly seems to react until I get to what Efta and I found in the Offices.

"You haven't found Warden Redgelyisch's personal log?" he asks.

"No. Efta and I were searching her office when Tompka—"

I stop because Brogden is nodding in a way that makes it clear he stopped listing at 'no.'

"Likely what Yost was looking for at the residence," he says.

He doesn't say it, but the look on his face is clear. One way or another, that logbook is central to his purpose here, perhaps his entire purpose. It might even be all of ours. I know I won't get a straight answer when I ask, "Does this logbook have some particular significance?"

Brogden shrugs and leans back.

"It is an artifact of some significance to understanding the progression of the disease," Brogden says. "And what about communication with the mainland?"

"Yummat and Jones are still on the plateau attempting to purge the beacon and clear the channel," I say.

"An interesting assignment, no?"

"To say the least. I just hope it does not keep getting more interesting."

"They say the first three days are measure of pace for surveys," Brogden says.

"I hope not," I say.

"Same," Brogden wheezes, "or else I'll be dead by nightfall."

Brogden seems about to say something, but Tompka opens the flap and sticks her head in. Her attention focuses on Brogden first.

"Have you finished the serum?" she asks. When Brogden shakes his head and takes another swallow, she looks to me and says, "The tents are secured. Need to show you the boat. Then, I must reinforce the camp."

"I will return," I tell Brogden as I rise. "We have more to discuss."

Brogden frowns. All his features seem to sag as if he's aged ten years in a blink.

"This conversation has already exhausted me," he says.

I exit, resolving to make a particularly generous note about the productivity of our consultation in the log. I will have to make sure he does the same in his. Otherwise, it will be only a matter of time before someone comes to question us about the conflict in our accounts.

* * *

I follow the engineer down to the dock. She walks at a steady clip, her shoulders leaning forward into her stride. The horizon explains why. The storm that approaches is more than formidable and towers into the stratosphere. Within it, lightning flashes. The bite of the wind is its harbinger. No doubt the camp must be fully secured by its arrival.

The wind blows against our backs from the plateau. I wonder if there is any chance that contagion could blow down to the camp from the Gollitok. Are we safe here at all?

I stop short at the dock's end as the smell hits me like a hammer. I would have noticed it sooner had the wind been blowing the other way. It is sharp, acrid, and burns my sinuses. An undertone in it reminds me, perhaps, of plum but bitter. It also makes me think of sticking my head in a bathtub full of bleach. There is smoke to it as well, burnt wires and melted plastic. I reach into my pocket and pull out a handkerchief I find there. I press the cloth over my nose. If I'd thought about it, I'd have brought a respirator.

The boat I rowed in on is straight ahead at the dock's end, but the compact patrol boat is to the left. It's a small, red and gray tug with a short flat meant to stack cargo crates chained to the deck. Tompka hops straight onto the deck, planting both feet at once. I grab the dock post and lower myself down.

The air is thick enough here with fumes that my eyes burn, and my mouth dries instantly. We will not be able to stay long, but the engineer doesn't waste any time leading me across the cargo deck. Astern, there is a double hatch that she pulls open in two fast heaves. A whitish-gray cloud billows up as she does so.

As the smoke clears, she swears profusely. The motor is only recognizable as such because I know it is supposed to be a motor. Otherwise, it's more like the metal equivalent of a badly melted candle. The steel is discolored with bright purple and green streaks where it is the most distended, and other places are streaked with black. A whitish corrosion seems to be spreading, creeping up some segments like a vine.

"It is progressing faster than I'd anticipated," the engineer says, crouching on the edge of the engine compartment.

I stare in disbelief. When she'd described the damage over the radio, I'd hoped she was overstating, but now I see she most severely understated.

"What in the hell could have done this?" I ask.

"Some sort of corrosive chemical," she says. "An acid I suppose, but nothing like I've ever seen."

"Did you take a sample?"

"Tshh," she snaps, pointing into the devastated hold. "You think I'm trying to collect what did that?"

"If we don't know what it is," I say. I don't like her tone or that her 'th's slur a bit. "It makes it harder to know how it got here."

"Whatever can do this, we don't let leave a laboratory," she says. "I don't even know if I have anything I can use to contain it."

Something crackles inside the hold. It's a sound like crumpled up sheet plastic collapsing under a heavy weight.

"Appears the smugglers have access to resources we did not anticipate," I say. "You must attempt to sample it."

She sighs, spits into the hold.

"Just don't you go expecting me to fix this," she says.

I wave my hand through the smoke as if it's going to improve my view. The entire engine is obliterated. Perhaps Tompka could have acted faster, but nothing about what has happened to the boat strikes me as something subject to intervention. What would the agent do to a human being, I wonder?

My throat tickles, and my lungs buck. I let out a hack of a cough and know it's time to get away from the fumes. I cross the small deck and hoist myself up onto the dock. Behind me, I hear the engineer rummaging through one of the storage crates. I don't quite get to shore however, before I freeze.

Across the cove, beyond the bluff where the old loading elevator dangles uselessly over the plateau's edge, a large bird alights with a sharp screech, followed by another, then another. They depart in twos and threes, and then in little clumps that look to range from several to maybe a dozen. I don't need to be closer to feel certain, based on their color and wingspan, that these must be the same birds that cascaded down upon the jellyfish and nearly killed Brogden.

I shiver and feel myself cringe, instinctively trying to pull back as if I can vanish into my jacket. They are on their way out to hunt, so I don't really have anything to worry about. However, I do wonder if there is a connection between their departure and the storm. Perhaps the jellies rise to the surface before severe weather.

I start walking back toward camp, continuing to watch the birds take flight. More still beat their way into the air, and I find myself awed by their number. Of course, Albertachen is a perfect roost provided they can find food within a close enough radius, since there are no natural predators. Though more than one of the epidemics originated among birds, the birds rarely seemed particularly susceptible to their deadlier symptoms.

At least a thousand must have embarked. I am reminded of the cities and the bat colonies that formed in the basements of some of the derelict skyscrapers that had yet to be, and likely never would be, reclaimed. Before my mom and I took the train out to the country, I used to stop on my way home from school at sunset to watch some of the colonies empty. There was one particularly empty block where the colonies would spiral up almost simultaneously, a half dozen arching columns like the double-helix of a DNA ladder. Every once in a while, a couple of the colonies would break into wars in the process, sending clusters into each other's columns, tumbling out of the sky biting and grappling.

These birds don't bite and grapple, but as their departure thins, the stragglers become increasingly more distinct. Several clearly suffer from what I can only conceptualize as feather disorders. One has a wing visibly longer than the other. Another sports a massive bulge on its side that seems to drag it into a tendency to skew its fight to the left. A couple appear to have vestigial, half-formed limbs, even one which struggles to remain aloft that appears to have four wings, two of which seem non-functional. That one rises and falls in its flight as its wings flap erratically, each struggling to do its job.

I note several wandering around on the plateau, either failing to get off the ground or failing to possess the necessary accoutrements for flight altogether, such as one without any wings at all. A couple stagger and fall repeatedly. Another simply stumbles off the edge of the plateau and vanishes with a modest splash into the water precisely in the shadow of the non-functional elevator. Feathers fly off the single beating wing of one that keeps tipping onto its side, and another is pushing itself along with its only leg. It does not have a recognizable head.

A sadness fills me. Of course, any population will have its share of genetic defects, but I wonder if the isolation of the island may have led genetic lines to thrive that would have otherwise died out in more competitive environments. I can't help thinking about my parents. How I am, in many ways, that marred line struggling not to die out.

CHAPTER 12

SECURITY, PAPERWORK, MOM

When I return to the camp, I am ravenous. I should have eaten more this morning. It is easy to forget the calorie expenditure in the field. Unfortunately, no one sits around the campfire, and nothing cooks on the low flames. Mikael stands by the gates chewing thoughtfully on a pale protein wedge and gazing at the plateau. The clouds have not yet reached the island, but they are drawing near, so maybe everyone decided it would be best to eat lunch within shelter.

Mikael attempts to raise the technicians. Hungry as I am, it worries me to have two team members out of contact with a storm on its way. Nothing moves on the plateau except the malformed birds on the bluff. If only the broadcast array was visible.

"Any luck?" I ask.

Mikael shakes his head.

"Thought I caught a bit of a garbled transmission a few minutes ago, but nothing else. We've begun to experience signal degradation in our local transmitters as well."

"Have you ever worked with Yammut or Jones before?" I ask.

"No," Mikael says. "I've not worked with any of you before."

I raise an eyebrow. I'd been certain he knew Yost. Strange as it would be to learn more connections among team members, I would have liked to hear the techs were experts, but the truth is that even high-profile assignments often receive undistinguished grunts. I have a gut feeling none of us are viewed as high profile candidates.

"What about their records?" I ask.

"Haven't read them," Mikael shrugs.

He flips a couple frequencies, attempts a couple more hails.

"Is it possible that they might—"

"Damage the beacon further?" Mikael asks. "Maybe. I've never trusted anyone to do their job properly. If I don't get to pick them, I'm going to judge them on what they do, not on what a file says about them."

I gaze up at the plateau for just a moment, but my stomach churns. The beginnings of a headache strike me. Over the years, plenty of folk have told me what a good leader they are because of how they deprive themselves to focus on work, but in general I've noticed the better ones take care of themselves. I can't risk not having a clear head because I'm too hungry.

Mikael makes a third attempt on the radio and swears when it fails. After returning his transmitter to our general channel, he inspects the junction box for the wiring of the motion lights. A half dozen neatly bundled wires are soldered into a simple circuit attached to a silver toggle switch. When set to the middle setting, all the lights come on. When fully thrown, only the motion sensors cause them to illuminate.

"Hope they've enough sense to come down from the plateau before the storm hits," I say.

"No doubt you'll see them during the afternoon excursion."

Satisfied by the wires, he kneels down and shifts some large rocks piled around the base of a fence post. There, planted but not armed, is a claymore mine. I hate working with the military.

"Guess we shouldn't head out to take a piss at night," I say.

"Latrine is in camp for a reason," Mikael says. "I don't fancy sleeping tonight without defenses with teeth."

"Won't argue," I say. "But I like to know when someone plants explosives around camp."

"Letting you see now, aren't I?" Mikael asks. "And I need to finish. If you need me—"

"I won't need you to come with us to the plateau," I say. "Yost should be sufficient."

Mikael scoffs. "Guess I'll need to add digging your grave into my schedule."

I cock my head. Is the mine armed? I presume not since he's fiddling with it, but I can't say I've spent enough time messing with mines to be sure. I shrug. "Yost will do what Yost will do, but after the sabotage of our transport, we can't afford to neglect camp security. No number of lights and booby traps will keep an under-guarded camp safe."

Mikael straightens.

"They sure do help though," Mikael says.

* * *

In camp, Brogden stands in front of the tent, fully dressed. His legs wobble, and he is standing with the assistance of a pair of metal crutches. He holds the same mug he did before, but what-ever it contains is no longer steaming. In the muted afternoon light, his complexion is even waxier than it was in the tent, but seeing him on his feet makes him seem more substantial. I place a hand on his shoulder.

"Please tell me you do not intend to attempt to mount the plateau today," I say.

"I plan to look at it today," Brogden says. "I will feel more able tomorrow."

His voice is thick with phlegm. He clears his throat and takes a deep breath. The congestion rumbles in his chest. I don't think he could cross the camp right now.

"Do you have a focus in mind for this excursion?"

"Not facing off with Yost," I say. "And I believe we will prioritize the Disciplinary Hall."

"Understandable," Brogden says. "I must admit my curiosity piques with it."

"With the stories of what happened here, how can one not wonder what they thought needed to be kept behind closed doors?"

Brogden shrugs and adjusts his crutches.

"An old philosopher once warned that when you gaze into darkness, the darkness gazes into you," Brogden says. "Sometimes it's good to see what looks back so you know that you are still better than it."

"Surely you overstate," I say.

Brogden points vaguely to the plateau.

"I'm tired of the road that brought me here," he says. "I've participated directly in fourteen executions for the Oversight Committee. I've taken eight lives in the field."

I shudder at the thought. I've made it my whole career killing no one.

"One time, my partner on assignment and I found the body of a child on the side of the road. He had been run over by one of the transport trucks like a deer. I could tell by the tire treads left on his clothes. We requested by radio permission to delay for burial. We were denied. That partner brought a large thermos of coffee on our excursions. Together we drank our coffees and smoked cigarettes while we walked. The boy was still dead on the road."

"When I was a teenager," I said, "before my mother took me from the city, I worked in the substructures, cleaning storm drains, unblocking sewers."

"Surprising," Brogden interrupts. "Your family's standing should have let you enter a higher tier of labor on entry."

"My father insisted I learn the bottom before he bandied his title," I say. I pause. It's strange to be talking about my father, I realize. My mother said little and steered the conversation to different footing whenever I brought him up. "I've not killed anyone, but I've pulled more bodies out of the piping than I care to remember. I don't know if they went down there because they couldn't find somewhere else to live or if they went there to die. Maybe both. Either way, though – that was the beginnings of why I decided I too would one day join the Bureau."

"Perhaps you should have gotten out when you had the chance," he says.

"Someone has to work for a world where that doesn't happen," I say. "I know you have better stories. Do you have family?"

"A sister. Ivitzi," he says. "But she has hard life. Bore her children too close to a contaminated zone. The ones that lived will never be able to live more than a few minutes from hospital. The others... Oba was born with heart outside of her chest."

"Someone has to work for a world where that doesn't happen either." I grimace.

"I don't know why she chose to keep having them," Brogden says.

"Because the alternative is to die out," I say.

"Perhaps is better that way," Brogden says. He pulls a cigarette from his coat and lights it. I doubt smoking is a good idea, but I say nothing. The first drag elicits a weak cough, but he meets my eyes. He says, "I understand what you say. Even Ivitzi's children together. Ivitzi and I used to laugh too. I tickled bottoms of her feet in crib when we were supposed to sleep."

I say, "Think on that the next time you look into darkness. That is in the dark too."

I squeeze Brogden's shoulder, bid him to eat something, and duck into my tent. I need to eat as well, but I also need to make an entry into the logs about the morning's exploration, the *Sarru*, and the difficulties faced by the technicians, fill out an update of incident report on the progress in Brogden's recovery, fill out a new incident report about the engine, and log at least a preliminary intent of filing a disciplinary grievance about Yost's actions outside the Gollitok administrative facilities. I've put off the survey's paperwork for too long already.

I slide the ration box from under my cot. I would prefer a hot meal, but, as they say, comforts are things you deserve tomorrow. Instead, I eat two protein bars, fruit and vegetable pastes, and set a couple cubes of starch seed in water to reconstitute.

Then, I set about filling out the paperwork by kneeling on the floor and using the cot as a desk. Despite the time pressure of the approaching storm, I need a moment to let my mind unwind. When I leave the tent, I will need to deal with Yost, to continue the search, to round up the techs. The methodical nature of completing the official forms has always helped me organize my thoughts. On the forms, there is a place for everything that is needed. What to put is clearly indicated by labels, and how much to put is clearly indicated by the size of the boxes. People don't fit so neatly into boxes in the field. Paperwork is its own world, and it is one I can grasp. Comprehend. Navigate.

It is all pointless, of course, or rather it is part of an illusion, a reality that exists in the squeak of file cabinet drawers, the click of staples, and the cool whoosh of manila envelopes sliding across desks. To look at the Bureau on paper, one would believe it in a level of order on par with the Kingdom of Heaven. Instructions were perpetually issued. Everyone was always in motion.

The reality is that everyone sat at a desk scratching dandruff from their temples wondering what the hell they were expected to do with their bodies.

I take up one of the starch cubes. It has expanded into something resembling a dinner roll but far soggier and far saltier. Biting into it shares textures with a cheap bar of soap that has been left in a bucket. It carries an odd bitter taste that leaves me wanting to spit. More than likely it is well past its expiry. A lot of field rations are. They're good for energy though. Protein for the day, starch for the hour, they say. It does not leave me full, but I suppose it leaves me sated enough given that I can only imagine that over the last twenty-four hours I must have burned enough calories that three days of rations would not suffice.

When I am done with my tasks, I crack my back. The writing has made my wrist even stiffer and achier than it already was. I turn off the interior light and am about to get up when I find myself caught for a moment, looking at the darkness of the tent wall. My mind is suddenly on that train with my mother beside me. Though I do not imagine we are holding hands, the memory of the warmth of her hand surfaces, and I smell chicken feather and excrement. The smoke of a train engine, oil. The taste of soot.

My face is pressed against the window, and there is the nothing of the tunnel. There is the everything of void. The small square of canvas can fit the whole of the plateau, all of Albertachen. The ocean surrounding. The shifting shoulders that wore a reef, the rising sea floor. Two great opening eyes. How their gaze does not relent. How it digs. They see my fears about Yost. My worry for the missing team members. The worry of being trapped now that the boat is disabled. The eyes see through the glass into the train car of my memory and of my now.

If I reach toward the darkness, things will reach from it toward me.

If I can't see the hands that take hold of mine, I will never prove they are not there.

I realize I am hearing voices outside.

I snap out of the spell of the darkness with a jerk. My spine is sweating. So are my armpits. My hands shake as I close my logbook and stow it in my pocket. My wrist throbs a bit under its bandage.

By the time I rise to my feet, my body is normal again, and the hazy afternoon light greets me like a tired friend as I step out of the tent.

There, I discover that everyone stands around Tompka, who has returned to camp. Her face is red and sweaty. She is covered in grease, and her hair is unkempt as she speaks rapidly with wild gestures. It only takes me a moment to gather the crux of it: the boat has sunk.

* * *

"I could not stop it," the engineer says. "Whatever they poured into the engine ate through the hull too."

She points to the dock. The craft is now invisible except for its prow, which points upward at a sixty-degree angle.

"And other boat," Tompka adds. "The motor will not turn over."

The boat that brought me still bobs against the posts, but we'd be a tight fit, and without a motor, we'd never beat the current. Mikael sits heavily onto one of the camp chairs. Efta squats by the fire pit and pours herself a cup of cooled coffee from a kettle. Brogden lights a cigarette. Yost stands facing the Gollitok with her shoulders squared and her hands loosely clasped behind her back.

No one speaks for several moments. It is to be expected. None of us want to be stranded here. We have rations to last for at least a month if we're disciplined, and water for at least fourteen days. If we do not establish radio communication with the mainland within a week, in theory at least, they should dispatch an investigatory team.

I look up to the mess hall at the edge of the plateau, and my heart drops a bit. Clearly, they'd been in no hurry to send a follow-up.

I look to Tompka and point to the plateau.

"What about the *Sarru*?" I ask.

She scoffs.

"It's on the fucking plateau," she says.

I shrug and point across the cove.

"If we can lay her on a sledge and drag her to the cargo elevator and repair the mechanisms, we might be able to get her down to the water."

"We don't know if her engine works," she says. "And she's contaminated."

With a gesture to the dock, I say, "I'm pretty sure she's a better bet than what we've got."

"Varka is correct that the possibility should be investigated," Efta says.

"I agree," Yost says, without breaking her attention from the plateau.

"Okay," I say. "Mikael will stay here to maintain camp security."

Mikael pinches the bridge of his nose and then lifts himself out of his chair. He looks exhausted as he curves around the firepit and picks up his shotgun from where it leans against a crate. Though I am leaving him as guard because it is imperative that we guard against further sabotage, I'm also relieved that it will separate him from Yost. Efta is tough, but she and I just wouldn't balance against a pair of trained soldiers.

I turn to Tompka.

"You will inspect the *Sarru* and determine whether she can be salvaged. Efta, stay with her. Keep a watch."

"But—" Efta interjects.

"No one alone," I say. "Once you've determined whether the boat is sea-worthy, make visual contact with the communication array from the safest vantage you can find. If you see Yammut and Jones, bring them back. If not, do not investigate further."

"How long until the storm reaches us?" Efta asks.

The engineer looks at the horizon, then to a small flag fluttering in the breeze off one of the fence posts, then to her watch.

"About three hours," she says.

"Then we need to be in decontamination in two hours and forty-five minutes," I say.

I take up my respirator and pass one to Yost. I bid her to follow me and walk out of the camp. It is greatly relieving that she follows without argument.

Mindful of the perimeter after seeing Mikael laying down the claymores, I lead Yost to the water's edge where the sand is still soft from the receding tide. The water ripples with a silver sheen, reflecting the sunlight filtered through the clouds and the particulate haze. When I was a child, the world went about its business under a perpetual twilight. I don't know how old I was when I realized that the sun could make my eyes ache if I looked straight at it during the most lightly clouded of days.

Yost gazes at the cove with me for a few moments before she says, "I assume we will do more here than watch the tide recede?"

I turn to face her. She, the same to me. Her physical presence I find imposing. She leans forward just slightly enough to make it feel like she will lurch forward if my heart beats wrong. Her face has a hard beauty and grace to it, but the muscles of her shoulders bulge against her neck. Her tendons betray both an impulse to act and a forced restraint. Despite how rash she has been, her being is one of physical control and discipline.

"I have already entered a disciplinary grievance into the log about your actions before your entrance into the warden's residence. An oral report will be transmitted as soon as comms are reestablished," I say.

Her jaw flexes. Her shoulders tighten, but she draws her feet slightly closer together and clasps her hands behind her back. Sweat beads on the back of my neck and on my forehead despite the cold air. It would be very easy for her to kill me right this moment. At any moment she chooses.

"You will not repeat that incident or any similar insubordination," I say. "If the team fragments, the consequences could be disastrous."

Yost rolls her eyes.

"My orders superseded your instructions," Yost says.

"And will they do so again?" I ask.

"Yes."

"I cannot accept that," I say.

"Then I cannot accept your command," Yost says.

I grit my jaw.

"This survey is under civilian oversight and jurisdiction," I say.

"I am not allowed to accept that jurisdiction," Yost says.

"Then resign, stand down, or I will force your arrest and trial."

Yost narrows her eyes at me. Everyone in the camp will be watching our exchange. Her only recourse would be to violently remove me from command, and she would need clear evidence of a failure of my competence to justify it after the fact. It occurs to me that she could attempt to intimidate the other team members to corroborate a fiction, but she would have to be able to maintain that corroboration after the survey had dispersed and we'd all been reabsorbed back into our respective departments.

"I also need to know if you have found Warden Redgleyisch's personal log in her residence," I say.

"No," Yost begins, but then she looks to the side, and something deflates from her shoulders. "Not in its entirety."

She reaches into the chest pocket of her overalls, pulls out a folded paper, and passes it to me. It reads:

To my dearest Olig,

In the event that this damned post defeats me, please know that you were loved and missed. Know that I will pass confident the world will be better with you having grown up in it to help shape its future.

Love,

Mom

At the bottom right hand corner, there is security barcode and watermark, indicating the paper was manufactured explicitly for government record purposes. Next to that, there is the date written in barely legible pencil.

I turn the paper over. The back side is wholly blank aside from the watermark pattern characteristic of pre-war records stationary. I return to the message. I keep coming back to the signature – 'Mom'. It is strange to think of Warden Redgleyisch, the Gollitok's warden, as someone's mom. The Gollitok's reputation was of torture and cruelty. Did she discipline her child by having him dig a hole deep enough to be his own grave and force him to spend the night at the bottom? Did she order her son's pediatrician to pull the most prominent teeth out of his smile?

Then again, maybe she arrived here meaning well. Maybe she didn't learn to create until she was presented with a waiting canvas. Maybe she looked at all the poor half-naked souls trudging about on this harsh naked island and came to the inner realization that the only way to save them was to break them.

"Is this all you found?" I ask.

"It is all I took," Yost answers.

I frown and hold the paper a little closer, shifting the angles of light.

"The date is wrong," I say, even though I have no doubt that Yost has already noticed. Though I don't know the Gollitok's history so well as to remember something like who was assigned to it and when, the date would have to be fifty years off at least. Maybe Efta could give me the exact number. Unfortunately, we don't have time to delve into the vibrant history of this place, so I ask, "What is the meaning of this paper?"

"I believe it to be a code or combination," Yost says. "The date."

I fold up the paper and slide it into the inside pocket of my coat.

"If you find the door that it might open," she adds, "do not try to open it."

Then, as if on some predetermined signal, Yost and I simultaneously shift our attention to the thunderhead, to the camp. Efta and the engineer both stand ready. Tompka wears a large caliber pistol on one hip, and she's cinched her jacket back to keep it accessible. Efta is still unarmed, but she wears a flare pouch on her thigh.

Mikael has begun a tight circuit of the inside perimeter of the fence. I am loathe to leave anyone alone right now, but we have two tasks to complete in short order and a camp to protect. At least Mikael has razor wire, motion sensors, claymores, and a shotgun to defend himself.

"Alright, everyone," I say. "We have no question that we're not alone, and whoever they are, they were skilled enough to sabotage the boat in broad daylight without leaving a trace. At no point should one of us be engaged in an activity if the other isn't actively standing guard. Do you understand?"

Their assent comes over our general broadcast channel, but it is laden with static, leaving everyone sounding a bit robotic. I am not unaware that should the signal further degrade as we spread apart, we may find ourselves unable to communicate. I feel kind of like someone is gradually closing my throat off and that soon my voice will be destroyed. It occurs to me that something about this place disturbs my thinking. Or, maybe, it reaches inside my thoughts and places its own inside.

CHAPTER 13

HORSE STALLS, MOSS, CLOVE HITCH AND STOPPER

When we arrive on the plateau for the second time, dread curdles my stomach like smoke in a bottle. I try again to raise the technicians at the top of the stair. Static crackles, and for a moment, I'm convinced a distorted voice says, 'Varka'. No one else comments, so I dismiss it as my mind reading into the white noise. Both the mess and warehouse stand between me and the antennae array. Could one or both of the buildings block my signal?

It occurs to me that the sabotage of the boat might have been a distraction rather than an attack. What if the real trap had been the damaged transmitter? It would have been a savvy place to isolate two members of the team. There'd been no gunfire, but anyone who could get to the docks unnoticed could stage an ambush among the buildings of the Gollitok. Unfortunately, if that were the case, whatever was going to happen had most likely already happened, and as such, no doubt the Bureau would prefer we spend our time completing steps of the official investigation.

I try again to raise the techs; again, static answers. I turn to the rest of the team.

"We should minimize open channel traffic," I say. "Watch your backs. From here on out, let's call ourselves scratched and swim as if we know the sharks smell us."

"Shit, bet sharks in the cove can smell these damn disinfectants," Efta says.

"Better than smelling like that shit hibiscus they put in all the outpost soaps," the engineer says.

Efta starts a laugh, but Yost speaks over her sharply, saying, "We need to move."

Then, the lieutenant shoulders her Kalashnikov and starts forward up the gradual slope toward the offices.

Efta and the engineer peel off into the mess; I must trot to catch up with Yost. As before, nothing moves across the plateau. The roost from which the birds had alighted is now obscured by the mess, but a couple return and vanish into the bluff, their claws laden with jellies. The moment I recognize those little, black tentacled-monsters, I freeze and scan the sky, but the anxiety passes that they will drop on us here like in the boat. How did those birds possibly evolve to eat something like that? How many must have died before finding that one who'd been born with the talent for enduring or deflecting that agony?

Ahead, Yost reached the split in the edge of the fence that cordoned off the administrative buildings. Straight ahead, the offices; to the right, the armory; to the left, the warden's residence. We don't cross the break in the fence, but rather follow its right side toward a long, low building with a peaked roof. It is the building marked on official maps simply as "Disciplinary Hall," a building that everyone who has heard of the Gollitok has heard of as well. They say that when blood is spilled by an atrocity, it leaves its stain upon the place. If that is so, every square millimeter in the disciplinary hall must be infected.

I pause and scan the plateau. The half-broken buildings weather their burdens in silence even as they decay one second at a time. Is there something hiding inside one of them, waiting for us? As the wind drags its claws across the open ground, sweeps of dirt cavort and twist in the places where the air currents buffet each other. Strange that the night's storm has so quickly dried up, but perhaps the soil is coarse and sluices the water beneath.

The only motion I find is on the bluff by the cargo elevator, where more birds have landed with their clutches of prey. Now, there must be a hundred of them. Though it is difficult to tell from this distance, it appears as if they dump the jellies upon the dirt and rocks and strut around pecking them at their leisure. With each snatch, they tilted their heads back and snapped up their morsels. One of them grabs a jelly by the sack and whips its whole body up just as another grabs one of its tentacles. For a moment, the two birds appear to be in a tug of war, but then they are lost among the moving crowd.

I shift my attention to the mess hall when a slip of motion catches my eye. I glimpse Efta's face passing one of the windows. I do not like that our team has been divided into such small contingents. Efta can handle herself, but I wouldn't expect anyone non-military to withstand active assault from an enemy possessing a clear tactical advantage.

I pivot to scrutinize the windows of the offices, of the warden's residence. The door of the armory. What's to stop the smugglers from watching our progress and then simply occupying a place we've already been? There are too few of us to maintain a permanent watch, especially with the techs missing. It occurs to me that the very practice of a survey's preliminary sweep is largely predicated on the assumption that no serious opposition will be encountered. I find it speaks to the Bureau's arrogance that they assume they can send five civilians and two soldiers to the fringes of the territory and simply expect us to negotiate whatever pitfalls may await.

The one thing I know for certain is that we could be under watch from a dozen different places across the plateau. God help us if the smugglers have a sharpshooter.

"Varka, put your head back on your body," Yost's voice bursts into my ear in a hissing whisper. Then, as if she'd been reading my thoughts, "We're too exposed."

I break from my reverie and trot toward the doorway of the disciplinary hall.

The door itself is still intact and on its hinges, but now it is propped open with a rock. The building doesn't appear to have a single window, but a segment of its roof has been damaged, so there may be enough light to see inside.

When I step up beside Yost, I squint into the darkness. Though it has not rained since before dawn, water drips from several unseen reservoirs, the patters magnified by the stone walls and tile floor. The room we gaze into is approximately ten meters square. An entry area is demarked by a barrier of crisscrossed steel cables that resembles a chain link fence with an open gate in the middle. Beyond, a five-meter-wide corridor runs down the center of the room, and the floor appears to have a downward gradient from each side that meets in the middle. Three grate drains are evenly spaced down the center of the trough.

Each side is divided into three cubicles with meter high walls, almost like stalls in a stable. A mesh of thinner cable completes the space from the top of the walls to the ceiling, and it is apparent that at some point, each stall had a gate, but the gates are all gone. From the ceiling above each stall hangs a naked bulb socket – only one of which contains an intact, dark bulb – and a series of meat hooks that sway in the draft from the damaged roof.

Though it is difficult to make out, and my view is partially obscured by low walls, I'm pretty sure that mounted to the back wall of each stall are metal arm and neck cuffs. Judging by their height, they are designed to suspend the prisoners off the ground.

Yost produces a pair of skinny flashlights from inside her coat. She passes one to me and presses the other against the barrel of her rifle. The beam is focused but bright, illuminating countless motes in the air like swarms of fruit flies, and we slide their circles over the surfaces. The tiles are the muted gray of a dead body, and both the walls and floor seem infested with tracts of some sort of bluish-green mold or fungus. It is the closest to plant life I've observed since our arrival. How has it failed to establish beyond this building? Photo-sensitive? I am glad for the respirator. I don't want to be breathe in spores from whatever grows in this place.

"Switch channels," Yost says, holding up fingers to show me what frequency setting.

We shuffle forward, even our clothes audible. The rocking chains groan and clink as the hooks glance against each other. Yost keeps her flashlight trained on the door at the far end of the central corridor while I shine mine into each stall.

The first on the left contains a metal card table with a green velvet top that has been stained brown in an enormous swath. What appear to be poker chips are scattered everywhere.

The first on the right contains a rotting saddle, riding crops, and bridle.

The middle left is empty, but the middle right has a set of wooden stocks bolted to the floor. There are only two holes, so I can only assume it must be for the ankles. I imagine someone futilely shielding themselves with their hands against an unescapable attack.

"I don't like this," I whisper to Yost.

"What's to like?" Yost says.

The last on the right has a metal chair with spikes all over its seat. I don't bother to look to the left.

Yost and I pass through the door into the next chamber. This room is a single open space with what impresses itself as a 'station' in each corner. My light falls on a table equipped with manacles. One end of the table is cut away to allow the head and shoulders of whoever is confined there to drop over a large basin, I assume for waterboarding.

Next, a true medieval rack with a large pulley at one end wrapped in rotted rope.

Then, a vertical table on a hinge with pulleys attached to the ceiling above. In front of the table stands a firepit, the mechanism designed to lower the prisoner attached to the table above or onto the flames.

Finally, the last corner simply has cuffs on chains attached to floor and ceiling from which a prisoner could be suspended in the air. All around lie an assortment of prods with cables that run to outlets along the wall.

Despite the implications of pain and suffering behind each device, they are from the world before the war. After all, the Gollitok was abandoned and left off the books nearly forty years for all that went on here. If the smugglers are here looking for something, I'd let the smugglers have it. What if the Bureau wants the prison itself? The thought is almost too disturbing to consider. The Bureau is not without its flaws, but I cannot have worked for them so long without seeing the kind of malice that would lead them to begin placing prisoners afresh in this place.

"This whole island is a torture chamber," I say. "Why need a building for it?"

"Suffering is a living thing," Yost whispers through the comm. "This is its beating heart."

I walk up to the fire table. The wood is dented all over in the spot where the back of one's head would rest. There is no neck restraint here, so I can only imagine it was intended that the head be free to move. Perhaps the thrashing was part of the show. The will it would take to kill someone this way is beyond my capacity.

The texture of the floor beneath my feet becomes squishy and unstable. Beneath my soles, the fungus has thickened. It doesn't cover everything, but it's like a river system and its tributaries, running in crisscrossing bands across the floor and up the walls. Even stranger, it has not grown in the mess or the offices. Why here of all places? Is it linked to the nature of the place?

I crouch down and shine my light into a thick tuft of it. With the light up close its teal tone becomes more iridescent; it lusters with purple and gold.

"It's like a moss," I say, though it actually reminds me more of fur. No, it actually reminds me of the Orlot in Midway.

"Maybe it is a moss," Yost says.

I pull my knife from its sheath and drag the blade through. Bits of whatever it is cling to the blade, leaving behind them little streaking scars that almost pulsate. A clear liquid beads up along the lines.

"It seems a lot more alive," I say.

"Moss is alive," Yost says. Her voice is as edged as my tool, though her obstinance is out of tension, not in earnest.

The chuckle can't be stopped, but I also feel giddiness behind it. I'm about to rise, but I happen to note my boots. The moss clings to the sides of the soles. I scrape it off with the blade, but it seems to be embedding itself into the leather. I straighten and wipe the blade with disinfectant before I return it to its sheath and discard the cloth wipe.

"We should burn our clothes as soon as possible," I say.

Yost raises her rifle to her shoulder.

"We should press on," Yost says.

She proceeds forward, her steps graceful, almost silent. At the far end of the chamber stands another door, this one intact and shut. I follow behind as Yost lowers her barrel to the side so she can take the knob.

A cold wind swarms from the portal as Yost opens it. It's like being caught by a weightless ocean wave. The respirator's filtration is fine enough that I can't smell the air, but the moment my light shines into the space beyond, I am glad for it.

In the circle of my flashlight, a woman's body lies bent backward over a metal chair. Her head is thrown back along with her arms, and her knuckles lie curled in the pool of her hair on the floor. The skin of her throat has torn in a jagged line from the force of whatever flung her backward. Her shirt, which has fallen upward to expose her abdomen, is also torn above her left breast where two penetrative wounds, each about as thick as the pad of my thumb, bloodlessly gape paths that must lead straight to her heart. Rich tattoos sprawl in a ring around her stomach at the level of the naval, but it's difficult to recognize what they depict because vivid bruising mars the coloration and lines.

Her feet are nailed into the floor with thick spikes. Her spine must be broken in a dozen places for her body to make such a shape.

Yost's light illuminates a second corpse, positioned a meter behind and a meter to the right of the woman's body. This one is a man with broad shoulders seated in a meditative position, except that he has been decapitated. His head rests in his lap with his hands neatly folded over his crown. He too is nailed to the floor with a spike through each thigh, his back affixed to some sort of metal rod. He bears the same twin piercings in his left breast.

My light finds the next body, this one a meter behind and a meter to the left. He is arranged identically to the other man.

Then, in a semi-circle behind the tableau is a line of what appears to be four more bodies.

No blood whatsoever. Anywhere. A numbness wells around my heart, and my fingers feel fat and useless. I grip my light tighter because the way it shakes in my hand tells me I'm about to drop it.

Yost steps forward and nudges the woman's arm. It rocks freely at the contact.

"She's been freshly killed," Yost says. "No rigor."

"Less than three hours," I say. "They were killed while we were in the administrative block."

"Impossible," Yost says. "That's seven people dead."

Yost sweeps her light and rifle barrel in a grim circle around the room, pausing at the doorway at the rear. Stairs lead down and curve out of sight. She shifts her light back to the bodies and systematically checks each of their breasts. Every one of the bodies around the edge bear signs of mutilation. Abrasions, gashes, chunks cut out. In every case, internal tissue is exposed, but it's as if they were drained elsewhere.

"No blood," Yost says. "Impossible."

I spout off an old saying, "If you see only impossible things, then maybe it's the possible things that can't happen."

"This isn't some damn city committee meeting," Yost snaps. "You don't torture and kill seven people unheard by someone a hundred meters away."

Nausea roils in my stomach like a rock made of oil. I swallow hard. Vomiting in my respirator will be disaster. Worse, it will force me to be exposed.

"Well, we have a room full of bodies that says something like it sure is possible," I say. "And the way they're arranged..."

Yost nods.

"It's meant for us to see."

She steps closer and examines the tattoo on the belly of the woman broken over the chair. I work to keep my breath steady as she does so, drawing in through my nose and out through my mouth. Yost's breaths over the radio are steadier than mine, but a slight hitch at their stop and start suggests that she too experiences anxiety. I look up to the ceiling in the hopes that clearing my vision of the corpses will help clear my head. My pulse is in my eyes, creating a slight stutter in my sight.

"Knots," she says, and I focus back to the tattoos. "Alternating pattern of clove hitches and stoppers."

"The Clove and Stopper, then," I say. The familiarity of the phrase calms me a little bit. Upon inspection, the pattern is clearer than I first thought, despite the bruising. Smuggler crews often tattoo themselves, and each other, while at sea to pass the time during their voyages. They are not all good at what they do, nor do they seem to care. However, these have some nuanced shading and attention to detail. "She's on the wanted lists."

"Yes, and this was her captain," Yost says, pointing to a sigil overlaid on the center of each knot. Then, she moves from body to body, confirming the identification. "Appears to be nearly her whole crew. Two missing."

She inspects the two headless men and identifies them as the first mate and warrant officer. I'm glad that she is sufficiently schooled in the smuggler tattoos because I do not want to get any closer to the bodies. My anxiety is at bay for the moment, but I had not expected something like this.

"I suppose we've found the smugglers then," I say. "Maybe this is the work of the remaining two?"

Yost doesn't answer nor does she need to. Even as the words leave my mouth, they feel hollow. Not only does it not make sense that they'd turn on each other like this, but even if two of them had managed to do this without us knowing, there was no way they could have also slipped down to the docks to sabotage our boat. Could the crew have taken aboard extras? Or maybe there was a third player involved.

"I don't like this," I say.

"You keep saying this," Yost says. "A mission doesn't give a fuck what you like. Just what you need to do."

"Easy for you to say," I say. Then, I shine my light to the stairs. I don't want to go any further. Whoever did this might be waiting for us down there. "Maybe we should pull back and regroup."

"No," Yost says. "Whoever did this may well have the techs. I believe their silence is by design. They could be dead by the time we get back with the others."

"They could be dead now," I say. "They could also be out by the transmitter with no clue that any of this is happening."

"Then you go," Yost says. "Leave me without backup."

She strides forward, angling her barrel to follow the curve of the stairs as she begins to descend.

I attempt to raise Efta and Tompka on the comm, but static is my only answer.

"Yost," I hiss. "If we die, damn well know my ghost will file a complaint report."

I stop at the top of the stairs and pan one more time around the room. Why the display? A terror tactic? I press my flashlight to my palm, plunging the room into darkness. The doorway to the torture chamber is a faint gray arch, and from here none of the torture stations are visible. Just enough light makes it in here as my eyes adjust for me to make out the shapes of the dead. I wonder if any of them had families. Who it was who loved them and watched at windows for their return.

Then, I reveal my light again, take a breath, and follow Yost down the stairs.

CHAPTER 14

TINNITUS, ROCK WINDOW, THE EXPANSE BELOW

The stair winds down below our feet, our descent throwing echoes like shards of glass no matter how soft we step. The moss has infested here too, but it appears to prefer the walls, seeming to root itself in masonry cracks. Purples and pinks begin to dominate, and in the shifting glare of our flashlights, I almost feel like I'm walking down a tunnel of amethyst.

A cold wind rustles my hair and sweeps up the cuffs of my coat as I descend further, and a low rumble rides it. The stone vibrates my feet like it grows impatient.

"The ocean," Yost says.

Immediately, I recognize the rise and fall of rolling breakers into the grind. This stair must lead to the lighthouse gulley.

"That explains how they could have gotten the bodies up to the disciplinary hall unnoticed," I say.

"It does," Yost says, "but it doesn't say how or why the crew was killed."

A crunching sound like someone stepping into hard-packed snow brings Yost and I to a stop. Yost seems to shift in the darkness, causing several softer crunches, almost like someone chewing dry cereal. She shines her light at her feet. The moss appears to have grown hard and brittle and spread fully to the stair tops. The phyllids have grown bulbous and angular at the edges – almost crystalline in their geometry. Yost sweeps her feet to the side, and they snap off at the axes.

"Watch your step," Yost says, and descends further into the spiral's curve. The slope of the path is tight with less than two and a half meters from step to ceiling – were I to jump, I'd crack my crown. The darkness and the path's spin are disorienting; the walls seem slightly angled, inward in some places, outward in others. Altogether, it makes every couple steps land with a waver.

My own boots land on the hardened moss, but it doesn't feel like stepping on crystals or fragile stone. Though I can't see what's under my weight, I feel like it moves before my weight lands, as if it's adjusting itself to accommodate me. Obviously, it is my imagination, but every step disquiets me as the stairs seem to choose how I step on them.

At the same time, the transition to a crystalline nature has become much more pronounced in the 'moss' that now nearly carpets all surfaces of the descending stair. The formations are larger, the lattices finer. I wonder if the moss is turning into crystals or if the crystals sprouted the moss. Either way – my mind butts against the impossibility of a transition from vegetable to mineral, or vice versa.

Yost holds up a hand.

"Did you hear that?" she whispers.

I freeze.

The ocean's rumble is louder now, my own breath heavier, more mechanical through the respirators. What if there are crystals in the air? What if they're clogging the filters? What if they're growing on the filters? The slightest shift of my weight causes a churn from the steps that seems amplified in the confined space, and pulverized dust wafts about. Above, the sharp piccolo of something dripping. Beyond that, nothing.

"What is it?" I ask.

"You don't hear that ringing sound?" Yost says. "It's high-pitched. A slow pulse."

I listen again. The same drips, the same breaths, the same crunch. A bit of fabric rustling as Yost tugs at herself. Still nothing.

"Not a thing," I say.

Yost curses but resumes her descent. Maybe it is just tinnitus or Yost's mind imposing substance into the silence. The mind deals poorly with absence.

The wind from below strengthens with each meter of incline. The moan of the ocean echoes more vibrantly, almost like some great beast groaning in its slumber.

I'd say we are at ten revolutions down when Yost comes to a complete stop and shakes her head furiously. She stuffs her flashlight into her belt and slaps her ear three times. A stream of curses burst over the comm.

"What are you doing? You're going to break your seal," I say.

"It's so fucking loud," she says.

She steps sideways and lurches against the stair wall. Her foot lands on the edge of a step. Crystalline dust sprays in a glittering, iridescent cloud that sparkles in my light as Yost's form drops. Her side and hip collide with the steps in a different sort of thudding crunch, and she slides down several steps before coming to a stop on her belly. Her rifle clatters with a cacophony as it slides around the curve and out of sight.

Careful not to step on her fingers, I descend beside her into cramped space, my back brushing against the crystal-coated wall. I kneel behind her even as she stirs with a groan. Miraculously, she kept her mask from striking the ground, but she hit hard.

I clasp my hands on her shoulders both to reassure her and to make sure she doesn't make any sudden movements. If she's badly hurt, she could reflexively shift and damage herself further.

"Are you okay?" I ask.

Yost groans again, reaches to her hip where it struck the edge of the step.

"I don't know," she says. "Help me rise a bit."

I ease her up by the shoulders as her hands find the stairs beneath. She rolls to her side against the wall and clasps both hands against her left hip. Fragments of crystal cascade with a clatter like pebbles shaken from a gravel bag.

"Can you move it?" I ask.

Yost nods slowly.

"Some range, yes," she says.

"Then it is probably not broken," I say.

"I've been in a dozen engagements, and I almost kill myself by falling," she says.

"My father survived the Wasting Years without so much as a sniffle," I say, "and a can of spoiled beets killed him."

"The world hates those who survive against it," Yost groans.

I pat her on the top of the shoulder. She winces and I suspect she may have bruised the muscle in her fall as well.

"Don't move. I will retrieve the rifle."

Yost says, "Watch your step."

I rise up. I want to light a flare and throw it down ahead, but I'm afraid the smoke will be too thick in the passage. I will be blind and choking. Still, something in my gut churns at the thought of walking into that darkness.

I draw my pistol and step forward.

The growth on the walls thickens, growing bulbous and jutting out from the stone almost like coral. The available path narrows to less than a meter. I wonder if it is possible that I will find the passage blocked near the bottom. The steps become uneven and treacherous. There is no telling how much the lattices will collapse under any step. The ones on the ground have not yet taken on the bulk of the ones on the wall, but they're clearly increasing in volume. Maybe someone carved these steps into a massive geode.

I reach the rifle a full rotation down the steps. If I cover my flashlight bulb, a dim glow shines below after my eyes have a few seconds to adjust.

Over my shoulder I call, "I think I see light below."

"Well, hale-fucking-lujah," Yost responds.

The rifle's strap has caught on a crystal formation. I crouch, steady my balance as something collapses beneath my left boot, but freeze as I reach for the weapon.

The crystals themselves, all manner of purple and pink with streaks of blue, individually appear chaotic, but there is a flow to their growth, much like above there'd been flow to the growth of the moss. All sorts of veins branch off as haphazard as tree branches, but the central arteries loop in distinct formations – taken as a whole, it is quite clear that they are in the shape of knots. Clove hitches and stoppers. How the hell is that possible?

I snatch up and sling the rifle, then crawl back up to Yost.

She's sat herself upright, and she is prodding her hip with her fingers. When she sees me, she looks up and says, "The sound. It's stopped."

"Good," I say.

I reach out and place one hand on her quadricep and another on her shin. She holds her hands up in objection.

"I'm fine," she says.

I shake my head. With a slow, steady pressure I bend her knee and push her thigh upward so that it rotates at the hip. Yost sucks in a sharp breath but says nothing. I then guide her leg out to the side as wide as the walls of the stair allow. She groans.

"We need to get you back to camp," I say.

"No," Yost says. "We continue down. Either I won't make it up or I'll walk it off and there's no point to turning back."

I further examine Yost's leg as best I can through her overalls and then shift attention to her shoulder. She slides one arm out of her coat so that I can pull her collar back enough to examine where she struck the stone. A purple bruise is already forming on her scapula.

There is some unusual ridging as well, almost as if a broken fragment of bone is pressing underneath the skin. When I probe the spot with my thumbs, she jerks away the instant I contact her skin. Perhaps a hairline fracture. She may have trouble discharging her weapon.

"I've had worse," Yost says, covering up the injury. "We can't stay here any longer. Please help me..."

She breaks off, nodding at her coat sleeve. I help her writhe her arm into it even as she makes a soft whimper. I envy her fortitude. Were our roles reversed, I'd likely be blathering over the comm for a medical evacuation.

Then, I help Yost to her feet. Her leg nearly gives under her weight, so I wrap an arm over her shoulder and press her side to mine.

"You do not need to take this risk," Yost insists. "No contact on the plateau."

"Leaving you for dead in a stairwell will represent poorly in the official log," I say.

"Do not be so sure," Yost says. "I am of the suspicion that none of us have been sent here because we are popular with the central authorities."

I freeze.

"Why do you say that?"

Yost grunts.

"Because I do not believe any of us are expected to return," she says, as we begin an awkward descent.

Every step, our shoulders crush crystals off the wall and send powder from them cascading to the floor. Every step, the uneven growth beneath our feet cracks. As we pass the spot where I retrieved the rifle, the brittle crunch takes on a squelching quality. I shine my light to my feet.

The crystals ooze a yellowish puss-like liquid from where they've broken off, and as I lift my boot, the liquid takes on a tacky and viscous quality – stretching in strings like gum. The texture reminds me of what I would imagine it would feel like to step on a carpet of beetles. I hope the substance can't seep through my boots or through my skin, though if it can, I'm fairly certain I am already in mortal danger. Thankfully, the growing strength of the wind reassures me that we might be nearing the lower exit.

Ninety degrees further into the curve, we stop again. Built into the wall, there is a rectangular window recessed into the wall. It is two meters high and a little over half a meter wide. The moss-crystals have left it completely untouched, growing thick and dense at the edges but not obscuring its view for a millimeter. Yost lets me lead slightly, leaving less of her weight on my shoulder. She pushes aside her coat, placing a hand on the butt of the pistol in her belt.

I lift my light, but the brightness throws our reflection onto the window. I press my flashlight to the glass as tightly as I can. Yost buries her own against the fabric of her overalls. I lean forward, cup my face to the window. As there is not enough space for both of us, Yost asks, "What do you see?"

"A room, three meters long perhaps, two meters tall, a meter wide. Bones on the floor, half-crumbled. Looks to be from a couple different people, though I cannot say for certain."

I take a step down. Yost's hand slides off my shoulder and grabs hold of an outcropping of crystals. I wince as her grip crunches some of the material, and the same fluid that stuck to my boots sluices between her fingers and runs down the back of her hand. One of us will have to come back down here to take down a sample to test at the camp, but for now, I warn Yost to minimize contact with anything in the stair. Again, I suggest we return to the surface.

"If anything in here is going to kill me, I started dying when I fell," Yost says. "And again, head back if you feel you need to."

She presses her other hand against the glass and pounds it twice with the flat of her fist.

"This isn't glass," she says. "A pre-war polymer. Even a thin sheet can withstand a powerful concussive force. Judging by the recess in the wall, this is six inches thick."

"So, they didn't want the prisoners to escape," I say.

"They wanted this to survive an explosive detonation," Yost says.

"Guess these guys really fucked up then," I say.

"Go to hell," Yost says, even as she slides her arm back over my shoulder.

A wave of claustrophobia sends my heart pounding. The slope of the roof, of the revolution we just completed, hangs within arm's reach of my face. How many circles have we made now? How much weight in stone is above my head? How much of that crystal? I picture myself being overgrown by it, trapped and consumed, watching in the darkness as my flashlight fails for a massive eye with a pale green iris –

I take the next couple steps and a couple long, slow breaths, hoping that Yost doesn't notice the tremors in my muscles.

Those tremors only amplify as the next window comes into view. This one contains actual skeletons, three, slumped in their shackles. No doubt the slightest nudge would send them to dust. We don't linger, but pass by like one might a museum exhibit.

The skeletons behind the third window contain the last vestiges of muscle, still contain the last tatters of their clothes.

Yost pats my shoulder with her fingers twice. She points her flashlight to the steps at our feet. The crystals have begun to breathe. I hardly believe I see it at first, but the stairs rise, perhaps a full inch, and then decline. The crystals ripple and surge in waves the way fur might in a breeze. Indeed, they only seem to resemble crystals now in form; their texture appears soft, almost supple, like crystals made of skin.

At the fourth window, a single body lies in the center of the tiny space. The flesh is marbled, blotched, and split in large gashes. He wears military-style suspenders and shirt, and there is a special forces insignia on both shoulder and collar. It is difficult to determine how long this body has been decomposing given its highly-sealed confinement and the complete lack of normalcy to the condition of this place, but it is quite recent. Weeks.

I hesitate when Yost asks what I see. Her weight leaves me, and she pushes past me to the window. Her push, neither light nor rough, focuses me on maintaining my footing on the absurdity in which my boots are planted as she shifts by.

Her face presses to the transparent barrier, and then, an instant later, she'd sliding down onto her knees. A whimper that forms a syllable like 'bah' leaps from her mouth like a thing with wings.

Then, she lurches to her feet despite her injuries, draws her pistol and fires three rounds against the plastic. Two ricochet past my head so fast I can't even react as the force of the reports bash my ears, like being hit in the head with a baton. A flash of white light floods my vision, and I stumble down step after step, my mind barely able to keep my feet under me as my shoulder strikes the wall.

Over the comm, Yost sobs, "Baby brother."

Fury surges inside me that she discharged her weapon so recklessly. My head reels from the damage to my inner ears, and a lush ring floods my mind like a thousand fingers on a thousand wine glasses are inside my skull. My vision tunnels. Then, it is I who falls to the stair, landing hard on my rump. Things spin, and I lurch sideways, bracing myself against the living crystal with my elbow.

The ringing leaves a sour taste on my cheeks, and all I can smell is hibiscus. Somehow, the smell is bright, bright pink.

My equilibrium returns in layers, kind of like bandages are being wrapped around my head, tightly. I'm sitting on the spiral staircase like I might sit on a park bench, watching the vendors load their carts, ladle soups from braziers, or arrange their garments to better show their colors in the dim sun. The rifle has slid on its strap and lays across my lap like a closed umbrella. Everything feels distant, like I'm watching through trapped sea foam.

Something hot trickles out of my left ear canal. It runs down my lobe and along the strap of my respirator, vanishing into my hair. A rhythmic breeze pulses through the air, and I realize my flashlight is out, its hard form jabbing my thigh under my weight.

Nonetheless, I can see quite fine. The light is poor, but my eyes adjusted to the dark in my daze, and the afternoon light rises from below.

I tilt my head to look up to Yost. I cannot make out her face at all, but she sits with her back to the glass, her hurt leg bent up, her hurt arm tossed over the knee. Slowly, she bumps her head against the window with a soft, rhythmic thunk.

I try to stand but find I am unable. My feet won't move, and my thigh seems stuck to the stair. I try to pull my flashlight out from underneath me, but it too is stuck. I reach into my coat pocket and pull out a pack of matches. I light three at once and lower the flame toward the stairs. I gasp.

The places on the leather where the viscous contents of the crystal smeared are themselves growing crystals, and those crystals seem to be merging into the ones growing on the stairs. Were I disoriented longer, how far would they have enveloped me?

I take up the rifle and plant the butt against the stairs. With a tremendous heave against the weapon, I throw my weight to the side. Things shatter and a pull on my legs like a powerful vacuum yields its grip all at once, and my body suddenly frees with a lurch. If my shoulder didn't meet the wall, I may well have simply tumbled down the stairs like a giant ball.

On my feet again, I reach out my hand toward Yost.

"If we don't get out of here now, I'm not sure we ever will," I say. My voice comes out like it's spoken by someone a mile away.

Yost's chin lifts in a slow nod, and she closes her fingers around mine. The growth on the stairs has taken a hold of her too, but between my pull and her push, there is no difficulty getting her to her feet.

At the bottom of the next revolution, we find two things: a final window and a twenty-meter stretch of tunnel that opens up onto a rocky beach. Small breakers churn and a fresh wind gusts in with a howl. The crystalline growth fades approaching the egress, giving way to barren stone walls. The soft incoming light might deter its development.

In a slow shamble, Yost approaches the final window.

Yost speaks, but it is difficult for me to understand through my ringing ears. I have to listen to the whole statement and hold it in my head all at once to identify the individual words. After a moment, I process that she has said, "Blood on my mother's grave. There's someone alive in there."

The woman in the sealed chamber is attached to the far wall by a thick metal restraint around her neck that keeps her neck from dropping. Her face is pale and angular, her cheeks are withdrawn as culverts with shadows gray as stone, and her eyes are sunken hollows with bright pink rims edging dark splotches. Their vacant gaze wobbles like a chunk of ice in a slow-flowing eddy.

She wears the layered linens typical of smuggling crews, and a black marble-toned overcoat with white highlights. Her pants are shredded below the knees, and her legs drag in a futile struggle up and down the stone floor. Her shoulders rock back and forth as much as the neck cuff allows, and her fingers pull against the metal. They bleed at the nails from where she has bullied them in desperate hope for freedom.

There is no real fight left in her motions. They are mechanical, the body and will on autopilot in a vehicle crewed by a broken spirit.

I raise my hand and pound the glass twice, but she does not break from her stupor or flinch. No relief nor hope for freedom washes across her face. Yost prevents me from raising more noise.

"She's not reacting," she says. It is a little easier to understand her now. Now, it feels like I'm sitting on the far side of a room. "Not to sound, not to our lights. We don't even know if she CAN hear or see us, and even if she could, we have no way to break through to her right now anyway."

Indeed, the smuggler woman twists against her restraint as if she is trying to lay on her side, but her motions look like those of a wind-up doll caught against an obstruction.

"But if she knew we were here—" I start, but Yost cuts me off by placing a hand on my wrist.

"Use your head," she says, softer than I would have expected. I am amazed I can hear her. "We will be lucky to get back up that stair. You think we're coming back down given what we've seen? Better she doesn't know we were here at all."

I don't have a lot of sympathy for the smugglers as a whole, perhaps because they're often as much a ghost story as they are a real threat, but I find it hard to stomach leaving someone in these conditions. What kind of thoughts pass through her mind given those motions? If she recognized our presence, would she think we were real?

"It's unfair," I say.

"Just after training, on a routine hump between stations, one of my squad mates was blown in half by a mine. Thing must have been buried there a hundred years just for him. There was a flash and smoke, and then he was gone from the waist down. He landed on his back and seemed peaceful, senseless, staring," Yost says. She forces herself to speak louder than necessary, perhaps to accommodate my hearing or her own, and her voice trembles a bit at the ends of her words. "Our medic fought to save him. Gave him painkillers and jolted him with smelling salts to keep him awake while he tried to stop the bleeding. Half our mate's intestines were gone, and the moment those salts hit, he just started screaming like a train whistle. He screamed every last second of life he had left."

"There—" I begin.

"Is nothing we can do right now. Our medic should have left well enough alone. So should we," Yost says. She points to the mouth of the tunnel. "We must get out of this tunnel."

Yost shuffles ahead of me without looking back as I follow slowly behind. It is clear that she intends to communicate that she can walk on her own, though her slow pace and the drag of her right leg at each step betrays her difficulty. Her gait does improve a little as the crystals diminish.

She freezes at the point where they seem to terminate altogether and holds up a staying hand to me. I approach cautiously and remain a few feet back. The floor grows suddenly smooth half a meter ahead of Yost; not stone smooth, but perfectly smooth like the windows into the prisoner chambers. The top and bottom of the opening are irregular, but the barrier stretches from wall to wall of the tunnel. In order to proceed, we will have no choice but to cross it.

At first glance, the tunnel floor might as well be polished laminate or some other some such material. The dull way the light reflects off it reveals it to be made of the same substance as the transparent cell barriers. It would then stand to reason that the floor is transparent too.

Yost lowers her weight to the side, using her hand to extend her right leg because her hip lacks the range of motion to drop her into a crouch. She rests one elbow right at the edge of the window and shines her light in.

After she angles it around a bit, she turns to me and says, "Nothing. Either there is no cavity under this floor, or the cavity is too large for my light to reach any of its walls."

Though I would prefer the former, I believe the latter to be the case.

I come up beside Yost and drop into a squat. The butt of the Kalashnikov clacks against the ground, and I adjust the weapon before I angle my light about the window as Yost did. Then, I track the beam around the edges.

"I believe the window goes under the stone," I say. Then, I frown as a thought strikes me. I shine my light all around the corridor. The stone walls are roughhewn, almost like the walls of a mineshaft. However, in a few spots, the contours and bumps seem to also give way to flat walls; what appears to be tarnished metal.

My light finds a spot near the roof. Through nearly the whole breadth of the visible tunnel, the edges are rounded, but in this spot, wall meets ceiling at a precise right angle.

"I don't believe they carved this tunnel into the stone," I say. "I believe the stone has grown over a tunnel."

Yost brings her light to the same spot as mine.

"Not possible," she says.

"I'm growing less interested in what's possible the longer I spend on this island," I say.

A sudden bang on the glass at our feet makes us both jump. Our lights jerk to the dark surface simultaneously, just in time to see something elongated – maybe like a forearm – drag away from the glass. Behind it, some sort of opaque-gray slime drips into the darkness in clumps, leaving a faint residue.

A burst of static erupts in my ear. For three or four seconds, my radio blares with chatter – a mix of white noise, the island's beacon, and what I believe to be Efta's voice. Between the overlapping signals and the damage to my own hearing, I am completely unable to understand whatever it is Efta attempted to say. I try to raise her several times with no success. The reason is clearly that we are underground, and the solution is clearly to cross the window and exit the tunnel.

However, something in me bristles with anxiety at the convenient timing that, just as I arrive at the edge of this void, I am suddenly given fresh reason to cross.

I find myself drawn to the opaque transparency, leaning forward to bring my eyes and light as close to the surface as possible without touching it. Is that empty darkness I see or is there something moving just at the edge of my light's reach? Some dark, rolling mass, a mix of angles and curves? Do I see projections and protuberances, or is that just pure blackness as my light fails to find a surface to reflect from? What if I'm shining my light through some massive pupil and the barrier is the eye's lens?

Yost, too, hesitates. Of all the things we can do, staying put is not an acceptable course of action, but ascending the spiral stairs sounds more arduous than crossing a plane made of something I know can stop bullets. So, I rise and step out. My boot heel lands with a thunk.

Beneath me, the dark.

Beneath me, myself in a train car pressed against the glass watching me walk across it.

Another step and nothing breaks. Nothing collapses. I'm neither gripped by a frenzy of flesh nor do I plummet into an abyss. Yost gains her footing and adjusts her gloves. I expect spiderwebs of cracks to launch from the points at which my weight is most concentrated.

But they don't.

Nothing writhes in the dark below or rises like a mythic creature. There is no great flash of eyes. Instead, the light grows from outside, and the air on my skin cools and becomes brisk. I imagine if I did not wear the respirator, I'd smell the brine. Perhaps the pungency of whatever failed to make it back with the tide.

My steps quicken and eat the meters, and then I'm nearly across.

I almost slip on a pool of blood and dirt sludge to match the deep gray stone. I shine my light to the rock. The blood begins right at the edge of the glass and still glistens in the contours. It streaks in a trail toward the tunnel mouth, and I follow it into the daylight.

There, I emerge into the lighthouse gully, and immediately I feel staggeringly exposed in a savage wind, a natural side effect, I assume, of a substantial time spent in such confined, underground passages, and the ferocity with which the wind whips into the space. The steep cliffs rise with a mouth consisting of just over a quarter circle. The gray stone has been weathered since its exposure, but it's also clear from the visibility of the sedimentary layers that the gully was blasted or channeled rather than being naturally formed, something I'd learned abundantly from my time in the quarry.

The lighthouse itself rises from a platform of cement atop a cradle of boulders at the gully's center and still shows signs of gleaming paint up its sides. However, unlike most lighthouses, the staircase to the lantern room spirals up the outside of the building. There is no visible point of entry, though it may be on the other side.

I want to know why they'd create such a space specifically for a lighthouse given that the very nature of the place they built undermined the purpose of the lighthouse.

However, I know that is not my immediate concern. My immediate concern is a trail of blood. It is then that I find that the smeared path terminates not ten meters away at the crawling form of what by my best guess should be the final remaining member of the smuggler crew.

CHAPTER 15

WARRANT OFFICER, LIGHTHOUSE, FRESNEL LENS

The blood trail curves and meanders due to the channels of the shore rocks. I'm amazed that he is still mobile, though his pace is admittedly tortured. I watch my path carefully. The rocks are covered in urchins, mussel shells, and numerous black jellyfish, left by the receding tide. Behind me, Yost's breath is ragged through her respirator. Perhaps she has broken a rib. She will need to rest soon. She will need attention when we get back to camp.

I consider drawing my firearm, but both the man's swollen and bloodied hands are visible as he pulls himself along. I catch a glimpse of an insignia on his arm that I believe indicates his ship rank as warrant officer. Though we've done nothing to conceal our arrival, he seems insensible to us, and blood coats his visible cheek. The man is not wearing a respirator or protective gear of any kind. Neither had the woman in the cell, nor had any of the bodies above. Had their precautions been taken by whoever had killed them or had they simply not believed they needed any? I instinctively reach up to my own respirator. A buffeting gust blows open my peacoat like a parachute.

Yost glides forward, suddenly graceful despite her injury. Her trajectory curves in a sweeping arc that spirals toward the man, her own weapon in hand and trained to fire. When she arrives beside the man, he has still not responded to her presence. The lieutenant cannot easily bend over, so she taps his ribs with the toe of her boot.

The man continues his path unabated. Does he hope to make it to the lighthouse? Or some destination of which I'm not aware, such as a vessel? Perhaps he meant to drown himself in the water. If the latter, the poor man must curse this low tide.

Yost looks about to nudge the man again, but I hold my hand up and crouch on the rocks beside him. I don't know what to say. I almost don't want to trouble him.

"Who has done this to you?" I ask.

The man continues his attempted crawl.

"Was it one of your crew?" I ask.

The man's breath rattles. His fingers clench and unclench on the stones. I want to roll him over to better examine his injuries, but while I've broken protocol to assist Yost, I have no connection to this man who breathes the island air unfiltered.

"What happened to your people?" I press.

The man wobbles, and the spring leaves his arms. His body sags to the rocks.

"Water," he gasps, his eyes straining to focus on me. My hearing hasn't fully returned so it is the movement of his lips I most recognize.

I shake my head and hold my empty hands up. I have nothing to offer and can think of no reason why he should tell me anything I might find of use.

So, I ask, "Is there someone I can tell that you have died?"

"Everyone I know... dead on... the bluff," he says with some effort.

His face holds the tone of a raw oyster. His lips quiver like one too. Yost reaches inside her pocket and pulls out a yellow sucker on a white stick. She unwraps it and holds it to the man's lips. To my surprise, he opens his mouth just enough for Yost to insert the candy between his teeth and his cheek.

Then, she produces a pouch of small ampoule and a syringe. She preps an adrenaline injection and administers it into the smuggler's neck. His eyes instantly widen. He draws a deep breath as Yost lets the needle fall to the rocks.

"My name is Yost," she tells him. "I am a special operative under military command. You are going to die from your injuries, but I have morphine to ease your passage. Before I can give it to you, I must know: has your crew located the blast door?"

The man tries to crane his head but seems unable to turn it. Instead, his fingers clasp the rocks, and he pushes himself onto his back with a heave that sends stones scattering. His shirt is heavily soaked on his left breast, but the heaviest bleeding appears to have come from his abdomen, left of his navel.

"Open," the man says, drawing a sharp breath and pressing his filthy hands against his side. "When we got here."

"Is it in the lighthouse?"

"No," the man says. "The warden is in the lighthouse."

The warden?

I can't bite my tongue. "Warden Redgelyisch?"

The man blinks the slightest nod.

"How is that possible?"

Yost steps over the man and interposes herself so tightly between him and I that I must take a shuffling step back lest I be bowled over.

A prolonged squelch out of my radio damn near stops my heart.

"... you read?" The voice is heavily distorted, almost robotic. Several unintelligible words are followed by a long static whine, then Tompka clearly says, "Where the hell are you?"

"At the base of the lighthouse," I say. "We lost signal in the passage down here."

"I've been trying to get a hold of you for hours."

Hours? I look up. The bright stain through the cloud caps and the particulates suspended in the air has travelled much further than the descent down the spiral stair should have needed. How long were we in there? Maybe we were dazed by Yost's gunshots for longer than I'd realized. It was a powerful concussive force in a confined space, something to which I am unaccustomed, and Yost was in a state of dismay.

It does not seem fit to mention this however, so I simply say, "We have discovered the smuggler crew. They are all dead."

While I know two of them are technically alive, I doubt either of them will be by the time anyone would have an opportunity to make their introduction, so I don't feel I am deceiving her. I will clarify later and be accurate in the log.

After a pause, Tompka says, "How?"

"Unknown," I say.

"Fantastic," she says. "Hope one of them showed you how to fix the radio array. The *Surra* is slagged. We will need an alternate form of extraction."

"Shit," I say. "Perhaps the smugglers' vessel remains."

"Well, either way, you'd better get back to camp fast. The storm is nearly upon us," she says.

I check the sky again. Though the overcast above has thickened, the storm banks must be obscured by the bluffs. The bluffs themselves have taken on a glistening quality different from the cliffs on the camp-side of the plateau. It's almost like they are sweating.

"Have you seen any sign of the techs?" I ask.

"Negative," the engineer says.

I curse under my breath.

"It's going to be a haul to get back to camp from here before the storm," I say. "You and Efta get back to base camp ASAP. We'll see you there."

When I return my attention to the rocks and Yost, the warrant officer is dead. Yost is holding a silver medallion on a broken chain and gazing pensively over the water.

"Did he say anything else?" I ask.

Yost drops the medallion to the rocks next to the body.

"They made shore on a raft they stowed in the lighthouse."

Yost and I both gaze at the lighthouse. The lighthouse is not the bright white of a typical lighthouse but rather its stones are a light gray with a bluish tint. The weather has, of course, scoured the surface, but it still gleams in swaths, especially against the surrounding stone of the gully. The tower is an oddity – especially with its external staircase. How would a keeper even make it to the top in a storm? Could it really contain Warden Redgelyisch, who by all rights should have been dead, possibly by hanging, for forty-some-odd years? Given the nature of the disciplinary hall, alongside the well-established general cruelty of life on Albertachen, the interests she held as warden makes this all the more ominous.

All this is idle speculation of course. It is risk assessment, but at the end of the day I will be expected to sit down at my logbook and describe the ways in which I proceeded with the survey. They will have considerable interest in an examination of the lighthouse, just as they will have considerable interest in my account of the disciplinary hall. Whether they believe my account of the spiral stair is another matter, but one thing no one will be able to say is that I turned back easily. It was like in the train tunnel with my mother. No doubt many would have been disturbed by the darkness, but I found it more comforting to gaze deep into it.

"Do you believe it to be a trap?" I ask.

Yost makes no physical expression or gesture, but says, "With the crew dead, there is no purpose other than spite."

"Or to complete their mission," I offer, well aware that spite is no small motive.

"You can't think like a Bureau-man here," Yost says. "The smugglers don't have a central organization. They don't have missions. Missions mean you fight for someone else. They have the luxury of fighting for themselves."

"You almost sound like you envy them," I say.

"Forgetting what we saw in the hall, wouldn't you?" Yost asks.

I hesitate. I am not sure I know the distinction between who the smugglers are and who the propaganda says they are. The hard-liners would have us believe they're little more than barbarian raiders out of some old Viking tale, but in general most of the moderates I know regard them as foolish malcontents who have deprived themselves out of futile idealism. Having lived in a city, I cannot ignore how destitute the marginalized could be within our own borders. Nothing like a little realism to puff some color into an ideal.

"Could they have called for help?"

Yost shrugs.

"I didn't have time to ask," Yost says. "Likely they're blocked by their own sabotage of the array, but even if they got a call out, the Bureau would have us believe the smugglers much more orga-nized than they are."

I take a step toward the lighthouse as Yost rises.

"You'd better pass me back the rifle, just in case," she says, a request to which I readily comply.

We approach the tower base carefully across the rocks, me taking a considerable amount of Yost's weight since each step seems treacherous as the rocks shift. A tiny crab darts out from underneath one and skitters into a tidal pool. I've seen so little life here other than the birds. Where are all its friends? Where is the meat upon which it feeds? Perhaps it hunts things that wash up with the tides. Maybe the water contains enough algae to anchor the food chain.

The temperature seems to drop ten degrees as I approach the tower. All my garments are growing damp. The waves are insuffi-cient to generate a soaking spray, but perhaps there is enough water sloshing among the rocks to mist the air, or perhaps the gully somehow traps high levels of condensation. Strange then that they have not begun to fog.

At the base of the lighthouse stair, it is clear the stonework is not traditional stonework. Rather, it is coated in some sort of porous substance that both provides texture to the steps but also an eerie give that makes it feel like I'm walking on a sponge. All over again, I feel underground, walking on substances foreign to my understanding.

I consider taking my chances on the spiral staircase back to the disciplinary hall, but even the thought fills my heart with a foreboding. Even conceding that someone initially carved that tunnel, there is something far more unnatural about it than it being man-made. The idea of rafting around the spurs of the island feels more comforting, despite the incoming storm.

Yet perhaps I am meant to feel this way. Perhaps this is by design. The thought is irrational, of course, given that such a design defies any identifiable causal logic, but it feels compelling, nonetheless.

"Wouldn't it be lovely if they'd simply stowed the raft at the bottom of the steps?" I ask.

Yost gives an empty chuckle.

We proceed upward. Yost brings one foot up each step, then drags her other foot up. Though her motions betray her discomfort, she bears it without complaint. As we rise, my attention shifts to the sides of the gully. Small openings riddle the cliffs. Depth is difficult to gauge because of a lack of scale, but my guess is that the hollows are two, maybe three meters deep, and each one contains a heap of debris. It looks mostly like cloth, some dead branches, bunches of something akin to straw.

Nests, I realize. All empty, but hundreds of them pocking the whole gully wall.

"Perhaps they nest here in the warm months and spend the remainder on the far side of the island," I mutter.

"What's that?" Yost asks.

"The birds," I say, pointing vaguely toward the cliff.

Yost grunts but does not comment.

The spiral is a little looser up the lighthouse than it was on the downward stair, so two revolutions bring us quite a way up the neck. A stout wind roars from seaward, strong enough to make me stumble. I extend my hand and brace myself on the lighthouse wall.

My hand recoils abruptly even though I haven't quite recovered my balance, and I wobble. I look at my palm and then the wall. The wall gives every appearance of stone, but it felt warm and oily, far more like human skin than I am comfortable with. I take a step back from it. Then another. Then, I jar against the stair rail. My weight tips backward.

A flurry of steps erupts, and hands grasp my coat. Yost's sharp jerk stabilizes my careening trajectory, and my weight settles onto my heels. Just hours ago, I might have been afraid that Yost would have let me fall. That she might have pushed me over the edge herself. How wrong I was about her. How glad I am that I was wrong.

"I don't know that I can drag your corpse back to camp, raft or not," Yost says.

"The stone," I say.

Yost doesn't look. She simply walks past me, her limp more pronounced. I doubt it did her much good to rush up to help me.

"I don't think it's stone," she says.

"Then why the hell are we climbing it?"

"Because there might be a raft on the top."

I continue on. Something makes me want to touch the wall again, to remind myself of the strange living texture. Is the stone made of it? Is it something that coats the stone? Its faint blue hue looks more mottled as I draw closer, almost blemished. The surface is covered in minute pores, and I almost wonder if this is like a compact version of the gully walls. What if those 'nests' are really pores in the stone skin of some massive living being, and I'm simply walking along its back?

I brush away the thought. Bad enough that I have to face the reality of seemingly living crystals and the possibility that the prison's warden, supposedly long dead, has inhabited this light-house for over forty years. Am I simply being overwhelmed by the unreality of everything I'm seeing? I don't know if I'm accepting it or simply rejecting the experience wholesale.

The wind grows stronger around me, now in a perpetual gale that whips the edges of my peacoat and chills my exposed skin to the bone. Then, underneath its howl in my ears, a scraping sound, like someone dragging a chisel along mortar, behind the stone. I step closer to verify the origin of the sound.

Now, it sounds more like a mortar grinding against a pestle, and I'm struck with the image of something inside pressing strips of flesh against the stone and grinding it into masonry like grinding grain, pressing the living material through the stone to fuse their qualities together.

The image is, of course, absurd, but my mind accepts it as wholly real. Part of me is aware that something may be affecting my thoughts. Why is Yost so composed? Perhaps she is not. Perhaps she entertains the same things that I do, and it is simply that her outward appearance has become increasingly discon-nected from her internal being. Could the end result be separate individuals?

I slap myself hard, and it leaves my cheek hot and fat-feeling. I catch Yost looking at me, but she does not comment. I watch her hands on her rifle. She has not brought the butt to her shoulder, nor are her fingers near the trigger. I do not yet believe her rifle to present an imminent threat to me. Yost turns her eyes back to the steps and proceeds on, so I proceed on too.

We are nearly to the top when all at once the stone façade bris-tles with goosebumps. There can be no mistake. One moment it was smooth, now it is covered densely in little domes. Most importantly, a tiny, crimped filament extends from the middle of each one. They flutter in an incoming breeze then snap rigid. Blemishes streak the surface, large patches where sheets of stone seem to be peeling away from glistening patches. Discoloration swaths these places, and tiny cracks weep a beige, viscous fluid.

I don't want to go on, but I can't simply leave Yost to ascend alone. It is not just because she is injured, but because she is taking a risk that could save the whole team. I cannot stand by and let her face all the danger herself. Twice the travelers mean twice the chance for success. I also want to say something to Yost about what I'm witnessing, but part of me wonders if I'm really witnessing it – and I am not sure there is anything either of us can do about it if we confirm each other's experience. Perhaps it is better that I pretend it is only in my head if it allows me a moment's respite from what assails my reason.

Then, we are at the top of the lighthouse.

The lantern deck is surrounded by intact glass panes, except for its own doorway. Through that portal is a gigantic lens. The lens is folded like the Fresnel lens I would expect to see, but it is shaped like a human being.

The impact of what I'm seeing is instantly uncanny. The light is out, and I have serious doubts that it would be capable of illumination. It looks much more like an artist's sculpture than an actual functioning lighthouse bulb. Maybe it is, in essence. After all, when viewed as a lighthouse, the lighthouse's placement seems irrational. However, if I view it as a sculpture, its scale becomes the most distinctive feature and perhaps a statement.

I step onto the lantern deck and examine the lens from all angles. The way its corrugations wrap around the body features, the arms crossing the chest, reminds me of a mummy. It's face has no distinctive features, but rather a smooth convex, almost like a pill.

Despite how long it has stood here with an exposed opening, it is completely devoid of dust, dirt, or debris. The floor is a centimeter-bar grating over what appears to be some sort of machinery, perhaps for turning the 'bulb' on its pedestal, and the grating is shiny and polished like it was just fabricated and installed. The entire lantern deck appears meticulously maintained other than a pile of deflated rubber, an outboard motor, and a duffel bag that appears to contain a pump and battery just inside the door. Those are crusted with salt and grit of all kinds.

At the far end, a hatch is propped open and the head of a ladder juts out. The ladder does not appear to be made of the same metal as the rest of the materials around us, and it strikes me that perhaps it was placed there by the smugglers. It would make sense that they'd utilize the interior of the lighthouse to conceal their presence and whatever goods they might wish to stow.

A deep clang like a heavy wrench striking a steel beam rises from the hatch.

Yost checks the chamber on her rifle, shoulders it, and creeps over to the hatch. She aims into the darkness.

"You see anything?" I ask, taking a step closer.

"The drop is too long to see the bottom in the dark," she says.

A second clang sounds. The ladder visibly shakes. I feel the concussion through my boots. I remove my flare gun and a flare from the pouch on my belt.

"Shall I launch a flare down there?"

Even as I say it, I know I do not want to do it. Something electric crawls around in my belly. I almost feel like an invisible thread runs from my center of gravity to something down there in the darkness. Yost's eyes are wide and alert. The pressing of her lips is the closest thing to true fear I've seen her display.

A third clang. This one is louder, harder. Maybe closer. The reverberation makes it difficult to determine distance.

Yost shakes her head and steps back.

"We need to leave immediately," she says.

I turn to the raft. I don't know how we can retrieve it quickly. The raft itself will likely weigh fifty kilograms, and the motor at least seventy. I grab the duffel holding the inflation compressor pump and sling it over my shoulder. It is a bulky model, one obviously reverse-engineered with available technology, but it still only weighs a few pounds.

"You're going to need to drag the raft," I tell Yost. "Move slow, let your weight do the work."

Yost nods and immediately complies. The rubber seems to churn as it drags, and I hope it does not fissure on the descent.

I crouch in front of the motor and lift it. As I feared, its weight is significant, and the only way I can manage the bulk is to let it dangle against my hands with my arms fully extended. Though it is not nearly too heavy for my legs, I cannot take large steps, and it is immediately clear that my grip will struggle. Angles I cannot seem to avoid already press into my fingers even as I waddle toward the door. I feel like I'm carrying a person – though in a sense, it might be more accurate to say that I'm carrying the weight of us all.

Another three clangs in succession, each louder than the last, as I traverse the simple two meters to the staircase landing. The cold sea breeze washes over me. It has grown more significant even in the brief moments we were in the relative shelter of the lantern deck, and the light has failed further to the choke of the storm cover. If we do not get the boat into the water soon, it is likely we will be unable to sail at all until the storm has passed. I do not relish spending a night in the tunnel, on the lantern deck, or on the rocks where the smuggler died.

At the top of the first step, my knees wobble as I adjust my grip to keep blood flowing to my fingers, and another clang helps me find strength and stability. My heart stutters like a pigeon trapped in my chest as I descend the first step. Will my ankle give if all this weight lands wrong? Will the dampness riding the wind make the stair too slippery? The image of sliding down the stairs on my back with the motor on my chest leaves the imagined sound of my ribs and vertebrae cracking echoing in my ears.

At the next metallic crack, there is no doubt that its source slowly ascends. It seems to be in no hurry, but I feel that same invisible tether to the origin of the sound as it rises up the throat of the lighthouse.

I check below. Yost is almost half a turn ahead, dragging the raft one heave at a time. The slickness of the fleshy stone may be assisting her, and it may be keeping the raft's wall from scoring through. She curses with each step, and her breath rasps in fits through her respirator. I empathize. The resistance of the filters demands more force from my diaphragm, and my lungs work harder than they would like. The cold invades deep into the bronchial passages like frozen threads searching for needle holes.

My hands start to throb before I've finished the first revolution of the spiral down. My resolve to get the motor down doubles because, even forgetting about the growth in the tunnel up to the plateau, there is no way in hell I want to climb up another spiral staircase today. The clang that follows that thought only nudges me further. I distribute as much of the motor's weight onto my knee to let the blood flow back into my fingers before I re-heft the bulk and continue my descent.

The swearing from Yost accelerates from a brook to a river. Her movement has grown erratic as the strain she is placing on her hip clearly worsens her injury. The rifle wobbles on its strap across her back with her motions and for a moment I have an image of it discharging accidentally and shooting me in the face.

"Do you need a rest?" I call down, but the loudest strike yet from inside the lighthouse answers for her. It is much higher now, almost risen to our level. Once it reaches the lantern deck, only a short stretch of stairs will separate it from us.

As I hobble one step at a time, I begin to imagine the source of the noise as something inhuman. Though I lack any sort of empirical evidence, it seems the only thing congruent with a tower of flesh-like stone, living crystals, and the abattoir we found in the disciplinary hall. I, of course, will leave such misgivings out of the official record and merely report that we perceived the sound to represent an approaching threat. The Bureau would disdain unproven speculation.

All at once the great, green eye I saw on the ocean channel crossing fills my mind. I stumble, my feet slipping just enough on the step to let my mass careen toward the stair rail. I feel the momentum of the motor threatening to throw my body into the void over the rocks.

Clang.

Higher still up the lighthouse throat, so sharp my vision pulses.

My heel finds a strip of grit on the step that halts the swing that presses my ankle to buckle. My weight lurches back a little less, then a little less like a twanged string losing momentum. I heave breaths. My fingers are agony from the press of the motor casing, but my grip has held. Yost has ceased her toil on the steps below and stares at me.

Clang.

Adrenaline fuels the both of us, I assume. Maybe Yost presses forth with the machine discipline of her training. The lantern deck landing is no longer visible from any angle, obscured by the wrap of the stair above. Though I know I can look out over the railing, I find myself picturing that I'm still descending the underground spiral, coated in crystals, with its prison windows. Maybe it's just how similar our movements are or how heightened my anxiety was in both places, but my mind wants to merge the two experiences.

Maybe, I wonder wildly, I'm still in that stairwell. Maybe I'm in one of those windowed cells, chained to a wall. Maybe the clank is the warden come to question me.

I realize I am weeping within my respirator. There is something happening here that I do not know my mind is equipped for. Or perhaps my mind is too well equipped to receive what is happening here.

Clang.

It is either near or at the lantern deck. My face burns with exertion. My ears are burning, and hot sweat trickles from my hairline just as the chilled gusts from the storm sweep it off. Everything about me shivers and shakes from the cold and exhaustion. My field of vision gradually narrows, and in the peripheral darkness I imagine looming teeth and claws. Twitches in my spine threaten to simply unspool my taut muscles and let the motor drop as I imagine something creeping down the stairs, ponderous and bulky, oozing slime and bristling with spines. I imagine it descending patiently, unstoppable, knowing its arrival at my back is a foregone conclusion, that it will be able to trace a razor nail from the nape of my neck to the base of my spine, slide its scaled fingers into the slit, and debone me like a fish in one brutal snap of its mass.

I try to turn my head to look up the stairs, but my arms have lost too much strength for them to do anything but hold on.

Then, my feet hit the gravel skirt around the lighthouse base. Yost is there spreading out the raft, her limp massive and loping. No doubt her hip can barely support her weight, yet a moment later she stands in front of me and is helping to ease the motor to the ground so she can get the pump bag off my shoulder.

A brilliant flare erupts across the whole gully. Yost and I look up simultaneously to see that it's almost as if the top of the lighthouse has erupted in white hot flames.

The lighthouse lantern has been lit.

Yost attaches the pump to the inflation valve and powers it on. The whir is soft, but clear over the groan of the sea and the toss of the spray of the swelling waves. The wind rakes its way into the gully like a grinning devil throwing white foam this way and that.

The light swells. Though I cannot see the lens, I know that it is no longer fixed in place, that it is moving to the stairs.

The raft swells too, rising on the shore. The creases and folds of rubber smooth out, and all of a sudden, the heap looks like a boat. Yost and I mount the motor onto the back of the raft. As we struggle with its bulk, the friction powers on the old-tech measurement device on my belt. I am unable to read the numbers it displays, but it emits an urgent and piercing groaning, clicking sound that I doubt signifies anything I want to know more about.

"Move your ass," Yost snaps.

Above, the light slowly descends, curving down the side of the lighthouse.

Yost pulls the raft from the front while I push from the rear. We both strain to lift the weight as much as possible to diminish how hard it scrapes against the unforgiving rocks that shift and tilt under our steps. Over my shoulder, our pursuer is halfway down, and the device on my belt intensifies with a matching pace to the light's approach. The shine refracts in beams through the spray, throwing prisms to the rocks around us. Though I cannot see the places on my back where the light strikes my coat, I could swear I feel a burning warmth digging through the fabric to my skin.

A cry from Yost precedes a splash and a clatter of stones. She has fallen into the shallow surf, in water close to knee deep. The raft barrels forward on top of her legs and nearly forces her under the surface even as I throw my weight to shove the raft to her side. The boat hits the chop, and I grab the side with one hand while I throw my other hand toward Yost.

Her reaching fingers find mine, and I am pulling her to the raft. With a tremendous thrust with her good leg, she pours herself over the boat's edge and then I am in behind her.

The motor ignites with a smooth crank, and we are pulling out from the shore toward the gully's mouth. I look back as a figure that appears to be made of pure light emerges from the stair bottom with its arms outstretched. I don't know what I am seeing or how it is possible, but the brilliance of the glare leaves a glowing imprint on my vision that lingers with me well after the gully bluffs obscure my vision of the tableau.

Then, we are left with the churn of our motor in the water, the heave of our breaths under our respirators, and the beating of our hearts under our ribs.

Ahead, the storm is no longer on the horizon. It has neared the shore, and underneath its shroud a torrent of rain cascades. No doubt that had we been any later in our departure, the waters between us and the dock would not have been navigable.

I raise Tompka on the comm.

"Yost and I are coming in by the cove," I say. "You need to set up some sort of decontamination space on the dock immediately."

"I'll do what I can," the engineer says.

I flick off the transmitter. Yost leans back against the raft's wall. She clutches her hip with both hands and though her mask obscures her face, the pain in her eyes is visible through the lenses.

"So, tomorrow, we take the day off, yes?" I ask.

Yost shakes her head. I don't think she has it in her to react with anything more.

CHAPTER 16

WRONG FACES, STRUCTURAL INTEGRITY, CRIME SCENE

By the time we pull up to the dock, the storm has brought upon us an unnatural twilight. Yost said nothing enroute, not even about whatever the hell we saw at the base of the lighthouse, and she left me to navigate and watch the storm approach. Though I've never seen one, I've heard of hurricanes that tear roofs off and uproot trees on the Western coasts. The sky during those must look something like this. We are about to face a bear.

Tompka waits for us at the dock, about ten meters from the edge. She has set three, small wooden crates at the mooring post on the shallow side of the dock. It will be insufficient to simply tie up the raft. Not only is the storm approaching, but after what happened to our engine, I'm not willing to leave our only trans-channel transport untended, even if the smuggler crew is dead – not after what we saw at the lighthouse.

As the boat nudges the dock, I cock my head at Tompka. It is almost jarring to see a human face rather than a respirator. I feel alien. Despite the failing light, my eyes pick up on blemishes in her skin, hair-thin wrinkles, a sag under her chin. Is that silver around her temples or is it just light?

"No time to gawk," the engineer says, crossing her arms. "No time for proper disinfection. Tie the raft to the dock, grab a box and strip your shit on the rocks. Scrub with bleach. Clothes will be waiting on the path."

Yost needs my help over the side of the raft into the water. She holds her rifle above the low cove swells with one hand and slides her other arm over my shoulder once I join her. I place one supporting hand across her back and take one of the crates in my free hand. It is heavy, but the buoyancy of the water helps me keep it steady even as the chop sends the bottles inside rattling about. The cove still protects us from the storm surge, but I doubt that'll last.

"Are you injured?" Tompka asks.

"I'll live," Yost says. "We will see to it in camp."

The engineer unfurls a tarp onto the edge of the dock and prepares to hoist the raft from the water onto the plastic.

Together, Yost and I hobble to shore. She sits herself on the rocks and lays the rifle beside her. By the time I return with the second crate, Yost has removed three bottles of bleach and a bundle of rags from her crate. Mine contains the same.

Then, Yost removes her respirator. It is even more jarring than seeing Tompka. It feels almost like Yost is removing her face. With the mask away, I'm shocked at how pale her skin looks against the gray rocks, the gray sky. Her eyes are pink and weary, and deep lines from the pressure of the gear streak her cheeks, temples, forehead, and chin. Her cheeks are flushed.

I remove my own mask and throw it into the box. No doubt I look wretched. Nonetheless, Yost fixes her gaze directly into my eyes.

"You are the only reason I know I haven't gone mad," she says, her voice low. My ears have not fully recovered from the gunshots in the stairwell, but the only other sounds are the wind and the water.

I take a deep breath. The air cools my throat and lungs like strong mint.

"I don't see how we can operate under any assumption other than what we've witnessed is real," I say.

"If I were alone, I would doubt..." she says, but she trails off.

"I do not think we should tell the others. They can't – shouldn't – accept it without empirical proof, and if they do not accept it, our authority will be irreparably undermined." I glance to Tompka to make sure that she has not heard. If she has, she offers no sign as she methodically scrubs the raft from one end to the other. Then, I lean a little closer to Yost and add, "They do not need to know about your brother, either."

Yost says nothing. Did she hear me? Can she? Being used to gunshots doesn't make them less concussive. She looks away and begins removing her clothing. I do the same. The air on the beach bites my skin. My arms become a mat of goosebumps. I dump my clothes into my crate and make a small pile of my possessions even as the shivering sets in.

Yost has stripped to the waist. The front and straps of her overalls dangle down to her knees. She seems almost entirely unaffected by the cold, though her breath is barely visible. The tiny cloud dissipates. It's almost like watching her damage the air.

"I need assistance," Yost says. "I won't be able to bend my leg enough."

I step beside her and pull the fabric away from her skin. The edges of a massive bruise become immediately visible. By the time I've pulled the clothes down her hips, I've exposed a fist sized purple blotch with an angry red rim. She sucks air through her teeth when my knuckles brush it.

"How are you standing?" I ask.

Yost does not respond. She simply shifts her hip and flexes her knee just enough to remove her pants completely. Another large bruise darkens the side of her knee. I probe gently at it. She scowls at the pressure, but when I try to check the hip injury again, she pulls away entirely with a small gasp.

"You're going to need to be off your feet," I say.

Yost shakes her head, she seems about to speak, but she stops herself. After a pause, she says, "I'm sorry for countermanding you outside the warden's residence. I have my orders, but I no longer believe you simply don't belong here."

"Thank you," I say.

I kneel down and pick up the bottles of bleach. I pass one and a rag to Yost while I scrub myself down. My body burns all over from countless scrapes and abrasions I'd not realized I'd suffered. I discover a particularly long gash down my ribs that has staunched with blood. Perhaps it was inflicted by the motor. More uncomfortable, however, is the chill of the cold liquid washing over my skin. I've bathed in plenty of streams, lakes, and creeks so it is not a terrible ordeal. If nothing else, it has nothing on the waters in the Northern territories. There, I would swear the temperature of the water drops well below zero without any solidification.

When we are done dowsing ourselves with disinfectant, we turn our attention to our gear. Yost gives me an odd look as I wipe down the piece of old tech.

"Do you know what this is?" I ask.

Yost hesitates. It is clear to me from her face that she knows what it is, but she gives her head a slight shake and returns to her work. I want to press her on it, but we are both miserable, and I do not want to risk this new accord we appear to have reached.

We dispose of the bleach-soaked rags in the crates with our clothes. I sling Yost's rifle, the strap and weapon frigid against my exposed skin. It strikes me that I can see my own breath as I bend over to gather up the rest of my belongings. Everything of Yost's appears to be attached to a single belt and holster she'd worn under her clothes.

I help Yost to the path at its point of arrival at the dock. There, another pair of boxes holds fresh clothes, boots, and jackets identical to the ones we removed. They might even be our clothes form morning, though I doubt Mikael had time to deal with the bundles of clothes we left in the admitting building after we first came down from the plateau.

Yost again asks for my help, this time dressing. For a moment, I appreciate the rough strength of her thigh as it disappears into the fabric. I force myself to look at the water and chastise my mind for letting my thoughts wander. While there are no explicit protocols concerning the possibility of physical engagements between members of the survey, it would be privately considered inappropriate and would not read well in the reports. I dismiss the thought as a side effect of undressing together and the intensity of the experience we endured.

At the end of the dock, Tompka finishes cleaning the raft, squinting against the bleach fumes. I'm surprised she does not wear a respirator, but since we must wear them the whole time on the plateau, I don't blame her.

She rises just as Yost and I finish getting dressed. I still shiver from the cold, but the bite of the wind subsides.

"You going to stand there," the engineer says, "or help me drag this back to camp?"

* * *

The first rumbles of thunder arrive as we struggle to carry our burden. Tompka carries the raft at the stern while I manage the prow. Though the engineer bears the brunt of the motor's weight, the raft is broad and slippery, and I can't seem to find a way to settle its weight in my arms. I'd suggested we simply drag the boat on the tarp, but the engineer hadn't wanted to tilt the motor.

Yost attempts to help, but her limp has grown more pronounced. The sooner she is off that leg, the better. For her part, Yost seems lost in thought with her gaze fixed on the plateau, even as she presses one hand to her hip while she drags each step. Despite all of the things she has every reason to be preoccupied by, I sense that something unknown occupies her mind.

Thunder rumbles again, and I have a flash of our first arrival in the hailstorm. How different the survey had felt then. Despite Brogden's injury, we were just beginning – and there was exciting work to look forward to. It still felt like a survey. Now, two of our team are unresponsive, two injured – three if you count me. The raft means we're not stranded, but we've been sabotaged and soon the whole plateau will stink of the bodies in the disciplinary hall. I feel like I've slipped out of my own world into someplace new where the rules I know no longer exist.

Though it's not yet night, the camp lights ahead emit a bubble of glow in the growing gloom. It feels more welcoming than I'd imagine tents behind razor wire ever could, but that same welcome feels isolating. Safety shouldn't be so small a space. I wonder if the inspector is upon the Midway watchtower watching us. Even though we've found something other than insurrectionists, will he think that he told us so, shake his head and walk away?

When we arrive at the camp, the fire is burning, and Efta tends a simmering pot and a rack of cubic oceanic protein blocks. She looks up at us as we arrive. Her face, like the rest of ours, looks harried and worn. When she takes in our burden, however, she scowls.

"I do hope I should not take this as a sign that you mean us to leave," she says.

Yost scoffs and limps toward her tent without a word. Tompka and I shuffle to the edge of the encampment where we set the raft down on the dirt.

"I will secure this immediately," the engineer says. "You rest by the fire. You look like you got your ass kicked."

After a failed attempt to raise the technicians, I insist that I help secure the boat, but even as I make the offer an enormous weight settles onto my shoulders. My joints creak even at the possibility of moving, and numerous muscles have already begun to stiffen. I cannot keep going much longer.

"To think that just last week I walked through my family

orchard thinking happily that I was done with leisure for a while," I say.

"Do you mean to say you regret accepting this assignment?" Tompka asks.

"I do not," I say. "Do you regret accepting?"

"For me, there was no accepting," Tompka says, releasing the air from the raft. A steady hiss begins. "'Do this job or you and your daughter will starve,' is what they said. We are not all so lucky to have a family orchard."

"What is your daughter's name? How old?" I ask.

"Lyenni is twelve years old," the engineer says. We crouch down and press the sides of the raft, trying to guide the air to the vent.

"Does Lyenni have a guardian?" I ask. "You said about your partner—"

"We have a secure lodging with walls and a good roof," Tompka says. "And she has enough food to hold her through until my return. It is the best doing we can. We are not all so fortunate as you in our refuge."

"Twelve is a hard age for her to be on her own," I say.

Tompka shakes her head. I cannot fathom the anxiety she must feel. She did not say, but I suspect she likely lives in one of the cities, though perhaps one smaller than the capital. How afraid her daughter must be to fall asleep alone amidst the sounds of one of the apartment blocks – or how sad it is that she was forced to accept that as fine.

"The orchard was the result of my father's life work," I say. "It physically represents his life, and he gave it for us."

Tompka's face softens just a bit. "May I speak openly?"

"Of course," I say.

"I do not believe we were given sufficient forward intelligence for this duty," Tompka says. Between us the raft has almost fully collapsed, so we fold it by quarters until it is small enough for one person to lift, and she says while we do, "Forgetting the smugglers,

I suspect this island faces regular, intense storms. Structurally, our equipment's integrity will not be able to withstand this for long."

"Do you have an estimate on how long it will hold up?"

"This storm just as well as the next could be the one that rips the tents down," she says, pulling a rag from her pocket and wiping sweat and oil from her palms. "We can't navigate the storm on this craft, and it would be unwise to risk the channel at night, but otherwise we should leave at dawn."

"I will not have us evacuate as long as the technicians are still MIA," I say.

Tompka throws her rag to the dirt by her feet.

"Understand that the choice may be that we go back without them or none of us go back at all," Tompka says.

"We are all expected to put our affairs in order before we depart on a survey," I say. "I understand that it's not quite so simple—"

"As putting my daughter in order?" Tompka snaps.

Of course, it is tempting to evacuate and call for help. However, there is no conceivable way I can abandon Yammut and Jones. The Bureau would never allow it. Will never forgive it in a review. I wouldn't forgive myself.

"Our duties are clear," I say. "This will need to be the last word on the matter, or I will have to put in the record my official censure."

A dark cloud passes over Tompka's face as she glares at me, and I recognize in its shadow the fear that roils like a storm within her. I do not blame her. We are not operating under safe conditions nor normal parameters.

Then, she breaks her gaze and lashes down the now compact raft with no further word.

Such a happy family we have become in so short a time.

* * *

At the fire, Efta gestures to the empty chairs. One for each member of the team. Tompka, of course, is physically fine, and I've not heard of anything happening to Mikael, though I've yet to see him since our return. Otherwise, though, the canvas seats practically sag under the weight of the absence upon them. I heave myself into one with an explosive sigh. Immediately, I feel an overwhelming sense of privilege.

"I take it that following your examination of the *Surra*, you found no success in locating the technicians?"

Efta shakes her head.

"We found no one at the array," she says, "and they appear to have moved considerably across that end of the plateau. Tompka believes they may be attempting to trace underground conduits."

I remember Yammut talking about that after the debriefing. Perhaps they're safely tucked away in the mine out of the storm's reach and out of radio contact. The thought makes me feel more secure in my choice to continue attempting to locate them.

My belly gurgles as Efta prods the protein cubes with a skewer, but the tip pierces too easily. The fishy, earthy scent reminds me of how much I've exerted myself and how little I've eaten. These have the same bitter tinge my lunch did, but I'm so hungry I don't think I'd care if it was a year spoiled.

Again, I attempt to raise the techs. This time, in case they can hear but not respond, I instruct them to find cover if they haven't already and to hunker down for the storm.

"It is not too late to return to the plateau," I say. "Perhaps Tompka and I—"

"Tompka?" Efta asks, raising an eyebrow. Then, "It would not be prudent. If they are simply out on the surface, they would have been found already. I can only imagine they've sought shelter, or they are in a danger a pair of civilians would be ill-equipped to resolve."

I sigh heavily. I rummage through one of the boxes near the fire and grab a skewer of my own. I prod at the cubes until I find one that is cooked firm enough that it won't just slide off the skewer, and pierce it.

"You feel guilty for the things that have gone wrong, yes?" Efta asks.

I nod as I blow the steam from my bite.

"Good," Efta says. She pierces one of the protein blocks and dumps it into a plastic bowl. Then she slops a ladle full of the reconstituted vegetable stew simmering in the pot. "At least someone from the Bureau should eat the shit they've served the rest of us."

"I've done nothing—" I start, but Efta cuts me off.

"Oh please. You Bureau-men are all the same," she says. "Just doing your jobs. Just playing your parts."

She spits into the dirt by the fire pit.

"Supporting myself is not a crime," I say. "And I am no one of real consequence. If I leave, they will find someone else."

"Try to murder someone and see how far it gets you to say, 'If I don't murder someone, someone else will.'"

"Hardly the same."

Efta falls silent and gazes into the flames a moment. She produces a small knife, slices a corner off the protein block, and eats it off the blade. I simply take a bite off mine on the skewer.

"Is it not?" Efta says.

"Do you have reason that could convince me it is?"

Efta sighs and sets her bowl down.

"Do you still not understand who you work for? After all you've seen today?"

Something cold slithers through me. How does she know what I've seen? Or maybe she simply means the prison itself? One thing that I do know is that I am far too exhausted and far too strained to sit here and play guessing games.

So, I slap my hands on my knees.

"Efta Yopteminik, today I have seen things that defy all understanding, and I do not wish to add more such things to my memories. Please, come out and say whatever is on your mind."

"Does it not bother you what happened here?" she asks. "Does not every damn stone of the place infuriate you? Or are you as indifferent as everyone else?"

I shrug. I pick up a bowl and fill it with stew and protein. A drop of rain spatters my hand as I do so. I take a moment to fill a second bowl. Brogden will likely not emerge from the tent before the storm hits. No doubt he will appreciate being able to eat dinner.

"It was a long time ago," I say. "I don't even have memories that far back."

"Well I do," Efta says.

"Your grandparents."

"Dissenters," Efta says. "Wealthy and connected, dangerous to some."

"I understand that you—"

"NO!" Efta throws her bowl over the flames. It smacks against one of the other chairs, its contents spraying in all directions. The remains of her protein block splat like mucus across one of the fire-pit rocks. Immediately, the gelatinous substance boils on the stone with pops, crackles, and then a little plume of white smoke that stands out against the flame. "You don't understand. You keep thinking you do, but you don't."

"If I misspoke," I say carefully, holding my hands up, palms out, "I apologize. I didn't mean—"

"Of course you didn't," Efta says. My mind races to try to pin down the cause of her sudden anger. "No one in the Bureau ever does. Nothing human ever pops into your narrow, orthodox, little minds."

I take a deep breath and roll my shoulders back. I clasp my hands and lay them in my lap.

"I'm sorry that you lost—"

"Bah," Efta says. "You keep trying to speak without a damn clue what you're saying."

My face gets hot. I rise up.

"Then tell me," I snap. "Do not berate me for not knowing what you refuse to produce. Your grandparents—"

Efta strides forward, her whole face quivering angry, and she stops with her nose an inch from mine. Out of my peripheral vision, I see her arm jerk rapidly and I believe that imminently I will be struck. I brace but do not blink. However, her motion ceases, and I realize that she points to her scars.

"This isn't about my grandparents, you idiot," she shouts. "This is about me. This is about them burning my face and chest with boiling oil while my parents watched, to force my grandparents to sign false confessions." Tears erupt from Efta's eyes. Her voice rasps. "This is about me being raised in their system as if they owned me. 'Little broken girl' was my nickname until they realized I was more capable than they. They realized all the uses they could put me to, all the work I could do for them. They forget to me what had been done. They had the nerve to forget about to me what had been done."

Her voice drops to a whisper.

"This is about being able to return to the scene of the crime."

"Efta," I say. "I had no idea, but the ones who did this to you, they are long, long gone. Dead and buried. That whole government collapsed."

Efta shakes her head. Her breath is hot on my face, coming in rapid gasps, almost hyperventilating.

"Do you really think they all died off when the bombs detonated?" Efta asks. "Who do you think lead the rebuilding? Drafted the Articles of the Bureau?"

"I—"

"You delude yourself even now," she says. "Do you really think we are just here to conduct a survey?"

"I can only go on the information I've been given, the guessing I've made, and the things I've seen," I say.

"Ask Yost, Mikael maybe. I don't know," Efta says, her face darkening. She reaches by her foot and picks up the portfolio she brought from the warden's office. "A lot of the warden's documents are written in cypher, but some of the requisition forms lead me to believe this island was more than a prison. Tomorrow, I go to the plateau even if you leave with the boat, and I will search every room, every corner, until I find proof of not just what was done to me, to my family, but whatever on earth they were doing here."

Efta turns and strides into her tent. I'm trembling, and my knees feel about to give, so I sit down. I cup my hands over my mouth, blow into them, and rub them together. The friction feels distant and provides no warmth.

Then, rain patters down all around the camp. Efta's voice carries from inside her tent. I don't know if she's speaking to Tompka or at Tompka, but after a few moments, Tompka emerges looking flustered, hastily pulling a coat over her shoulders. I watch for Efta to emerge after her, but her hand reaches up, grabs the zipper, and jerks it down.

I stretch my aching muscles as best I can. Part of me wants to attempt to calm the situation, but I do not have the first idea of how to do so. I have simply been through too much today. So, instead, I pick up my and Brogden's food and carry them inside my tent in the hopes that perhaps I may be able to find simpler companionship or maybe just sleep.

CHAPTER 17

STEW, FLARE, WORM

The tent smells like old fruit rind and vinegar. Brogden sits in almost exactly the same position he'd been in last we spoke in here. He sits a little straighter, and his color is a bit improved. Otherwise, he could be entitled *Still Life with Oversight Officer*. In his hand, a cup of steaming liquid. The steam has a bluish tint to it. The vein in his temple stands out.

He looks at me when I enter. His jaw flexes. I offer him his stew, but he simply gestures for me to set it down. I place it on the floor by his feet.

"Have you had anything to eat?" I ask.

"My stomach's been sour. Mikael's broth is only thing."

I sit on my cot and stir my meal. My appetite is also absent. I did not relish my altercations with Efta or Tompka tonight, but I also know that I've exerted myself severely today, so I force myself to take a bite. The reconstituted vegetables—zucchini and mushrooms—are rubbery, and every chew seems to lace more strings of them between my teeth. The whole mess tastes terrible, but I doubt my taste buds are up for any sort of a challenge right now. Brogden takes a sip of his drink. We continue in silence for several moments.

"Perhaps we should have taken you to the mainland right away," I say. "To a hospital."

"No," Brogden says. "I am making recovery. Hardly been twenty-four hours."

"A lot has happened in that twenty-four hours," I say.

"Such is what I understand," Brogden says.

"When we locate the technicians, we will be departing."

Brogden clears his throat and tugs at his collar.

"Departure would be ill-advised if they are uninjured," he says. "Perhaps it will not surprise you that I now believe our return from this assignment may not be anticipated."

"Yost said the same," I say. I want to be angry, but it feels useless. Instead, I help Brogden back onto his cot. "I'm afraid that after the events of today, I agree."

"If it is true, then return to the mainland will be, at best, received with rebuke. Possibly even prison," Brogden says. "I believe our purpose to be more significant than I'd believed."

"How so?"

"The engineer has confidentially provided me preliminary work-up of her soil analysis of plateau samples."

"Confidentially?" I ask.

Brogden sips his drink and shrugs.

"Do not pretend to be naïve. You know well our posts do not share the same purview."

"Then why tell me this?" I say.

"Because I am to pass on information as you need to know," he says, setting his drink on a hotplate under his cot.

"Are you kidding me?" I say, rising to my feet. "The technicians are missing, and Yost is injured. I feel like I've gone three rounds with a bear. What Yost and I saw at the lighthouse – and you still keep intelligence from me?"

Brogden rises too. The sudden motion along with his size startles me, and I take an involuntary step backward. I trip on my cot. My dinner flies up and out of my hands, spattering the tent's canvas wall as I tumble. My ass thuds hard against the back side of the cot's frame and the bed flips up onto its side. My back strikes the tent floor, and all the wind goes out of me.

"My superiors know exactly what I know," Brogden snaps, pointing down at me. I remember his story about Liaison Leotov. "They would not look kindly if your reports made clear, directly or otherwise, that you'd acted upon knowledge you were not supposed to have."

Then, he staggers and falls to one knee. He gasps and braces himself on his cot with an outstretched hand. The veins in his temple pulse as each breath gets longer, slower than the last. I slide my legs from the cot frame. Clearly, he has not yet sufficiently recovered to make such abrupt exertions. No doubt he could no more overpower me than I the stone steps to the plateau.

I right my cot and help him back onto his own. I pass him his mug of medicinal broth. He cups it in both hands.

"Thank you," he mutters. "Apologies for my outburst. My constitution is not what it needs to be."

If it had been, what might have happened? I do not comment on it. Somehow this just feels like another part of this day. Outside, large rain drops begin to spatter the outside of the tent. If there is anything still cooking on the fire, it won't be for long, but I don't feel like rushing out to refill my bowl. I grab sealed rations from my stock – a fruit bar and a waxy protein block whose texture will remind me of cheese. We sit in silence for a moment, consuming our respective 'meals.'

Then, Brogden says, "I am sure it will not surprise you to learn that I was given access to your full record."

"Indeed, I would be surprised if you had not," I say.

"Your father did not leave a favorable reputation in his wake," Brogden says. "And his death was redacted from outward-facing reports."

My back stiffens.

"He died of food poisoning," I say. "Botulism. We spoke of this earlier."

"I saw no need to contradict the family account earlier," Brogden says. "It seems, however, that he'd been attempting to extract himself from the Bureau on a matter of ideological difference."

"Neither he nor mother ever told me much about his work," I say.

Brogden waves me off.

"I doubt the circumstances of his passing are accidental as you believe. Late in his career, his superiors regarded him as erratic. Some of it may have been centered on this very prison. Did you know that your mother is still listed as wanted/at flight in some circles?" Brogden says.

"Why are we talking about this?" I ask.

"Because this is not your first lead, but first lead of note. You come from family out of favor. Your own record reads without specific fault and is adequate, but, and forgive me for saying, you are nobody."

I raise a finger and open my mouth to speak.

"Neh," Brogden says with a sour glance. "I mean no judging. My family has its dark blotches. You're a nobody, I'm a has-been. We both have just enough past successes to make us credible candidates. We both were excited to take this appointment because we both saw in it our futures. If we don't return..."

Brogden shrugs.

"That falls in line with my thinking," I sigh. "What did Tompka discover?"

Brogden pulls out a little notebook much like my own ledger. He licks his thumb and flips through many pages of notes written in a dense script and interspersed with many tables and charts. Has he composed so much in just one day while infirmed? Finally, he appears to find what he seeks.

"That the soil is clean of active and dormant viral pathogens,"

Brogden says. "Not even traces of capsids. I do not believe there to be any traditional risk of infection."

"Why the hell have we worn respirators? Why the decontamination protocols?" I ask. I don't ask, 'What did Yost and I see growing under the disciplinary hall?' I continue, "Why did Tompka have Yost and I scrub ourselves in bleach not thirty minutes ago?"

Brogden holds his hands up. Thunder swells and the thrum of rain intensifies outside. The drops hit the tent sideways. The canvas ripples as if being raked.

"We follow the protocol and wear the respirators because we were told to do so," Brogden says. "The tests aren't conclusive, and they don't mean that the soil has never been—"

"Yes, yes," I say, "But do her results—"

"Indicate something more?" Brogden finishes. "Indeed. She did not find pathogens, but she found the soil rich in exotic minerals, all structurally unstable. 'Undergoing radical recombination' she said. She's just field tech, but she says the soil displays properties unlike anything she's encountered."

"I don't need a technician to tell me this island is fucked," I say. "Does any of that have practical meaning?"

"I believe we need to watch for evidence of more... unusual contamination," Brogden said. "Tompka spoke of crystallization and changes of state."

Just like the crystal growth in the spiral staircase and the fleshy materials the lighthouse was made from. I consider revealing to Brogden what Yost and I observed in the stairwell, but I'm not sure it's in my best interest to inform him of anything that might lead him to believe I am compromised. He doesn't seem altogether fazed that he believes both that we should stay to complete the survey despite our poor condition, and that we should not expect to leave at all.

"If you ask me," Brogden says, "it tells us that the protocols are wise, unless we discover something more conclusive or a better method. We don't know what we're being exposed to, so we'll continue to protect ourselves in a way we know."

I remember what Efta said about my piece of old tech, that her team had used it to take some sort of measurements, and I wonder if what Tompka found relates to the device. I reach to my belt. The device is missing. I discreetly scan the floor and my cot. Did it come off by the fire? I'd hardly paid attention to it. It's been off almost the whole time, and I have no idea what anything it's indicated means nor what numbers it displayed.

As if he could read my mind, Brogden says, "You were issued an old-tech device, right?"

"Yes," I say. I am hesitant to admit that I don't know where to find it. I would prefer not to have such a slip on my record. Nonetheless, saying anything else would be even more detrimental if its inaccuracy became apparent. "But I do not know where it is."

"Perhaps it was lost on the plateau," Brogden says.

"Could be," I say, but I remember disinfecting it on the shore. Yost took note of it. Could she have lifted it off me while I helped her to the dock?

"It does not matter, I suppose, unless it is found," Brogden says. He appears lost in thought a moment, his gaze drifting, his jaw sagging. His fingers flex and release around his mug, and he clings to it like it's some precious thing. It looks as if he's considering something. Then, he says, "So, tell me what happened up there. I am to understand that you found the smuggler's crew?"

Brogden listens quietly as I recount our exploration of the disciplinary hall, only occasionally asking for some clarification about a detail. A demeanor of sadness weights his frame, and I can, of course, sympathize. The smugglers were strangers to me, enemies, but to imagine the state in which they'd been abandoned aches me to consider. I tell him about the descent down the stairwell and peering into the 'cells' along the way, though I leave out everything about the moss and the crystals, about Kirsch, about being pursued down the lighthouse steps by what, to my experience, tells me was some sort of living Fresnel lens. I suspect he can detect that things are being omitted, but I don't feel guilty because he has not told me everything I might need to know either.

When I get to the death of the smuggler on the beach, he pauses me.

"This crewman," he says. "Are you sure they said nothing of use? Perhaps about why they are here? Or their port of origin?"

I shake my head.

"Perhaps to Yost, but not more than a sentence or two," I say. "She asked him about a blast door."

"Blast door?" Brogden empties the last of his cup and sets it idly on his cot. He cracks his knuckles. He tries to crack his neck but fails.

"Yost did not elaborate," I say.

"I wouldn't expect she would," Brogden says. He pulls a cigarette from out of his coat and lights it. He blows out a plume of acrid smoke. "The tension between the Civil Bureau and the military will be the death of us all."

Brogden and I fall silent, and I find myself overcome by exhaustion. My mind fights to race, to maintain a high level of alertness, but all my thoughts become recursive. I just don't know where to focus. How to parse things. Forty-eight hours ago, I literally anticipated today to be a simple walking tour of half a dozen broken-down buildings. I thought my biggest concerns would be structural instability and the unpleasantness of pathogenic protocols. Now, the things that I picture when I close my eyes don't feel like they should belong to a world I know, and I wonder if they feel I don't belong in theirs.

* * *

I don't know when I fall asleep, but I do so sitting up with my head drooped to my chest. The next thing I know the tent is dark, and Brogden is lying on his cot under a heavy blanket. The storm rages outside, wind shrieking, rain battering, thunder roaring, and hail shattering, but some sharp report sends my head jerking up from my slumber.

The tent flap zipper jerks and rips down from the outside. Mikael bursts through. It is full dark behind him. Water pours from his hair and spatters droplets off every part of his clothes. His cheeks are bitten red from the cold. He's wearing a headlamp and carrying a shotgun with a drum clip.

"You need to come out now," he says. "Both of you."

We both stand. Brogden rises slower, groggy, clearly unsteady, especially at the knees.

"What is it?" I ask.

"Movement coming toward us from the plateau," he says. "And Yost has left the camp."

He ducks back out of the tent, letting the storm whip in through the flap. Hail stones the size of my thumbnail clatter into the vestibule and scatter across the reinforced vinyl floor, coming to a stop right by my feet.

Though I fell asleep fully dressed, I retrieve a poncho and a stiff rain hat from my footlocker and pull them over myself. Our peacoats will protect our bodies from the hail and the hats will at least shelter our faces from the worst of it. Brogden huffs a little as he readies, and no doubt he will need to move carefully lest he further damage his recovery with exertion.

I step out of the tent into the night and the rain just as Efta emerges from her own. She carries a brilliant lantern and a heavy-duty umbrella.

The storm drowns out her voice, but I can read her lips when she says, "What the hell is going on?"

Tompka moves between the tents. She holds a pistol with a flashlight attached to the barrel extended in both hands, and she is scanning the perimeter fence with rapid, controlled movements. Mikael moves laterally across the camp toward the entrance. I draw my own pistol in one hand and my flare gun in the other. I step up beside Mikael as he drops to one knee and sights down his barrel along the road to the plateau.

The storm is so loud I practically have to shout to hear myself.

"What do you mean Yost has left the camp?" I ask.

"She's gone," Mikael shouts. "Maybe an hour ago. Left with her rifle, a small pack, and a respirator."

"Did she say what the hell she is doing?"

"Not a word," Mikael says. "I tried to raise her on our local comms, but something has fried my receivers."

"We've lost the team channels?"

"Maybe yours is different than mine or the backups," Mikael says, "but we appear to have experienced some sort of surge."

"Okay, and what did you see coming from the plateau?" I ask. "Could it be the techs?"

"No chance," Mikael says. "Didn't get a good look, but some sort of animal if I had to guess, huge."

"An animal?" I ask.

"Quadrupedal," Mikael said. "Very large, bear sized. Came down the steps, but I lost it in the shadows around the admitting building. We have not reacquired."

I gaze into the darkness toward the cliff. The perimeter lights throw sharp shadows from even the small rocks into the empty stretch between us and the admitting building.

"How are our defenses?" I ask.

"Well, anything that gets within ten meters of the fence is liable to blow itself to kingdom come, and we've got a large skirt of open ground around the whole of the encampment," he says. "The camp entrance is the only safe ingress."

The floodlights illuminate clearly more than half the distance to the admitting building, but after that, shadows dominate. A few rock outcroppings provide potential shelter, but any approach would be vulnerable. We'd have an excellent line of sight if the storm weren't so intense. I feel like I'm looking through mesh screens. I check my transmitter and try to raise Tompka, but Mikael is right. I don't even get static.

"Keep covering the road," I say. I give him a pat on the shoulder and make my way toward Tompka. She's taken position at the far side of the camp. Unlike Mikael, who'd seemed rock steady, her hands shake as they grip her weapon, and her face looks drained. Her eyes are wide, and she bites her lower lip.

"Anything?" I ask.

One of her hands falls from her gun and she swiftly wipes a stream of water away from her eyes and forehead.

"I can't see a damn thing," she says. "This rain is impossible. They could walk right up to us and shit on our doorstep before we knew it."

"They?"

"I saw at least two points of motion around the admitting building before the floods kicked on," she says.

"That means something came close enough to the perimeter to trigger the floods?"

"Yes," Tompka says. "But what I did not see."

I step toward the fence to try to see just a bit farther, but Tompka takes me by the forearm.

"I should not tell you this," she says, "but I fear we may all be compromised."

"Compromised how?"

"The camp food has been laced with something. Certainly all the cooked food as well as some of the sealed rations," Tompka says. "The sample I studied contained a neurotoxin. It's hard to say its exact effect, but I believe hallucination to be likely and my tests suggest it would be slow to metabolize."

"Are you sure?" I ask. "Does Brogden know?"

"I'm certain, yes," Tompka says. "But I have not informed Brogden. This is the work I was doing in my tent before Mikael informed me of the movement."

I gaze into the terrain. It's strangely difficult to see past the edge of the light field. I almost feel like the lights make the island beyond much darker. What if someone or something is moving across the field right now, and I simply don't see them? Claymores and floods aren't subject to hallucination, but the path to the gate is unmined. Then again, it's possible that whatever Mikael and Tompka saw is a hallucination itself. Something had to trigger the floods, but maybe we're poring over the darkness for something that doesn't exist.

Then, I remember the inspector giving us the bundle of Orlot. What if it had been put into our food?

"Did the customs inspector at Midway give you any Orlot?" I ask. When she stares at me blankly, I add, "He insisted I bring some. Said it strengthened the immune system."

Tompka snorts and shakes her head.

"If it's still in our supplies," I say, "you could match it against our food?"

"Yes," Tompka said. "Easy enough."

"And if it's not," I say, "then that makes it a pretty good bet too."

I don't need to add that we need to figure out who has betrayed us because as far as I am concerned, the odds lie on Tompka just as much as anyone else. Of course, Yost has also cast herself in doubt with her disappearance, especially if she stole my old-tech. No doubt, whoever did it is in league with the smugglers. Or maybe I'm simply compromised and following paranoid trains of thought.

I drop back from Tompka toward the camp center where Efta stands with Brogden. Brogden leans on a metal crutch while he holds a pistol of his own. Efta is still armed with only a lantern and umbrella, but she's set a machete on one of the camp chairs beside her.

"Have you identified the danger?" Efta asks as I cross back to Mikael, but I simply give a quick shake of my head.

When I reach Mikael, he rises.

"I can't see anything from here," he says. "I'm going to sweep along the shoreline and get a new angle on admissions. When I give you the signal, fire a flare toward the plateau."

Mikael extinguishes his headlamp. I want to protest, but he's in motion even as I tell him to wait. He does not react to my request.

When he has moved about fifty meters along the shoreline, his headlamp flashes twice quickly. Again. In the dim light, he continues moving. I extend the flare gun at a high angle and fire.

The red bulb launches in a fury of sparks, its light casting a burning sphere into the sheets of rain through which it passes. Its ascent slows and angle curves toward a decline. Then, for a split second, the glow vanishes.

The magnesium payload ignites and expands a large starburst that illuminates the entirety of the beach that skirts the plateau. Everything becomes orange. All across the open space, shadows throw in new directions, and for a heartbeat the open field feels alive with movement.

Then, my eyes catch movement along the base of the plateau headed toward the rock wall that curves onto our peninsula. I can't tell what I'm seeing; it's something large and bulky, something that almost looks to be stone itself. The motion vanishes into a deep shadow just as soon as I register it, and I'm left trying to reconstitute what I saw from my memory of the impression. Did I really see it at all? What if Tompka is correct and we can no longer trust our senses?

Mikael lurches forward into an aggressive approach toward the admitting building. The shotgun is pressed to his shoulder, and he moves with sure-footed purpose. He does not pursue the same point of interest upon which I'd just been focused, rather he seems to have found a target of his own. Tompka too has repositioned herself, now at the center of the fence, likely focused on the same thing that drew Mikael's interest.

I shout for Mikael to come back, but he cannot hear me. The

rain escalates its intensity even further, the hail stinging harder and faster. The flare fades, and the shadows crawl back to their sources as a deeper darkness swallows the landscape. A freezing gale howls around me, rakes me with hail, and fills my nostrils with stiff brine.

Thunder peals as Mikael's muzzle flashes. I don't even hear the first report, though the second reaches me like its own thunder. Whatever quarry he has found, I cannot see, but he shifts in a tight arc toward the stairs, maintaining his bead on the admitting building.

Tompka has moved back to her initial position. Best I can tell, she is trying to draw a bead to cover Mikael, but at this distance and in these conditions, her pistol makes a poor weapon. We need Yost and her Kalashnikov.

I step toward her just as something large moves just on the other side of the fence.

"Nine o'clock," I shout. "Tompka—"

But she's already twisting, her leg swinging out underneath her, her gun training. The light under the barrel clashes with something gray and glistening, something rain-soaked and hunched. Lank limbs are curled close to its body, and for split-second, teeth shine in the muzzle flash from Tompka's pistol. Whatever it is rears up and fans out its limbs like a man-sized cobra rising with hood unfurled.

A devastating blast shrieks through the camp, and a flash of light sprays fire and shrapnel into the fence. Stones rocket through the air in all directions. Something whizzes past me, glancing off my temple even as I slap my hands to my ears. Debris crashes out from a billow of smoke that illuminates in a streak of lightning that spans the horizon. A chunk of something ricochets off one of the reinforced tents. An arc of mud spatters everything. Then, the echoes of the blast vanish into the storm.

Rain drops on dirt blend with the clatter of falling pebbles and hail. The floods nearest the damage flicker erratically. A gale sweeps a mist off the puddles like sea spray, the wind itself a wall of banshee that shrills my ears. A pale cloud twists like a dervish up from the fence, the wires jutting and jiggling, the posts bent. I find myself picking up something that rolls to a stop at my feet. It's caked with rough dirt, but underneath, something hard and smooth and curved.

My thumbs sweep out a chunk of mud from a hollow on one side then from a hollow on another. Underneath the spattering rain, I recognize that I hold a skull. Tompka shoves herself on her back through the mud, away from the blast site, even though the explosion is over. She tries to maintain her weapon's aim in the space above her.

A small hail stone strikes me on the cheek beneath my left eye. It sears with a white heat, and I feel a warm bloom of blood. I stand frozen a moment, staring at the ruined fence, staring at Tompka frantically waving her pistol's barrel in search of her target, feeling the blood growing cold on my cheek before it reaches my chin.

Then, I drop the skull and run toward Tompka. Bones lie scattered all around in an ejecta blanket radiating out from the detonation site. The claymore blasted open a mass grave. I shake off that thought and scoop my arms under Tompka's arms and wrench her to her feet while backpedaling. Blood is running out of one of her ear canals, and her face is streaked with soot. Her forehead is gashed and shiny. At first, I am dragging her, her heels scooting and scraping in the mud, but then she twists against me, and suddenly we are both trotting into the center of camp with our arms over each other's shoulders.

We arrive at the fire pit and both pivot and aim our weapons at the broken fence. Brogden has seated himself in the chair nearest the gate and turned it so that he can maintain a line of fire upon the camp entrance. Efta waits by the gate and, judging by the direction of her gaze, is watching for Mikael's return.

"What caused the explosion?" Brogden asks.

"Claymore," Tompka says loudly. Her legs wobble beneath

her, but she stays upright. "That son of a bitch was turning a claymore to breach the fence."

"Well, that means we're dealing with something more than an animal," I say.

"More than an animal?" Tompka asks. "Gott in Himmel, did you see what I saw?"

"I don't care right now what it looks like," I say. "Just that we assess the manner of threat that it poses."

"It had six arms," Tompka says.

"Impossible," Brogden says.

Tompka spits into the rain and says, "I don't think we agree on what that means."

A shadow streaks along the outside of the fence toward the water, visible between the tents for a split second. I try to follow it with my barrel trained, but I need to look at the sights to draw aim. By the time I refocus outward, I've already lost the target.

In my peripheral vision, Tompka pivots sharply, sweeps another forty-five degrees, then curses. Efta seems to glimpse whatever Tompka targeted, but then she looks bewildered.

"There is more than one," I shout.

The hail has slowed, but the stones clatter just often enough to make it impossible to listen through the rain. Something fails in one of the floods, and its irregular flash turns into a relentless strobe. The wind blows sheets of rain, and in the flickering light, shadows sweep in ebbs and flows. There could be a hundred beasts in the darkness, or just one. Suddenly, it's as if the whole of the air has come alive with monsters that wink in and out of existence.

A second claymore on the cove side of the fence blows, but this one outward. I don't know if it was triggered by simple motion or another attempt at sabotage. Either way, the fence remains intact.

Nonetheless, everyone's attention is so fixed on the new smoke cloud rising through the storm that I immediately step away from that point and cross to the other side of the firepit, swinging my weapon as best I can toward the hole in the fence. In the same motion, my finger slides onto the trigger, and I am already pulling it even as the enormous shape darts into the gap. With all the sounds of the storm, the report is almost lost in the white noise, but the muzzle flash is a brilliant sun. The two shots I fire go completely wild, but whatever my target was, it darts out of sight as quickly as it appeared, leaving me none the wiser of its form.

It hits me that the second claymore was meant to distract. If our stalkers are smart enough to figure that out, they're smart enough to realize that we are incompetent with our weapons, especially if we have any more failed shots.

Motion draws my eyes to Brogden as he shifts in his seat and leans forward with his eye sighted down his barrel at the gate. I follow his line of sight out of the camp. With a gasp, I take a step to the liaison and say calmly but firmly, "Brogden, hold."

A silhouette in motion resolves itself in the floods; into Mikael arriving at a trot. He is mud-plastered and limping. His arms shake.

"Bastard dug narrow trenches all over the place out there," he sputters, out of breath. "Just a few inches deep, but enough to twist an ankle. What blew?"

I point to the fence. Mikael raises his shotgun to train the barrel light on the ruined segment of fence.

"Two claymores," I say. "They're here. Just outside the fence."

"They?" Mikael asks.

"At least two," I say.

Mikael nods.

"Guess the one I tagged didn't go down," he says. He sweeps rivulets of rain off his forehead with the back of his hand. His breath clouds. His cheeks are bright red.

"If they keep us out in this rain too long," I say, "we'll suffer hypothermia."

I feel the cold in my bones already. If my fingers get too much colder, I will struggle to wield my weapon. Then again, I struggle to wield it anyway.

Mikael takes several steps toward the fence breach. He waves me over, saying, "If we want any hope of sleep, we'll need to mine the breach and the camp entrance. Go—"

An enormous shape bears down on his back with a meaty thud and jerks back up out of sight as fast as I can blink. The impact sends Mikael skidding forward face-first in the mud. A chunk of his coat is gone, as is a chunk of the clothes underneath it, as is a chunk of muscle from just under his shoulder blade. Blood wells up and pours over the edge of the wound.

"Son of a bitch," I say. "Help Mikael! Take cover!"

Both Efta and I lunge toward our prone companion, but another dark shape crashes down onto his back in front of us. I see its talons dig into Mikael's torso like daggers, and he screams as the bird attempts to jerk him up into the air. His weight overcomes the bird's grip, and he falls onto his back, gasping for breath, writhing at the pain of his wounds.

Efta pulls me back as two more birds strike, one at his lower belly and one landing on his chest. The one on his belly clenches its talons into his stomach around his navel, plunging easily through the soft tissue. Blood bursts from his mouth as he thrusts his head back to scream.

The bird on his chest darts its head down to his face. With a precise snap, it rips the tongue out of his mouth with its beak. Illuminated by a streak of lighting, I see it toss back a length of the man's tongue like a worm and swallow it before taking off again.

More of the birds are upon him, tearing through his clothing with their claws, pecking at every patch they expose, as I register that they also seem to be receding into the darkness, diminishing.

"Come on, damn it," Efta is shouting as she drags me back with both hands gripping mine.

I snap to my senses, and we dive into the nearest tent and frantically zip the flap shut.

* * *

We shove ourselves backward to the floor, knocking the cots back against the tent walls. Efta's eyes are wide, and the tendons stand out on her neck. Her machete and umbrella are gone. Her face and hair are caked with mud, and she is drenched from head to foot. I touch my hand to her shoulder. She is cold to the touch. Our body temperatures must be dangerously low.

A strange clacking sound fills my ears. I have no idea where Tompka or Brogden sought shelter or if they made it there. What I do know is that I hear the birds shrieking over their prey and at each other. I can't see what they're doing, and for that I am glad. I look at the tent. I imagine the reinforced canvas might hold back the birds, but I don't know that anything will save us should the beasts enter the camp.

Efta is shaking all over. I reach with one hand to try to unbutton her jacket and notice my hands are shaking just as badly. I realize that the clacking sound is my teeth chattering. My other hand is heavy. I look down. I'm still holding my pistol. A lot of good it did me. I set it down on its side on the floor between us.

The absence of the technicians still doesn't exactly feel real to me. They're like every other person who turned off a street they occupied with me and vanished from sight never to be seen by my eyes again.

Mikael was killed right in front of me.

"We're going to die here," Efta says.

"I'm tired of people saying that to me," I answer. "You know what? We're not going to die. We're going to get the hell off this island and we're not going to die."

The wall of the tent buckles hard as something barrels against it. Two trios of talons, two curved one way, one the other each pierce the tent. Another body crashes against it from the other side. It too thrusts its talons through the tent at the moment of impact and though it again pierces it, it fails to tear.

On both sides now, the birds twist and pull at their purchases. The tent jerks and snaps back elastically until both sets of talons withdraw. I don't even have time to draw a full breath before the next one hits, and the next, and the next. Their wings beating the air and the canvas outside is as loud as the hail, and the tent fills with a thrumming as they bash themselves against it body and limb. One of their beaks stabs in through one of the holes left by the first set of talons and it snaps open and closed with clicks as loud as a pistol's cocking chamber.

The tent frame creaks as the taut canvas bulges against it. The supports flex back and forth under the weight as two more birds hit, and their claws and beaks all dart in immediately. Efta plants herself onto my lap with her legs behind me and we huddle together in the tent's center as the walls become alive with sharp swiping things. I can't even tell how many of them there are any more as more land and others give up, but there must be at least a dozen.

Then, the strangest pulling sensation comes from underneath me, and the tent around us begins to elongate upward.

"Oh my god," Efta whispers. "They're lifting us up."

The canvas beneath me stretches slowly under my weight, and the creak of the frame grows into a cry of thin metal giving. The cots slide inward against Efta and me. The footlockers clatter against the cot frames, their locks rattle, and the contents clonk inside them. Will we be lifted and dropped like the jellyfish? A hundred feet in the air and then crashing down on the rocks? The last of my weight leaves the ground beneath. Our rise is slow but unmistakable. The beating of wings is now thunder itself, the canvas being buffeted from two dozen angles. Though it protected us at first, the reinforcing matter of the tent now prevents the canvas from tearing away from their grasping claws. The screech of the birds rises to a frantic crescendo.

I snatch up the gun, jam the barrel through one of the holes left by the talons and fire three wild shots.

We lurch back down a few centimeters, and then their strength gives all at once. We crash back to the hard-packed mud under our tents and fall on our sides in a tangled mess with each other. The screeches outside grow frantic and scattered, and the thunder of wings gives way to a gentler thunder, to the thrum of rain, to the howl of wind.

Efta and I lay breathless in each other's arms. We do not speak. Soaked and cold, we shiver in our rain drenched clothes. She simply presses her cheek to my shoulder and wraps her arms around my chest. She holds onto me, and I to her. I feel certain that if I don't, something inside me will simply break beyond repair. The tremble of her grip tells me that in all likelihood, she feels the same.

DAY THREE

Chapter 18

Salvage, Disposable, Bonfire

I awake on a cot with a coat folded under my head as a pillow and a thermal blanket over me. The cot's legs under my own legs are broken. Sheets of plastic have been stapled to the tent walls to keep the weather from flowing in like the light does now through the myriad of holes. Efta snores on the other cot. Our wet clothes are in a heap by the entrance. I don't remember the rain stopping, changing clothes, or climbing onto the cot, but I'm grateful for all three.

My entire body aches like I'd just spent the night tumbling in an institutional dryer. My joints all move like creaky door hinges. My cheeks are bitten by chill, the skin rough and sore to the touch. I glance at Efta as I pull on the coat I'd used as a pillow. I assume that she helped me change into dry clothes since I have no recollection, and for that I am also grateful.

I unzip the tent flap and step out into the morning glow. The sun is heavily muted behind the haze and clouds, and the air has teeth from a frigid breeze. A gentle snowfall descends. Already, a light dusting coats the ground. I give a glance to the bluff from where I'd seen the flock take off to hunt jellyfish the day before, and then I survey the results of the prior night.

The camp is an absolute ruin other than a small fire that's been kindled in its center. Only two tents remain, the one Efta and I sheltered in and the one I presume held Brogden and Tompka. One of the other tents lies twisted on the shoreline rocks, and the muted canvas of another bobs on the cove. The folding chairs lay scattered all across the approach to the plateau. Every supply crate has been bludgeoned or destroyed. Some have been carried off.

I try to find the spot where Mikael was killed, but his body is gone; eaten or carried off. The heavy rains must have swept the blood away. The image of those darting beaks and slashing talons returns. From the moment the first blow struck him, he'd been good as dead. His shotgun is nowhere to be seen either. Was it staggering luck that our attackers did not return when the birds gave up on our tents? Or, maybe they did return but were no longer interested in us. After all, once we hid in the tents, what stopped them from walking through the main gate?

I approach the gate. Beyond, the ground appears to have sunken into a deep divot. Several similar divots pock the shore in a zigzag leading toward the plateau. I approach the one closest. What appears to be deep drag-marks run from its edge, and I realize I may be looking at collapsed tunnels. Was that how our attackers moved around last night? Did they dig like machines, or did a network of caves run underneath the entire island? Either way, a miracle that they didn't surface inside the camp perimeter.

I pick up a splintered slat from one of the crates that had fallen or been discarded, and I scrape at the edge of the divot. Immediately, some sort of yellowish steam rises up from the edge of the wood where it touches the dirt. It's noxious and rank, driving my eyes to immediately water. I drop the slat and step away, turning back into the camp.

Near the segment of fence broken by the claymore detonation, Tompka pokes through the remains of a shattered crate with a hunting knife, holding up mangled ration packs and tossing them aside. The entire site is littered with shredded vacuum packaging, broken plastic containers, and shards of human bone. Judging by the debris, we have at best the personal food stocks in both remaining tents.

Tompka looks up as I approach. There are tears in her eyes. Snowflakes cling to her hair and shoulders like shed skin. She absently scrapes aside broken rocks with her blade. The rocks are an odd yellowish tone, smooth and a bit rounded.

"It's all gone," she says. "Everything. Our food, water, our tents, Mikael..."

"I'm sorry," I say. "We were not prepared for an attack like that."

"We should have left last night," she says. "Ahead of the storm."

"We never would have made it to Midway," I say.

Tompka rises like a bullet and throws her knife blade-first into the dirt where it sheathes itself with a thunk in a spot surrounded by charred bone shards.

"And now we can't try at all, yes?" she asks. "They ripped the raft in a dozen places and bent the blade on the motor. The respirators are gone too."

I feel like a seam with the thread being pulled out of it. It's as if the birds knew exactly what to destroy to deal the most damage.

"And I've been digging holes all over camp," Tompka says. She crouches and grabs up a handful of dirt and bone. "Bones, everywhere. We pitched our tents atop a goddamn mass grave."

"Let's take it one thing at a time," I say, looking around for anything that might be at all salvageable and finding nothing. "We may be able to—"

"There's nothing to do," she says, throwing the handful of debris at me. The dirt and bone hit my chest with a thunk and tumble away like a broken snowball. "No rebuilding. No salvage. Not a single container is unbroken. Every package of food. How the hell can birds do that?"

"I don't know," I say. "Just like the thing at the fence—"

"What do you know?" she snaps. "Who knows? Who sent us in blind?"

"Tompka," I say. "Please. Calm down. This won't do us any—"

"Why the hell does this island seem alive?" Tompka says, grabbing fistfuls of my peacoat's fabric. "The soil samples from the plateau? The minerals replicate. Like cells. How?"

She gives my clothes a sharp jerk.

"They didn't tell me—"

"What the hell did you people drop me into?" Tompka shouts.

I put a hand on her shoulder, but she slaps it off. She pivots, and a quick rotation at her waist and shoulder brings her fist at my temple. I duck just in time for her blow to whip through the air just above my hair.

"Tompka, stop," I say, stepping back with my hands raised, palms out, in an attempt at a placating gesture.

"You should have listened," she says. She bends down and snatches up her knife, holding it blade-down in her fist. "We can't survive on the beach. We can't survive on the plateau."

She makes a darting slash with her knife, but I'm backpedaling now fast enough to stay out of her reach as she advances.

"Tompka, you need to stop," I say. "This isn't helping—"

"Nothing's going to help," Tompka says. "We can't help ourselves. Who's going to help my daughter? Who's going to bury my fucking body?"

She slashes horizontally at my throat and then at the stroke's end lashes diagonally across my body. Both attacks miss, but I hear them whistle.

I try to watch my feet as I retreat but I can't keep my eyes on the blade if I do so. My stiff joints struggle to keep up with the instructions I give them.

Then, my body jumps, and my eyes snap shut at a deafening report. My face is hot and wet, and small, hard things strike my cheeks and forehead like stinging hornets. I open my eyes as

Tompka lurches forward and hits the ground like a sack of flour fallen from a shelf. Something is wrong with her face, but I don't register what. Mud sprays, and I pinwheel my arms as I nearly lose my balance.

Blood dollops out of her missing forehead onto the dirt in heartbeat surges before stopping altogether. I look around, grappling to understand what just happened. Brogden leans on his crutch outside the tent he shared with Tompka with his pistol raised and the barrel smoking.

His face is wrought with anger, and he maintains his aim on the body as he approaches. Behind him, Efta stands wrapped in her blanket in the mouth of the tent we shared. Her eyes are wide with shock.

"That was wholly unnecessary," Brogden says, his voice devoid of any emotion. He holsters his weapon as he shambles toward me. When he is close enough, he spits on the back of Tompka's head. The foam clings to her hair. "And wasteful."

He places a cigarette between his lips and lights it.

"You shot her," I say, as my mind reels to catch up with the turn of events.

"Yes, friend," Brogden says. "Better I have let her kill you?"

"She has a daughter," I say.

Brogden nods and places a shepherding hand on my back. A nudge of pressure sets me in motion toward Efta and the camp's center. Brogden limps on his crutch at pace with me, clearly significantly more recovered.

"Parent should know better than to act in ways that leave her child abandoned," he says. "Had she killed you, what else would my recourse have been? Better lose her than both of you."

I certainly will not argue, but I also feel guilty. Could we have left the night before? Would the storm have drowned us? We still don't even know about the technicians, and now Yost is missing, and our raft destroyed. My eyes snap to the dock, and I discover that the vessel we rowed here is gone as well.

Brogden notes my gaze.

"Yes, she broke from her mooring in the night. Now, forgive me, but I'm going to take a moment." He carefully lowers himself until he is kneeling at the edge of the stone fire ring. As he does so, shivers wrack his body. He looks at his hands and chuckles. "A miracle I didn't shoot you by accident."

*　*　*

The falling snowflakes fatten as they settle across the beach and within a quarter of an hour, the entire beach is covered in pristine white. The crystals settle into the folds of Tompka's clothes, her body no longer warm enough to melt them. I try not to look at her face. It is hard not to look at her face. One of her eyes is still intact, and it has lolled off to the corner as if it's watching us move about the camp. Half her forehead is gone, but I try to look away when I catch my eyes straying there. It is no good to dwell.

Still, we will need to deal with Tompka's remains before we depart. No matter what she did, I can neither leave her to rot or leave her for the birds to rip to pieces. Maybe something even worse will come along. Though the Bureau has minimal protocol in regard to the dead, I feel it is my duty as survey lead to treat every member of the team with every respect I can afford them. It is only right.

After I clean Tompka's blood off my face as best I can with a tattered towel, I mention my intentions to Efta as we continue poking through the debris and the meager supplies that had been within the two remaining tents. Given their recreation together, I assume she would have an interest in contributing to the effort.

"If we must, it would be most expedient to stack the broken crates onto the fire and then lay her remains on top," Efta says as she examines what appears to be an undestroyed package of kale compress and a couple tubes of emergency nutrient paste. Her voice is sullen. Bitter. Though she'd likely not known Tompka long, there is nothing like the surge of emotion and endorphin that accompanied a fresh connection. Efta's is not the reaction I would have anticipated from someone as animated as her, but no one should ever tell another human how to mourn.

I nod and begin gathering the splintered slats. Brogden does not move from his perch by the fire. No doubt he has a lot on his mind, but I wonder what exactly. Is he contemplating that he just took a human life? Or is he thinking about whether or not he should have something more for breakfast before we abandon the camp? Perhaps he simply considers how to relay the most recent events in the reports he will file if we make it out of here alive. Fortunately, it seems everyone agrees we're all going to die here, so maybe the paperwork is irrelevant. No. Not irrelevant. Someone else's.

I chuckle to myself. How entrenched have I become in the workings of the Bureau that this is how I think when faced with my own demise?

Before long, the pile of wood has grown substantial. I hope it will create enough flame to burn Tompka's remains to the bone. I would prefer to bury her, but we do not have the time and I fear doing so here would disinter more dead. Looking around us, I wonder about the holes the beasts dug and the bones blasted every-where by the claymore. I wonder if the beasts didn't surface in the camp because we'd built it right atop the dead.

Efta drags one of the footlockers out of the tent we'd sheltered in. The lid is open, and she has emptied it of everything but the remaining food and water supplies. All we have are a few bags of water and perhaps enough rations to feed the three of us for a day or two. It might be possible to catch snow and rain to extend our lifespan, but I doubt we can last long enough on what we have here to hold out until a rescue.

Then, I look to the plateau. To the mess hall.

"There were canned supplies in the mess pantry," I say. "And on the *Surra*. If we have to—"

"We cannot trust that anything up there has not been contaminated," Efta says.

"There is no contagion here," Brogden mutters. "No truth to anything you were told before arrival."

"Is that right?" I ask. "And here you had the nerve just last night to play detective over Tompka's analysis."

"Albertachen was never placed on starvation quarantine," Brogden says. "It was annihilated from inside. After the *Surra* went missing, Yost and I were dispatched to find out why. If a larger investigation of Gollitok can be justified on public expense sheets."

"What about the rest of us?"

"Disposable," he says. "You can either create cover story or your deaths will create cover story. As far as the Bureau is concerned, you owe debt for your father, and Efta's history of dissent makes her perceived threat – especially after the incident at the Quarry. Tompka had amassed enormous debt to secure her daughter's future, one of the technicians was once customs inspector who took bribes, and the other repeatedly failed promotion exam."

"Yost's brother was a crewman on the *Surra*," I say.

"Yes," Brogden says, "which is why they felt she would succeed at all costs."

"And you?" I say. "How is it you're tainted?"

Brogden chuckles without smiling.

"I've been helping smugglers find safe waypoints, of course," he says. He continues laughing softly, shaking his head as he speaks. "I'd believed I'd been discreet; I'd hoped I get out before they caught on, but I think they always knew. When they assigned me here, I knew."

I find my hands shaking with anger, my face growing hot. Efta stares at him impassively with her arms crossed.

"You're a traitor?" I ask.

Brogden raises his eyebrows. His face is etched with bemusement and disbelief.

"Traitor to whom? You were sent here to die because your father disagreed with what happened here. Efta was tortured to make a point to her grandparents," Brogden says. He rises and spreads his arms to gesture at the ruin around us. "Look at this place. Look what people did here. Do you think they vanished when wars came? Reconsolidated under different name amid the ruins. The Bureau believes they own you, can dispose of you as long as suits purpose."

I step forward so that I am hardly a foot from the huge man. Though I know he is still weakened, his bulk is imposing. I do not allow myself to be intimidated.

"And you still brought us to die for them?" I ask.

"I did not expect to have been so incapacitated," Brogden says. "I was to meet crew of Clove and Hitch, and we were to figure out what the Bureau wanted so bad about this island and to take it first."

"And have you figured that out yet? You ready to share?" I ask.

"If only I could," Brogden sighs. "I know that this was a place of experiments, but among us, only Yost knew the specifics of what we hoped to recover."

"Experiments?"

Brogden shrugs. "Physics? Chemistry? Biology? I don't believe they put any chains on what happened here beyond those they placed on the prisoners."

"If you'd succeeded, what would you have done with the rest of us?" I ask. "What makes you any better than the Bureau?"

Brogden shrugs.

"No better. No worse. That is punching yourself in mirror. With the smugglers, I was set to retire," Brogden says. "With the Bureau, I was set to *be* retired."

Then, Efta steps forward and presses a pistol to the side of his head. His breath catches, and his hairline pulls back in surprise as he peers at her out of the corner of his eye. Sweat beads on his brow. I raise a hand in a gesture of staying, but words die in my mouth. I do not even know that I should try to stay here.

"That would be unwise," Brogden says. "And wasteful."

"Give me one reason—" she starts.

Brogden cuts her off.

"Because I know the location of the Clove and Hitch," he says. "Unless you want this place to be a grave to us all, it is our best chance of reaching some place less forsaken."

Efta's entire being seems to quiver. I feel like there is an anger larger than the island in her chest.

Brogden's voice seeps with disdain at her display as he says, "Now if you don't mind, I believe it time we burn Tompka's remains so we make plateau in good order."

Around us, the snow continues to fall, the ground to vanish, the ocean wind to rash red our cheeks.

* * *

It does not take long to stoke the remains of the crates into the fire, and when it is burning brilliantly and hot, the three of us hoist Tompka's remains out of her blanket of snow onto a stretched out blanket salvaged from the camp ruins. We carry her to the flames, the ruin of her face wobbling as she bumps and sways between us. Already, I'm uncertain what she looked like and can only picture her face contorted in fury as she tried to kill me.

At the fire's edge, Brogden asks for us to hold.

"Given the events of this afternoon and that neither of you have known her for more than forty-eight hours, I feel that having read her file I am the only one qualified to say a few words."

He clears his throat, but Efta scoffs with disgust and releases her corner of the blanket. She sweeps her hands together once, walks over to the box of supplies, and methodically stows them into a backpack.

Brogden looks at me. I lower my end gently, but I do not depart.

"Tompka made mistake of having someone she loved," Brogden says. "The Bureau likes everyone to be their own sheet of paper so they fit neatly into a single folder. They've always kept you in your father's folder because they have no way of knowing what he told you or your mother. You could never truly operate under such conditions."

I sigh.

"I assume you were familiar with the smuggler crew?" I ask.

"Only a couple. They were part of one of my survey teams in Eastern province." When he recognizes my surprise, he adds, "They're almost invariably Bureau defectors. Most who choose to depart are not fortunate as your father to have amassed sufficient capital to retire to the outskirts – it might well be that your family was only a couple steps removed from becoming smugglers themselves."

I pause. I remember how my mother had taken me from the city. I'd been too enthralled with the mountains and the tunnel at the time, but retrospectively, one could say I was myself smuggled to the orchard. However, it bothers me that Brogden is so willing to kill; it does not seem wise to spill the kettle.

I say, "I am sorry then for your loss."

Brogden offers a half smile and then gestures to the body with his chin. I pick my end up again, realizing that Brogden has been holding her weight without so much as an adjustment of his grip. If he was infirmed before, I'm not sure he is now, and I certainly don't have faith that we are on the same side. He was able to give Efta a reason she should not kill him. Could we give the same to him?

Tompka's face gapes at me. I don't want my eyes to focus, but I can see her brain and skull, and it is not something I want to process. My stomach churns, and I need to swallow down the saliva that slathers over my tongue signaling the urge to vomit. I didn't have children. I never even tried. Outside my mother, I don't know that there is a single person to whom I am consequential. I envy Tompka. Someone will spend their whole life remembering her.

We count to three and fling her remains onto the fire. The blanket is wet, and so it billows steam before it catches. Tompka too steams and sizzles. Her hair burns, and her skin blackens. I find myself wishing we could do the same with the remains in the disciplinary hall. They don't deserve that either, no matter what crimes they may have committed in life.

Really, this place, the Gollitok, the whole of Albertachen, would best be burned to a cinder and sunk into the ocean.

When there is nothing recognizable beyond bone, I turn away at last. I don't know how long I'd stared into the flames, but my nose and eyes burn, and the snow has deepened around the camp despite being kept at bay by the heat of the fire.

Efta steps up beside me. She wears her pack already and holds a flare gun in one hand and a machete in the other.

"None of this is your fault," she says, placing a radio receiver into my palm. "You are shit lead here, but maybe in an assignment not designed to fail you might have done better."

"No one has succeeded in killing me, and if I'm not mistaken you are as of now entirely uninjured," I say, putting the earpiece in. "Under the circumstances, I think I'm faring much better than you give me credit."

She smirks for a moment, but then grows serious.

"There is something else I must tell you," she says. "The keys and binder I'd found in the warden's office. They are now gone from my pack."

I nod.

"Tompka believed we were all being dosed with some sort of hallucinogenic neurotoxin," I say. When she cocks her head, I add, "In our food. I have a suspicion it is Orlot."

"That would mean—"

"It would almost certainly be Brogden who did it," I say.

"And here we are about to let him lead us to supposed safety?"

"Yes," I say. "And we also must be careful not to be too trusting of what we see and hear."

"Pezzo di mierda," Efta mutters. Then she says, "Regardless, we need to move. If we are not on our way by the time the afternoon storm arrives, I think we'll need to walk home via the ocean floor."

I walk to the tent to gather gear, but the tent is not mine, nor do I really have any gear to gather. Looking inside the tattered shelter, I'm not even sure what I would bring. There is nothing of me here, and everything useful has been taken by the birds or strewn across the island.

I meet Brogden and Efta at the gate. Efta passes me a couple of penlights that I stick in different pockets. Brogden has brought nothing but a length of rope he wears over his shoulder, his crutch, and his pistol. I am aware that I still wear both my pistol and flare gun, but they feel ornamental to me. Unless I need to light the night sky, I doubt I have any chance of successfully accomplishing a purpose with either.

We walk the path toward the plateau. I turn and take a few backward steps so that I can give one last look to the camp and its ruins. I'd arrived here thinking this would be a real chance to advance, and now I leave certain my life is all but over.

I collide with Efta as I try to turn so that I'm facing forward. She and Brogden have come to a complete stop, and they both stare at the cliffs.

On the far corner of the island, a pillar of black smoke billows in a massive column straight up into the sky, propelled like it was being pressured out of a funnel. The expulsion is so thick its sides appear ridged and churning. At its center, something glows ferociously green.

Brogden tilts his head back and grunts. Even from here, the fierce light within the smoke tinges his skin and the whole landscape. The air around the smoke almost seems to crackle and flash, like a power transformer throwing off sparks. Should I be terrified? I feel I've reached a point of exhaustion incompatible with such a reaction.

"Perfect," I say. "I can only assume the parameters of our departure have simplified."

"Like they say, 'When you're sick, you'll always find more to throw up,'" Efta says.

The column rises up tall as a cumulonimbus cloud in a matter of moments until I can no longer see its top. However, it does not dissipate, even in the wind, as if the particles of smoke are somehow bound together – or perhaps to the pillar of light in the center.

"No sense in looking now," Brogden says. "Our path is going to take us a lot closer."

Chapter 19

New Snow, Mess, Fissure

When we pass the admitting building, I halt us and break away from the group. The door through which I'd passed to decontaminate hangs open from one of its hinges, blasted off by Mikael's shotgun fire. The door on the far side of the undressing room is further damaged. I do not see what I would normally recognize as blood, but the walls are sprayed with some sort of blackish substance that takes on a purplish, iridescent sheen when I shine a light upon it.

"What have you found?" Brogden asks from the junction where the path continues to the plateau stairs.

I look back over my shoulder.

"Not sure," I say. "Looks like Mikael may have hit his target last night."

"Dead?"

"No, just blood. I think."

Whatever it is, it's pooled mostly around the far doorway, but a fat streak of it extends to the door at which I stand and disappears under the snow. I scuff away the snow a couple meters from the door, but it's hard to tell if I see the same substance mixed in with the dirt. The rain would have washed most of the traces away anyway.

I consider creeping through the dressing room and shower to see if perhaps Tompka had a chance to finish disinfecting our respirators, but I don't believe they will do us any good. Though I don't know how I could trust Brogden, I believe Tompka's soil analysis. There is no pathogen. Whatever infected the spiral stair to the lighthouse struck me as something that a respirator would not stop. We may already be so badly compromised that none of us should ever leave this place. I hope some of what we saw was hallucination, but Mikael being ripped to pieces by the birds was real.

"There were at least two of whatever it was that attacked first," I say. "We should not dismiss their threat."

"The other may have been wounded by both the blast at the fence and Tompka's bullets," Brogden says.

"And yet we did not find a body at the camp," I say.

"Better to assume that everything we see is threat and that a threat can come from anywhere," Efta says. "This whole place is a blight. An obscenity."

I shift my attention from the admitting building to the bluff by the cargo elevator. Though I cannot identify what, several pieces of camp debris are heaped on the height. There is, however, no activity.

We approach the steps. Every few meters, I check to see if I can find evidence of the blood trail, but it's not until I scrape the snow from the bottom step that I find something. Whatever it was that Mikael shot, it has made its way to the plateau. For all I know, it is crouched at the top of the stairs waiting for my head to emerge into view.

I draw my gun. It feels absurd in my hand. Even if I could shoot it, how can I believe it would harm something Mikael's shotgun failed to kill? The steps will be treacherous enough covered in snow; I can hardly imagine trying to draw aim and actually hit something while on them. The wind roars hard against the cliff. I press one hand to the rock and keep the weapon in the other, barrel pointed down.

Brogden limps in the middle of our procession, taking each step with both feet before moving to the next, but there is a stability to his step that reminds me of how he held up Tompka's weight at the fire. The crutch and limp are likely show, and no doubt Efta is too sharp to be taken by the act. So, for whom does he put on the show? Perhaps everything we've done here on the island has been nothing but theater, playing out a script we didn't know we were following.

I grow increasingly anxious every meter I rise. Every step, my feet threaten to slide out from under me. The wind is going to throw me over the edge. Perhaps Brogden will simply grab me by the back of the collar and jerk my weight sideways. Maybe Efta will just shoot us both and be done with it.

We reach the top of the steps. The blood trail has vanished. The pillar of smoke has ceased billowing. Its origin appears to have been the warehouse, a large section of whose roof appears to be missing. The column still towers overhead, but the green light at its core has vanished along with whatever cohesion had kept it cylindrical. The column is spreading into an enormous black cloud that deepens the gloom.

We survey the plateau for what I hope to be the last time. The snow makes it almost beautiful, the way it clings to the broken roofs and collapsing walls. Had it looked as such upon my first arrival, I might have been enamored with the place. Drifts have begun to gather against walls, forming new contours across the landscape. Nothing moves but the snow, and there is no sign that anything has moved through here since the snow began to fall.

Efta sets her gaze on the official offices and the warden's residence. A deep sadness settles into her features.

"A couple days," she says. "I just wanted a couple days."

"I think all of us wanted something different," I say.

"I needed to know," Efta says, touching the scar on her neck.

"To see proof of what they did to me, that my memory was real. Do you know what happened at the Quarry after you left?"

"Only that the survey fell under attack," I say. "Some local insurgence."

"It was a food riot," Efta says. "The distributors had cut off rations to everyone with cancers to 'ensure the essential work-force' would be fed. They were good as dead already, they said. The mob knew we had several months of supplies stocked. All they wanted was enough to make it a couple weeks. We were ordered to open fire. Teach them a hammer lesson. Do you know what it's like to open fire on a crowd of sick and starving people?" Tears glisten on her cheeks, and her voice catches in her throat. "We were forced to burn the bodies, and even though they couldn't stop stories from spreading, you won't find a shred of proof the massacre happened. They even destroyed the requisitions and shipping records for the ammunition we used." She swallows and takes a deep breath. All that comes out is a whisper as she looks up at me and says, "I just wanted to bring them some accountability, even if it was for something that happened forty years ago."

"I don't know that it would change anything," I say.

"That's not why you try," Efta says.

I nod. I know she's right. With everything we've seen since departing the mainland, I'd never see my duties the same way again. I'd seen this as a chance to advance, but advancement and fame only come from the Bureau when you are at the center of an atrocity. It's not that I'd never had reason to suspect this before, but sometimes you only imagine what you want to see when you gaze through the window into the darkness. It's a very different view from the other side of the glass.

"We can't go back to Midway," Efta says. "Or the mainland."

"I am convinced that was true before we were even offered this assignment," I say. "If not here, they will find some other use for us that will end in our disposal."

"Then we go with Brogden to the smugglers, let the Bureau think we all died here," Efta says.

So, I turn to Brogden and ask, "Which way then?"

Brogden gestures to the mess.

"Best to move in cover, in case the birds come out for the hunt again," he says.

Without a word, we adjust our path through the mess doors, and immediately upon entrance we all freeze. Upon the broken tables in the morning shadow of the *Sarru* lies the remains of some great beast.

* * *

If I had to guess, it is about twelve feet tall, but the way it is folded in on itself could conceal additional height. Its skin is waxy gray, hairless, but it bears a chevron texturing that initially reminds me of scales, but soon looks more like the layering one might see in crystals. As best I can tell it has eight functional limbs, four powerfully built motor limbs and four arms that end in something resembling hands with barbed fingers. A dozen other limbs dangle almost randomly off its frame, and they strike me as somehow more vestigial frills than something that developed for survival.

A giant, gaping wound dominates the thorax. Black filaments dangle from the wound's edges. Several of them appear to twitch, but I can't tell if it's from some sort of active nerve impulse or simply the wind sweeping in through the holes in the structure.

I curve slowly around it, keeping a wary distance. I keep my gun sighted on it, but it's so large that I'm pretty sure I won't miss it. One of its arms is thrown up and over the side of its head, so I have to make a ninety-degree arc to see the face. When I do, I freeze.

Though the skin there is also a pallid gray, and the face is covered with ridged protuberances and thorn-like growths, I recognize the face immediately. Yammut. If there were any doubt because of how briefly I'd known the man, Brogden steps beside me and says, "I suppose that is one less question this place has to offer."

"And about a hundred more," I say.

"What the hell happened to him?" Efta asks.

"I don't know," I say, but I think about the way the crystals in the spiral stair had seemed to be growing onto my boots. "Tompka said there was no pathogen here, but I'm not sure she had it right – I don't think she knew what she was looking at."

Brogden aims down the barrel of his firearm and shines a light into the wound. The beam glistens off the inside. Something in there moves. Pumping. The heart still beats. I take a step back. Before I can say anything, motion erupts, and what was the technician pushes himself up on two hands and knees.

Brogden and I both fire. The bullets appear to strike the technician, but the tissue seems to simply accept them like they'd been invited. As each slug hits, they leave a thumbnail-width mar on the skin. The technician stutters against the impact but reacts no further.

Neither does he move. It is as if he's undecided what to do next. When I was a teenager in the capital, I'd see people sitting in stairwells or at the base of streetlights. Someone could bump into them while walking, jostle them hard, but they'd simply resume their prior position like when you release after pressing hard on supple leather. Deformed as Yammut is, he somehow reminds me of those people. They were out of themselves. Maybe he is too.

I take a step toward him with one hand outstretched.

The air fills with thunder from the far end of the hall and Yammut shudders violently at a barrage of high caliber impacts. Chunks of flesh blast out of exit wounds along with some of the same blackish blood I'd found in the admitting room. The focus of damage sweeps up to the technician's head. Suddenly, the whole form collapses like a table with broken legs.

A muzzle flash spread like daisy petals vanishes as a magazine clicks dry. In the doorway to the kitchen stands Yost. Her face and neck are red and blistered, oozing with some sort of transparent fluid. One of her eyes is puffy and bloated, and her face seems to sag in such a way that it looks like it is literally sliding off her skull.

The rifle falls to the debris with a clatter. Her hands are equally burned as her face, and strings of tissue slough off where they'd grasped the weapon.

Yost wobbles.

Then she falls to her knees and vomits.

I run to her side. I'm scared to touch her because I don't know what has brought her to this condition, but I need to know if I can help her.

"What's happened? Where have you been?"

Brogden and Efta step up beside me, both casting wary glances at Yammut's remains.

"Vented the reactor," she says, her voice thick with phlegm, or something else. Her destroyed hand shakes like its being electro-cuted as she reaches into her coat and pulls out the old-tech device she'd stolen from me. She turns it on, and it clicks frantically. She casts it to the ground among the broken plates. "Reactor's been sealed. Cycling down."

"What reactor?"

"Beneath," Yost gasps. Her eyes roll back a moment, but one of them seems to refocus on me. Her lips seem like they want to stick together every time they close. "It powered the labs. Containment breach. Now it will starve."

"What labs? What will starve?"

"I thought entrance would have been warden's residence. Was in the mines. Tech like you can't imagine. Frontline as hell until they lost control. Inorganic life," she says, taking a sharp gasp at every pause. "The island will starve. You must–"

She convulses and a rush of vomit fills her mouth. She doesn't project it out though. It simply sits there and runs out the corners of her lips. There is a catching sound in her throat. Instinctively, I slap her on the back, but I feel her skin and muscles slide on her frame over the blow. A spray of bile and blood erupts from her mouth, but she also pitches forward with the impact and collapse to her side like a marionette whose strings are cut. Her eyes flutter and her joints twitch for several moments before she stills.

I rise up from her body. Four down now without question, Jones still missing. Judging by what's happened to Yammut, I can assume something equivalent or worse has happened to Jones. Mikael, Tompka, and now Yost. I've seen people die before in the cities and at our survey sites, but not so violently, so viscerally. I've never shared an experience like Efta's at the Quarry, nor do I have the unflinching resolve to kill as I must like Brogden appears to.

Maybe that's why my father had wanted to part ways with the Bureau. Maybe he knew from the start that something about me wasn't suited for the way I would need to carve my path. I believe that someone truly orthodox would simply accept the loss and move on, but I feel a profound sadness for Yost's passing. Perhaps it is simply that we survived such a harrowing experience together in our trek to the lighthouse, but I have grown to admire her.

"No time to mourn," Brogden says. He is standing at one of the breaks in the wall, gazing across the plateau. "Something moves out there. At offices."

"It must be Jones," I say. "No doubt he heard the gunfire."

Efta pokes at Yammut's remains with a piece of rotting wood she retrieves from the ground.

"It's astonishing," she says. She scrapes at the edges of the gaping rifle wounds. "There is still activity in the tissue despite the amount of damage."

"His head's been obliterated," I say. "Is he not dead?"

Efta shrugs and drops the piece of wood.

"Hell if I know," Efta says. "You seem far more confident than I that we should be calling that 'he.'"

"I don't give damn what we call it," Brogden says. "And we waste time entertaining such questions."

Brogden adjusts his rope on his shoulder, loads a fresh magazine into his pistol, and steps through the door into the kitchen. Efta gives Yost one last sad look, and then follows.

I hesitate as they step out the door. I gaze at Yammut and remember what Tompka said about contamination in our food. I do not doubt that the thing before me is real. It is too tangible and clearly shared among us. However, the Bureau has been known to use psychotropic substances in both training and in interrogations to make the subjects more susceptible to suggestion. Could it have been given to us to distort our judgment?

From outside, Efta hisses for me to quit my delay.

Though I don't want to touch it, I take Yost's Kalashnikov. Doing so almost feels like I'm desecrating her body, but we need to be able defend ourselves. She emptied the inserted clip, but she attached an upside-down clip to it with black tape. Our pistols were insufficient to drop whatever Yammut became, so it stands to reason they would fail to bring down a second beast. I'm not sure the rifle will fare much better, but it seemed to do more damage.

As I adjust the strap on the folder, the hull of the *Sarru* catches my peripheral vision. I trot over to it and pull myself up to the deck by the rail. I pop open the storage container full of ammunition. I grab a pair of clips for the rifle and pocket three hand grenades. They are heavier in my hands than I expected. I hope the weight reflects their capacity for damage. I know the claymore blast didn't kill whichever beast triggered it, but it was a shaped charge. This might fare a little better.

Then, I climb back down, check my pistol and flare gun, shift the rifle, and depart the mess. The grenades thunk against each other in my jacket pocket.

* * *

The cold breeze swirls snow in the air. Brogden kneels at the corner of the mess and peers across the plateau toward the offices.

The expanse is still, other than the drifting flakes and falling ash. Efta watches the cargo elevator bluff. Three of the birds have emerged and strut around the camp debris, pecking here and there. One of them snaps at what appears to be a sock or some other thread of clothing and gives it a sharp shake of its head before throwing it down into the snow. Another bird flutters up from the unseen cliffside and lands on the corner of a shattered crate. It snatches up one of our foil-wrapped ration packs and gulps it down whole. No doubt the birds were disturbed by the gunfire. I worry that should we discharge our weapons further, a significantly larger group of them will arrive.

"For all the stories about this place, to think the greatest danger has been a bunch of birds," Efta whispers.

"I don't think those birds are natural," I say. "I think they've grown under the influence of whatever was released on this island."

"What the hell were they doing here?" Efta asks.

"It's above my station to know," I say with a glance to Brogden.

Brogden looks over his shoulder and gives us a mild shake of the head.

"Mine as well, I'm afraid," he says. "We are simply supposed to pave the way for something further."

"Where do we go from here?" I ask.

Brogden points to the warehouse and to the radio array beyond it.

"To the array," he says. "We descend the bluff there, follow the beach through the graveyard. The boat's anchored offshore behind the rocks."

"Offshore?" I ask. "We don't have a boat."

Brogden sighs.

"We swim."

I shiver immediately at the thought of trying to swim in the waters around this place. I don't know how we'd manage without dying of hypothermia, being killed by the jellyfish, or just outright drowning.

"Doesn't matter much if we don't get there, yes?" Brogden says.

The warehouse lays ahead, a long, wide building with a gaping hole in its roof from where the 'venting' occurred. The walls were once coated with some sort of external veneer, but that has since eroded exposing cinderblock construction. Like the disciplinary hall, there are no windows. The building was clearly meant to survive a formidable assault – it could itself be mistaken for a prison.

It's not a long run to its nearest corner, but there is no cover whatsoever between us and it. The span is almost entirely flat, though it does seem like the wind blows a slow and rippling contour through the snow atop it. I wish we had an alternative to crossing the space between buildings so openly, but the Gollitok offers little cover. By design, of course.

I look back to the birds. Two more have joined them. One of them is severely deformed with what appears to be the nubs of two vestigial wings protruding from its breast. It stretches its primary wings back to a startling span that makes it appear almost human in size before it relaxes them back in on itself. With any luck they'll take off for their jellyfish hunt before long.

"There," Brogden says. "It's on the move."

I peek over Brogden's shoulder and follow his gaze to the edge of the armory. The remaining beast's bulk moves with an awkward grace behind the snow-clung fence. I can't see him well enough to tell if his attention is on us, but, being realistic, how many more things are there on Albertachen for him to take an interest in? Fortunately, he appears to be headed toward the offices and the warden's residence, but that would also bring him more in line with the gap in the fence. I don't know how fast he can move, but the Gollitok is not an especially large place.

"Do you know anything about Jones?" I ask.

"His file was pretty thin," Brogden says. "An immigrant from Old America. No family. No connections. No prospects for advancement. The definition of disposable."

"I would add human to the list of traits," I say.

"You won't find that on paper," Brogden says. "Which version of him do you think will exist in ten years?"

"I know which one I believe exists now," I say. "And that's the one I believe we will need to engage with."

"Nonsense," Brogden says. "We wait until it breaks line of sight. As long as we get to the warehouse before it emerges, we should be fine."

"If Jones gets to the ropes before we're down the cliff, we'll be taking the fast route to the rocks, I suspect."

"Strange that you keep calling it Jones," Efta says. "Do you think there's something left of him in there?"

I shrug.

"It just feels right," I say. "In my gut. Tompka said our judgment and even our senses might be compromised. If nothing else, I think it's best to presume that its more than just some animal or we may underestimate the threat or opportunity it presents."

"The only opportunity it presents us is evisceration," Brogden says. "It's in the offices. We move. Now."

We break cover immediately, doing our best to make a full run. However, my aching body struggles through the calf deep snow, and Brogden's limp onto his crutch makes his whole gait look like some great wounded animal flopping its way forward. Efta alone moves with some sort of grace. I note in a glance that the birds have ceased their meandering and stand with their attention fixed, their bodies twitching and wings jerking.

My heart leaps in my chest as they all at once take flight.

As they rise, a sharp rumble rises too, escalating to an intensity of vibration that rattles my whole skeleton. The ground beneath our feet suddenly rolls with a great heave that sends all three of us rolling to the ground. I crash to the snow, my shoulder pushing straight through the fluff and jolting hard enough against the dirt to knock my breath out.

"What the hell was that?" I ask between gasps.

"An earthquake?" Efta offers as she pushes herself onto her hands and knees.

A fresh burst of smoke erupts from the warehouse roof. The green pillar of light is again at its center, but it also shoots off beams in upward directions that seem to ignite the particulate haze suspended in the higher elevations of the air. It's almost like a fireworks display put on by the sky itself.

"I think whatever Yost did is still happening," I say.

A new rumble rises, this from deep within the ground. Wildly, I imagine it to be some giant stomach wrenching within the island, starving, as Yost put it. The ground ripples like waves in a cove. Then, with an ear-splitting crack, a fissure opens on the plateau halfway between us and the disciplinary hall. The tremors intensify as the split widens to well over a meter and then it stills.

Above, the birds circle and a steady stream of them now takes off from the cliffside. I don't know if they're hunting us or have simply been spurred into flight by the seismic activity, but as they rise, several of them burst into flame as they cross the air over the warehouse. Charred bodies fall from the sky around me, thudding to the snow. The sky itself seems a field of small fires flashing in and out of existence.

The fires vanish, and I am left breathless and dazed. The remaining birds flap desperately away toward all horizons. Something alive seems to fill the air; it's almost as if the world is sucking in a massive breath.

Whatever is happening is not done yet.

A low vibration begins. I feel it in my fingertips, my teeth, my scalp, my spine. It grows slowly in intensity. Things around me rattle. I don't know if they are things that I carry or if I'm hearing a chattering among the rocks themselves. My muscles grow numb and paralyzed from the feeling and all my nerves become overwhelmed. My joints feel like they're coming apart, and I can't tell if I'm still lying on the snow or suspended centimeters above it. I can't tell where I end and the vibration begins.

Still the air seems to be sucking into some great void at the island's center. It doesn't feel like an air current, but rather that something else is being pulled from it.

Then, everything cuts off all at once.

The world fills with a brighter light than anything I've ever known, and it seems as if everything has become that light.

Then, there is no ground beneath my feet, and I am falling.

CHAPTER 20

THE SHAFT, WHITE METAL, THE BELOW

I strike a slanted metal surface and find myself sliding through the dark. All around me, rocks and pebbles clatter, the reverberations bludgeoning my ears. When I reach out, my hands squeal against more metal. I thrust my shoulder to one side and my legs to the other.

The jolt is agonizing as my momentum jams to a halt. The wrist I'd injured during my altercation with Yost jams again and comes alive with white hot pain. Falling stones slam into my body and tumble off to the side. Friction burns my shoulder through my clothes, and my knee hits hard just before my movement dies altogether. I draw several panicked breaths as rocks continue to pass by. A miracle that no large stone cracks my skull.

When I collect myself, I realize I've wedged myself in some sort of ventilation shaft. The entrance through which I fell when the ground collapsed is dark, blocked by debris. Another miracle that I was not crushed.

Below, darkness as well, but a dim light flickers within. The distance is hard to gauge, but I approximate fifty meters to whatever space the vent empties into. There must have been some sort of grating, but likely falling rock punched it out. About halfway between here and there, there is some sort of ruined mechanism. Much of it appears time-tarnished, but there are shining silver edges from where whatever was mounted was sheared off.

The radio bursts alive in my ear and my heart skips hard enough I nearly let up the pressure holding me in place.

"Varka?" Efta's voice is distorted and the signal dense with static. "Varka, do you read?"

"Efta?"

"Where are you, Varka?"

Even with the robotic tone of the interference, distress edges her words.

"Wedged in some sort of vent shaft."

"Say again? A shaft?" she asks. "I'm barely able to read you."

"The exit is blocked," I say. "I'm going to need to go deeper."

I try to shift myself to alleviate the pressure my position places on my neck, but my grip slips altogether as I do so. For a breathless moment, I feel almost weightless as gravity pulls, but I manage to jam myself in place again.

"Are you okay?" I ask.

She replies, but it is too garbled to understand. I try again, but only static answers.

I fumble in my pockets and pull out a penlight. I'm positioned pretty far from the surface, but the darkness makes the distance difficult to gauge. My muscles already burn from the effort of holding myself still. Given the difficulty keeping myself pressed in place here, I doubt that I'd be able to move the debris blocking the top of the shaft. Most likely it would collapse on me anyway, sweeping me down the shaft and crushing me.

So, I scoot myself downward a few centimeters. The light below continues to flicker. Though I don't know how many chambers could be hidden within the plateau, it feels reasonable to assume this is connected to wherever Yost and the techs went. Yost claimed to have shut down the reactor venting, but for all I know whatever burned her to death is waiting for me down below. A minor tremor churns through the island, and chunks of debris clatter down around me. I scoot myself down a little further.

Once on the way down the shaft, the radio bursts to life, but nothing intelligible comes through. My muscles burn. Sweat soaks my hair and runs down my back. The air grows stale around me. Am I rebreathing my own air? Am I going to suffocate? I grow short of breath. The hot fist of panic laces its fingers around my heart.

A few centimeters at a time are all I can manage. I could move faster if I didn't need to exert my muscles so hard to stall my weight, but I'm not certain I could stop myself should I let myself slide too fast. I try to shine my light below, but it's impossible to tell how far I'd drop out the shaft base. It could be three meters; it could be ten. Either could break a leg or an ankle taken wrong or at too high a speed.

I grow angry as my heartrate picks up and the sweat deepens. I can smell my own must, and my palms are slick. Inside my boots, moisture squishes in my socks. I want to punch the walls. I want them to let me go. I want to let go.

The curses that escape my lips should echo around me, but for some reason they sound completely dead. I barely hear them through my own jaw. My vision tunnels hard and I feel like I'm recessed within myself looking at the shaft from a shaft made of my mind's own darkness. My mouth grows cottony, my tongue thick. Colorful stars dance in the black in my peripheral vision.

The Orlot, I tell myself. It must be the Orlot or whatever it was I've been poisoned with. Perhaps the sweat and exertion are somehow forcing it through my system. Had something similar happened at the lighthouse? Had I really seen the light come alive, or is my body metabolizing a toxin?

I almost slip when my brain tells me that the walls of the shaft are no longer there. Every place I'm pressing against metal tingles with numbness like a limb sat on too long. Is it real or an illusion? My heart pounds, and bile rises up my esophagus like mercury rising in an old thermometer. The burn at the base of my windpipe sends me into a spasm of coughs, and I fight to keep my ribs from convulsing enough to shake me loose from my position.

I flip on my radio.

"Efta?" I ask. "Brogden?"

No response.

"Efta?" I ask. "I could use some grounding."

The radio crackles and hisses. Is that a voice? It's guttural, groaning, like a steel cable twanged by shifting weights during an equipment failure. I heard such a sound once in the quarries right before an inch-thick line lifting a quartzite slab snapped. The cable slashed through the air like a bullwhip, and it embedded itself nearly a full meter into the cliff wall. Afterward, as its momentum jolted a vibrating wave down the taut length, was when I'd heard the sound. The sound makes my bones ache, so I pull the earpiece out of my ear and shove it into my jacket.

I continue my descent. Another aftershock grinds through. Something in the shaft wrenches, and dust showers me. I shine the penlight above to where the seam between two of the metal panels buckled. Some ridge of mineral has ruptured through the gap under the shifting forces. Even as I see it, another tremor drives the shard of the mineral deeper into the shaft.

I cannot linger. The integrity of the shaft cannot be trusted if the quakes continue, and it's only a matter of time before some of the debris at the top of the shaft breaks free and sweeps the whole damn length clear with its mass. Though I feel my weight shift loose and wild, I allow myself more swing in my slides.

I must slow, however, when I reach ruined machinery. Some sort of heavy gear with broken cogs hangs off a bent axle. The remains of a pump apparatus disappear into the wall, and a greenish fluid leaks from a pair of disintegrating rubber hoses. The bulk of the unit appears to have at some point hung across the whole shaft, judging by sheered mounts on the other side and jagged ridges of metal welded to the wall. I look back up to the surface. Surely, whatever this shaft was, it did not reach the surface, or we would have noticed its egress. How deep had the fissure through which I'd fallen opened up?

I maneuver through the damage, twisting to avoid the razor-sharp edges. One of them slides against the shoulder of my peacoat and slices through the thick wool effortlessly. Another simply glides a scratch into my forearm just above the wrist as I brush a little too close. I don't even realize I've cut myself until I feel a bead of hot blood run down the back of my palm. I am forced to suspend myself into the center of the space with my feet and hands pressed as hard as I can to the sides as I shimmy down one centimeter at a time. Sweat makes every movement feel like it will be the one that fails and I'll fall, gashing myself open on some metal shard, then breaking my legs below.

When I'm through, my muscles scream for oxygen. My arms shake from the strain like they're being electrocuted. I refuse to let myself stop because there is no real rest no matter how I jam myself against the walls. My eyes water, or perhaps I cry from the exertion. Am I sobbing or gasping? I groan like thick syrup.

At the shaft's bottom, there is a small rim, no more than an inch, but enough that I can wedge the soles of my boots onto the support. The moment my weight transfers to my feet, my entire body shudders, and I let out a long quivering sigh. I press back against the shaft wall to distribute my weight, and I can practically hear the echo of my pounding heart beat off the metal.

I only allow myself a few seconds of rest. Below, all I can see is some sort of narrow corridor between one white wall and one black wall. The floor is maybe ten feet below, but it's mostly buried under a pile of rocks that must have fallen through in the initial quake. I slide myself into the closest to a crouch I can manage, reach down, and press my hands against the lip upon which I stand, and drop my feet through the hole.

* * *

The rocks shift under my feet as I land, and I wobble as I reach out for the two walls. What I'd believed was a corridor is an aisle in a much larger room. The white wall is solid and uniform floor to ceiling, and it appears to run about fifteen meters. The floor and ceiling both are metal grating, and through both there appears to be a dense network of wires and conduits. White strip lighting along the meeting of wall and ceiling flickers and fades, never staying lit for more than a blink, but never going completely dark.

Beside me is an almost two-meter-long, black, stacked-shelving frame that reminds me of an industrial kitchen rack. Each shelf contains an oblong, black box from which bundles of wires run into larger bundles that vanish into vertical conduits between the shelving units. Each black box appears identical, and each has a smooth face except for a vent plate concealing a fan and two rows of tiny yellow, red, and green lightbulbs. Many of the bulbs have burst. None appear functional. At the base of each shelf, there appears to be some sort of tank with hoses that run up and through the units. The tanks are labeled 'Coolant' and 'Warning: Extreme Cold.'

The room is as cool and stifling as a cave, and a haze of dust hangs in the air. On either side of the shelving unit, a one-meter gap separates another shelving unit. The gaps are cross-aisles that lead to another row of shelving units. I sidle to the aisle and peek around the edge of the shelf. The room appears to have four rows of shelves. What the room is for, I don't know, but I've never seen so much old tech in one place. Given that everything seems connected together by the precisely organized wires and conduits, I can only assume that it was something far beyond my knowledge.

I find Yost's rifle lying on top of the rocks. It appears undamaged other than scratches in the surface. I'm uncertain whether or not a fall can break a rifle, but should I need to discharge the weapon, could it blow up in my face? Sometimes you need a little more menace added to life and death self-defense, I suppose. I shoulder the strap and step between the racks.

The central aisle of the room is a little wider than the others. One side ends in a broad computer terminal, with a three-by-three grid of monitor screens mounted to the wall above it. The other side stops at a massive, hydraulic door jammed open about half a meter. I approach the door, crouch, and shine my light into the gap.

Beyond, a short, narrow, corridor with smooth white walls terminates at a bluish glass door. A jagged crack runs down the middle of the door. Through the door appears to be some sort of decontamination airlock. I recognize UV banks similar to the ones that Tompka installed for us to use coming down from the plateau. One wall is made of shallow storage cabinets, and a row of hooks hangs on the other above a washing station. The ceiling appears to be ventilation.

I wriggle on my belly under the door. My back scrapes a row of pegs at the bottom of the door meant to close into a row of holes on the floor. I imagine as I pass through the gap a quake breaking the door loose and its weight crushing me into the floor. Would it rupture something fatal? Or would it simply pin me in place until I die of thirst?

Once through, I approach the door. The handle won't budge. Above it, there is a twelve-button numerical control pad. I hover my fingers over the panel for a moment as if I know the combination. I withdraw my hand.

I unsling the rifle, remove the clip, and check the chamber. Then, I smash the butt of the rifle against the glass. A spiderweb of cracks explodes around the impact and joins the already present break. I lunge into a second blow, and glass smashes into the decontamination chamber.

The white strip lighting goes dark. A klaxon blares. A red strip light beside the white throbs on then off. More lines of red illuminate beneath the floor across the decontamination chamber and out the opaque door on its far side. A mechanized, tinny voice

emits from a hidden speaker, saying, "Containment breach, cont
—" then it dies.

White gas erupts from nearly invisible spouts in the ceiling but
fails as quickly as the voice. Cold paralysis squeezes my spine for a
moment as I realize I probably triggered an automated defense
system. I turn around and notice on the door behind me a small
plate that says "Servers – Clean Room."

I step onto the shards of broken glass with a crunch, and check
the unlabeled cabinets. I find plastic sealed gloves and a box of
paper booties. There are several sealed bottles of disinfectant,
several chemicals I don't recognize, and several large syringes. I
look back at the "Server Room" door. What the hell kind of
precautions did people take to enter? What am I just walking
out of?

Another cabinet contains respirators hanging from hooks. I
take one, but the rubber crumbles at the edges under my grip.
With a pinch, I break off a nugget and poke out one of the plastic
lenses with a nudge from my thumb. Even if I managed to pull it
on, any seal it managed would collapse. I throw the mask to the
ground. The next time I trigger gas, it might not fail. I suppose I
should think three times and sniff the wind before the next time I
break a piece of glass down here.

The door at the far end of the decontamination chamber
opens without resistance, and I step out into the middle of a
hallway which runs ten meters in either direction. There are two
doors on the wall opposite the decontamination room. A door on
either end of the room. The ceiling contains the same red pulsing
strip lights, but the white ones are lit here too.

The wax and wane of the light throws shifting shadows off the
three bodies collapsed on the floor. They are remarkably well
preserved, nothing like the disintegrated remains in the stair
leading to the lighthouse. What is left of the flesh has taken on a
mummified quality. One of the bodies, however, is also garbed in
the remains of a laboratory coat, while the other two wear low

rank, pre-war military uniforms. A clipboard lies on the ground by the one in the lab coat, and the handle of a shattered mug still hangs off its fingers. Whatever happened here killed them where they stood.

The soldiers still wear belts with sidearms attached. I consider taking one, but I have no guarantee they'll function. I feel enough risk with the Kalashnikov after its long fall.

Instead, I consider the doors. On one end, the door is marked 'Habitation.' The door on the side wall of the corridor in that direction is marked 'Administration.' In the other direction, the door on the side is marked 'Elevator.' The door at the end is unmarked. There is no handle or knob, but a heavy numerical lock is mounted where one would usually be.

I press the button for the elevator, but it is, unsurprisingly, defunct. A fresh tremor, mild, deep below my feet tells me that I don't want to be aboard even were it operational. Still, if I find nothing else, perhaps I can pry open the doors and attempt to scale the shaft.

I turn toward Habitation since it's most likely to have an emergency exit, but even as I turn to head that direction, I stop and consider the Bureau, especially as it existed pre-war. It is not like it is a secret, simply something none of us prefer to acknowledge. Efta was right – the same people who brought the world to ruin were the same ones who took power to rebuild it. They lit the sky afire, took the sun from my childhood. I don't know which power attacked first, but they'd all planned it. They'd run a million scenarios, and the only thing that had ever stayed their hand was knowing they wouldn't win. When the pandemics laid whole populations low though, they saw it as time to run the numbers again. One of them thought conditions looked favorable.

I ask myself which would they prioritize: getting their people out quickly or their experiments?

I look back to the heavy lock. To the steel door. If the center did not hold, the people who saw the population of the world as an obstacle to victory would likely want the secrets to stay below the surface.

The door itself I consider.

The rifle could not possibly pierce the steel, and no doubt fail-safes would prevent shooting the lock from being effectual. I chuckle and shake my head. I doubt they gave the people stationed here the code freely. Just expected them to trust that catastrophic failure was outside possibility. They never knew they worked in their own mausoleum.

I look at the bodies on the floor. I wish I had something to cover their faces with. They are not the ones who deserve to lie dead on cold metal. I check their pockets but find nothing that might clue me toward the combination.

Then, I pause. Yost's face comes to mind. I remember confronting her about the warden's residence. I remember the note she gave me to the warden's daughter. The incorrect date at the bottom. I doubt Yost foresaw a situation quite like this, but no question she wanted me to have that information.

Without hesitation, I punch the numbers in. The keys squeak as I press them.

Nothing happens.

I punch the numbers in again. One of them shifts slightly and I feel something crunch inside the box.

Inside the door, something gasps. A seal exhausts. The door jolts. It does not open, but something about it seems to fall loose. The outline of a panel becomes visible in the middle of the door. I pull it open.

The panel exposes carefully threaded wires. A row of three ports. Two flip switches labeled with a power symbol. A handle with a groove to allow the handle forty-five degrees swing. Though I'm not familiar with the panel, I take a guess and flip the first switch. A tiny blue light comes on.

I flip the second switch, and something hums inside the door.

I pull the handle.

With a squeal of servos and then a screech of aged hydraulics, the door lurches up until it is like it no longer exists.

Beyond the door, a large pentagonal chamber with a doorway in each corner. At its center, a half circle desk. The ceiling is much higher here, ten meters. Emergency lighting still glows in the corners, but the air is suspended with a field of particulates like there'd been a fire. Around the edges of the room are several work-stations. Some appear clerical, desks characterized by a broken computer, file folders stacked in inboxes and outboxes and open on blotters. Other stations appear scientific. I recognize the micro-scopes scattered on many surfaces, but there are numerous machines of whose functions I'm fully ignorant.

In some ways, it reminds me of the official offices, but it seems far less personal and lacking in whatever paranoia had ruled that place in its final days.

Also, unlike the offices, there are bodies here. Like in the hall, they too have failed to fully decompose. The first one is laid on the floor between a desk and a chair. Another has fallen over one of the desks. Both wear lab coats. A third in plaid shirt and brown slacks collapsed on top of some sort of metal serving tray covered in plates. The plates are broken everywhere. The tray is bent under the body's weight.

I circle around the central desk. A fourth body in a soldier's uniform is on the floor there beside a chair that has been pulled back. This body has a square of cloth laid over its face.

On the desk, there is a computer console and a device I recognize as a video camera. The Bureau uses them to record debrief-ings. The video camera is wired to the console. The console's screen has a glowing green light beside a button in its bottom right-hand corner.

I press the button.

The screen comes to life with a static hiss. It amazes me that the system still functions, but then I notice on the counter a number of computer circuits, several fine-point screw drivers, a tiny wrench, a couple cans of spray, and chemical cleaners. Someone has worked on the computer recently. When the screen comes on, it contains several small images. One of them is a right-facing equilateral triangle labeled, "Touch me."

I don't know if I'm being too literal, but I press my thumb to it.

The screen flickers, and then Yost's face appears in its center. Her skin is already blistered and burned. Patches are splitting and peeling away like she is an overcooked tomato. Something oozes out of the corners of her eyes and mouth. She coughs a spray of blood onto the camera which she then wipes away with her sleeve. Her voice is broken and hoarse.

* * *

"My name is Lieutenant Yost Aldrinaya. I have been exposed to a lethal dose of radiation. I believe I will be dead within the hour. I am located in the front rooms of the sub-Gollitok laboratory complex. I have returned from the below and hope to attain the surface to die. The emergency containment protocol within the reactor has been engaged. Radiation levels should reduce below the threshold once venting completes. The substrate should be null in an indeterminate period of time.

"At the time of this recording, the survey team with which I arrived on Albertachen is likely under assault in the beach camp. The survey lead, Hammel Varka, the historian Efta Yopteminik, Sergeant Mikael Byell, and Engineer Tompka Mercitian are, to the best of my knowledge, still alive and in acceptable health. Second Liaison Brogden Hayes was seriously injured on the Midway crossing but is recovering.

"First Technician Dellyan Yammut and Second Technician Steven Jones are both... compromised... after they inadvertently discovered access to the laboratory complex. To the best of my knowledge, they were exposed to the Cekic Compound and have succumbed to its principal effects. Despite the camp's fortification, I find it unlikely that the remaining team members will survive the extant threats. If they do, the safest course of action will be extermination. It is uncertain whether they carry the ability to spread the compound, and to risk any sort of assessment protocol is unacceptable.

"Finally, I believe that further examination of the remaining records will determine what we have assumed to be true. The operant condition change that precipitated the initial strike was the research underway here, but the containment failure prevented the completion of the strategic initiative. It is my hope that the venting procedure may repair some of the damage.

"I will go to choose my grave now, like so many on the Gollitok before. Damn us all who are part of the mechanisms born from the ruin began here. Damn you for sending Kirsch first."

I turn off the screen, put my receiver back in, and try to reach Efta with no success. The conclusion laid out by Yost's video is little different than the one I'd reached just outside this very door, little different than the one that drove Efta's anger and criticism since before our arrival on Albertachen. I've done nothing but serve those who brought it all to ash in exchange for a few dying cinders. No wonder my parents fought so hard to secret me from the Capital – and here I was now, exactly in the type of position they'd never wanted me to be in.

Extermination?

Damn us all indeed.

CHAPTER 21

SORRY, BOTANY, WHITE WINDOW

A door opens with a screech and whine somewhere out of sight, and I immediately drop into a crouch behind the counter. My hand falls onto the shoulder of the dead body. The tissue underneath is almost crisp in texture through the disintegrating military uniform. I'm glad I missed the face. I just know it would have collapsed under the impact.

A thunk from some room beyond the far wall echoes. Somewhere, something falls.

I crawl out from the central desk. It might hide me from 270 degrees of view, but one way in means one way out. I move around the side farthest from the wall the sound came from and peek up over the top of the counter. I don't know what approaches, but I can only assume it is like the thing that we found in the mess or something else I do not desire to meet. The rifle on my shoulder does little to reassure me.

On the other side of the room, stillness. Odds are the air has hardly moved in this room for years. Was Yost the first to make it this far? Who's to say what has killed the prior teams? Seems unlikely that we've discovered every threat in this place.

However, it occurs to me that if Jones is coming, he is coming from the surface. Perhaps whatever door he enters from is the door that will lead me out. Of course, if something else lurks in this facility, then it may well be approaching from even deeper in. I remember the way Yost and I fled as something rose up the throat of the lighthouse. Was it the thing of light, or did it simply ignite the sculpted bulb?

I squint to try to read plates beside the door on either side of the room. I believe the one on the left corner says 'Virology' while the one on the right says 'Botany.' Aside from the irony that there was once a portion of a facility on this island dedicated to botany, I would much rather attempt a transit through that room than through one labeled virology. Tompka found no signs of active pathogens, but that doesn't mean that a viral laboratory in a defunct facility might not have something waiting within.

Something hard scrapes against metal on the other side of the wall between the two doors. It's a grating sound, like a rusty hammer being dragged on coarse iron.

I glance behind me. The two doors on my side of the room are 'Chemistry' and 'Reactor.' Should I retreat into one and hope that whatever approaches passes through another door? It would only have a twenty-five percent chance of picking my route on the first attempt. No matter what, I feel like 'Chemistry' would be the smarter bet. Yost's recording indicated that the radiation should drop, but I can't imagine the levels get better in proximity to the reactor.

My heart lurches as my radio bursts with static in my ear. Efta's voice blares out, then cuts off, blares out, then cuts off. Though the sound channels directly into my ear, it is frightfully loud. I want to answer, but I'm afraid that in here even my whispers could echo.

I clamp one hand over my ear in the hopes that I can block any sound that might escape as I duck back into cover.

"Varka," she says. Her voice is choked. "Do you read? Where the hell are you?"

"Some sort of underground research facility. I believe Jones may be stalking me. Unable to reply further."

"Understood," Efta says softly. Her voice almost becomes one with the hissing interference, but the interference itself seems to form the words too. "Brogden is dying. He was crushed from the waist down when the ground collapsed. I've secured myself in the cabin of the *Sarru*. I don't think I'm alone out here."

"Lay low," I say. "I'll be there as soon as I can."

I cut the transmitter. I peek above the counter and suck in my breath as the door to 'Botany' opens with an ear-splitting shriek of grinding metal.

With no more than a glimpse of a dark mass, I drop back onto all fours, hoping I'd not been seen. I unsling the rifle. I'm not sure I intend to use it, but it would be easy for the butt or barrel to thunk against something while I move.

A deep guttural breathing rattles across the room, and the sound of hard things dragging on metal whines and grinds through the room. It cuts to the left from the botany door toward the door through which I entered, so I creep slowly back toward the opening in the central desk. I hope it vanishes through the door toward the server hall and the entrance to Habitation.

Carefully, I try to peek around just enough to better assess what stalks me. I glimpse a hulking knee, glistening, cord-like muscles sliding under the skin. The foot is a massive paw with a circle of taloned digits gripping the steel grating of the floor in all directions. A pair of the talons on each side clacks impatiently.

A ball of flesh shudders on what I can only think of as its calf and slides off. It strikes the floor with a wet splat and quivers. Another chunk of its meat falls off something higher than I can see and lands beside the first.

I don't dare lean out any further to see more. I would hope its attention is fixed on the door I entered through, but I don't even know for certain this thing just has one head. Instead, I creep later-ally, crossing the gap that leads into the desk, to the monitor that played Yost's final report, the mummified body with its face covered. I peek around the other side, glimpse the spur at the back of what appears to be a scaled, backward knee. The fleshy ring around the base of the spur flexes and pulses, and a small stream of milky liquid oozes from the point of the spur. It splashes onto the grating and sizzles into a little steaming cloud.

Then, the beast is on the move, away from the door through which I entered and toward the door to Chemistry. I slide around the edge of the desk, nearest the Virology door. The ground between myself and the door is relatively clear, but small wisps of steam rise up from the grating in a trail all the way through the still-open passage. Whatever the creature excretes has been dribbling out for some time. Fortunately, the door is open, so as long as I can get into the passage quietly, I may be able to slip away unseen.

Then, a door opens. By the direction of the sound, it can only be the passage to Chemistry. My heart freezes in my chest as I listen for the dragging sound that has signaled the creature's movements so far. All I hear is its breathing and that soft sizzle of the milky venom. The air takes on an ozone quality, and my eyes water. I don't know that I can linger long. Will it pass into the lab beyond? Will it keep its attention fixed in that direction?

A couple more wet splats reverberate. My eyes water harder as the sizzling continues and the smell intensifies. Maybe the thing will just fall apart. If it really is Jones, certainly his physiology is staggeringly unstable. Maybe it's a matter of time before his frame can no longer support that scale of transformation.

The acrid scent takes on a metallic quality that coats my tongue. The inside of my nose and cheeks begins to tingle. Whatever those secretions emit, I can no longer question if it is toxic. I glance back to the doorway through Botany. If I make a break for it and get spotted, if there is no passage to the surface, I'm a dead man. I wish I had even the vaguest understanding of the layout of this place.

I try to make it around the edge of the counter, but I would need to crawl back across the opening to be able to glimpse the legs of the creature. If I want to know what it is doing, I will have no choice but to peek above the countertop.

A bit of movement catches in my peripheral vision. By the door toward Habitation, the two quivering balls have begun to bulge and pock. Are they disintegrating further?

Then, a sharp spike breaks through the viscous outer membrane. A long, jointed needle of a limb thrusts out of one, flexes, and then stabs itself into the metal grating. Then another. My throat grows raw and my lungs ache. I must get out. I rise, peeking as little as possible over the countertop.

Whatever stands there before the open door marked 'Chemistry' does not have a head, but its upper third is covered in eyes. They all snap focus onto me. They ooze a brownish-green fluid as if they're crying swamp water, and several of the eyes bulge out from their lids like inflating balloons. One of them bursts, and I hear its innards spatter across the room.

I unsling my rifle as it spreads its four massive, webbed arms in silent grace until they brush the ceiling in their full extension. The butt of the rifle meets my shoulder, and I grip it firmly. The creature's sides split open like the seams of an overstuffed shirt, revealing tooth-filled vertical mouths that run up the whole length of either side of its body.

"Mother of God," I whisper as I pull the trigger.

The world goes white with heat and light and my upper body is overtaken by a strange numbness. It seems worlds away as the rifle suddenly becomes two pieces flying in either direction with its breach twisted and ripped. I'm staggering backward through a room that feels the size of the whole world until I'm suddenly leaning over something hard and angular.

A desk. I've fallen over the desk. The rifle misfired and blew out the chamber.

My face is hot, and there is something wrong with my hand.

The pain surges as I see that my right hand is missing my index and middle fingers.

Something massive breaks behind me, so I roll onto my back. The creature has smashed half the center desk. The monitor and camera have both fallen to the floor. I thrust my good hand into my coat pocket, pull out the flare gun. Without thinking, I fire it straight into the center mass of the beast.

The shell strikes with a sickening thunk, and it vanishes into the soft tissue in what I would call the beast's belly. For a moment, its eyes simply stare at me as its arms raise up from the smashed desk around it. Suddenly, the eyes feel more human than anything else about the creature, and they are filled with profound disappointment and sadness. I can't say for certain that this is Jones, but I know there is something human about it. A surge of guilt strikes me despite the unquestionable menace of the form before me.

I let the flare gun fall from my hand. It clatters to the ground, a tendril of smoke still drifting up from the barrel. I hold up both my hands, blood pouring freely from my ruined knuckles. I wait for the flare to burst like the one I'd launched over the camp in the night. I wait for bright red light to explode from the creature's torso, for it to thrust about in agony as its insides burn. For a moment, I believe it awaits the same. I'm oddly relieved when we are both proved wrong.

I push myself standing and inch toward the Botany door. I become aware of how difficult it is to breathe. The fumes in the air are stifling me. I taste blood. My lungs don't want to expand. I don't know if the flare was a dud or somehow this Jones-thing simply consumed it. Its eyes track my movement thoughtfully. Does it understand?

"Jones?" I rasp. "Are you in there?"

Some of its eyes blink. I don't know if that is supposed to indicate recognition. All I know is that it hasn't killed me yet.

"I don't know what's happening to you," I say. "But something they made here is changing you."

I don't particularly have a reason to keep talking other than it hasn't killed me while I'm talking, so I hope that if I continue talking, it will continue not killing me. Its radial talons flex on the debris it clutches under its massive feet. Sinews and tendons all over its body twitch, tighten, relax. Bile rises in my throat as my esophagus convulses at my next breath.

"I don't know what you're changing into, but I'm sorry that you're changing," I say. It takes all my will to keep my voice clear, my pace of delivery even. I can't alarm it. "I'm sorry that I can't do anything to help you."

I don't want to look over my shoulder, don't want to let Jones know my only real focus is on the exit. My entire respiratory system is now on fire.

"I'm sorry that we were sent here to die," I say, my voice rasping like I'd raked my larynx with hot coals. "And I'm sorry that I agreed to lead us to our death."

My good hand finds my pocket. There is something heavy in my coat pocket. I throw up into my mouth. Stomach acid dribbles between my lips even as I struggle to swallow it back down.

Several more orbs of flesh tumble off Jones's shoulders. The ones that fell first have grown a bundle of spindly limbs that are setting about the work of cleaning the membranes off themselves. One of them raises itself up on four of its legs and wobbles. It tries to take a step.

My hand closes around a hard orb. My finger finds a ring sticking off one of its ends. Slides through the ring. I close my palm around a protruding handle. I try to speak but this time a mouthful of bloody acid lurches from my mouth before I can stop it.

Jones straightens. Rolls its four shoulders. A wet tearing sound wrenches from the thing's body and its shoulders fan forward as if the invisible line down the center of its chest is a hinge. The twin mouths bend so that they're side by side facing me, opening and closing, their teeth twisting and wriggling in their gums, dripping saliva. The spurs at all its joints ooze the same viscous fluid as before in bursts like a broken faucet.

The ring slides from the housing and I feel a spring tension. The only thing holding the striker lever in place is my hand. I step backward, almost into the doorway.

The grating breaks beneath my feet where the oozing fluid has eaten into it. The striker lever pops away from the grenade inside my pocket as I collapse to the floor. The Jones-creature lurches forward, but the floor, damaged by its own excretions during our standoff, collapses too.

Frantic, I grip the grenade and jerk my hand. The metal catches in the fabric. I tug frantically for a split second, but then force myself to relax. Ease my hand forward then back.

The grenade clears the pocket's mouth. With a flick of my wrist, I lob it toward Jones. Then, I thrust my hands down despite the agony from my ruined fingers and lurch myself to my feet. The floor breaks further as I careen into the hallway toward Botany. I slam my good hand against a button on a control panel on the other side, praying it will bring down the door.

It does.

A slab of metal grinds down between me and the flailing form of the Jones-beast.

Then, the hall shakes at a thundering reverberation that throws me onto my side. I land on my devastated hand. Something of my mind leaves myself. I think I belt out a scream, but I don't really know for sure. It could be someone who shares my body screaming.

* * *

My voice simply stops working before I stop trying to scream, and I throw up repeatedly. My eyes are a blurry mess of tears and some sort of oozing pus. Everything inside me feels like it is on fire. I want nothing more than to collapse into a deep sleep. I don't know that I have strength for anything more. I feel my chest rise and fall as if in ragged breath, but I don't feel like I'm getting any air. Is that why I'm dizzy or is it my loss of blood? I need to focus.

I turn on my radio.

"Efta?" I croak in a voice I don't even recognize as my own.

Silence.

"Efta, please," I say. I don't know what pours from my eyes, but I'd like to think it is tears. The liquid blurs my vision and tints it orange.

I pat along my pockets and pull out a canvas bundle marked with a red cross.

"Can anyone hear me?"

It's tricky to open the med kit one handed, but I manage with the help of my teeth. Something is wrong with my face too, something that also happened with the misfire. I feel it as I bite down. I want to touch the side of my head, but I'm afraid of what I will find.

Something crackles over the radio. There is a hum in the signal, like when a cable is improperly connected to a speaker.

I focus on finding a bandage and gauze. The plastic sealing the gauze tears under the grip of my molars. I try not to look at the stumps as they disappear under the gauze pad and then the layers of wrap.

The hum rises and falls. It's almost melodic, but the notes are arbitrary. Underneath, some sort of clicking chatter, like wasps chewing behind a wall in an otherwise silent room.

I wrap my hand as tightly as I can no matter how much it hurts, though I'm surprised at how little blood is pouring from the wound. The gauze soaks red quickly, but it does not grow sopping before it's gone altogether.

The field cocktail syringe is cold between my fingers. Capped in plastic which I also pull off with my teeth. Funny how your mouth is like an inverted hand. I giggle at the thought, and giggling sends my chest into convulsion. Deep as I expand my lungs, it still feels like I'm sucking vacuum. Something pools at the back of my throat, and I gag violently. I nearly drop the syringe in a nasty convulsion.

I inject the cocktail into my stomach muscles because I don't know if I can manage to expose any other part of my skin other than my neck and head, and I do not know if it would be wise to inject myself there.

The rush is like being caught in a river current and then entering an eddy at speed. Suddenly, everything feels far enough away that the pain isn't as relevant, but my thoughts are significantly more present.

I sit up. I know that the sudden rush of energy is artificial and very temporary, so I push myself standing as fast as I can manage despite a massive wave of vertigo that threatens to topple me before I'm even halfway up. I press my good palm to the wall and take stock of my surroundings.

I'm in a hallway with several doors on either side. The walls are three feet of metal, three feet of glass. Though only the track lights function, it is clear that behind the glass on either side is some sort of greenhouse laboratory. The rooms are filled with vertical racks covered in botanical specimen chambers and tables lined up side by side with more chambers and incubators. Much of the glass is broken or cracked, but all through the rooms on either side grow things that on first impression remind me of plants: ferns, cacti, dwarf trees, young bushes, flowers, and even vegetables.

However, as I totter closer to the glass, their edges are all wrong, and I realize they are all composed of fine crystals. The crystals here are much like the crystals that coated the stairwell under the disciplinary hall except that here, they haven't coated anything. The stone hasn't grown over metal and sprouted the lattices. Instead, the entire plant does not seem to be a plant at all but rather crystals grown in the shape of a plant.

I also note that crystalline roots have spread from the base of the crystal plants and embedded into the surfaces beneath. I cannot tell from this angle whether or not the crystal tunneled into the table or simply converted channels of table into crystal. A cluster of crystalline fungi catches my eye just as the fungi unfurl their vents and release an almost invisible cloud of spores.

I do not believe that I will be opening any of these doors. It is a miracle that neither the quakes nor the explosion broke the glass.

Cradling my damaged hand to my chest, I limp my way toward the far end of the hall. My vision is too damaged from the fumes released by Jones's toxins, but I know there is a door at the end.

"Varka," Efta's voice whispers. "Where are you?"

"I'm moving," I say. "Underground still."

"I need your help," Efta whispers. "Something is here. Right outside the mess. Can you get here?"

"I lost two fingers," I say. "Might bleed to death."

My ankle ceases for a split second to hold any weight, and I slump against the wall. On the other side of the glass, the crystal plants sway in unison as if swept in a strong gale.

"I'm seeing some really messed up shit in here, Efta."

"I'm unarmed, Varka," Efta says. "If they find me—"

I throw up a river of green bile. It sluices into the grating and vanishes from my awareness. So much the better.

"I'm not sure I can do a whole lot if I can get to you," I say, but I don't like to hear myself say it. The door is just ahead. I can force myself forward. Efta is the only person I have not managed to fail. I shuffle one foot forward, then another.

I'm almost there. Almost to the door, and then, maybe stairs up? Maybe another hall? More labs? A room full of creatures like Jones? Like the living Fresnel lens? Perhaps the worst would be welcome. My body might not withstand the climb to the surface.

A thud behind me reverberates strong enough I feel it through my boots even with the cocktail buzzing through my system. I look back just in time to see the door to the central hub shiver as a second blow strikes it. Is it Jones? The things that were falling off him? Something else entirely? Can it smash its way through that steel door? I can only assume the blast must have damaged it so that it can't open. Thank God for small favors.

I shuffle the last few steps to the door. The control panel blurs and doubles in my vision. I try to press the central button but miss it by inches. I'm not even sure the panel is in the spot I think it is in, but I plant my thumb against metal again and again.

Behind me, a crash with stunning volume and force. My teeth hurt from the impact of the vibrations. Something agonizing cries from the door. It cannot withstand long what struck it.

Again, I try to hit the button, this time slapping my whole palm on the panel, hoping to trigger something. Anything.

Something whirs in the door, and it shoots straight up.

Immediately, I sob, and the sob causes me to retch.

In front of me is a long staircase down.

* * *

Another deafening blow sounds behind me. Something that sounds like a fracture in a frozen pond follows. I look back over my shoulder, though it hurts terribly to twist my head that far for reasons I don't quite understand. A zigzagging, white crack runs from one end of the botany glass to the other, skipping only the doors. Another blow or two and that glass will shatter. I lift my foot to take the first step, but my depth perception distorts. One moment the step seems a couple centimeters below my foot, the next its half a meter. My inner ear tells me that if I try to shift my weight forward, I'll simply tumble face first down the flight.

I press my good hand against the wall. It's good to feel something hard and rigid under my palm. Something that doesn't yield. I feel like I can count on it. Though my ankles don't seem to want to flex right. I slide off the edge of the top step more than I step down to the next. I take the next step the same way. Though I don't hit any switches, the hallways lights attempt to illuminate. The door shuts behind me, again of its own accord.

Another blow from the far end of the botany hall.

"Who is calling?" I ask. Or I think to say it. I'm not really sure. With a wild flick of my wrist, I say: "Efta, see who's at the door."

Then, I laugh. It hurts so bad to laugh, but I laugh, leaning my shoulder into the wall, rolling my feet down step after step.

I take a few more steps before the next blow. The glass shatters with a raucous crash. Thankfully it's really far away. It's funny because it's as if glass continues falling in the hallway. There, another piece.

The radio comes alive again, but I don't know in what language Efta's voice speaks. From the outer provinces, I'm thinking, maybe one of the remote dialects. Something is wrong with my hearing too, I think. Maybe it's still damaged from when Yost fired in the stairwell. Or the misfire. There's something wrong with my face after all.

I reach up to adjust the radio earpiece. My hand misses my ear altogether.

I try again, this time slower.

I don't miss my ear. My ear isn't there. Neither is the hair on that side of my head. My finger brushes my burned scalp.

If there is no ear, there is no earpiece.

"Varka, where the hell are you?" Efta whispers. "Are you almost here?"

Metal cries from up the stairs and down the hall in a way I've not yet heard. I don't know what the sound indicates, but I'm no longer certain what is or is not real. I pull out the remains of my med kit. My fingers feel fat and massive, but I manage to get a second syringe out even as the rest of the kit falls to the stairs. My vision is blurry, but I'm pretty sure I make out the field symbol for a stimulant.

I don't know what this second injection will do on top of the cocktail I already took, but if I don't do something to bring myself into focus, I don't know how I'll ever get to Efta in time.

I plunge the second dose into my stomach and lean against

the wall. I take a deep breath. Time seems to slow. At the bottom of the stairs, a short corridor ends in another door. In good shape, I'd be there in seconds, but now it seems impossibly far.

A new reverberation, more violent and distressed than any other so far, snaps through the structure around me, into my joints, my bones, like a thunderclap.

Something swipes from my mind like steam wiped from a mirror. I become immediately aware of my missing fingers, of the distant, searing pain on the side of my head where my ear was. The pain is not overwhelming because of the opiates in the initial cocktail, but rather it helps return me to reality. I don't know how much of what has happened since the Kalashnikov's misfire has been real, nor do I even know if that was the point where my experience began to diverge with actual events.

What I do know is that the bottom of the stairs is only a few steps away and the door out of the stairwell is only a few steps further than that. I complete the descent and arrive at the next door. This one has its own key panel like the one into the central laboratory hub, and the warden's code works here as well. The door opens to a long hall.

I limp down it, cradling my forearm to my chest. The lights flicker around me. They're all white metal, featuring only a handful of doors and nameplates. I appear to be passing through offices that belong to doctors and officers. It is tempting to search them. If anywhere will hold clear explanations of what they were working on here, this will be the place.

However, I am in no shape to do so. If I don't find Efta soon and have not departed for some place that may offer medical intervention, I will die. Then, it will not matter how well I understand what killed me because I'll just be dead.

I keep my eyes fixed straight ahead. The door at the end of the hall becomes a singular focus, the only thing in my world. I try to block out the ramifications of the fact that I've been holding imaginary conversations with Efta and that I have no idea if she even survived the quake. Is Brogden dead?

I shake my head. I can't think about this. Those are thoughts for the surface. For when I am in a world of which they are a part. Here in these tunnels, I'm in a world that belongs to something else, that belongs to Jones and whatever else lives that is like him.

I hesitate.

What if I shouldn't leave? What if I do belong here now? Tompka had told me that we were all compromised. Can I believe myself safe to return to civilized areas?

I look back the way I've come. What if I return up the stairs and open the door to the botany labs? Just take a deep breath, give myself over? Is Jones unhappy as he is? Am I being presumptive that whatever is changing this place is something to be avoided?

I shake my head again.

The door is ahead. It is near. I must reach it. Just one step at a time. It occurs to me that the battering on the door to the central laboratory hub seems to have ceased. Did Jones break through or give up? A minor tremor in the floor reminds me that I cannot count on stillness to mean safety, but a doubt gnaws at the back of my mind that I'm in any danger at all.

The tremor does not subside. It feels like I'm standing at a station and the train is speeding by. The memory of my mother on the train holding my hand as we talked about the smell of animals returns. The memory of descending into the belly of the mountain. Of staring through the window into the blackness of the rocky throat of the earth.

The walls here are white but they are no less a dead template. It is arguable that white is more violent than black because the darkness does not overwhelm, it does not close your pupils with its presence. It invites you to open yourself to it, to dilate and let it rush in.

I want to press against the wall even as I pass it by, the way I passed the walls of the tunnel in the dark. The rumble does not stop. It grows slow, steady, the way a basin of water heats slow as boiling water pipes into its bottom. The door ahead has a plate in the middle. The letters are out of focus. They will tell me where it leads. What level of hope I have.

I need something to write itself onto me.

When I reach the door, I know that no beautiful orchard awaits on the other side, but whatever is beyond feels like it must be paradise.

The door reads: "Emergency Exit."

The rumble grows and my legs wobble. I must brace myself against the wall, and several seams between the wall panels down the hall twist and wrench apart.

The door has a simple push latch in its handle. I press it. It opens.

The world turns into sound and light.

CHAPTER 22

PIPE, BLOCKED LIGHT, BLUFF

The klaxon pierces my good ear. I don't know from where it originates. I half wonder if it originates inside me. I would be convinced of such if I did not feel it through my feet and my palms as well. It even vibrates in the stump of my severed fingers. Had I not taken such strong pain killers, no doubt the sensation would be agonizing. Now, it's a distant flare of throb.

The lights attempt to strobe in sync with the klaxon, but they are far too degraded. Only a handful of segments achieve a peak intensity while most simply go dark after a dull to moderate flicker. Everything light and reflection of light takes on a fuzzy, haloed quality.

Ahead, the short tunnel terminates in an ascending ladder.

The rumble returns as a fresh quake takes hold of the passage behind me in a crushing grip. The metal walls collapse with a grind like a tin can in a vice. The torque lifts the grating under my feet several uneven centimeters, and I stumble a step to maintain my balance.

I reach the ladder. It extends up into the darkness and vanishes. Unlike the corridors of the facility, there are no running lights in the corners. Just a straight shot up into a black pipe. I take one last look at the collapsed hallway behind me. The jagged rocks have crushed in like molars. However, it seems likely that were we below sea-level the tunnel would have flooded. Perhaps this facility was carved into solid rock, but I would rather believe I'm above sea level. That would mean I have less than a hundred meters to climb. I don't remember the building regulations, but I think that would mean no more than five hundred rungs.

I examine the ruin of my hand. I don't know if I can make this climb. Between the physical damage to my hand, the exhaustion from the ordeal, and blood loss, I really just want to sit down and drift into sleep. I realize how thirsty I am. Though the painkillers and stimulants are dulling my appetite, no doubt I'm severely calorie deficient. Efta has our food. Will I ever have a chance to eat again? To taste water?

The throat through which I'd just passed won't be letting anything through it, and I don't want this space to chew me up in the next quake, so I take hold of the first rung with my good hand. I don't know that I'll be able to actually grip, but I can simply take things one move at a time and do the bulk of the work with my legs. The pipe is narrow enough that I might even be able to rest slightly by pressing my back against the back of the passage.

Of course, it's also narrow enough that it could collapse while I'm climbing and crush me into pulp and liquid. Unfortunately, the bulbs of both penlights Efta gave me are broken. I drop them to the floor. The tunnel and the darkness are the only way out, so away I go.

I regret the decision by the twentieth rung. My muscles hate me. My whole body is in a state of fatigue beyond anything I've ever experienced. A tremor buzzes my teeth. Bolts rattle in the ladder at the joints where it meets the wall. Some have sheered where they enter into their sockets. The previous quakes have done damage. No question the forthcoming will do more.

I keep climbing. I try to speed up but find myself moving the exact same speed. I can't see the rungs anymore. Rather, I can and I can't at the same time. Visibility has dropped below the point where it can confirm the reality before it. I reach for what I believe to a be the next rung, and my hand finds nothing but air. I grab blindly with my damaged hand.

A roar of pain dazzles my senses as my hand strikes the pipe wall, but my arm also happens to come down on a rung. I let my elbow hook it. Waves of ache ride my bones and muscles from wrist to shoulder despite the painkillers. I hiss over and over between my teeth. My breathing verges on hyperventilation, and my temples pulse.

Gradually, it all subsides. My heart rate remains elevated, however, in a nasty combination of the exertion, the stimulants, the exhaustion, the pain, and the lack of sustenance. I worry that I might cause some sort of stroke or embolism.

Nonetheless, once I feel I've gathered myself enough, I resume my climb. Rung after rung, I pass through darkness feeling for every next grip. Now, I am the train in the darkness, something inside me looking out the glass. How much further? Is the pipe crushed above, the ladder vanishing into a medley of rock and mineral? Or will I find some sort of sealed barrier? Tears of anxiety burst in my eyes and run down my cheeks. I try to think of anything – my mother, the orchard, of my father or my childhood. I think of Efta and Yost, of Brogden shooting Tompka. I try to remember the faces of the technicians before the island took them and fail, try to picture Mikael in any way other than having his tongue ripped out, and fail.

Rung after rung. I try to recall the day I interviewed to join the Bureau. I was a shoo-in, of course, or so I thought at the time. I'd been unaware that my father's name was not a ticket through the door, but they'd seemed fine to let me think so. I was a good candidate – young, idealistic, self-sufficient, but not enough that I knew life where one bad turn wouldn't let it crash and burn. They let me keep the orchard, let me stay there on my longer breaks. Let my mom live there. Had Brogden been lying when he said she was still well-regarded in some circles, or had they been content to look the other way so long as I served their ends?

I pause a moment to take slow breaths and suppress a growing giddiness. I feel something hot running down my lip. I sniff and blood runs down the back of my throat. Not a good sign.

Still, I keep climbing. One rung at a time. Keep the weight on my legs, not my arm. I take a moment to rest, pressing my shoulders against the back wall of the shaft, but my throat and mouth are paper dry. My head hurts. I realize that my lower back is running with sweat. My armpits and the backs of my knees are sopping too.

I look up and strain into the darkness. Is there an exit anywhere up there? What if the climb just continues on and on? My arm is shaking. Striking my hand against the shaft wall also appears to have broken open the wound. The bandage has soaked through, and a slow trickle runs down my wrist. Whenever my hand points downward, no doubt the drops fall down past my feet and streak the wall of the pipe.

Below, the darkness is complete. I see no sign of the glow at the shaft's bottom.

Have the lights in the corridor gone out? There was certainly enough damage that I can believe that.

However, something in my gut tells me that the light is still lit. The pipe is just blocked.

Something is climbing beneath me.

* * *

I take a deep breath and carefully hook my elbow behind a rung. With my good hand, I fumble around in my pockets. My hand brushes past the remaining grenades through the outside of the pocket. If I were to drop one now, the concussion would probably liquify my innards.

In another pocket, my hand closes on a pack of cigarettes.

Another. Below them both, a lighter. I take out a pack of cigarettes and unwrap them. I pull one of the sticks out of the box and place it between my lips. With a spark of flint, the flame lights, and the paper burns. I hold the lighter up. The light from the flame doesn't reach far enough for me to see my destination.

Then, I look down and drop the cigarette between my legs. The ember wobbles as it falls. Five meters. Ten. Then a burst of sparks. Did it hit the wall or the blockage? Fifteen meters? Twenty maybe?

For just a moment, I listen into the darkness. I feel like I should be hearing something. Something squelching or grinding or growling. Every movement I make, every scrape of the fabric of my clothes, echoes in this damn pipe, but below – nothing.

My gaze still fixed below, I reach for the next rung. The pain rings me like a gong. I reached with the wrong hand and jammed the finger stumps against the rung. By reflex my good hand snaps toward the pain. A moment of weightlessness overtakes me as my mass shifts backward. As my good hand continues its flight to grab my wrist as if it can choke off the pain signals, I thrust back with my legs and bash my shoulders hard into the back of the pipe. The impact knocks the wind out of me, but I manage to fight the urge to try to curl inward.

My next breath sounds like I've surfaced from two full minutes under water, but I manage to exhale it with a wavering bellow.

Something flutters the air around me. A chill wraps my skin as the air draws past. Whatever is below has drawn a breath. I know it.

Despite the fact that the pain has my entire body buzzing, I grab the rung with my good hand and pull myself to the next rung. Why hasn't it rushed up toward me from beneath?

"What the hell are you waiting for?" I croak.

My fingers tremble on the ladder. The muscles feel loose. I can't keep up this climb much longer. Is it waiting for my strength to give out so that I just tumble down the shaft? If it comes to that, I'll just pull the pins on the grenades.

"I'm not going to stop," I whisper as I take another step up. My quadriceps shake like they've got palsy. Muscles in my lower back and around my ribs spasm. My body feels suddenly heavy. Like my energy is converting to mass and gravity is increasing.

One step up. Reach. Pull. One step up. Has it gotten closer? Did I just hear a breath? A slight tremor buzzes. Dust and scattered pebbles fall around me, spattering my face with painful little stings. There is no question that I'm not being chased. I'm being stalked. Whatever it is, it's biding its time.

Another few rungs as the tremor intensifies into a rumble. The concern of collapse returns. How far have I come? How far to go? It's hard not to feel like maybe the ladder is getting longer or perhaps it is descending at the exact rate I'm climbing. I reach again – and my hand hits something solid with a jolt. I pat the ceiling my palm. The surface is convex with a round protrusion in the middle. A wheel. No, the handle of a hatch.

I look down below, but of course I see nothing but pulsing colors as my mind attempts to assert some sort of stimulus onto the nothing. I can't even see my own body. If I couldn't feel my feet on the rungs, I'd not even be sure they were there.

I grip the handle and twist. It doesn't budge. Is it locked? Wedged? Rusted?

I adjust my grip and try again. No movement.

This time, I take my feet up another rung and press my shoulder into the pipe wall to increase my leverage. I strain as hard as I can. Did it move? A drip falls onto my face. I have no idea from what. I strain again. This time, I'm certain it moves but my grip fails, and I must draw a deep gasp. I don't think I can open it with one arm.

I slowly raise my damaged hand. I don't want to try. It's going to hurt. A lot. I remember banging the stumps just moments ago. My body revolts at the thought of going through that again. I try to look down. I want to climb down. There is something below me, but I want to climb down.

My breath comes in ragged pants. I'm hyperventilating. I force myself to slow, so I don't pass out. Whatever is below hasn't attacked. Hasn't reached up from the darkness and taken hold of my feet. It hasn't growled or gnashed any teeth.

Maybe I can just stay where I am.

I close my eyes and grit my teeth. I flex my remaining fingers.

Then, I take hold of the wheel. The agony is immediate and obliterates my awareness of reality. It's like I am the pain that throbs down my arm in searing waves. I feel my consciousness attempting to slip away. I jam my legs to the rung, my shoulder to the wall, and twist.

The wheel gives with a piercing cry. I cry out along with it. I give it a full half turn before I release it. Blood sprays away from the soaked bandages onto my face and chest and down into the darkness. I grab the handle again, this time with just my good hand and twist. Another half turn. Another half-turn. Each one chokes on its rust and cries like a burnt child.

Then, the wheel spins loose. I shove up hard.

Sunlight pours onto me from a crystal blue sky. Something beneath me gives an inhuman shriek like nothing I've ever heard. I look down in time to register something dropping from view, leaving behind nothing but a cloud of smoke or steam.

I want to try to find some sign of what I'd just escaped, but I see nothing and have no time to linger. I pull myself out of the pipe and find myself emerging from a hatch concealed in a hollow among several large rocks. I pull my legs out of the tube and immediately slam the hatch shut behind me. I have no way to lock it.

Fortunately, it is hard to believe that whatever was below me would not have come up already if it could. So, I lay on my back across the hatch while my muscles ache and twitch and the stumps of my severed fingers sear with pain.

Above, a sky blue like I've never seen. Where is the haze? The clouds? A weaver didn't have dyes so vibrant. It's like a painting of the sky from old books stretched from horizon to horizon. Is this the result of whatever Yost did? Is this what this place was meant for? I feel like I could die staring into its endless sapphire. What would my mother think? My father?

Tears run from my eyes over the burns on my cheeks. The salt stings, of course, but what a small price to pay for this. I don't know how long I just lay there in an exhausted daze, but I can't imagine wanting my eyes to take in anything else.

I realize there is a spot in the sky my eyes just won't look. It hurts too much to even try. It's the sun. How had people lived underneath this for so many generations? How had they survived it being taken?

Then, a strange trilling draws my attention away from the sky. Maybe it's new, maybe it's been there the whole time.

Careful not to raise my head too high in case something is watching, I peek over the edge of the rocks at the warehouse ahead. Or, what's left of the warehouse. The front half of the structure has collapsed into a massive sinkhole. On the other side of the hole, the mess is still intact. If Efta really is hiding inside the *Sarru*, she might still be safe – but I also remember that my conversation with her was entirely imaginary. Perhaps I invented that from my memory of the journal I'd found in the *Sarru's* cabin.

To my left, the plateau drops off, and I am looking across the cove. On the far side, the beach. The remains of our camp. The abandoned barracks. At least all the snow is gone. The clear sky has already raised the temperature by several degrees. How much warmer would things be?

The rocks that conceal the recess where I am crouched are high enough that they obstruct my vision to what lies in my immediate vicinity, but I grow increasingly aware of a shuffling sound mixed with more odd trills. I raise a little higher so I can see a bit closer to the base of the rock formation. The hatch from the laboratory has deposited me square in the middle of the flock of monstrous birds.

* * *

There are hundreds of them, all jostling and cramming against each other. The smell hits me first. Sweet and musty. Like a chicken coop. The overtones immediately thrust my mind back to that train car, back to my mother. But underneath, there is something vile. Something dead. Unlike before where the only birds I saw on the plateau from a distance were the deformed stragglers, now they comingle with the healthy in a heaving swarm like ducks crowded by a pond. Even then, it only takes moments to pick out the misshapen ones. The ones with two heads. Three. Two heads dead, one head alive. One head dead, one head alive.

There, a single wing grows out of the crux where shoulders and neck meet.

There, legs dangle helplessly from one's lower back.

All throughout the flock, mounds of flesh bulge on various different birds. Tumors? Cysts? Bone spurs? Even the ones I'd thought healthy suffer from all manner of issue. Bald patches where their feathers have fallen out. One with scraggly tufts of hair jutting out among its feathers. Another where its entire body seems to simply sag off its frame like a wet sheet thrown over a drying rack.

Had they been this diseased when they'd struck our camp? When they struck the jellyfish bloom? The smell of sweet decay grows the more I breathe it in. How many of them have rotting parts hanging from their frame? I see putrid boils oozing under unkempt feather bristles at the joints where wings meet torso. One of them excretes something brown and waxy from its anus and falls over sideways. Another one pecks the face of the one beside it until the beak comes off. The victim does not protest. It simply stares up at the sky. At least three quarters of them do.

Their eyes are all dead black beads that could decorate someone's shirt. Whatever level their misery, they seem accustomed. How can life like this happen? I feel like the universe should just collapse inward at this spot and leave them all crushed as some sort of existential mercy. What are they watching for?

I want to be scared of them after what they did to Mikael, but I simply loathe them, pity them. No doubt they are the direct offspring of this place. Whatever the Bureau or their predecessors had done here made them the abominations they are. That is not something I can condone or accept. My mother moved me out to the countryside, to the orchard. She did not move me far enough. I have to guess that they'd seen more than I had. What was their breaking point? Why would mom ever stop running?

A few of the birds seem vaguely aware of me, but they don't seem interested. Instead, the flock as a whole seems to mostly be pressing to each other, perhaps for warmth, with a few grooming themselves or others. Again, one draws blood from another, and I watch as it pulls, from somewhere underneath its skin, some sort of long, parasitical worm. The image of Mikael's tongue being swallowed immediately resurfaces, and I gag a bubble of blood up to the back of my throat.

I take another look at the sky. It is both soothing and terrifying. The color sends shivers of pleasure down my spine, but I also feel strangely vulnerable. I'd not realized how comfortable the perpetual haze had been, the way it seemed to hold the sky to the earth. At night, when the stars were blurs through the suspended particulate, it made them feel more there, closer, more substantial.

Now, the earth seems stripped of her clothes from the bombardment of the cosmos. Her cloak burned away.

It is then I realize why the birds watch the sky. They used the haze to hunt, to hide. What if they already know that this might mean the starvation of their whole colony? How long until starvation drives them mad? What if they are growing hungry already?

I pull myself so I can look right to the base of the rocks around me. The birds don't press right up to it, but I'd have to physically push my way through them in order to get clear of the flock. I don't know that I could imagine a better way to increase the odds that they'll turn on me.

I return my focus back to the mess. I need to find a shelter the birds can't penetrate easily until I can figure out how to get myself off the island. The smuggler's boat is anchored offshore, but I know I couldn't make it there without help in my condition. Perhaps if I can sustain myself until my hand has sufficiently healed, I could build myself a raft and paddle myself out to the craft. The mess has food, and I feel I owe it to Efta to check for her there.

Also, I recall the account in the captain's log of the first mate's final shelter in the *Sarru*. While it is clear that they failed to protect themselves, I actually prefer the thought of holing up in something not from this place. Somehow, everywhere else here feels too corrupted.

Unfortunately, there is a bit of ground between me and there.

I reach into my pocket and pull out the remaining grenades. There are more on the *Sarru*, so I can use them both without worry. I don't allow myself time to second guess myself. I pull the pins, let the housing pop away and lob them both over the rocks into the flock.

I duck, curl up in the fetal position as tightly as my battered body will allow, and cover my head with my arms.

The blast is deafening. Pebbles, rocks, dirt, meat, and chunks of bone sail up into the sky and then fan out like a blossom before cascading back down to the earth. Grit stings my cheeks. Stones strike my shoulders and side. One of them gashes open my cheek, another leaves a savage scratch down the back of my already devastated hand. Innards splatter everything. Wet. Stringy. Pink.

And I'd thought the smell was worst when it just came off their bodies.

Immediately, I rise. The birds on the peninsula stare at me as if they're all sharing the same mind, but the flock between me and the mess has been reduced to heaps of quivering, smoking pulp.

Planting my good hand on the rocks, I swing my legs over and land on my feet. A shock of pain runs up my shins, but nothing gives, so I break into an awkward run, barely aware that I flail my arms as I do so, that my head bobs on my neck like a turkey.

Then, a fresh quake seizes the island. I tumble face-forward. I fling my arm out sideways to try and prevent my stumps from striking the ground and let the rest of my body go limp. I flop to the ground and roll like a doll. Despite my best efforts, my hand hits twice. Each time turns my entire world white, and my body seems to vanish in a slamming gate of pain.

Then, my momentum ceases but my motion seems to continue as the earth roils underneath me. I crane my head sideways and see Efta emerging from the mess toward me at a full run. Behind her, a fracture in the plateau widens like the island has grown its own mouth and is now settling into a waking yawn.

CHAPTER 23

ARRAY, THE WALKING SUN, HORIZON

When I sit up, my eyes fill with pulsing blotches of light. Everything is a blur, and the world around me is brilliant. I remind myself that the snow is gone and that the sky is a brighter blue than anything I've ever seen. A radiant heat presses upon my entire body like the peak of summer. Sweat runs down my forehead and cheeks, down my spine.

A fresh rumble shakes the island. Geysers burst across the plateau. Stones break off and fall down the fissure widening across the plateau's center, rifting where I am away from the administrative buildings.

Efta arrives in front of me, skids to a stop. She wears Brogden's coil of rope diagonally across her body. She is reaching toward me even as she recoils at what she sees. Immediately, her fingers snap back to her chest and knead her burn scars. No doubt I must look like hell.

"Can you walk?" she asks.

I nod and blink.

"The sky is blue," Efta weeps, pointing. "Gott in Himmel, the sky is so blue."

I shield my eyes and look into the brilliant blue field above us.

There is a place I'm unable to gaze toward because it is so intense it's like daggers are thrust into my eyes.

"I did not know what blue really is," I say. It is difficult to focus on anything for more than a couple moments. Everything around us too has taken on a radiance my mind is unprepared to process. The nuances of the grays and browns and blacks are stunning excess.

The whole of the sky isn't quite clear yet, but rather a massive ring of clearness in the haze gradually expands in all directions. How far will it spread? How is it happening? What did the island release?

"Was this our mission?" I ask.

I turn my back to it because only in the company of my shadows can I keep my eyes open without pain. I never knew that seeing such light would be so hard.

"I don't know," Efta says. "Maybe Yost knew?"

Smoke rises from the fissure. In fact, the entire plateau has begun to fount tiny geysers of smoke.

The tremors intensify. All across the plateau, the ground seems to undulate and pulse. The walls of the offices collapse, and the roof comes down in a heap on top of them. The disciplinary hall simply seems to sink in on itself. The ground surges under my own feet, and it's all I can do to keep standing.

"If we don't go now, I don't think we ever will," Efta says.

Yet, for one more heartbeat I hesitate. If we linger, I have no doubt that we will die, but part of me wants to see the chain of events through to the end. I don't know if I'm watching something cataclysmic or some sort of birth.

Spikes of rock thrust up from the earth like giant talons clawing at the air. Every step feels like it's going to throw me to the ground or like the ground will rise up beneath me, or like it won't be there at all when my foot lands. Two more fissures open, one on each side of the first crack, and the first crack widens further meter after meter. Stone pillars thrust up along its edges like the island is growing fangs.

We get to the edge of the chasm where the front half of the warehouse stood. I chance a glance down as we run along its edge. The pit looks like some massive excavation. Broken walls of reinforced concrete reveal a vague floor plan, but whole swatches of the human construction are outright missing. Beneath it, the rocks themselves glisten and pulsate like flesh. As the tremors deepen and grow more violent, we curve away from the edge to make sure we can't accidentally fall in.

The peak of the bluff where the radio array once stood comes into focus. Now, all that is left is a melted slag heap, but it gives us as good a destination as any to try to spot the Clove and Hitch from. We're hardly fifty meters away, and for the first time since Yost and I returned to camp with the raft it feels realistic that we might make it off the island.

A devastating crash erupts from the middle of the island that pitches me face-forward onto the ground, unsure if I was knocked over by a fresh tremor or the shockwave from the noise.

I roll onto my back and feel my eyes widen as they take in what is happening.

A massive pillar of living stone has burst up from the fissure and towers at least a hundred meters above the island. It's at least ten meters across and buds of rock swell all over its mass. I feel like it had to be something coiled up in the center of the island's stone foundation waiting to be free. Had I somehow alerted it with the grenade detonation, or had it simply reached some sort of breaking point?

Some of the rock buds elongate rapidly into something resembling tentacles while others sharpen and taper into barbs and spines. Great eyes shining with green light open up all over it, blinking heavy stone lids. It crackles and groans. Patches of flame all over its surface ignite, throwing off its own shroud of black smoke.

Then, I'm on my feet and practically throwing Efta onto hers. We stagger and weave as the ground cracks around our feet and stone outcroppings break the surface. I feel like a flea on a dog's back trying to dodge the animal's snapping teeth.

The living pillar sways, casting a sweeping shadow across us. The whole of the island surges with it as if the island wants to wrench itself from the ground. I don't look back as further thunderclaps erupt from the plateau behind us.

Efta and I reach the radio remains. The metal has all melted, but knobs jut off the slumped structure to which Efta ties off the rope before she throws the rest of the bundle over the edge.

Below, it unfurls two-thirds of the way toward the rocky beach until a tangle in its length leaves the rest of it a dangling ball. We will simply have to deal with that when we get there.

"There's more of them," Efta says breathlessly. I don't bother glancing back. Multiple enormous shadows swing across us and tell me all I need to know as Efta attaches a handle-like device to the rope. "Do you think you can hold onto this until the bottom?"

I nod. I don't really know if I can, but I don't really have a choice but to try.

I scan the ground below. The rocks underneath us give way to a dirt-covered beach lined with hundreds of graves. The stones are all simple markers, many of which have broken or fallen over. A retaining wall was built along the waterline to prevent the graves from eroding, but a portion of it has broken and has spilled a delta of erosion into the divot.

Despite the chaos I feel behind me, I keep my focus off the island. I do not see a boat, and the sun glistening off the waters pierces my eyes and hurts my head.

I take hold of the descender and carefully step so that my feet plant against the cliff. My fingers immediately want to give under my weight, but I squeeze the device. I slide down a half a meter, stepping my feet down the stone face. I move in stops and starts even as Efta attaches her own device. She should, of course, wait for me to be off the rope, but I don't think this is the time to think heavily about safety protocols.

Somewhere out of sight, things shatter and break. What sounds like an avalanche into the warehouse cavern churns like an endless peal of thunder. Things bash and burst. Pebbles spray us from above.

The side of the cliff has eroded away, so for much of the descent I dangle suspended in open air by one arm as the device lowers me a half-meter at a time. Efta hangs on with both hands and, oh how I envy her. The tremors that wrack the whole island cause us to sway side to side a little and the rope vibrates a bit like a plucked guitar string. I imagine that my hand and the device are the same thing. That tired as my hand is, I can't let go. Somehow that seems to work.

I chance an outward glance. From here, the whole of the bluff blocks the sun, so I'm able to see the pure blue above the island in all its glory. It's like a dome made of some precious gem or rich silk covers the entire world. No matter what follows, for this view I am grateful.

Then, above my hands, up the rope, the edge of the bluff takes on a shimmering quality. An iridescent white light reflects off the crown of the bluff like something stretched a phosphorus wire across the stone and lit it. The shine intensifies steadily like turning up the heat, and I know instinctively that even as I climb down, something approaches. The rope itself takes on the same shine. Smoke billows over the cliff's lip, and flames burst in the air above. I don't know what the glow is, but it's not the sun. I can only imagine it is whatever chased Yost and I down the lighthouse. Whatever it is, it approaches the point where we began our descent, growing brighter and brighter.

I remember the intensity of the light of the nuclear detonation, the one that took from me years of sight.

Then, my feet are on the tangle. It's not a knot, but rather a single loop that has caught a small bundle of loops. Nothing in the universe hates something more than my hand hates me, but I maintain my grip even as I pull the loop lose with my feet. The rope unfurls, and I drop as fast as the descender can allow. At the point where it meets the array, the rope now shines like phosphorus and billows steam or smoke, I can't tell which.

My feet hit the stones, and I stumble back, getting clear so that Efta can come down fast. She lets go of her device just as the rope breaks, and she lands hard, stumbling backward. I grab her by the collar with my good hand and let us both swing with her momentum in a circle that brings us both down to the ground on our knees.

I look up and see a brilliant orb that seems almost as bright as the sun itself peek over the cliff's edge. It is indeed the same thing that pursued Yost and I down the lighthouse. As Efta and I clamber down the rocks to the dirt beach, it watches us escape its proximity for the second time.

* * *

On the beach, Efta and I locate the rock outcropping. Choppy surf batters it with a foamy white spray that glistens in the bright light of day, and I'm still unable to actually spot the boat itself. It occurs to me that Brogden may have been mistaken or lying. After all, even if he'd been in active contact with the smugglers before my arrival on Midway, anything could have happened to the boat after the rendezvous. If nothing else, it has been anchored and unmanned through two fierce storms already.

Furthermore, between us and it, countless rocks under the surface and what appears by the surf to be a frenzied current. The distance is impossibly far without a boat. We'd either drown or die of hypothermia long before we reached the boat – if the boat was there at all.

"This is suicide," I tell Efta as we approach the retaining wall. To our right along the cliff base runs the graveyard, all the way to the island's spur. On the other side of the spur is the cove. Atop the spur is the cargo elevator.

On our side of the spur, the cliffs are pocked with alcoves much like the bluff around the lighthouse. They are mostly empty now, though a couple of them seem to house writhing forms, most likely the birds too deformed to be capable of flight. At first, I wonder how on earth they survived, but I notice that several of the alcoves contain remains from our campsite, and I wonder if the healthy birds bring food back for the damaged. How odd that they should be self-aware enough to care for their infirmed.

A violent quake reminds me that we cannot linger. Rocks tumble from the bluff and an enormous horizontal crack forms at its base. I realize how vulnerable we are here should the cliffs collapse from the seismic activity.

"We need to move now," I say, throwing off my coat. It's a strange feeling to be without it. I've worn one peacoat or another almost perpetually for years except when indoors, and to feel the ocean breeze in the sun-warmed air, I could almost simply stand here until I died and die content.

I lunge toward the retaining wall but halt as I feel Efta's hand suddenly grab my sleeve.

"Look," she says, pointing across the beach graveyard.

There, at the far end, half out of the water on the rocks is the boat we rowed here from Midway. We'd never be able to row it against the current to Midway, but perhaps the currents might take us to some smuggler's base or to some habitable island that's been forgotten on our charts. We could also drift until we die of thirst.

Yet, I prefer those odds over chancing an impossible swim toward a vessel I'm not even sure is there.

The earthquakes intensify as Efta and I run side by side across the beach. The ground heaves and fists of rock shove their knuckles out of the ground. A rotted casket breaches the surface and explodes like a matchbox under a piston. Bones tumble out.

We weave around the irregularly placed stones as more knobs of rock break the surface and another casket roils from the ground. This one comes up whole, and it rolls onto its side. I hear what's inside rattle like dice in a cup.

We are hardly ten meters from the rocks at the far end when the retaining wall collapses, and the entire beach begins to slide sideways underneath us toward the sea. We fall onto our sides and find ourselves climbing laterally. My fingers close on the edge of a surging casket, and I claw my way over it. I don't even realize when I start screaming at the pain from beating my stumps against the coffin, but so much adrenaline surges through my system that it seems to be happening in some other world entirely. Finally, I find something more stable under my fingers even as sea water reaches my legs and I pull myself onto a boulder at the base of the cliff. I turn and throw my hand out for Efta.

She catches hold of my wrist even as her shoulders dip below the new sea-line. I don't know how much of the island has fallen away beneath her, but it's clear her feet have no purchase as she flounders against the new spray.

I manage to get my other hand around her wrist. Blood spatters from my hand onto her face, but I manage to thrust up and back with all my weight and strength. She slides from the water and lands on top of me. My breath evacuates with an 'oof,' and I have to gasp hard to draw my next breath.

Then, we're on our feet again, scrambling to the edge of the boat. We part along either side of it and use our momentum to shove it down from the rocks onto the surface of the water and pile in. I free two of the oars strapped to the inside of the hull. The water below is shallow enough that we simply shove the blades into the ground and shove ourselves along the shoals. I can only work one handed, but I jam the oar handle under my armpit so that I can put my weight into it. The breakwaters sweep us back toward the shore against our efforts, but we gradually seem to gain distance.

There is no comparable feeling to the moment I feel the boat take on a motion of its own, lateral to the island instead of toward it. I slump down and fall back against the bulkhead. Tears run down my cheeks, and I hold my hand up toward the sky as if the sun could heal it. Efta appears beside me and injects me with something. Then she sets about tending to my hand. I don't pay any attention to what she does.

I let my eyes drift half shut and chance a final look toward the Gollitok. There, against the sky, swing three titanic pillars, each teaming with rock tentacles and studded with long, sharp spikes, tipped with savage barbs. Dozens of luminescent green eyes like tokens of jade gaze out up and down the length of each. I don't know what the island has become, but I hope that Yost is right: I hope that whatever she has done will cause it to starve.

Efta and I both pull our oars into the boat. The current has us in a swift hold, and I have no idea to where it takes us. Efta still wears her pack of food and water, so we have enough supplies to hold us out for a couple of days. Maybe by then we'll find a place to port.

THANKS

Thank you to everyone who has contributed to the process of the composition of this book. Most importantly, thank you, Mom. If you'd not told me about Grandpa and his internment at Goli Otok, I might never have found this story. I owe a lot of my successes in writing, in part at least, to you helping me discover and embrace the Croatian side of my roots.

Thank you too, Amber, my dear wife, for putting up with me during the writing process and for helping as my most valued reader. Thank you too for all the laughter and love.

In addition, thank you to my former teachers, Michael Knight, the late Allen Wier, Dale Bailey, Marilyn Kallet, the late Arthur Smith, Elizabeth Gilbert, Kathleen Driskell, Greg Pape, Molly Peacock, and Debra Kang Dean. So many folk have helped me on this journey, some directly, some indirectly, but I value each and every person who has lent me their time.

Another thanks as well to the folk I've met through the Meacham Writers Workshop, *Symposeum*, *The Dread Machine*, and *The Showbear Family Circus*, as well as all the other editors and staff with whom I've worked. I've been long privileged to work alongside incredible folk in various organizational, editorial, and assisting capacities that have helped me grow as a writer and literary citizen.

Finally, thank you to all the other friends and family who've helped along the way: the kids (Gillian, Elliott, Alex, Ashton), Tiffany Najberg, Dad, Curt Allday, Matt Urmy, Michael Allen, Travis Payne, Tyler Kraha, Richard Jackson, Earl Braggs, Mike

Jaynes, Alex Quinlan, Katy Yocom, Christian Collier, Elissa and John Anticev, Autumn Watts, Caleb Jordan, Vanessa Gonzales, and John Compton. I know I'm forgetting folk right this moment, but I think of the people whose lives intersect with mine all the time.

About the Author

Andrew Najberg is also the author of the horror novel *The Mobius Door* (Wicked House Publishing, 2023) and the forthcoming young adult dark fantasy novel *The Neverborn Thief* (Olive-Ridley Press, 2024), as well as the collection of poems *The Goats Have Taken Over the Barracks* (Finishing Line Press, 2021).

His short fiction has appeared among others in *Prose Online, Psychopomp Review, Bookends Review, The Colored Lens, Utopia Science Fiction, The Gateway Review, Dark Dead Things, Creepy Podcast, Fusion Fragment, Translunar Travelers Lounge,* the *Gods And Globes III* anthology, and more.

His poems have appeared in dozens of journals, including *North American Review, Asheville Poetry Review, Louisville Review, Nashville Review, Cimarron Review, Another Chicago Magazine,* and *Good River Review.*

Currently, he teaches for the University of Tennessee at Chattanooga where he is a senior lecture, teaching courses in creative writing, Japanese literature, and rhetoric and composition.

When he is not writing, Andrew loves playing video games, board games, and Dungeons and Dragons with family. He enjoys movies, gardening, playing the drums, martial arts, and is an absolute sucker for anything related to the Alien franchise.

Learn more about his work and projects at www.andrewnajberg.com, or follow him on Facebook or Instagram.

Printed in Great Britain
by Amazon